Also by Jan Burke

Irene Kelly Mysteries
Kidnapped
Bloodlines
Bones
Liar
Hocus
Remember Me, Irene
Dear Irene,
Sweet Dreams, Irene
Goodnight, Irene

Other Fiction
The Messenger
Nine
Flight
Eighteen

DISTURBANCE

AN IRENE KELLY NOVEL

Jan Burke

SIMON & SCHUSTER

New York   London   Toronto   Sydney

Simon & Schuster
1230 Avenue of the Americas
New York, NY 10020

First Simon & Schuster hardcover edition June 2011

SIMON & SCHUSTER and colophon are
registered trademarks of Simon & Schuster, Inc.

For information about special discounts for bulk purchases,
please contact Simon & Schuster Special Sales at
1-866-506-1949 or business@simonandschuster.com.

The Simon & Schuster Speakers Bureau can bring authors
to your live event. For more information or to book an event,
contact the Simon & Schuster Speakers Bureau at
1-866-248-3049 or visit our website at www.simonspeakers.com.

Designed by Jacquelynne Hudson

Manufactured in the United States of America

1   3   5   7   9   10   8   6   4   2

Library of Congress Cataloging-in-Publication Data
Burke, Jan.
Disturbance / Jan Burke. —1st Simon & Schuster hardcover ed.
p. cm.
1. Kelly, Irene (Fictitious character)—Fiction. 2. Women journalists—
Fiction. 3. Serial murderers—Fiction. I. Title.
PS3552.U72326D57 2011
813'.54—dc22   2010041942

ISBN: 978-1-4391-5284-3
ISBN: 978-1-4391-5755-8 (ebook)

For Kathryn Moriarty Killeen,
who elegantly blends class and sass

DISTURBANCE

ONE

Some people claim to be able to feel trouble coming, the way they might feel a storm approaching from a long way off. They sense a disturbance in the atmosphere, something stirs the hairs along the backs of their necks or makes them wary when old, slumbering injuries awaken and ache. My own sense of such things is not entirely reliable. Just as I am more likely to be caught in a downpour than I am to be the only one with an umbrella, trouble has blindsided me more often than it has announced its approach.

Hindsight being so sharp-sighted, when I look back on that June afternoon, I can say that my sixth sense, if it was working at all, was fully occupied by the distinct possibility that I would be out of a job within a few months. That didn't make me different from ninety-nine out of a hundred of the country's newspaper reporters.

So as I sat at my desk in the newsroom of the *Las Piernas News Express,* rewriting a city council story that wasn't likely to excite anyone, my thoughts were taken up with trying to find a better angle on it. What I felt, when the phone on my desk rang, was not fear but irritation at the distraction.

"Kelly," I answered, using my headset.

"Irene? Aaron Mikelson."

Mikelson used to work for the *Express*, but he had moved up north to Sacramento several years ago. He covers California state government for a news service there, reporting on everything from the legislature to the prison system, and putting up with all the jokes about the inhabitants of both being similar.

"You hear about Nick Parrish?" he asked.

"No," I said, and my next, exhilarating thought was *He's dead.*

"You know he regained the ability to speak, right?"

"Yes." During the first months after Nick Parrish had sustained head and spinal injuries, he had gradually recovered speech and movement in his hands and feet, though he wasn't walking. The speech impairment had cleared up as the swelling from the head injury was reduced. That he had fully recovered his speech wasn't news to me, and Mikelson knew that—he was the one who had let me know Parrish was asking about me at the time.

"You haven't talked to him?"

"Nothing has changed in the last few years," I said. "I have no interest whatsoever in talking to him or in hearing what he has to say."

"He tried to sue you, right?"

For a stunned moment, I wondered if Mikelson could possibly believe that my only complaint about Nick Parrish was a frivolous lawsuit. Aloud I said, "Tried. The courts rejected the suits he filed against me and the paper, so after that . . . well, that was more than enough of hearing from him."

"Understood. He's one sick bastard."

"Yes," I said, thinking that "sick bastard" didn't come close to describing Parrish. Mere words couldn't draw a line around him and hold the monster he was within.

"You know about the Moths?"

I sighed. "His online fan club? Yes. Almost too predictable that some group like that would form, right? If the Internet has given us anything, it's some idea of how much psychosis goes undiagnosed."

"Amen."

"Look, Aaron, you cover a prison beat, so you know how this goes. Parrish has doubtless had a dozen marriage proposals, too."

"That's true. I don't claim to understand it. I don't know if I'll ever figure out why anyone would want to marry a serial killer. How could anyone ignore what he did to those women before he killed them? And not just women, right?"

Images I'd rather not recall started flashing through my mind.

Body parts scattered over a rain-drenched field.

Parrish shoving my face into the mud, nearly suffocating me.

Photos of one of his victims found in the grave he had forced her to dig.

I could hardly concentrate on what was going on around me. As if from a great distance, I heard Mikelson's voice in the headset. I was vaguely aware that he was saying something more about the women who wanted to marry Parrish. Asking me if I had read anything on the Moths' blog or social networking pages lately.

I swiveled my chair, stood up, and looked out across the newsroom.

A normal Monday afternoon. Everyone else bent over their keyboards or on the phone, working toward deadline. Far fewer reporters than I would have seen even a year ago, but a normal day for these times. I took a deep breath.

As the rush of memories faded, my brain kicked into gear. Mikelson had news about Parrish, and Parrish wasn't dead, or he would have told me that right off the bat. He wasn't speaking of him in the past tense.

I thought about hanging up, letting voicemail catch the call if he called back, leaving my colleagues to wonder why I ran out of the building looking as if I had the devil on my tail.

I let the breath out, told myself to get a grip. I sat down again, turned to face the computer.

"Anyway," Mikelson was saying, "you may not know this, but when he was first injured, the doctors didn't realize he had something called central cord syndrome—they thought he'd be tetraplegic. But then some spine specialists were called in, and they started treating it differently. They stabilized his neck. He was on anti-inflammation drugs, and they did several surgeries. Then there was a long process of rehab."

"Look, Aaron, I really don't—"

"He's walking."

"Walking?"

"Yes. On his own. And not just walking—he's got full use of his limbs, with very few limitations. Apparently the type of injury he had is one of the few that have such a good prognosis. His doctor says that, for his age, he was unusually fit. And he was incredibly determined, really worked hard. I guess the trickiest thing was this last surgery on his neck. They've kept his progress under wraps, waiting to see how he did after the surgeries, and with the rehab."

"Oh?" I managed to say.

I looked down at my hands. My fingers were shaking. I pressed them against my cheeks. It was like sticking my face in a bowl of ice.

"Yes. His docs say he's doing much better than most patients his age."

I stayed silent. This time, Mikelson noticed it.

"You okay?"

"No," I said. I tried again to marshal my thoughts. "Um—this isn't an interview, is it, Aaron?"

"Jesus, Kelly. No. Just a friend calling a friend."

I apologized.

He said not to worry about it, then added, "Listen, later, if you'd be willing—"

I bit back a few choice phrases. "I'll have to talk to my editor about it." But the anger was good. It drove off some of the panic.

"Sure. Sure." He paused. "Look, Parrish isn't going anywhere, even if he can walk—now that he's finished rehab, he'll be transferred out of the prison hospital and into maximum security."

"Of course," I said.

"I keep thinking about that guy who lost his leg because of him. The forensic anthropologist—what was his name?"

"Ben. Ben Sheridan." God. I'd have to tell Ben.

"Yeah, that's right. I mean, how ironic is it that he's not walking and Parrish is?"

"Ben walks just fine," I said, unable to keep the anger out of my voice. "He lost part of one leg below the knee, but he's got a prosthesis. He leads an active life. In fact, he's still helping to put away assholes like Nick Parrish."

Mikelson paused just long enough to let me know my reaction had surprised him, then said a little too brightly, "That's great. Glad to hear it—I mean that. So he's doing okay. Maybe I'll try to give him a call."

I shut up again, thinking of how unhappy Ben was going to be with me if Mikelson called him. Aaron could have looked up the information he needed anyway, but I had made his work a little easier, and I wasn't happy with myself for that.

"There was a partner, right?" Aaron asked. "The original Moth. Parrish's partner is still in the slammer, right?"

"Yes." I left it at that, my resentment rising a notch. He knew damned well that Parrish's accomplice, who had helped him escape and lured victims into his grasp, was serving an LWOP sentence—life without possibility of parole.

Aaron isn't stupid. He knew he needed to stop pushing if he wanted my cooperation down the road. So he changed the subject and asked me about mutual friends and former *Express* employees, and caught me up on news of a couple of people I knew at the *Sacramento Bee*. Eventually, he said, "Sorry if I upset you about Parrish. Just thought you should know. And you'll let me know first if John cuts you loose to talk to other media?"

"Sure. Thanks for the heads-up."

I called Ben Sheridan's cell but got his voice mail. The outgoing message said he was away and out of cell phone range but would be returning late Tuesday. Leave a message.

I decided I couldn't leave this news of Parrish as voice mail, so I simply asked Ben to give me a call when he got back to town. I hung up, wondering if Mikelson was already in the process of tracking him down.

Calling Ben had forced me to collect my thoughts. My blood might be running cold, but I still had enough ink in my veins to realize that this was a breaking story, and one the *Express* needed to cover. Mark Baker, our crime beat reporter, was at his desk, so I got his attention and filled him in. He's known me a long time and quickly figured out that overt sympathy was probably going to make me lose it, so we mutually pretended this news wasn't personal.

He called the prison hospital and confirmed the details. At that point, we got together with our editor, John Walters, and the city editor, Lydia Ames. A few more meetings were held, and plans for the front page changed.

I didn't really want to be writing about Parrish or reminding the public—or myself—of his crimes. But under current conditions, every day with a job at a newspaper felt like a stay of execution, so I didn't shy away from the work, however much it amplified my fears.

Rumors were at a fever pitch at the *Express.* No one had any doubt that the paper was in financial trouble. If a buyer wasn't found soon, we'd close. Bets were being laid on whether our publisher, Winston Wrigley III, was going to resign or be canned before the place shut down entirely. Some said he stayed on because he had nothing else to do with his life, others that he seemed to believe the captain ought to go down with the ship. Most of us felt that this particular captain should have been thrown overboard a long time ago.

But the general state of the industry wasn't his fault, and as much as I disliked him, I couldn't help but find him a pitiful creature now. His shame surrounded him like a force field, repelling his critics even as it protected him from our anger. His grandfather had founded the newspaper, his father had built it into one of the most powerful businesses in the city. Yet the newspaper business was one the next son had never understood, and now it punished him for his ignorance. Although his father had seen Winston III's weaknesses and had been smart enough to set things up so that he answered to a board, too many family members were on that board, and they often protected sonny boy. Luckily for us, these days he avoided his employees—Winston III spent most workdays wandering aimlessly through the many parts of the building that were now all but empty.

For the staff, morale was at an all-time low. We stomached the group "good-bye parties," fought against the pressure put on senior staff to retire early, and went to too many funerals—the heart attack rate among our oldest male reporters and retirees should have triggered a study by the CDC. Admittedly, these were the guys who, in their salad days, had never touched a salad, and I'm sure the high-pressure work, the years of hard drinking, and the once smoke-filled workplace took their toll.

But it was hard not to believe that loss of dignity was the final nail in their coffins.

Old newspapermen were dying. The rest of us had to listen to people who believed all in-depth professional reporting could be replaced by text messages. The saying might have to change to "Don't believe everything you read . . . on your cell phone."

It wasn't just the *Express* that was being measured for a coffin, of course. The whole profession had been hearing eulogies while it was still on life support.

That afternoon, though, the newsroom was stirring to life in a way it hadn't in some weeks. Stories about Parrish, our local monster, sold papers. We could provide the kind of detail that wasn't going to be available on television. I had doubts that anyone living in the city needed a recap, but I dutifully told them of that time when Parrish—manacled and heavily guarded—pledged to help us find the body of one of his victims. It was part of a plea bargain, in exchange for which he would receive a life sentence rather than the death penalty. At the request of the victim's family, I accompanied the group that journeyed into the Sierra Nevada to recover her remains. We walked into a trap. I was one of the few lucky ones—I lived.

Parrish escaped and continued to terrorize Las Piernas and other cities while he was on the loose. When he was finally captured, he was injured and almost completely paralyzed. Between that and his conviction and imprisonment on additional murder charges, the good citizens of Las Piernas breathed a sigh of relief. They were safe.

Those of us who had been in the mountains with him never felt completely safe again.

By the end of the day, I was a wreck. When I came home, I told myself I was glad that my husband, Frank, was away on a camping trip with our next-door neighbor, Jack. Glad that they had taken our two dogs with them. Frank needed the break, and the dogs loved going to the mountains. Maybe by the time they got back, I'd have calmed down.

Except for the company of my elderly cat, Cody, I was alone.

Not for the first time, I reminded myself. After all, when you're married to a homicide detective, there are plenty of nights when he's not home. Although the dogs were usually with me, this wasn't the first time Jack—who is in many ways as much their owner as we are—had taken them camping.

Nick Parrish was in prison. He might be able to walk, but he wasn't going anywhere. I made dinner for one and watched television. Avoided all crime programming, which turned out to be about half of what was on. Other channels I flipped because I didn't want to shop from my TV or watch someone cook. I still found enough to stay amused. The distraction worked for a time.

I was safe, wasn't I?

By the time I went to bed, though, I could believe that for only a few minutes at a time. I tried to sleep. After an hour of tossing and turning, I switched on the light and grabbed a book of crossword puzzles. I was still awake when the alarm went off.

I kept telling myself I had nothing to fear.

I was wrong.

TWO

Kai Loudon pointed the Smith & Wesson at the blurred photo on the computer screen. Not a great photo of her face. Just one of those small, low-res images from the newspaper's Web site. The same one appeared next to all of her stories. Irene Kelly.

He took aim between her blue eyes.

He made a popping sound with his lips as he clicked the mouse in his other hand, setting the computer to sleep mode. The image disappeared as the screen blanked.

He sighed and set the gun down on his desk. Not even close to the real thing. She was alive.

Kai seldom used guns anyway. They were good to have on hand for unexpected trouble, or to let someone know you meant business, but he thought them an unsatisfying way to kill. He had never actually shot anyone. He would rather use his own body to demonstrate his power over others. He was young and strong.

He stood and began to move restlessly around the basement. He paced past the bookcase, distractedly running his long fingers lightly over the spines of one row of books. He paused before a second set of shelves and touched various little mementos displayed there. Most weren't biological, but the few items that had once been parts of living things were the most exciting to him.

He picked up a lock of hair and inhaled. The shampoo scent had faded in all but his memory, where it came back to him now as clearly as the night he had captured the dark, silky curl. The woman who had been sitting in front of him in the theater hadn't even known he'd taken it.

At least, not at first.

He carefully replaced this small treasure and kept walking until he reached the computer again. He stared at his reflection in the darkened monitor.

He had been using the Internet to search for more details on the big story. The newspaper and television reports hadn't told him much. If you entered "Nicholas Parrish" in any news search engine, you got thousands of hits. Since this morning, when the story came out in the *Express*, the number had increased.

The recent stories started with the predictable phrases. "Convicted serial killer . . . perhaps as many as fifty victims, including six members of the Las Piernas Police Department . . ."

He took a deep breath and let it out slowly, forced himself to relax. He glanced at his watch. His mother was upstairs, waiting for him to make dinner. She would have to wait a little longer.

He smiled to himself, savoring his rebelliousness.

Others had always seen his mother as a docile creature, but he knew that she had a way of getting what she wanted. His very conception had epitomized her acts of passive aggression. She used to be fond of telling him that it was a miracle she had not miscarried after the beating his father gave her on learning of the pregnancy. One of these days he would ask his father and find out if that story was true. He was inclined to believe it. To him, the story was just another indicator of her ability to endure hardship in order to get what she wanted.

He did not consider this trait to be heroic in any way.

He paused, wondering if she had what she wanted, these days. She couldn't make it down the stairs now, which made him savor his hours in the basement all the more. Still, it was time to have dinner. He locked the room and slid the false wall back into place.

He climbed the stairs with some anticipation, but not for the meal, which would be something he would prepare without real effort, and would be exactly like the meal he had prepared the previous day, and the day before that.

His anticipation came from the knowledge that today's issue of the *Express* would be upstairs. His mother had been a subscriber for years. He didn't usually read it, but this morning he had noticed the name Parrish in the headline, and instead of his usual routine of putting the paper straight into the recycling bin, rubber band and all, he took it to the kitchen and opened it carefully, with something approaching reverence.

This regard was not for the newspaper itself, of course. Not the reporting, not the photos, not the layout. It was the subject of the article that entranced him: Nicholas Parrish.

The story had changed his whole day.

Kai grinned and took the stairs two at a time. He went to the freezer, removed a frozen dinner, and put it in the microwave. He grabbed a can of a nutritional shake from the refrigerator and fitted it with a straw. The evening meal would be the usual silent affair. Afterward, he would read the story about Nicholas Parrish aloud to his mother. Her current state of health would force her to listen to it, like it or not. She would not. For him, this would be as good as dessert.

He stood in the kitchen, listening to the hum of the

microwave. The air began to smell of steaming broccoli, melting cheese, and warming plastic.

He felt contentment as he looked out the window and watched dusk fall. It would be dark soon. As pleasant as his dinner plans were, he didn't expect to spend an evening at home. He had a game to begin.

He got a hard-on just thinking about it.

THREE

I dozed off just before the six o'clock news came on. I had caught about fifteen minutes of sleep before Nick Parrish's name was mentioned by a talking head—that woke me up enough to do some math. Fifteen minutes of sleep in the last thirty-eight hours.

Not good.

I listened to Parrish's surgeon, full of pride in his medical accomplishment. Parrish had jokingly told him he wanted to run a marathon. "Other than his incarceration, there is really no reason why he couldn't do so one day," the doctor said. He pointed to a diagram of a spine and indicated sites of injury, talked about the repair rate of nerves, and quoted statistics on central cord syndrome. I couldn't stop myself from wishing that he had found some other—any other—paralyzed individual to be his miracle man.

The newscast changed focus to the patient's notoriety, and Nick Parrish's face filled the screen. I aimed the remote at him and sent him off into television oblivion. If only it were so easy to ship him off to real oblivion.

But in real life, Nick Parrish clearly wasn't ready to sign off.

Despite my lack of sleep on Monday, I was at my desk by eight Tuesday morning. The room was buzzing—apparently someone on the Moths' blog had said that I'd soon be hearing from the friends of Nick Parrish, and that I'd recognize the message when I got it. The phone started ringing with interview requests. John asked me to write a follow-up exclusive for the *Express* but promised other outlets I'd be available the next day at a press conference. The paper had its own need for publicity. But at least I'd be spared one day of repeating empty phrases:

"Yes, I heard his doctor say that Parrish wants to train for a marathon."

"No, I know he's not getting out anytime soon."

"No, I don't know what the Moths have in mind, and I'm really not too anxious to find out."

"No, I don't think I would feel better talking it over, but thanks all the same."

I understood why John wanted the story and why I had to write it. What would have been a small item in other papers, one more bizarre note in the bizarre life of Nicholas Parrish, would take up most of the A section of the *Express.* Parrish had taken his victims from a number of communities, including several in other states, but no city had suffered as much horror at his hands as Las Piernas.

Writing the story brought back more memories, of course. Of being hunted by Nick Parrish. Of bodies. Of bones. Of betrayals.

It took me all day—most of that time spent staring at a blank computer screen, or fending off overly protective colleagues. After about the tenth "Are you okay?" I picked up my laptop and scouted the building. I found an empty desk in a place full of empty desks—our now almost vacant features department. But it was a sunny, airy room where I could hide out while I wrote, so I finished the story there.

Just before I left, Lydia Ames offered to come over that evening. But Lydia was recently engaged, and I knew her life was crammed with wedding plans. My mood wasn't exactly going to be a good match to hers in any case, so I told her not to worry. On the way home, I tried calling my therapist, the one who had helped me deal with my PTSD after my first experience with Parrish.

She was on vacation. "Is this an emergency?" her answering service asked.

"No," I said quickly.

Not yet.

I could handle this.

After forsaking the news, I distracted myself by watching old Marx Brothers films. When I'd reached my limit with that, I thought about playing games on my computer but knew that would only keep me wired. So instead I went through the newspapers in our recycling pile, pulled out the crossword puzzles, and took them to bed with me. Before long, I grew drowsy and dozed off.

At one in the morning, I awoke again. I had heard a sound — a dull thump.

I turned the lights on, checked the locks again. Twenty minutes later I was back in bed in the darkness, berating myself for being a spineless wimp and wondering if I could hope to fall back to sleep.

I did, but a little after two my slumber was disturbed again. This time, the sound was continuous. Not what had roused me earlier but something different. Not unfamiliar but out of place.

It took me a moment to recognize it — water running through the pipes. Not at high volume but enough to make me certain that was indeed what I was hearing.

I swore, stumbled out of bed, and went into the bathroom, expecting to discover that the toilet was running. I jiggled the handle, then woke up enough to realize that wasn't where the sound was coming from. The shower, the sink—those faucets were off.

Southern California was in the middle of one of its too frequent droughts, and residents of Las Piernas were on mandatory rationing—overusage of water was illegal and expensive. Hell of a time to spring a leak as big as the one I was hearing.

I pulled on a robe and turned on some lights.

Kitchen faucet was off, too.

No problem with the dishwasher.

I went out into the garage, half expecting to find a flood.

The sound was louder here, but to my relief, everything was dry. Including the washing machine.

I stood still and listened. The backyard sprinkler system controls and a faucet were just on the other side of the garage wall. The sprinklers had been off for weeks. But was the sound coming from a hose that had been left on?

I made my way to the door leading to the backyard, reached for the dead-bolt lock, and hesitated.

I hadn't been in the yard at all that day. There was no way on earth that I had been the one to leave the water on. Staying inside, I flipped on all the outdoor lights.

The water sound stopped.

I swallowed hard. How strong was the dead bolt?

I waited, standing still, straining to hear any sound from the yard. I heard nothing.

I tried to work up enough nerve to open the door, couldn't. I ran back inside the house and relocked the door between the house and the garage. I stood inside the kitchen, unsure of what to do next. I saw my cell phone on the counter, reached for it, and sent a text message to Ben Sheridan:

Are you awake?

The phone rang less than a minute later.

"Hi," I answered. "Things are going bump in the night and I'm scared shitless. Would you be willing to bring the dogs over?"

"Okay if Ethan and his dog come along, too?"

This is what I love about Ben. Call him after two in the morning and his only question is not "Are you nuts?" but "How about reinforcements?"

FOUR

I felt better after making the call, better yet when they arrived. At different times, Ben Sheridan and Ethan Shire had each lived in our home. In many ways, they were the brothers I'd never had. Ben, a forensic anthropologist, also handled search dogs. Ethan, currently his roommate, worked at the paper with me.

I received a warm greeting from their shepherds, Altair and Bingle, and from Bool, the bloodhound. Cody leaped from a counter to the top of the refrigerator and gave me a look that had the accusation "traitor" written all over it.

The dogs seemed puzzled when they realized our own mutts weren't present, but the moment Ben and Ethan took out Bingle's and Altair's working harnesses, their focus changed and they were all business. Ben gave me the bloodhound's leash — Bool wasn't being put to work yet, but there was always the chance they'd need him later. Or maybe Ben knew I'd feel a little better going outside with a big dog next to me. Bool is as friendly and harmless as they come, but whoever was out there wouldn't know that.

"Let's have a look around," Ben said, unlocking the sliding door that leads to our patio.

I walked a few yards behind Ethan and Ben. We soon discovered that my garden hose was stretched over to the house next door—not Jack's house but the one on the other side, the one just north of mine.

"What assholes," Ethan said. "Stealing your water! Let's go have a word with them."

"We wouldn't get far," I said. "That house has been empty for just over a month. It's in foreclosure."

We broke off conversation because it was clear the dogs were interested in a scent. We hurried with them as they made their way down the street, away from the beach. They came to a halt at something one doesn't find too often on a June night on a Las Piernas beach street—an empty parking space.

"Don't suppose you remember what kind of vehicle was parked here earlier?" Ben asked.

"No, sorry."

He looked back toward the house. "I think the . . ." He made a motion with his hand, as if stirring the air would help him find the word he wanted.

"Hosers," Ethan supplied.

Ben rolled his eyes. "Whoever is trying to play tricks on you—they were probably parked here."

"More than one?" I asked.

"No way to really be sure. From the behavior of the dogs—just a guess, mind you—I suspect just one. But that's a guess. It could have been however many could fit in the missing car."

"Wouldn't take more than one to stretch a hose over a fence," I said.

"No. But it might take more than one to work up the nerve to play a prank."

"The Moths . . . you know who I mean?"

"The idiots who blog about Parrish?"

"Yes. They posted something saying I'd get a message from them. Do you think this is it?"

"Could be," Ben said, "but what the hell is the message?"

We ignored Ethan's various attempts to find a humorous interpretation and walked back down the street, looking for footprints or other signs of the prankster—or pranksters—but didn't find any.

Back at the house, I thanked them for coming over and said I'd be fine. Ben wasn't fooled. "Ethan, you can take the guest room. I'm taking the couch." He looked at me. "You, try to get a little sleep."

I started to protest, but Ethan interrupted to say they had brought overnight gear. "Including stuff for the dogs. Ben's even brought what he needs for his classes tomorrow."

"And you?"

"My classes are all online."

"You know what I meant."

"I'm going to ride in with you in the morning."

"And who's going to take you home at the end of the day?" I asked.

"You. We're staying here until Frank gets back."

"He'll be back tomorrow night."

"Okay, we'll be here at least until then."

I wasn't sure I liked all these decisions being made without my input, but I couldn't deny a sense of relief. Still . . .

Seeing my hesitation, Ben said quietly, "I got a call from an Aaron Mikelson today."

"Shit. I did *not* give him your number."

"I know you didn't. I can imagine how you felt about getting that call yourself."

I looked at him, saw what I hadn't registered before—he hadn't been sleeping, either.

Ben and I were among the few who could say we'd survived

an attack by Nick Parrish. It was an extremely small club. The dues were damned high.

Ethan and I had been through a separate hell. Once a hard drinker, he had caused a scandal at the paper that alienated his fellow reporters—I was one of the few who stood by him when he returned from rehab. He returned the favor when we were taken captive one night—he saved my life, although he suffered a near-fatal gunshot wound in the process. So there was a bond of survival with him, too. He was the slightly pesky younger brother, I suppose. The one who shared my ability for finding trouble.

I wouldn't trade either of them for the world.

"Well, we're staying here," Ethan said.

"Thanks," I said.

I felt safe. Until the first body showed up.

FIVE

onovan Cotter checked the locks on the door to the studio and stepped carefully on the paving stones that led back to the house. His boots stayed dry, but he wiped their soles on the rough mat all the same. He moved inside, sliding the glass door shut behind him. He locked it and listened for a moment.

The house was quiet.

He liked that so much.

It had not been quiet when his second wife lived with him. She had been unhappy, and what she would not say to him directly she expressed by loading and unloading the dishwasher in a noisy way, by banging pots and pans on the stovetop, by starting the vacuum cleaner when he would lie down for a nap.

When Donovan refused to acknowledge these acts for what they were, she escalated her attempts to get a combination of revenge on him and his attention. If, in the evening, she felt displeased with him—and near the end of the marriage, she so often was—she would set her alarm to go off the next morning with loud music and a buzzer an hour before the time for which his own was set. He would try to fall back to sleep, but she would pour cereal in a bowl and eat in a manner that he thought worthy of a chimpanzee annoyed with its keepers—she would cause the bowl to ring in a maddening arrhythmic staccato as she tapped her spoon against its sides.

When this failed to get a response, she prolonged her morning campaign. After breakfast, she would enter the bathroom off the master bedroom. She would flush the toilet, sing off-key in the shower, and just when the water was off and he thought he might get a minute of peace, she would turn on her blow dryer.

Once Donovan was up, she would wait until he was in the shower to run the washing machine and the dishwasher, so that the hot water was gone within seconds.

Donovan let her get away with it for a while. One morning, he rose from the bed and strode naked into the kitchen, took the bowl of cereal from her, and calmly dumped it down the sink. He said, "You should stop this little warfare. You don't know who you are up against."

He had not raised his voice, or lifted a hand to her, but there must have been something in his face or his stance that conveyed a little of his real nature to her, because she shrank back from him. He could not suppress—or hide, in his state of undress—his arousal when her eyes widened, her lower lip quivered, her breath quickened in fear.

Disgusted with himself, he left the kitchen and took a shower.

When he emerged from it, she had left the house.

The first thing he had noticed was the quiet.

She filed for divorce, did not ask for anything from him—he had bought the house before he met her, but she might have had a go at his military pension—and she never came back to retrieve so much as an article of clothing. He did not fight it, attempt to reconcile, or seek a new partner. He had already decided that marriage was not the answer he had hoped it would be.

He had tried it twice. The first experiment had failed mostly because of mutual immaturity, but over time, he was sure, the result would have been the same. She had protested when he went into the service, claiming she couldn't stand knowing he was in so much danger. Shortly after he shipped out, she filed for divorce. Ironically, getting on the freeways in L.A. proved to be more dangerous to her than his military duties were to him—after the divorce was final, and long before he returned home, her mother wrote to tell him that she had died in a car accident.

He turned his thoughts away from her, back to the quiet.

No, marriage was not for him. If he ever changed his mind about that, he knew he would have no difficulty finding a woman willing to be his wife. Without entirely understanding why, Donovan knew he was considered to be attractive. He did understand, because he worked at it, that he was in excellent physical condition. He had a good job, and knew how to be personable. But he didn't want to think about any woman in the way he had started to think about his most recent ex-wife, so he would probably stay unmarried.

Donovan's ex thought he didn't know where she lived now. She was wrong about that.

So far, he had been able to control his impulses in that direction.

Self-mastery meant you didn't have to become what certain people predicted you would become. Self-mastery meant you, yourself—and not your past—defined you. Self-mastery was the key to his happiness.

It was time to leave the house and earn his wages. He did not like to look in mirrors, but neatness was important to him, so he compromised by studying the uniform carefully and merely glancing at his own face in the reflection.

He savored the quiet of the house for another moment, then it was time to go out into the noisy world.

No sooner was he out the door than his personal cell phone rang. Caller ID blocked.

He took the call but didn't speak.

"I love that you're so cautious," a man's voice said.

When he still didn't speak, the man laughed.

"Did you see the television interview with his doctor?"

"No," Donovan said and considered hanging up. He knew he wouldn't. He was angry with himself for his curiosity. It made him weak. It kept him listening.

"I didn't think so. The doctor spoke the code phrase—innocently, of course. He mentioned the marathon."

"Coincidence." He would hang up. He would hang up now . . .

"You don't believe that any more than I do. It's time to begin."

Donovan stayed silent. He felt a little queasy. He wasn't ready for this, even though the news about Nicholas Parrish being up and walking had left him expecting it.

"Don't let it upset you—we are what we are."

He winced, thinking, *I'm not what you are,* but said, "I'm not upset."

"Good. I'm going to contact the other one."

"That might not be wise. What if it isn't really starting?"

"Cold feet?"

It would not do to let the caller play these games.

"Call me again when you really have something to say," Donovan said quietly and hung up on him.

SIX

I first heard about Marilyn Foster as a missing person case.

Marilyn Foster's husband managed the swing shift at a manufacturing plant forty miles from Las Piernas. Dwayne Foster routinely arrived at home well after midnight, ate the light meal his wife left waiting for him, took a shower downstairs, and wound down with a beer or two while he watched TV with a headset on before going up to bed.

He got caught up in an old movie in the early hours of Wednesday, so it was about three in the morning when he went upstairs. To his surprise, the bed was empty. He called his wife's name, wandered through the house looking for her, feeling a mixture of annoyance and fear. He went into the garage. Her car was missing.

He tried calling her cell phone. He heard it ringing and discovered her purse still in the kitchen.

He called the police.

"It's not a crime to be missing," I once heard an old cop say.

"It's not a crime to be dead, either," I replied, "but you still investigate when someone calls to report a body."

What he had said, though, is true—as far as it goes—and he was only expressing the frustration that many in law enforcement feel when it comes to missing persons cases. All too often they use their time, energy, and resources trying find a missing adult, only to discover they're not looking into a crime. As it turns out, many adults who go missing just want to escape whatever they've gotten themselves into—debts, bad relationships, boredom, overbearing families, abuse, you name it. The police run into that so often, it leads to a kind of cynicism that in turn leads to a lack of investigative effort.

In recent years, Las Piernas has taken missing persons cases more seriously. The *Express* has always given those cases special attention, which has brought some pressure to bear on law enforcement. Nick Parrish, I suppose, brought a different kind of pressure to solve missing persons cases.

So the Las Piernas Police Department called a news conference late Wednesday morning. Mark Baker was on the road, sent up north to cover the Parrish stories, so John sent me out to it and asked me to try to get an interview with Dwayne Foster.

The public information officer for the LPPD handed out several photos of a thin thirty-eight-year-old woman with short, dark hair and blue eyes. Although there were no signs of struggle at her home, they believed she might be in danger. Their press release included photos of her blue Chevy Malibu, gave a plate number for the car, and mentioned a fact that made me understand why they might have been quicker to move on this case than on some others.

Marilyn Foster was a type 1 diabetic. She was dependent on insulin, and had not taken her insulin supply with her.

If Dwayne Foster was suspected of doing away with his wife, the police weren't giving any indication of that. They might be keeping an eye on him, or have information I didn't, but from everything I could see, Dwayne Foster was devoted to his wife, genuinely worried about her, and hadn't a clue where she might be.

He agreed to my request to meet at his house and tell me more about Marilyn, hoping my story would increase interest in her case.

Dwayne had known Marilyn since high school, although they hadn't dated then. "She was kind of wild back then," he said. "I think because she had to take insulin and all, she wanted to prove something. She used to drink a lot, which was really dangerous for her. I don't know, she wanted to show everybody that she could be just like any other teenager, I guess. Wanted people to like her. Every kid does, right? Anyway, she got pregnant by this older guy, dropped out, and went to one of those places where girls get cared for if they agree to give the baby up for adoption. I guess because of the diabetes, the whole thing was even harder on her." He paused. "Later, when we tried, she kept having miscarriages. Last one damned near killed her, and we decided maybe we'd adopt but never actually took the steps to do it. She kind of has funny feelings about adoption. I know she still regrets giving the baby away." He paused. "She always feels sad on his birthday. He'd be twenty-two now. She's tried to locate him and joined a couple of online groups that help people connect up with their adopted kids." He wiped at his eyes. "That's another reason I know she didn't run away! She's waiting for that kid to show up here. If he shows up now, what do I tell him?"

The question caught me off guard, especially because apparently it wasn't rhetorical—he seemed sincerely to want an answer. "Tell him what you told me," I said.

After a moment, he nodded. "I'll welcome him. I'll see if he'll stay here until she's found. I think his birth father was

probably an A-number-one Asshole, but that doesn't mean he
is. Shit, my own dad was a real piece of work. Nothing dooms
you, you know?"

"I agree. Any chance Marilyn's old flame is still around?"

"No. He wasn't a flame really, just a one-night stand from
what she told me. I mean, the dude had to know she was under-
age. But she'd never tell anyone who he was. Her parents tried
really hard to get that out of her, but she always said she'd been
drunk and didn't know who he was. She knew, though. Once I
joked that if she found the kid, she might end up reconnecting
with his dad. She told me there was no chance of that, and not
just because the kid's dad was in prison for life but because she
had wised up since then, and I was the only one for her. I asked
her how she could know he was in prison, but she got all upset
and said she never wanted to talk about it. Ever."

He grinned ruefully. "When Marilyn says something in
that tone, you don't argue. Besides, I didn't want her to think
I thought less of her. I never have. Never. She's the only one for
me, too."

"So, she hasn't been acting strange in any way lately? No
tension, no odd behavior?"

"No. Not at all." He looked me square in the eye and said,
"She's not cheating on me."

"I'm not suggesting that," I said and meant it. Although I'd
known plenty of people who had been surprised by the devilry
of supposed spousal saints, most of them had deliberately closed
their eyes before the moment of revelation. Nothing about
Dwayne said he had his eyes closed. And the more he told me
about his wife, the less it seemed likely that she had been looking for an escape. I'd have to check that out with other people
who knew her, though. For now, I asked, "Any new acquain-
tances? Strangers approaching her? People hanging around the
neighborhood who haven't been around before?"

"Not that I know of. And we talk. She'd tell me. Police asked about that, too."

"So life has just gone on as usual lately? Nothing out of the ordinary?"

He hesitated.

"What?" I coaxed.

He shook his head. "It's so stupid. It doesn't have anything to do with her being gone."

"Tell me anyway."

He seemed embarrassed. "Hell, she's going to kill me for telling you as much as I have already."

I waited.

"The other night," he said. "Not the night she went missing, but the night before? She did do something that's not like her. But it was just forgetfulness, that's all. I didn't even mention it to her."

"What?" I asked again.

"You know, when she's upstairs asleep, she turns the fan on—makes white noise, so she probably didn't hear anything, or it wouldn't have happened. But I came home, usual time, and here's the garden hose, turned on and running. Like we're building a pond in the backyard. Please don't print that in the paper, okay?"

SEVEN

I talked to Marilyn Foster's co-workers at the dentist's office where she was employed as a receptionist. She was a reliable worker. The dentist and his wife, who was a hygienist in his office, looked upon Marilyn almost as a daughter. They were sure she would have confided any troubles to them, and had no indications of unhappiness in her marriage. She was the last person, they said, who would ever simply disappear.

I talked to her mother and sister, who lived in the San Fernando Valley. Again, no sign that her life was troubled, that she had a secret romance going, that she was feeling restless or wanted a change of scenery.

The contacts I had at the police department didn't have a lot to say beyond what had been said at the press conference—no leads, hoping that any publicity the *Express* could give the case would help to generate those. It was clear they didn't think this was a voluntary disappearance.

I wrote up the story and tried to pull myself together for a completely different kind of press conference—the one Wrigley had arranged for late that afternoon. As I walked downstairs with John Walters, he glanced at me and said, "You look like a cold slice of hell on stale toast."

"Always so kind," I said.

That made him laugh, not something he was doing very often these days, so I had a smile on my face when we went into the room Wrigley had designated for the event—a large space that had once been used for staff meetings. That was in the days before you could fit the staff into a phone booth and still have room to dance.

I was relieved to see that while the turnout wasn't embarrassingly low—local television, a few local papers, two radio stations, and a couple of online news outlets—the room wasn't crowded enough to cause me to panic. All the same, the subject wasn't one I wanted to talk about. I prefer being one of the people asking the questions in these situations.

Wrigley gave the introduction, putting on that public persona that actually makes him appear serious and competent. Anyone who looked hard enough could see that he was enjoying himself.

I wasn't too surprised to notice that Ethan had left his desk in the newsroom and managed to slip into a chair in the back row, where he alternately tried to signal me with an occasional thumbs-up and glared ferociously at anyone who asked a question that he deemed out of line. It was enough to amuse me into remaining calm.

After the Q & A ended, Wrigley stayed behind to chat up some of those who lingered. John, Ethan, and I headed back upstairs. I heard someone rushing down the stairwell just as John was asking Ethan if he had enjoyed making an ass out of himself for the entertainment of the competition. Lydia came to a halt on the landing above us. "They found her," she said, looking shaken.

"Who?" Ethan asked.

"Marilyn Foster."

"Alive?" I asked, knowing the answer even before Lydia shook her head.

"In an abandoned warehouse, near the harbor."

"What aren't you telling us?" I asked, knowing that no one who works as a city editor would be looking like she did over a garden-variety homicide.

"She was tortured." Lydia shuddered. "The killer drew things on her in some kind of indelible ink. Moths."

I went to work on a rewrite. Ethan was sent to talk to the police—he had to borrow my car. Now that it was a homicide investigation, John was hesitant to send me, even though it wasn't going to be Frank's case. Before Ethan left, I took him aside and said, "This may sound strange, but mention the hose to them. A couple of nights ago, someone pulled the same trick on Marilyn Foster."

His eyes widened.

"Yes, it scares me. No, I won't try to find another way home. I'll wait until you get back and can stay with me."

"Good," he said. "What time does Frank get back?"

"Depends on traffic," I said. "Probably late this evening."

"Call him."

"He's probably out of range of a signal."

Ethan looked skeptical.

"And I really, really don't want to fuck up his time off," I quickly added. He started to leave, but I had seen the mischievous gleam in his eyes, and I caught his sleeve. "Ethan, don't you call him, either!"

"I make no promises," he said, freeing his shirt from my grip.

"Ethan!"

But he was out the door.

If John thought I looked bad before the press conference, he should have seen me after I called Dwayne Foster.

Sometimes families of victims take out their understandable rage and feelings of helplessness on the press—they can afford to alienate us but not the police who are investigating their loved ones' deaths, so we get the force of their reactions. But I soon discovered that Foster wasn't hostile, he was just bereft, lost in that numb state of denial and pain where a person tries to deal with every intruding thought that isn't the essential one. I was someone who had listened to him when few others had paid attention, and he needed a listener now, however disjointed his conversation might be.

"I don't know what to do," he said several times.

I asked him if there was anyone in his family, or a friend, who might come to stay with him. He told me that his brother was on the way from Santa Monica.

"They haven't found her car yet. I was thinking about driving around, looking for the car. If he's in it—"

"Do you think that's a good idea?"

"No," he said, defeated. "No. But—moths. Why moths?"

From the moment Lydia had told me about the decorations on Marilyn Foster's body, my thoughts had gone to the warning on the Moths' blog. Had this woman been killed as a warning to me? The idea that the Moths might go to that extreme horrified me.

I thought of Marilyn's ex-boyfriend in prison—someone who was LWOP, as was Parrish. Like me, Marilyn had dark hair and blue eyes—Parrish was known to choose victims with those features. And there was that weird business with the garden hose.

But Parrish was in prison. There was no doubt about that. And the Moths on the blog had always seemed more likely to bluster than to act. Surely they knew that if they started committing murders, computer forensics experts would track them down.

I had no real evidence, though, and wondered if I was making connections based on my own fears. I was sleep-deprived and stressed nearly to my limit, in no shape to see things clearly.

So when Dwayne Foster asked me about moths, I didn't give him the answer that seemed likely to me, but he didn't seem to need one. The question was just part of that emotional pinball game playing in his mind.

"I can't help but think about . . . about what he did to her. Why? Why her? She was so sweet. She never did anything to anyone." He took a big, gulping breath, let it out on a sob.

"Tell me more about her. Tell me how you met," I said.

It worked. For a few minutes, he focused on something other than the last day of Marilyn's life. His brother arrived, and we ended the call.

My phone rang again almost as soon as I hung up.

"Irene? Ethan. I'm with Reed and Vince," he said, naming two homicide detectives with the LPPD. "I told them about the hose. They want to know if you'll meet them at your house in about an hour."

"I've got a rewrite, and you've got my car, remember?"

I heard him talking to them.

"Reed says, when we're both done for the day at the paper, give him a call and he'll meet us."

All of that seemed as if it might work out just fine. Ethan and I had turned in our stories. Reed and Vince were following us back to my house from the paper. But then, just before I turned down my street, I saw something that made me slam on my brakes and nearly get rear-ended by the unmarked car behind me.

Marilyn Foster's blue Chevy Malibu was parked in the space that had been empty the night before.

EIGHT

I got out of my car, but before I had taken three steps forward, Reed ran up to me and grabbed hold of my shoulders. "Wait," he said as Vince hurried past, using a radio to call for a crime scene unit and a couple of units for traffic control.

I was semicoherently telling Reed that the space had been empty the night before, that the dogs had led us to it. He was getting similar information at the same time from Ethan, who had also rushed to my side. Vince put gloves on and was reaching for the trunk button when I screamed, "Vince, no!"

He looked back at me, puzzled.

"He's used explosives in the past," I said, hearing shakiness in my voice.

"Who?"

"Nick Parrish!"

The three men exchanged glances. "Nick Parrish is in prison," Reed said, in the sort of quiet, patient tone one reserves for three-year-olds frightened by thunder.

But I was cringing, because Vince was pushing in that trunk button. It snicked softly, and the trunk lid came up. No explosions.

"Oh, Christ—" Vince said, and Ethan, Reed, and I moved closer.

At first glance it appeared to be a woman cloaked in a colorful blanket. Except there wasn't a blanket, just her softly rounded nude body, wrapped in thin, clear plastic, and the skin beneath that plastic was covered with moths.

Artistically drawn moths, colorful, and richly detailed, but with a fanciful quality—if real moths exist in matching designs, I've never seen one locally. If not for the chosen canvas, I might have thought them beautiful.

Her straight blond hair was pulled back into a short ponytail. Because of the moths and the plastic wrap, I could not see much of her face, but judging by her hands, which were not painted, I guessed her to be a young woman. Her eyes were closed.

Vince reached in and touched her with a gloved finger, then drew his hand back suddenly. "Jesus! She's frozen!"

Someone honked a horn, and Vince quickly shut the trunk. Our cars were blocking traffic. I saw a martial light come into his eye as he walked back toward the horn honker, badge coming out of his pocket.

I looked back at the closed trunk. "Parrish did that, too. Froze some of his victims."

"Don't touch anything," Reed warned me, quite unnecessarily. If he hadn't been holding on to me, I think I would have run home. Maybe something in my body communicated that to him, because he asked Ethan to drive me home and wait for them there.

"I can drive," I said.

He shook his head. "Ethan drives. Both of you, wait outside the house. Before you go in, I want to make sure you don't have any visitors."

———

We had just pulled in the driveway when my cell phone rang. I recognized Frank's number.

"Irene?" I could hear the worry in the way he said my name. Jumping to a conclusion, I was ready to kill Ethan for calling him, but then Frank said, "I just heard the news on the radio. Are you okay?"

For a wild moment, I wondered if the events of thirty seconds ago were already being broadcast. "What news?"

"You. The press conference."

"Oh, that."

"Yes, that."

"I didn't think it would air outside the local area."

"You sounded shaken. And you sound shaken now. What's going on?"

I ignored an impulse to gloss over events until he got home. I'd have too much explaining to do. And since he'd heard the press conference, trying to hide my feelings from him was an equally bad idea.

"I'm not really doing so well, to be honest, but Ethan and Ben have stayed with me, and now Reed and Vince are here. Kind of. They won't let me go in the house, but Ethan's waiting with me. Vince and Reed are at the end of our street, looking at a frozen body in the trunk of a car. She has moths painted on her. Or maybe inked."

There was a silence, then he said, "What?"

I didn't blame him. It wasn't exactly a clear explanation. So I started over, with the story of the call from Aaron, then went on to the stories of the garden hose, Marilyn Foster, and finding the car. Although I hit a couple of rough patches in the telling, on the whole, talking to him about it calmed me down. I suspect it had the opposite effect on him, but he said, "I'm going to get home as fast as I can."

"More important to me that you get here safely."

"We're still a couple of hours away from Las Piernas. God, I'm so sorry I haven't been there with you, Irene."

"Just tell me you and Jack and the dogs had a good time."

"We did, but—"

"But nothing. I'm going to be so glad to see you."

"Me you, too. Let me talk to Ethan."

I handed the phone over. Ethan listened for a minute, then said, "Of course I'm staying here until you come home. Ben will be here any minute now—I texted him while Irene was talking to you." He glanced at me, then away. He added in a too casual voice, "Give Vince and Reed a call, will you? . . . Not yet, but you know how they can be. . . . We'll be okay. See you soon."

He handed the phone back. Frank repeated that he'd see me soon, told me to call him if I needed to talk again between now and when he got home. He told me he loved me, and I said the same back, not caring who overheard us.

I hung up and turned to Ethan. "I should have known he'd find out, but—thanks for not tipping him off before now."

He shrugged. "I was tempted, but I figured it was your decision to make."

I took a deep breath, let it out slowly. It didn't help. "I need to wait outside the car."

"Claustrophobia kicking in?" he asked, as we opened the doors.

"Yes."

"I'm calling the paper," Ethan told me.

I nodded, even as I wondered what the hell was happening to me that I hadn't thought of that on my own.

After Ethan had talked to him for a while, John asked to talk to me. I told him what little I knew, which was no more than what Ethan had given him.

"I have to go," John said suddenly. "Wrigley wants me at the board meeting. Tell Ethan to get something to me before dead-line." He ended the call before I could ask him what, if any-thing, he wanted me to write up.

I paced on the front lawn, watching as half a dozen patrol cars and a crime scene mobile unit pulled up at the end of a street.

"Wonder if Wrigley's going to hold another press confer-ence," Ethan said, clearly trying to distract me. "He was in his glory this afternoon."

The comment made me halt my pacing and stare at him.

"What?" he asked.

"Wrigley's up to something."

"Isn't he always?"

"He's asked John to come to a board meeting."

"That's happening a lot lately. You know how things are. Probably means more layoffs, which means I'm about to lose my job."

"You don't sound too broken up about it."

He looked away, and in that moment I realized how wrong I was. When he looked back at me, he said, "Aren't you in the same place? I mean, the threat hangs over you long enough, you half wish it would happen just to get it over with."

"I don't know. I don't have a lot of hope, but—I don't know. Right now, I'm just trying to figure out Wrigley. He's never invited other media into the building. Even when newsworthy events happened in the building itself. Did you see who he was hanging out with after the show?"

"The show, is it? Well, I guess it was. No. I was too inter-ested in making sure you got out of there without being button-holed."

Two of the patrol cars headed down toward the house, and minutes later, a couple of uniformed officers went into my backyard. A police helicopter began hovering overhead.

I didn't believe for a moment that the killer was lounging around the neighborhood, let alone inside my house. But I kept thinking of Nick Parrish's love of concealed traps and decided to let Vince and Reed and the uniforms clear the house. They did this quickly, and the patrol cars and the uniforms drove off. Reed stayed behind and asked me more questions about the time of night I first heard the water running, and other details, but it was hard to see how my answers could be of help. He thanked me, though, and hurried off to join Vince. Before long, the helicopter left as well. Fortunately, when the media helicopters arrived, they were focused on the activity near Marilyn Foster's car.

Ben texted Ethan that he had been asked to help the coroner's office but would join us as soon as he could.

I paced again. Ethan, who had taken out his laptop and started to write the story, suddenly halted, looked up at me, and said, "The universe is expanding."

"What?"

"I just thought I'd let you know. Saw that on a science program. A show about Einstein and Hubble and a bunch of those guys. The Big Bang theory. There was this British scientist named Hoyle, and in the program—believe it or not, on this show, they actually used the phrase 'according to Hoyle.'"

From this I understood he was making a determined effort to amuse me. He proceeded to give a recap that had a few black holes of missing information in it, but his retelling kept me distracted and probably more entertained than the original show would have. When he finally ran down, he said, "I just try to keep that in mind, you know. When things get shitty with work and all. There are bigger things than the *Las Piernas News Express*. Than assholes who try to bother you with garden hoses. And bigger than even—" He broke off and shook his head. "Well, no, I don't want to make it sound as if I don't care about those women, or as if I don't understand why you're scared."

"Bigger even than Nick Parrish and his minions," I said. "You're right, Ethan. Letting myself become obsessed with him plays it just the way he wants it. I've got to keep perspective, not give him the attention he wants."

That resolve would have been easier to maintain if Parrish and his friends had stayed a galaxy away.

NINE

In later years, Quinn Moore wondered if his mother would have told him the truth about his birth father if she had not been on drugs.

They were perfectly legal drugs, taken for pain. She was dying. Though he was fairly sure that dying in and of itself would not have been enough of an incentive to tell him the story. She began by saying that Harold Moore, the man who had divorced her when Quinn was ten, was not his father. In her confusion, she had forgotten that he already knew Harold Moore was his adoptive and not his birth father. Had her mind not been wandering between past and present, she might have recalled that the matter of his adoption was public by the time he was eighteen.

She wasn't aware that Quinn had actually learned he was adopted two years before that. He had learned it, of all places, at a shopping mall. By chance he had encountered Harold Moore there, while Moore was out shopping with his timid second wife. Quinn, given twenty bucks by his mother's latest boyfriend—who was very far from the worst of the men she had brought into his life—and told to stay out of the house for a while, had been deciding between going to see a movie and visiting an arcade when he saw the approach of the couple and the look of surprised recognition on Harold's face.

His memories of Harold were mostly of coldness and cruelty, but he gave a half wave and said, "Hi, Dad."

"Hi, Dad?" Harold said. He turned to his wife and announced to her that Quinn was not his son, that he had been tricked into adopting him, and that Quinn was a bastard.

"I've never heard better news in my life," Quinn said.

Harold turned away, red-faced, then spun back around and sucker-punched him, knocking Quinn flat. Unfortunately for Harold, he did so within plain sight of a pair of mall security guards. He was arrested for assault. Although the D.A. ultimately decided not to pursue charges, during the brief time he was in custody, Harold's second wife took advantage of this opportunity and left him.

Quinn did not tell his mother the truth about his bruised face or what Harold had said to him. He told her he had been mugged. He had been bruised before, and suffered far worse than a blow to the face, but something about that public punch and disowning awoke a long-simmering rage in Quinn Moore.

Quinn's mother chose to believe the story of the mugging, which was easy for someone with a long-standing habit of pretending not to see the truth. She told herself that the mugging was why he took up strength training and self-defense. She was disapproving but not surprised when she learned he had bought a gun.

She probably didn't know that he never practiced enough to fire it with real accuracy. She also failed to realize that he had developed a penchant for reading about poisons and household accidents and other ways a person might die before his time.

He searched in vain through her papers and belongings for a reference to someone named Quinn, deciding that he must have been named for his real father.

About two years after the mall incident, Harold Moore tried to reunite with his first wife, Quinn's mother. By then Quinn was no longer living at home—he was attending Las Piernas University. He had started out as an art student, as his mother had once been, but had changed his major to business.

When his mother told him of Harold's renewed courtship, Quinn could see that she was flattered by Harold's attention. The man had made a fortune in commercial real estate, and a prenup and excellent attorneys had ensured that the runaway second wife had received only a minuscule portion of Harold's wealth.

Harold believed Quinn's mother was the only person who had cared about him when he was poor and struggling, or so he said. Quinn thought that this was probably true. Harold also told her that was the reason he wanted her back in his life. Quinn didn't care whether or not that was true.

Quinn had supposed that his mother would be disappointed when Harold did not keep the date they made one Friday night, but while she may have been a little hurt by it, she didn't seem to be crushed, or to think it was out of character. Quinn was angry with her for even accepting the date, but he didn't show her that anger. Women were stupid creatures, after all. Whores at heart. She certainly never knew how to say no to a man.

When Harold didn't show up for work the next Monday, inquiries ultimately led police to check on his home. Harold's car was in the garage.

As police entered Harold's house, they found his car keys, wallet, and cell phone on the kitchen counter. He was not in any of the rooms of the home, or in the backyard. They began to look for indications of whether he had left his home voluntarily. Moore's toothbrush, razor, and other personal care items were in the bathroom. His empty suitcase was in a spare closet. Yet there were no signs of a struggle or forced entry.

These and other indicators made police question his few friends and family members, including his ex-wife and adopted son. None of these people were able to provide any information that resulted in solid leads.

Further investigation showed that Harold had last used the phone and one of his credit cards on the previous Thursday, the last day anyone had seen him.

Harold Moore had vanished.

The story ran for a day or two in the local news, then all public concern about him seemed to vanish as well.

Police quickly learned that Harold Moore reserved what little charm he possessed for business relationships. Most who dealt with him in real estate transactions knew him only for his ability to negotiate deals and for his knowledge of the local market—and a kind of ruthlessness. He was a workaholic who spared no time for friends.

From his attorneys and the few others who had more than a slight acquaintance with him, detectives heard again and again that he often worried that anyone who wanted to get close to him was only after his money. Most of the neighbors they spoke to described him as difficult and secretive. He was one of those people who seemed to make a hobby of estrangement.

As time went on, legal processes were brought to bear. The probate court created a conservatorship to care for his business and property. After five years, the same court declared that Harold Moore was presumed dead. His will, which his attorneys had been urging him to update long before his disappearance, left his estate to his first wife and his adopted son.

By then, though, Quinn's mother had been dead for four years. The entire estate of Harold Moore came to his stepson. At the age of twenty-three, Quinn Moore was a wealthy young man.

During her final days, not long before she lost the ability to speak coherently, Quinn's mother seemed especially restless. She was in a strange state, he thought, so anxious that even the painkillers hadn't completely taken the edge off. They simply removed the barriers of secrecy she hid behind.

She said to Quinn, "Remember Meredith, from the airport?"

Quinn easily recalled his mother's co-worker from the days when she worked as a waitress in the airport coffee shop. Meredith loved to ignite drama, loved to pry into other people's business and spread gossip or cause conflict, while she remained at a safe distance from the outcome.

"Of course," he said. "What makes you think of her?"

"She came by yesterday. To visit."

"Did she upset you?" he asked, happy to think he might have a reason to settle a score.

"No . . . no . . . I mean, not intentionally. She asked about you."

I'll just bet she did, he thought. But he didn't say anything. He could tell his mother was going to say more—he had only to wait for it.

"There's a man I used to know. Used to fix airplanes out there. He's been gone for a long time. A long time. I thought he was gone for good."

Still he waited, mentally saying, *His name is Quinn . . .*

But that wasn't what she said.

"Meredith told me . . . he's moved back here. His name is Nicholas Parrish. I wanted to warn you about him."

"Warn me?"

"Yes." She twisted the bedsheet in her hand. "Quinn—Quinn, he thinks he's your father. But he's not!"

"Why should he think that?" he asked, able to tell, as he always was, that she was lying. But what part of it was the lie?

"Stay away from him, Quinn. Please! Promise me."

"Why?"

"He's very dangerous. That's why I was so happy when he left. He left before I found out I was pregnant with you, or God knows what he would have done. It doesn't matter, because— Well, he's wrong. I was so angry when Meredith told me she'd mentioned you to him. But . . . well, she doesn't know. I'm hoping she'll go back to him and tell him she was wrong. But either way, stay away from him, all right? Promise me."

"Okay, I promise." He was the better liar.

"I was always afraid Nick would come back. I married Harold because he was big, and I thought he could protect us."

"Some protection. Harold beat us both."

She looked away, then looked back at him. "He was mean, but he was mean enough to keep Nick away. Nick would have killed us. Nick is a killer."

"A killer?" He almost laughed. "You should tell the police."

"No good. Can't prove it."

"All right, but there must be more to the story than that. How do you know he's a killer?"

She didn't answer, but even through the haze of drugs, her fear was palpable.

She stayed silent, brooding, until the weariness that had hold of her in those last days of her life allowed her to drift off. When she awoke, she said, "I wonder if he did it."

"Who did what?"

"Nick. I've always wondered if he killed Harold."

Perhaps, he thought, *she's being devious. Trying to trick me into an admission.* What was the natural response? He wasn't sure. "Really?"

"Yes."

"What makes you so sure Harold is dead, let alone murdered?"

"Harold never would have left money and his car and his house behind."

"True," he said. "But . . . probably he just had an accident."

"No. Maybe. I don't know."

She was staring at him. Time to change the subject. "So if this Nick Parrish isn't my father, who is?"

"He's dead," she said quickly.

"How sad. But who was he?"

"It doesn't matter," she said. "I've forgotten his name. But he was good. A good man."

She was lying, of course. She was such a shitty liar, he wondered why she even bothered. Even if he had doubted Nick Parrish was his father, he wouldn't have believed this story of hers about an imaginary good man. Quinn knew she had never been attracted to a good man in her lifetime. But that wasn't the real reason for his rejection of the fairy tale she was trying to sell him.

He knew himself. No one who was good had anything to do with the making of Quinn Moore.

Quinn drove out to the airport that afternoon. At nineteen, he met his father—a man who would, within a few years, be infamous. The day after that meeting, Meredith failed to show up for work. Other than a mention in the annual article on local missing persons cases in the *Las Piernas News Express,* she was all but forgotten.

TEN

I slept better that night than I had for several days. I suppose
it could have been a matter of sheer exhaustion, but no one
will ever convince me it was anything other than having
Frank and the dogs back at home.

When Frank came through the door, I didn't care about the
"been camping" funkiness, the week's growth of beard, or who
was watching—he gave me a fierce hug and a kiss that under
any other set of circumstances would have had me taking off
my underwear. As it was, I managed not to let the dogs trip us,
or to forget to say hello to Jack, who just grinned knowingly,
set down the gear he was helping to carry in, and said, "I'll be
next door if you need me."

"Let me give you a hand with your gear, Jack," Ethan said
and left with him.

"Ethan, giving us privacy?" Frank asked when they were
gone.

"You're wasting the four or five minutes of it we'll get," I
said.

Once the dogs had completed their exuberant rituals to celebrate the reunification of the pack, and Frank had cleaned up
and stowed his gear, he asked me all the questions Reed had

asked and a few more, doing all he could not to make it seem like an interrogation. It really wasn't—he wanted to be caught up, but not so that he could take over the case. I understood the way his mind worked. We both were in professions that require a person to be inquisitive, and the only way to the real answers is through the right questions.

Ethan came back to say he had walked down to the end of the street but complained there was no getting anywhere near the crime scene. He gave Frank a hopeful look, but Frank shook his head. "I'm not going to get my ass chewed out for interfering just for your sake."

Ethan shrugged. "I wasn't down there for my sake."

Frank looked chagrined. "Of course. Look, thanks for coming over here last night. I owe a lot to you and Ben for that. But as much as I'm grateful, this would be the worst time for me to try to butt into Vince and Reed's investigation."

"Yeah, I understand. Besides, even the television news 'copters can't get a view of it. Coroner's got those privacy barriers up."

We watched the late news together and saw that Ethan was right—the coroner's office had essentially tented the car, protecting the body—and most of the car—from being seen by cameras. The television reporters didn't have anything we didn't know—in fact, we had more details. The police hadn't released the information that the body was frozen, or that it was painted.

"Better check with Reed and Vince before you write anything about that," Frank warned.

Ethan and I exchanged a look, and Frank swore under his breath but didn't say more.

Ben came to the house to pick up Ethan. He told us that the police had no leads on the identity of the woman in the trunk, but we all knew that if none of her personal effects were in the car, and she wasn't a known criminal or otherwise familiar to the police, in all likelihood much more time and lots of effort would be required to find out who she was.

A good portion of that work would probably fall to Ben, since the coroner's office often brought him in to help with any case where the body wasn't newly dead, or where it was found in an unusual condition. He'd use his expertise as a forensic anthropologist and that of whatever team he assembled to work with him to preserve as much evidence as possible from the trunk and her remains. He'd then try to determine the victim's identity—if not from her DNA or fingerprints, which might not be in any law enforcement–accessible database—then by studying indicators of age in her teeth and bones. He'd discover whatever her remains might tell about her general health, previous injuries or surgeries, whether she was most likely left- or right-handed, and perhaps her possible occupation or hobbies. He'd learn what he could of her dental health, and perhaps where she most likely had had any dental work done. He'd learn whether she had been injured before being killed. He'd also be looking for evidence left by her killer that might lead to that person's identity. He'd study the style and nature of the artwork on her body, the materials used, and determine whether she had been painted before or after death.

Ben looked troubled, but I didn't get a chance to ask him any questions—he was needed at the coroner's office and didn't have time to do more than pick up his gear and take Ethan home. By then, everyone was ready to call it a night.

I crawled into bed with Frank. I could feel his tension. I hadn't wanted his homecoming to be like this. I put my arms around him and used my fingertips to tap in a pattern on his back. I was halfway through the message before he realized what I was doing. "Morse code?" he said, laughing.

I replied: -.-- . ---

He knew Morse code, too, and I could feel him smiling in the dark. He waited as I repeated my invitation. He didn't respond to it in code, but he clearly got the message.

Frank was still asleep when I left for work the next morning. The day was postcard beautiful, and once I was away from the place where Marilyn Foster's car had been parked, I spent the rest of the drive telling myself I had much to be thankful for, to cheer up, and lots more along those lines. By the time the Wrigley Building came into view, the pep talk was working. The Wrigley Building was one of those imposing old newspaper palaces, complete with gargoyles. You couldn't look at it without knowing something important was going on inside.

When I turned down the alley to the employee parking lot, I got a shock. Something was going on, all right. The lot was full. I hadn't seen so many cars parked there in a decade.

And oddly enough, that told me something was wrong.

I parked on the street and went in through the front doors. Geoffrey, our ancient security guard, looked up. His face was tearstained.

"Geoff?"

"Go on in, Irene. Go on in."

Just then one of the accounting office workers came downstairs. She said, "Mr. Wrigley asked me to send you into the meeting, Geoff. I'm sorry."

For a moment I thought he was going to refuse to go.

"What meeting?" I asked.

Her brows rose as she noticed my presence. "They'll want you, too, Ms. Kelly. Everyone. In the room where they held the press conference."

I walked with Geoff to the stairs. "We're shutting down," I

said, knowing nothing else could bring so many people into the building at one time.

He nodded. "Never thought I'd live to see the day."

We took two seats at the back. Others filed in, including Lydia, who took the empty seat on my other side. Ethan came in a moment later and sat next to her. John was standing at the front of the room, arms crossed, leaning against the wall. Wrigley asked everyone to please give him their attention. Once he had it, he handed the meeting over to one of his cousins, James Anderson, the current chairman of the publishing board. It was a good strategy, I thought. Anderson was well liked by the staff. Someone who cared but had been given power way too late to use it to save the paper.

His words were soft and measured. About our history. About efforts made to try to preserve the paper. Something about "an untenable position." I was too numb to hear the rest of what amounted to a eulogy.

I kept telling myself I had expected this to come one day, but only then did I realize how fervently I had hoped that day would never come.

Anderson was saying something about the decision to shut down now, when they could still give everyone two months' pay in lieu of the sixty days' notice California law otherwise required. Someone from HR would give us more details about all of that, and insurance, pensions, and any other benefits.

If Wrigley thought he wasn't going to have to face the wrath of his employees because his cousin delivered the bad news, he was wrong. Anderson handed the meeting back to him, saying as he did so that he was sure Wrigley wanted to spend some time answering our questions, a patently false statement. Anderson added that they were here for us, and would stay to talk things out as long as any staff member had questions.

As Wrigley took the microphone, there were plenty of angry shouts, dozens of questions he was unable to answer, and a few he was afraid to answer. He looked nervously at me a couple of times, probably expecting anything from a verbal skewering to a physical assault, but I found he seemed more insignificant and unworthy of my attention than ever before. I heard a soft, choked-back sob next to me and put an arm around Geoff's skinny shoulders as his tears fell. There were tears on other faces, too, although I found myself unable to cry. A glance at Lydia told me she was in a state similar to my own. Numbness.

Wrigley handed the mike off to the head of HR, who said there were packets to be handed out, come and get yours when your name was called.

So I signed my name for receipt of my packet and went upstairs to gather "personal possessions only" under the watchful eyes of a set of security guards hired from an outside company. A few friends stopped me in the hallway to mention that they hoped to see me in church, which was a form of invitation to join them at Banyon's, a local watering hole popular with the press and off-duty cops.

I walked toward my desk and came to a halt. My desk—or the one I still thought of as mine—was the only wooden desk in the newsroom. It was a plain desk, nothing fancy about it, but it had belonged to Connor O'Connor, my mentor, and the thought of parting from it seemed unbearable to me. I started to empty it out, but the more I thought of letting it be sold off to some liquidator, the more I felt certain that I had to at least try to save it. I hurried back to the room downstairs.

Almost everyone was gone or in the newsroom emptying their own desks by then. A couple of people were talking to the chairman of the board, and John was still leaning against the wall. Wrigley was ambling across the room, heading for the door, when he saw me and came to a standstill, a look of alarm on his face. He had to be feeling guilty about something, given the way he kept reacting to me.

I walked toward him and, out of the corner of my eye, saw John straighten and begin approaching, too.

"Mr. Wrigley," I began.

"Irene, excuse me, I'm just heading out—"

"I want to buy my desk."

"The desk? Oh." He looked at his shoes. "I thought perhaps you—"

"Perhaps I what?"

He glanced back at his cousin, then muttered, "I am sorry if yesterday's press conference disturbed you in any way."

So Wrigley had been given a reprimand. Judging from the scowl on John's face as he approached, he was about to get another one. "It did, but it's too late to worry about it now. So apology accepted. About the desk—how much will it cost?"

"I'm not really sure the paper will want to part with it."

"What are you talking about?" I asked in disbelief. "There is no paper."

He turned red, then said coldly, "You want to start buying our assets? Fine." He then named a price that was ten times my annual salary.

"Wrigley, you are such a little turd biter," John snarled before I could reply. "Every time you open your mouth, shit falls out from between your teeth."

"Now see here," Wrigley said indignantly.

"You put her through hell yesterday, made her front for your last little attempt to boost your ego. Don't you think you could be reasonable about a desk?"

"What's going on?" a new voice asked. We turned to see Mr. Anderson approaching.

"Ms. Kelly wants to buy her desk," John said. "Mr. Wrigley has offered to sell it to her."

"Sell it to her?" Anderson repeated blankly.

"Oh yes." John repeated the price, and Anderson's brows rose.

Wrigley's face went redder still, but he said, "It's an antique."

"It's a beat-up piece of shit that you've tried to get rid of every year," John snapped.

"If that's so, Ms. Kelly," Anderson said, turning to me, "why do you want it?"

"It was O'Connor's," I said.

"Ah." He turned to Wrigley. "Winston, setting prices is really not within your authority at this time. Actually, there isn't anything more that will be needed from you. Perhaps you should go home."

Wrigley slouched away in defeat.

"The desk is yours, Ms. Kelly," Anderson said.

"Yes, that's the one I want."

"No, I mean, the desk is yours to take home."

"Oh, thank you. But how much—?"

"Not a cent." He paused. "I was very fond of O'Connor myself. I know he'd want you to have it."

"Thank you," I said and couldn't manage to say more.

He put a hand on my shoulder and said, "You let me know if I can be of any help to you. I mean that. We were always proud of the work you and your colleagues did. I'm so very sorry we couldn't continue."

And I knew, perhaps in a way I hadn't known before, that he was telling the truth, that if he could have found a way to continue publishing the *Express,* he would have done it.

He told me he'd leave word with Geoff to let me into the building whenever I wanted to pick up the desk, provided I could do so within the week.

"You're keeping Geoff on?"

"For as long as we can," he said.

John walked upstairs with me. "Thanks for sticking up for me," I said.

"What are editors for?"

I could hear the bitterness beneath that. "John—"

"Oh, never mind me. I should thank you for giving me a chance to light into him. Not one tenth of what I'd really like to say to him, but you have to take your opportunities where you find them."

"Come to church later on," I said. "I think there will be a choir there singing that same song."

I heard laughter from the newsroom. Ah, gallows humor. I was going to miss that. As we walked in, I heard the tail end of the next rude joke, and more laughter.

"You guys should have been downstairs just now," John said and told them how much Wrigley wanted for my desk.

That led to impolite speculation on what Wrigley planned to do with the money.

I finished packing up my desk. As I gathered my notes from unfinished stories, I found myself wondering who would tell the story of Las Piernas now. Who would write about Marilyn Foster, or the woman in the car trunk? Those stories were sensational, so maybe someone at the television or radio stations would. But sensational murders are a very small part of what goes on in a city of half a million people.

How would the people of Las Piernas find out about the high school baseball games, or how much the new school uniforms might cost? Who would warn them that a fee hike was being proposed for use of the biggest local park? Or tell them that the mayor was using taxpayer money for family vacations? That their state assembly representative didn't really live in the district and had defaulted on the mortgage for his sham address?

And what the hell was I going to do with myself all day?

ELEVEN

Frank was enjoying his last day of his week's vacation by doing some gardening. At least I didn't walk in to find him surrounded by dancing girls, which would have been a real kicker to a day from hell. Apparently he heard my car, or the dogs tipped him off to my arrival, because he was coming into the house just as I opened the front door.

"Hi, honey, I'm home!" I called out. "Possibly forever."

There was a brief silence while he processed that, then he said, "Fired or laid off?"

I laughed. A little hysterically, but I laughed. "When I go out, I do it in style. They're shutting the whole place down. I would have preferred fired."

"Oh, Irene," he said and opened his arms. I went right into them, not caring if I got dirt on my work clothes. What the hell did it matter? Are they work clothes if you're out of work?

After a while, he said, "We'll be okay, you know."

I did know. We had been preparing for this day for several years, and seriously planning for it financially during the last two. I was in a better position than most of my colleagues. My husband had a good-paying job that would provide health insurance, and enough time in with the LPPD to avoid any layoffs that might someday come to his department. We didn't have kids who were depending on us. I had sold the house I owned before I met Frank, and managed to do that at the height of the Southern California real estate bubble, so we had savings. We didn't owe anything on Frank's house, and neither of us was the acquisitive type, so we didn't have much in the way of other kinds of debt, either. We had enough for the upkeep and taxes on some mountain property Frank had inherited, and no other big obligations.

"Yeah," I said quietly. "I know. But I also know that you have days when you want to leave the department, and now I'm afraid you're trapped there."

"No, don't ever worry about that. I'm fine. If I need to change jobs, I'll find a way to do it."

"The universe is expanding."

"I'll take your word for it."

"It's something Ethan said to me. God. Poor Ethan. What's going to happen to him?"

"Do you seriously doubt he'll land on his feet?"

"No . . . I just hope he doesn't get too bruised on the way down."

We went through a litany of the people I was closest to at the paper. Stuart Angert had taken his retirement months ago. Mark Baker's kids had just finished college, and I'm sure there was some debt there, but his wife had a good job, so maybe they'd be okay. Like the rest of us, Lydia had been expecting this possibility, but she and I—and many others—were without definite plans for future employment. Her fiancé, Guy St. Germain, was an executive with the Bank of Las Piernas, and since it was one of those local banks that hadn't gone in for shaky lending practices, Guy's job was secure. He made enough to support them both, but I couldn't picture her being happy with idleness. I had no idea what John's situation was. I'd asked him once, and he'd told me not to worry about him.

"A useless command," I said now.

"Yes," Frank said. "And I admit I'm worried about you."

"Me?"

"Yes. You. . . . In a lot of ways, you define yourself as a reporter, and I hope you'll get to keep working as one. But what worries me is that you identify so strongly with the *Express* itself. You grew up reading O'Connor's stories—"

"That reminds me, we're getting his desk."

"Your desk from work?"

"Yes. Is that okay?"

He smiled. It was one of those you-are-crazy-but-that's-what-I-love-about-you smiles. I'll take one any time.

"Sure," he said, "but you're proving my point. You've been doing this work for a long time—"

"Don't remind me how long."

"A long time now," he said. "And except for a couple of years here and there, you've worked at the *Express* most of your adult life. Being a reporter for that paper was what you dreamed of doing as a little kid, and you got your dream. That's not something a lot of people can say about their work lives."

"No. I've always been lucky. Except at cards. So I won't try to become a professional poker player."

"What a relief. That was what I was working up to, of course."

"Okay, I get it. I'll stop trying to dodge the point you're making. You're right, but . . ." I broke off, tears finally threatening.

"Hey, it's all right," he said, pulling me closer. "My real point was, go easy on yourself. You'll find what it is you're going to do next. Or it will find you."

"Aren't you afraid I'm going to sit here eating bonbons all day?"

"I'm more afraid you'll run yourself into the ground. Or decide to redecorate."

That made me sit up. "You know, I do want to paint the guest room."

He sighed dramatically.

"What? I'm just talking about painting."

"It is never—never—just painting."

He was right, of course.

Two weeks went by. I did some serious drinking with my fellow former co-workers that first evening, was given an unpleasant reminder about hangovers the next morning, and called it quits. I realized that Ethan—who went to an AA meeting that night—and most of the other people I wanted to spend time with weren't going to step into the bar.

I sent off résumés to any media within commuting distance, knowing damned well they weren't hiring, but I was unable to surrender to this new state of aimless existence without a fight.

One of the hardest things, at first, was being cut off from the constant flow of information that was part of life in the newsroom. Waiting for local television news to come on and then listening to its four-sentence coverage of city stories was making me crazy. I felt a frustrating sense of isolation.

The police were facing their own frustrations. The woman in the car trunk remained a Jane Doe. There was no ID in the trunk, and her fingerprints didn't turn up any matches with criminal records. Ben's work had determined that she was between eighteen and twenty-five years of age and had suffered a stab wound to the temple with a slender object, possibly an ice pick. There was another, similar wound to her heart, one that had been much harder to find beneath the paint. Bruising indicated she had been bound and gagged at some point. Toxicology tests were still pending. No DNA other than her own had been found on her remains. Ben believed she had been thoroughly washed before she was painted, and painted after she was dead.

The coroner's office had submitted her DNA to the federal database for missing persons cases, but Ben told me that so few jurisdictions were making use of it and so few families knew about it, he didn't have high hopes of a hit.

The Marilyn Foster case hadn't progressed any further, either.

The police had no leads on the identity of the killer or killers. They were interviewing some of the people who posted on the Moths' blog, but that didn't seem to be getting them anywhere. Nor did they have any leads on who turned on the hoses in the middle of the night, but they did believe there was a connection between that and the killings. Which was of no comfort to me.

So I didn't go out too much during those two weeks.

Frank helped me pick up O'Connor's desk. At first it was in our living room, taking up more of one wall than I expected it to, until I could make space for it in the guest room. Frank kept telling me just to take it easy for a little while.

Ethan helped me move everything out of the guest room and paint it. "Least I could do after staying here rent free," he said. He helped me keep Cody and the dogs occupied while the floor was refinished. I gave away the desk we'd had in there, along with a small table, which made room for O'Connor's desk.

At the end of the second week, Ethan helped me put the furniture back into the room. He ran his fingers over the top of the desk. "He smoked?" he asked, looking at a burn mark.

"No, at least not in the years I knew him. The desk belonged to Jack Corrigan before it became O'Connor's."

"Wow. O'Connor's own mentor."

"And one of my teachers when I was in J-school."

"How old is this thing?"

I laughed.

"I didn't mean it like that!"

"I'm not sure how old it is—John Walters and Stuart both thought it was from the early nineteen thirties. It could be older than that. Maybe I'll visit Helen Corrigan and ask her. She and Jack were at the paper at the same time."

"I remember the story Hailey wrote about her."

Hailey Freed, who had been one of the first laid off. "What do you hear from Hailey these days?"

"She's selling drugs."

"What?"

"Pharmaceuticals. It's one of the family businesses. Her grandfather's, I think. He gave her a job going around to doctors' offices as a salesperson. She's really good at it. Making big bucks."

"Does she like it?"

He hesitated. "Not sure. She likes being good at it, and likes having money. But—I don't know. It's always hard to tell with Hailey."

"And what about you?"

"I've got some plans. And an idea for a business," he said but wouldn't tell me more. When I started to pry, he suddenly remembered that he had promised to go next door to visit Jack.

So I sat alone at my old desk. At O'Connor's old desk. At Corrigan's. I touched an ancient ink stain from a fountain pen. I pulled out one of the slides, could see little worn places where typewriters had sat upon it. Thought of all the words written at this desk.

I felt tired. I had finished my big project of sprucing up the guest room and finding a place for the desk. Now what? Sleep?

I folded my arms on that worn surface, laid my head down, and closed my eyes. I wanted to dream away a world that no longer cared about those words. I fought against a sense of loss so deep, it would have taken a hundred funerals to bury it.

I'm of Irish descent, and I was at a desk that had belonged to two men who were sons of immigrants, each a bit closer to the ould sod than I. So perhaps I can be forgiven for saying that a feeling came over me—others may prefer to say that, between my never-distant fears and an abundance of sentiment brought on by all that reminiscence, I was overwrought. They can explain it that way if it makes them happy. For me, a feeling came over me.

I didn't hear voices or see a vision or anything like that. But I thought of Corrigan, one of the most determined individuals I've met in my life, and remembered how he'd helped O'Connor when O'Connor's sister had gone missing in 1945. Her grave was found five years later, and O'Connor had taken his grief and forged it into a relentless campaign to ensure that missing persons cases and the unidentified dead weren't forgotten in Las Piernas. O'Connor had died solving one of those cases.

And the notion came to me that this legacy, of which I was one small part, wasn't dead. It wasn't about a building or a piece of newsprint on a driveway. It was about the story, whatever that story might be. Every story was a gift.

I had a story. I needed to go after it. It was as simple as that.

I needed to find out who that woman was, that young woman who had been left in that shabby tomb at the end of my street. Who had been hurt and frightened, who had been demeaned even in death.

I might not solve her murder, but I was going to do my damnedest to name her.

But how?

And almost as soon as I asked myself that, I knew that my search for her name had to begin with another name, one the city had already nearly forgotten: Marilyn Foster. I got up from the desk and made a phone call.

TWELVE

Dwayne Foster had a story of his own, of course. One advantage of not having a deadline was that I had the leisure to let him tell it. By turns he was angry with the police, then cognizant of the fact that they couldn't work miracles, full of half-formed plans for everything from pulling up stakes and moving to another part of the country to staying and delivering his own form of justice to the killer.

After he wound down a little, we started going over some questions I had. On the night Marilyn disappeared, he had come home at about half past midnight. Dinner had been waiting for him as usual. Marilyn's habit was to go to bed between ten-thirty and eleven. Police said computer records showed she had been online at about nine-thirty.

"I just want to make sure I'm not making any assumptions about Marilyn's routines and habits. Did she ever go for long walks at night?"

"No. Even though this is a safe neighborhood—" He broke off, then started again. "Even though we used to think this was a safe neighborhood, she was afraid to do that. Being diabetic, she didn't like to exercise alone, because, well . . . she was good about her meds and all that, but she wasn't always good

68 ♠ JAN BURKE

at gauging what she needed to eat to avoid going too low on her blood sugar. So just to be on the safe side . . ." The word seemed to catch on him like a small, sharp hook, and he looked away. He took a breath, then went on. "She had routines at the gym, and her trainer there was someone who knew about diabetes and what to do and all that. Sometimes we went walking together before I left for work, but if you're asking if she could've been walking around alone in the neighborhood at midnight or whenever it was, no ma'am."

"I'm just trying to figure out the logistics. Her car was gone, but her purse and phone were here. Any woman I know would have taken her purse and phone if she was driving somewhere at night, even—perhaps especially—in an emergency. There were no signs of forced entry. So one of two things happened—she went out of the house and encountered someone there, or she invited someone in who then forced her to go out to the car."

"The police said something like that. They had me give them a DNA sample, then took our trash. Said that if she had given him something to eat or drink, his DNA might be on something. But unless it's someone she met at the dentist's office, or one of the neighbors, I just don't know why she would have let anyone in, or gone outside in the middle of the night."

"From all you've told me, it sounds as if your wife was a helpful person. If a young man came to the door and said he'd been in a car accident, and had already called the police but he needed her to help him with his injured, pregnant wife until they got there, would she step outside to take a look? Or if he pretended to be crying and asked her if she could please tell him whose dog he had just hit?"

"I see what you're saying. Only there's no wife or dog or whatever."

"Right. Or he's wearing a uniform, or—whatever—does something to gain her trust. If she was taken between nine-thirty and midnight, then there's a chance it really wasn't all that late when he first arrived. None of your neighbors saw anyone come here that night?"

"No. But I'm not really surprised. No one around here pays much attention to anyone else. The police asked them all—over and over again. Someone said they heard a car, assumed it was mine. Frankly, I think that lady is lying and just wanted to be part of the drama—you know what I mean?"

"Yes. Maybe if we look at this from another angle—he arrived here somehow, on foot or was dropped off. Maybe he was given a ride by someone who had no idea what he was up to but dropped him off here." I paused. "But anyone who was innocent and unaware would have spoken up by now if they've heard the news."

He shook his head. "I think about that all the time now—all the news stories about missing people that I never paid much attention to. Stories about murders. I didn't really care, so maybe no one really cares about Marilyn."

"You can't think like that, Dwayne. Tell me—have people around here offered to help you?"

He sighed. "Yes, you're right. I've seen the good side of people, too. I'm in a mood, I guess. Kept hoping they'd catch the guy by now. But her family, people she knew, even total strangers have asked me what they could do to help me out. I never could figure out an answer."

"Give yourself time. You're probably still numb."

"Yeah. I am." He gave me a fleeting grin. "That is, when I'm not just pissed off. But I have to change my attitude. To be honest, I was totally surprised by how many people were at the funeral, how many told me that she'd touched their lives in some way. I've got a lot of thank-you notes to write."

He looked over at a table laden with sympathy cards, but I doubted he was going to tackle that task anytime soon.

"To go back to what I was thinking about," I said, "you didn't see a car parked in front of the house that night?"

"No. I'm sure of that, because I parked on the street, and there wasn't any other car near where I parked. My pickup is kind of wide, so I usually park on the street, so I don't block her car in the garage. I mean, I did. I still do . . ." He looked lost.

"The police still have her car?"

"Yeah. They're still hoping they can find some DNA somewhere on it."

"A couple of things occur to me. One is that her killer planned everything out and had a way to get here that didn't leave his own car parked on the street. Maybe he parked on a neighboring street, but it's also possible he had an accomplice who brought him here."

"What about a cab or a bus?"

"Possible, although he'd know that the driver might remember bringing him out here. The police have probably already checked on cab companies."

"Haven't they already done most of what we're doing anyway?"

"Maybe."

"So why are you staying interested?"

"I've found myself with extra time on my hands lately."

He studied me for a moment, and I grew uncomfortable with the scrutiny. "Naw. That's not it."

"Pardon?"

"You've been straightforward with me up to just now. What's going on?" He frowned. "Her car was parked near your house, the news said. When you found it. Right?"

"Right."

"Not just a coincidence it was there, was it?"

"Probably not." I told him about the garden hose, which made his face drain of color.

"Holy God Almighty," he said. "You think he's after you?"

"I don't know. Maybe. I don't know of any connection I have to your wife, and I have no idea who the young woman left in the car trunk might be. And I sure as hell have no idea why he would target me, or even try to scare me." For a moment I thought of talking to Dwayne about Nick Parrish, but he had probably already seen the news reports on the Moths and probably would say what everyone else kept saying to me: "Nick Parrish is in prison."

"Your husband is a homicide detective, right?" he asked.

"Yes."

"So he works late at night, too? Like I do?"

"Sometimes."

He put his face in his hands. "I think about the lousy shift differential, and I wonder, if I had worked day shift, would he have picked someone else?"

"Don't," I said.

He looked up.

"Don't play that game. Even a bodyguard can't protect another person every hour of every day. Don't do that to yourself."

"I can't help it."

"Okay, fair enough. Should I come back another time?"

"Sorry, no, I'll be all right."

"Do you think you could do me a couple of favors?"

I explained that I was fairly sure Marilyn or someone close to her had unwittingly given the killer information he would need for his plans—where she lived, if she had dogs, what Dwayne's work hours were, and other details.

"So I'd like to spend some time looking at what's on her computer, if it's still here."

"Yeah, the police just copied the hard drive. I know most of her passwords."

"I may need to ask a friend of mine who's a better hacker than I am to take a look at it, but we can make a start."

I also asked to be given the numbers of his wife's hairdresser, her pastor, her sister, her closest friends.

"Men and women?"

"Yes."

"Okay, and you know what? I'll write a note telling them that it's okay for them to talk to you, and that you are helping me out and not working for the paper anymore."

The kindness of that offer nearly made up for the hollow feeling its wording gave me.

"Anything else you want to look at?" he asked.

"Let's start with the sympathy cards," I said, deciding my own bereavement was nothing next to his.

So I went after the story.

I spent time becoming acquainted with a dead woman. I came to know Marilyn Foster by talking to those who missed her. Some were afraid—the lightning strike of violent death had pierced the pretense most of us adopt to some degree, that our lives are safe. As far as they were concerned, talking about Marilyn's murder just might be akin to holding up a metal rod on a stormy day. Better to hunker down until you could pretend again.

Fortunately, most seemed to find comfort in talking to me. For them, the grief and anger and helplessness that came with her sudden loss were eased a bit by doing something—anything—to try to help apprehend her murderer.

They trusted me.

I was going to try to be worthy of it.

It wasn't the only way I kept busy, but pursuing that story got me going again. Rachel Giocopazzi, wife of Frank's partner, Pete Baird, asked me to do a little temporary work at her private investigation firm. It wasn't unlike work I did as a reporter, mostly tracking down property records and the like. I also helped set up a database program she needed on her office computers and taught her assistant how to do the entry work on it, but I don't think any of that amounted to fifteen hours altogether.

Rachel used most of the time I was there to convince me to let her teach me more about self-defense. "I lost my workout partner, so this will be good for me," she said.

"I've seen you in action. I'm not up to your speed."

"Of course you aren't, but going over the basics with a beginner will be good for me, and if I need a tougher workout, Frank can join us." So we set up a rigorous schedule of lessons that helped me to work off some stress several times a week.

Working off stress wasn't my big motivator. I never needed to be persuaded to practice. Rachel was an excellent instructor. She even brought in other people to help me test my new skills. No matter who she put me up against, though, I always had one opponent in mind. I didn't believe for a moment that it was a marathon he was dreaming of from his prison cell.

THIRTEEN

Donovan Cotter kept his face expressionless as he walked over to the picnic table in the park. He was wearing casual clothing in order to fit in with the setting. He knew this park. He had already spent time assuring himself that the other two had arrived alone, as instructed. He had been amused to observe them making similar efforts, although he was quite sure neither had detected his presence.

The bench was filthy. He avoided sitting on the bird droppings spattered along one end and made sure that he gave no sign of his disgust. He sat first, and Kai and Quinn took seats on the other side of the table. He viewed this as a good sign. They were giving him more real estate, as it were, and allowing him a dominant position.

He was the oldest of the three, but that did not make him feel any real sense of seniority. He knew that they would not accept his authority in any real way—at thirty-two, he was almost ten years older than Kai but only a year older than Quinn. The idea of trying to relate to them as their "big brother" would have made him laugh if he had been able to find the least bit of humor in this situation.

Quinn had approached him and revealed their connection to each other a few years ago. This was his first time meeting Kai.

Donovan disliked him on sight.

He had felt the same way about Quinn when he first met him, and that hadn't changed. Fine tailored clothes, facile charm, and a captivating smile were not enough to prevent Donovan from seeing the shark who hid behind them. Even for this meeting in the park, Quinn had worn a suit. Perhaps he thought that would give him power. If so, he would be disappointed.

Kai was dressed in jeans and a T-shirt, neither of which looked or smelled as if it had been in a washing machine lately. His brown hair fell into his eyes. It seemed he didn't own a brush, either.

The three of them looked nothing alike, which Donovan found a relief. Quinn had light brown hair and blue eyes. Kai, dark hair and brown eyes. Donovan's own hair was golden blond, his eyes green.

Quinn made the introductions while Kai studied Donovan in a wondering way, much like the way Quinn had first observed him. The concept of brotherhood was doubtless odd to each of them, but Donovan would not allow himself to betray any curiosity.

"This meeting is not a good idea," he said.

"Kind of an insulting way to start a family reunion, don't you think?" Kai said.

"We are hardly a family. Half brothers at best."

"No, that's not it—he's still afraid we'll be seen together by the police," Quinn chided.

"Wrong," Donovan said calmly. "While I realize this meeting appeals to your flair for the overly dramatic, Quinn, it's foolish. There's no reason for us to meet in person, and it introduces risks we do not need to take. The police won't patrol here—at most a park ranger will drive past in an hour or so. But what if, down the line, one of us gets caught? Anyone who happens to be walking through this section of the park today might recall having seen us together."

"We're all intelligent enough to talk our way out of a situation like that," Quinn said.

Donovan decided not to say more. He did not believe in wasting his breath and was unhappy with himself for taking the time to express his displeasure in the first place.

Kai looked between them, then said to Quinn, "So let's get down to business. Why are we waiting?"

Quinn frowned in irritation. Clearly, Donovan thought, Quinn expected to be the alpha dog here. Kai had better watch out—Quinn wouldn't tolerate his younger brother nipping at his heels.

"It has taken me a while to get hired there. But I'm on staff now. I'll be in touch with you soon for your help." He turned to Donovan. "What has she been doing?"

"What you'd expect a reporter, even a former reporter, to do. She's investigating."

"Close to anything?"

"She may be. She's extremely thorough. She spent the first two weeks not doing much, she's spent the last two weeks asking questions of people who knew Marilyn Foster."

"Let me get rid of her now," Kai said.

"I'll find another outlet for your impulsiveness, Kai," Quinn said.

"I don't need your help."

"No, you don't." Quinn quickly changed tacks. "You know I respect your abilities, Kai. But I'm sure you can imagine why Daddy Dearest wants her for himself."

Kai subsided.

Donovan wondered if Kai would ever figure out that by saying "let me" to Quinn, he had already placed himself in subservience to someone who should not be trusted with control. Watching how Kai interacted with Quinn—he now sat brooding, tapping his fingers on the tabletop in impatience—Donovan doubted his capacity to make that evaluation.

Quinn spent the next forty minutes laying out plans and giving them a set of signals and code phrases. Donovan wanted to laugh in his face, to tell him he was no James Bond. But he merely listened and replied as briefly as possible whenever a response was asked of him. His own part in these affairs came near the end of the plan, which was more than fine with him. He didn't demonstrate the depth of his boredom. To do so would be as revealing as to show too much interest.

Kai, on the other hand, had quickly changed moods, and now eagerly drank in every detail, clearly engrossed. Let him develop a case of hero worship, then. Donovan didn't need this sort of foolishness.

He considered walking off, simply as an experiment, to watch them lose self-control and behave rashly. He spent a pleasant few moments fantasizing his own reaction at that point.

Quinn, ever the showman, brought his attention back by saying, "I should have told you this long ago, but—we aren't alone."

"What are you saying?" Kai demanded, looking around.

"Why, that we have another brother," Quinn said.

"And you've been dealing with him secretly, is that it? Well, I don't like it! Who is it?"

"Forgive me, Kai. I think it best—really, you will soon thank me—if I don't tell you any more. You won't be meeting him in any case."

Kai ranted for a while, seemed to notice that Donovan was showing no emotion, and turned to him. "Why are you letting me do all the arguing? Don't you care?"

"No," Donovan said.

Kai seemed almost ready to leap across the picnic table but checked himself, studying Donovan again. "Why not?"

"For all I know, in the years he lived here, Nick Parrish could have fathered a dozen brats. There are doubtless others in other cities. I should add, since Quinn has started this confessional mode, that for all Quinn knows, I may know others myself. Perhaps they aren't all brothers."

He was pleased to see a fleeting little widening of Quinn's eyes. He had worried and surprised him. Good.

Quinn recovered quickly, though. He smiled and said, "Maybe so." His tone implied that he thought Donovan was bluffing.

"After all," Donovan said, "the so-called Moths seem to have an inexplicable devotion to him, don't they?"

That time he had scored a hit. Quinn stiffened a little. Even Kai noticed it. Kai subsided again, watching his older brothers warily. Donovan was beginning to revise his opinion of Kai. He still disliked him, but he thought he might be more intelligent than he had first believed. Capable, at least, of learning.

Quinn hurriedly changed the subject back to their larger plans.

At long last, it was time to go, and this presented a problem that Donovan would have found laughable under other circumstances. None of them trusted his brothers enough to walk away and turn his back on them, or to leave the other two behind to forge new alliances. Quinn and Kai would not address the problem, so there was simply a lot of shifting of weight on their parts. Donovan took control.

"I'm the only one here without a weapon," he lied but was pleased to see their surprise at being caught at their own rule breaking. He was more pleased to see the measure of respect. "I'll sit here, and you two walk off in opposite directions."

They nodded and left. Donovan could have killed either one of them when they turned their backs. It was as he suspected. These two were hunters of the middling sort, the type that seldom thought of themselves as prey.

A mistake on their part, one that might prove costly to them.

FOURTEEN

"Hi, Irene," Reed Collins said, looking up from the sandwich he was eating at his desk. "You here to see Frank?"

"No," Pete Baird answered from beside me. Since no one goes walking unescorted past the reception area of the police department, let alone into the homicide room, my husband's partner had been the one who fetched me from the lobby. "Frank doesn't know she's here." He didn't spare me the tone of censorship, but I didn't care—all that mattered to me at the moment was that he hadn't left me sitting in the lobby. I didn't even bother to correct what he said about Frank, at least not right away.

The others in the room knew me as a reporter, and I could see them moving to turn papers over and slipping files into desk drawers.

"Relax," I said. "No newspaper anymore, remember?" Before their elation over that or their sympathy for me could make itself known, I quickly turned back to Reed and added, "Could I talk to you in one of the interview rooms?"

"I'll come with you," Pete said, and since I knew that trying to shake him would be a waste of effort, I didn't protest.

When the door closed behind us, Reed said, "Are you working for a news agency of any kind, Irene?"

"No. I'm unemployed. This isn't going out to the media." I took a seat, and they followed suit. Interrogation mode—I was alone on one side of a table; they positioned their chairs to block me in. I tried not to let my claustrophobia distract me. I wouldn't get anywhere if I didn't stay calm.

"That leaves me with some questions, then," Reed said. "I've been getting some phone calls."

"I figured you would. Probably from Marilyn Foster's friends and family. I've been going over her case."

"Irene . . . ," Reed said pityingly.

"For what it's worth, Frank felt the way you do. Wanted me to butt out, thought you and Vince would be pissed off at me for interfering with your case. Thought it was kind of sad that I wouldn't just forget all about it. Pete's wrong, though. Frank knows I'm here. I sat down with him and went over what I had found out, and he agreed with me that you should be made aware of what I've learned."

Reed frowned. "He's at lunch with Vince . . ."

"Yes. Neither of us thought Vince would hear me out."

"Jesus, Irene. It might be an even bigger assumption on your part—and Frank's—that I'd go behind my partner's back."

"You can tell him anything I tell you, but we both know Vince always needs four times the amount of time you do before he'll calm down and listen to what I have to say."

"Any reason why Frank couldn't have come to us with this information you have?"

"I wouldn't let him."

Pete laughed.

"Does your wife give you her casework to carry in here, or does she come in herself?" I asked.

That shut him up. Rachel got into her work as a private

investigator after many years as a homicide detective. It was impossible to picture Rachel handing her cases over to him.

"I don't know, Irene . . . ," Reed said.

"Whatever. If you don't want to know what I've found out, fine, I'll go home."

He made me wait it out for a minute or two. Then he said, "Let's hear it."

"Marilyn Foster had a son by Nick Parrish."

"What!" Pete shouted.

"Settle down, Pete," Reed said in his calm fashion. "You want to bring half the department running in here?" To me, he said, "What makes you think so?"

"When I interviewed Dwayne Foster for the story, he mentioned that she had given up a child for adoption as a teenager."

"I read your story. That wasn't in there."

"The article you read was a missing person's story that had to be rewritten as a murder story before it went to press. I never had a chance to write the follow-ups." I paused, struggling to prevent my thoughts from going down a well-worn path of grief over the closing of the *Express* and to stay focused on convincing Reed. "I think you knew she had a child that had been put up for adoption."

He didn't say anything for a moment, then seemed to come to some decision. "For the sake of argument, and to save Frank the pain of a really long lunch with Vince, let's say we know not only that she gave birth to a son but that she was looking for him. Let's say Dwayne Foster told us that much and her computer records supported it. All well and good, but how you can reach the sensational conclusion you've reached . . ."

"Did Dwayne tell you that the father of the child was in prison?"

"No," he admitted uneasily.

"Parrish is not the only man in prison," Pete scoffed. "For

god's sake, Irene, a father in prison could be any one of more than a million-and-a-half men in the U.S. I hate Parrish, too, but I can't tie every crime in the country to the guy."

"First of all, Marilyn told her husband that the father of her child was in prison 'for life.'"

"In California, that cuts out about eighty percent of them," Reed said, "but it's still a big number."

"And she might have just meant he had a long sentence," Pete added, "or she might have been reassuring her husband that no dirtbag from her past was coming after her."

I sighed. "Look, you two. You can keep arguing with me every step of the way, or you can let me lay this out for you."

"It's falling apart already," Pete said.

Reed gave him a quelling look. "Go on," he said to me.

"The age of her son—and figuring back to his conception—works out to a time when Parrish was living here in Las Piernas. So it's possible.

"With all the publicity surrounding her death, Dwayne received lots of sympathy cards, including some from people who had only recently been back in contact with her—several of them had contacted her in the past year through a social networking site. Two were her closest friends from high school."

I handed him a slip of paper with the names and numbers of the two women. "They've said they would be willing to discuss things further with the police."

He took the paper and frowned down at it.

"I talked to them about the summer Marilyn had an 'older boyfriend,'" I said. "He was in his late twenties—although who knows if he told her his real age—and she was fifteen when they met. She was in full-on rebellion mode with her parents. She had been secretive about the boyfriend, but her girlfriends were curious. So one night, they watched when she sneaked out of the house, and followed her. They saw the young man she met."

"And twenty-some-odd years later," Pete said, "happen to remember that the guy they saw in the distance in the dark was one of America's most notorious serial killers. Give me a break!"

"Pete," Reed warned.

"They didn't just see him from a distance. He caught them spying."

Pete sat back.

I told them the story as it had been recounted to me.

Marilyn's family lived near a park, and that was where she had her assignation with her boyfriend. It was after closing time, and she met him near a tree-lined path. A perfect place to spend time with a lover, with lots of concealing shrubbery. The girls followed the couple, hanging back a little, trying not to be seen.

They passed a lighted area near a bench, but Parrish and Marilyn didn't stop there. The path twisted and turned, and they thought he was with Marilyn, so when each girl felt a hand grip the back of her neck, they screeched simultaneously. He held them hard, painfully, just below their skulls, and controlled them as if they were puppets. He told them to shut up, but they had already fallen silent.

He marched them back to the lighted area and turned them so that they were facing him. They said—independently—that he didn't say another word, just stared at them, then smiled. It had the same effect on each of them—he might have been smiling, but they felt certain that he was damned angry, and if they didn't get out of there, he'd hurt them worse. He released his grip, and they ran home.

I took a breath and let it out slowly, pushing aside my own memories of having Nick Parrish take hold of me.

"Even though it was more than twenty years ago, if you heard them talk about that night—the intensity of his stare, the way he stood, the painful bruises on their necks—you'd believe they haven't forgotten that man or how he made them feel."

"You're sure it was Parrish?" Reed asked.

"Not from that, no. I thought of showing them a photo of Parrish, but I don't have one of him from that time, so . . ."

"Thank God for small favors," Pete muttered.

"Go on," Reed said.

FIFTEEN

So I told them about gathering all the information I could from the women about Marilyn Foster and that time. How she had shown up the next day with bruises on her face and arms, and completely stopped talking about her boyfriend. Not long after that, she learned she was pregnant.

"She never considered trying to contact the father for help, and infuriated her parents by refusing to name him. She went to an adoption agency that could cope with her special medical needs. After a difficult pregnancy, she gave birth to a boy, whom she held for only a few minutes before he was given up to an adopting couple. It was much later that she began her search for him."

"With adoption laws as they are, she couldn't find him?"

"Not at first. She had told Dwayne that at the time of the birth, she was afraid the child's father would try to find him by looking up any records that mentioned her, so it was a closed adoption, and she kept her records sealed. Even when her son turned eighteen, when he could begin the process of letting his birth parents know he was seeking them, she didn't start her own side of that process.

"Yet suddenly one day, she seemed to decide that it was safe to start looking for her child." I pushed a piece of paper across the desk. It was a copy of a form Marilyn Foster had filled out online, signing up for an organization that helps adoptees and their birth parents locate one another.

"Father is still listed as unknown," Pete said.

"Look at the date. Recognize it?"

They both glanced at the date, then looked up at me, puzzled.

"September twenty-seventh . . ." My voice trailed off. "Could you open that door?" I asked. "And could I get a glass of water?"

"Sure," Reed said, eyeing me with concern.

A few minutes later, I continued. "That was the date he was injured. Parrish. Early in the morning on the twenty-seventh of September. At the time it seemed likely he'd be a tetraplegic for the rest of his life. When that turned out not to be the case— still, he was captured. If there was some small chance he'd ever get out of his bed in the prison hospital, there was no chance he'd ever get out of prison."

"Should have gone for the death sentence," Pete said.

"The district attorney might do that yet," Reed said. "Especially now that Parrish won't have to show up in court in a wheelchair. They've got DNA on other cases."

I stayed silent. It brought Reed's attention back to me. "So you're saying that she filed this form because she felt safe from him."

"But it doesn't even mention Parrish by name!" Pete objected again. "And while I know that date means something to you, why should she remember it? Irene, face it, there is such a thing as coincidence."

I let that go. I put a small stack of printouts on the table. Reed picked them up and studied the first page.

"E-mail from someone who says he thinks he might be her son."

"It's not e-mail, really, it's a set of private messages on an Internet message board. Which is why you wouldn't find it if you looked through her e-mail. I don't know how far your computer guy has gotten with his efforts."

"Not far," Pete said. "He's swamped. He's due to testify in some other cases and hasn't had much time for anything else."

Reed frowned, his attention still on the papers. "No names. Just a bunch of numbers."

"For the protection of both parties, the service keeps real names hidden until they agree to release identifying information to each other."

"Not too anonymous—he's giving his birth date and the name of the adoption agency."

"It matches her son's birthday and the agency she used."

"'After reading your post, I am fairly sure I'm your son,'" he read aloud. " 'Do you by any chance have type 1 diabetes? I have it. I am told it is hereditary, so that might be one thing we have in common. If you don't, I might have inherited it from my father.'"

He read her response and the next few messages to himself, then said, "It looks as if she was careful."

"Yes. She was clearly excited but didn't just hand over her address and phone number. Keep reading," I said. "Look at the last two."

"'We haven't discussed this yet,'" he read, " 'and forgive me if it is painful to you, but I'm kind of anxious to find out if a man who now says he is my father really is. Can you tell me, is my birth father in prison? Maybe you gave me up for adoption because you thought I might become like him. I don't want to meet him, really, but I have been contacted by someone who thinks he is my half brother. He said his dad told him about me a long time ago. If none of that make sense to you, that's actually a relief to me. Otherwise, it's kind of the orphan's worst nightmare, if you know what I mean. I just don't know what to do, and if you are my mother, maybe you would be willing to give me advice. Here's the Web site about the guy he says is my dad.' And there's a link."

Reed looked up again.

"Yes," I said. "The Moths."

It didn't take more convincing. Even when Frank and Vince arrived, Reed and Pete managed to get Vince steered away from his anger toward me (and Frank) and onto the scent of a new line of investigation.

They were good enough to let me know what happened after they told me to go home.

By the end of the day, they not only had the cooperation of the adoptee contact group but had the name, address, and phone number of the young man who had claimed to be her son. Cade Morrissey.

He had recently moved to Las Piernas and rented a small apartment in an old building not far from downtown. Had a job as a cook at a nearby restaurant, had applied for college.

Morrissey didn't answer a knock on his apartment door, and his landlady said she hadn't seen him for a while; neighbors said the same. They tried calling him—it was a cell phone number and went to voice mail. When police checked at the restaurant where he worked, the manager—happy to do some venting—said that Cade hadn't shown up for work for several weeks, so he was fired. But if they found him, the manager said, his last paycheck was waiting for him.

At that point, it didn't take much to get a warrant.

What they discovered, on entering the premises, was that someone had been searching before them. No sign of Cade Morrissey himself, but his toothbrush, razor, and other personal items, including a supply of insulin in the refrigerator, were still in the apartment. An empty suitcase was in the closet. A desk, however, that had once held a laptop computer and a router now held just a router. The drawers of the desk had been pulled out, their contents strewn on the floor.

The cell phone company cooperated with the police, and with GPS tracking, they followed its signal to the same industrial area where Marilyn Foster had been found. In an abandoned cannery, they came across an odd sight: a pristine white home freezer unit sitting unplugged in the center of the concrete floor of a large room, surrounded by rusting machinery. The freezer was padlocked.

Vince called the cell phone again.

They heard muted ringing from within the freezer and hurriedly broke the lock off.

Cade Morrissey's moth-decorated body had already thawed.

SIXTEEN

I tried to console myself with the thought that if I hadn't talked to Reed, Cade Morrissey might have remained missing, left in an unplugged freezer to rot. I told myself that the investigation had been aided by my work. It didn't make me feel any better.

I sold two freelance stories about him, telling myself that I was helping to bring him some justice. By writing about his life, I was letting others know who he was, showing that he was more than a decorated corpse in a sensational murder—he had been an individual, there were people who loved him. And I still felt that the checks for those stories were forty pieces of silver marked up for inflation.

The backlog in the crime lab's DNA section—they were hard-pressed to have tests done in time for trials—meant that it would be weeks if not longer before we knew if there was indeed a biological connection between Nick Parrish and Cade Morrissey (in this situation, I could not bring myself to use the words "father-son relationship"). The director of the lab pointed out that Parrish, in prison, could not have killed Cade Morrissey, so looking for a connection was not evidence from his killer, it was more a matter of curiosity—they might get around to it at some point.

The police investigation seemed focused in three areas—trying to learn more about the bloggers who called themselves "the Moths," tracking down people who knew Cade, and trying to identify the woman who had been found in the trunk of Marilyn Foster's car.

I sold another piece freelance—to a magazine that specializes in municipal government issues, on the changes already being felt in Las Piernas's city hall now that the paper wasn't around to keep an eye on it.

At that point, I was back to wondering if I should face facts and give up on being a reporter. I was rescued from dismal reflections about what other work I might be suited for when I got a job offer: a low-paying gig at a local radio station. The person who made the offer was Ethan.

To my surprise, Ethan had talked the town's struggling public radio station, KCLP, into letting him run an experiment. He had done his homework, discovered the weakest show in the station's lineup, and then shown up in the manager's office, underwriters in hand, with a proposal to replace it with *Local Late Night.* The program would be a mix of news and opinion on all things Las Piernas and surrounding areas. He wasn't unknown to the people he pitched it to—he'd taken a few classes in radio production in his unending time at Las Piernas University, during which he'd done his best to network with the people who were now running the station. They went for it.

Long before the first show aired, he had built an online following for himself—started in part at the *Express*—and made use of social networking sites and other tech that the paper hadn't fully utilized, and as a result he was already something of a local celebrity. When he became the host of the show, that following increased, and he was now enjoying himself immensely.

One of the best things he did was to organize a Web site for the show that allowed those of his former print colleagues who worked with him now to write at length—any length—about the issues we discussed on the show. So while the part of the story that went on the air had to be kept short, the audience was always told there were more details on the Web. More underwriting and pledge dollars were generated from the site.

A few decades working as a journalist who focused on local politics didn't hurt my ability to find stories for the program, but it took me some time to get used to the job, which differed in some important ways from print work. Learning to use the flash mike and the sound-editing software on my laptop were mechanics—they didn't take too long, although I was nowhere near the artistry of some when it came to sound editing. I got used to carrying more gear and learned the hard way to always have an electronic Plan B (extra flash card, more batteries).

I tried to stop writing things down during interviews, a habit I couldn't quite break, and tried to find humor in the fact that, in the press conference pecking order, my old colleagues couldn't stop thinking of me as a newspaper reporter, which often allowed me to grab a better position than lowly radio reporters would usually get. On the other hand, I often caved in to the practical need to set aside my dignity and sit with my new colleagues on the ground at the feet of the television cameras for the sake of better sound quality.

Changes in my own thinking and writing had more to do with the nature of the medium. I found out how fast a minute could go by. I learned how much breath was needed to speak a long sentence on the air, so my sentences became shorter. I was expected to cover two to three stories in one day—that kept me moving.

While the on-air stories were shorter, the associated Web site allowed the reporters working with Ethan to develop our stories even more fully than we could have done at the *Express*, which had never made good use of its own site (failing to listen to the pleas of our computer guru, until she left in frustration for a much higher paying job). In the last few years, as the print edition's pages had dwindled, the *Express* had kept most stories shorter than the ones we were publishing on the KCLP site.

The KCLP site wasn't the equivalent of the *Express* in its heyday; it was going to be reached only by the computer literate who happened to be paying attention in the first place, and it didn't compare to even a small daily newspaper in terms of the variety of items it could cover. We knew that people who read newspapers would often look through an A section and become engrossed in stories they hadn't set out to find, while on the Internet the average reader might be picking up only one local story a day, and that as the result of a search. Still, it was at least one way to get the local news out and to keep some level of accountability in Las Piernas government.

Ethan had also hired Mark Baker, as well as a couple of people whose specialties were the local art and music scenes. We all got along well, and Ethan had us working together as a team in no time.

I was seeing a whole new side of Ethan. I had always known that his interests were wide-ranging, that he was bright and creative. Even in his earliest days at the paper, he had been ambitious and competitive, but—in large part because of problems of his own making—the *Express* had never allowed him a leadership role. KCLP, on the other hand, had given him major responsibilities and power. "All the rope I need to hang myself," he'd say to me with a rueful smile.

So far, he was using the rope to climb higher. After a little more than a month at the station, he was offered the position of news director—KCLP had fired the previous one, who had resented the power Ethan had already been given to cover local news on his show.

Not long after that, he called me into his new office, which was small, but at least it was an office. He hadn't had one before. Now he even had a narrow window that looked out onto the parking lot. He was standing behind his desk, looking through some paperwork.

"Yes, Mr. Shire?"

He looked up and winced. "You know I hate it when you do that." He looked at my arm and said, "How'd you get that nasty bruise?"

"Rachel's teaching me self-defense."

He seemed ready to make the obvious retort but changed his mind. "Have a seat."

I took one on the couch that occupied most of one wall, but he stayed standing. "I have a request," he said.

I waited, and for once in his smooth-talking life, he seemed to have a hard time coming up with what he wanted to say. Finally, he said, "You know John and Stuart made it clear to me they want to stay retired."

"Yes . . . ," I said warily.

"It kind of surprised me."

"They were in the newspaper business longer than the rest of us. I don't think they wanted to try to start over here."

He paced the two short steps the office allowed him, then said, "You've been best friends with Lydia since grade school, right?"

"Yes. Why do you ask?"

"I'm thinking that you'll be able to explain something to me. When I started the evening show, you and Mark were the only people from the paper that I wanted here and had budget enough to hire. Since then, about half the former staffers of the *Express* have asked me for jobs, but she hasn't even stopped by to say hello."

"You don't take that personally, do you? You know she likes you—she probably just thinks you're busy."

"I'm more worried she was insulted that I didn't ask her to work here."

"No, not that she's mentioned to me."

"Do you think she wants out of the news business for good?"

I hesitated. "I don't think so. But she knows that the chances of landing another job as a city editor are slim to none."

He was silent for so long I figured we were done and started to get to my feet. He motioned me back down. "You've never taken an editor's position?"

"No," I said. "I've covered for people a few times, but I didn't enjoy it. It's not what I do. I'm a reporter. Lydia—she's a good reporter, but writing and editing are where her real interests are. Can I ask where this is leading?"

"I have the title of news director now, but when they offered it to me, I didn't accept it right away."

"No? I thought you would've jumped at it."

He smiled. "I wanted to, but I negotiated."

I couldn't repress a laugh.

His smile became a grin. "Yeah, I know. A little over a month ago, I was out of work. Now I'm making demands. Anyway, the conditions were that I could divide the previous director's salary, take some for myself as a salary increase but use most of it to hire an assistant director."

"Ethan—I don't get it."

"The deal is, I can hire an assistant, and if the station starts to get better ratings and support, they renegotiate my own salary in six months. Otherwise—well, otherwise, up to them."

I just stared at him for a moment, then said, "I assume you have a plan?"

"I'm hoping Lydia will take the assistant's job. She . . . she has skills I don't have. Yet. I think if we all work together, we can pull it off. I know she's getting married and all that, and the pay won't be close to her old salary, but—do you think she'll be interested?"

As it happened, she was thrilled. On her first day at work, she sighed contentedly and told me she had missed that feeling of being at the center of the flow of information that comes with being in a newsroom.

"I know," I said. "The first week at home, every time I heard a fire engine—"

"It made you crazy not to know where it was headed and how big the fire was and if there were injuries and what type of structure—"

"Exactly."

Not many days later, I was again sitting in my boss's office, going over some possible stories, when his new assistant came rushing in, looking shaken—reminding me that when the news is especially bad, being at the center of the flow of information isn't such a fine thing.

SEVENTEEN

Josh Enwill, one of the four guards sent on this trip, sat back on the narrow bench seat. The prison could hardly afford their absence in these underbudgeted days, but the warden didn't want to take any chances where Nick Parrish was concerned. Bad enough that their regular ambulance had broken down months ago—there was no money to repair it.

There had not been any problems with this ambulance company, though, and it did have experience in transporting dangerous patients. This was not your typical ambulance. The walls of the van were thick and windowless. The van was separated from the cab, where the driver and Stan Rawls, another guard, sat.

They would be followed by two more guards in another vehicle. Josh could remember times when twice as many guards would be detailed to a trip like this. Luckily, Parrish was in no condition to put up a struggle.

Even so, the ambulance had been searched before the prisoner was loaded into it. Parrish was secured on the gurney, although there seemed to be little need for that—he was barely conscious. In the middle of the night, Parrish had fallen, screaming, to the floor of his cell. He received a brief examination by the prison doctor, who decided that he was out of his depth, and that the person who was best qualified to evaluate Parrish's spinal problem was his surgeon at the prison hospital. So Parrish was loaded up with painkillers and strapped onto a support board. He was now being transported back to the prison hospital where he had spent years before being transferred just a few weeks ago.

Josh didn't have a problem with Parrish. You worked around the prison population, you knew you weren't keeping an eye on angels. He knew Parrish's history, and that he had attacked both men and women. But in the short time Parrish had stayed at their facility, he hadn't caused trouble. He could even be charming. Which didn't fool Josh for a minute.

It was going to be a nine-hour drive. Josh was back here with Parrish and one of the paramedics. Air-conditioning kept it cool, but Josh was worried that he'd get carsick. Maybe Stan would switch with him.

The paramedic didn't seem bothered by it. He was a friendly young guy, full of curiosity about Parrish but professional. He had red hair and wore black, heavy-rimmed glasses. Geeky kid.

Josh hated not being able to see the road or where they were. The ambulance, which was about the size of a mail truck, had a specially reinforced patient compartment with no access to the driver's compartment. Which made it safer for prisoner transport but not much fun to ride in. Josh was just wondering why they couldn't have put in a few small windows near the tops of the side panels when the ambulance braked and swerved sharply.

"What the hell?" the paramedic said, as they were thrown side to side, almost landing on top of Parrish.

They heard a loud explosion behind them.

Josh got to the intercom before the paramedic did. "What's going on?"

"Something in the road," Stan said, his voice strained. "It

looked like a dead animal, but it must have been rigged with a mine or something. I'm trying to reach the car. I think they hit it."

Josh heard the sound of a door opening.

Stan shouted, "Don't— Hey! Come back here!"

"We've got to help them!" the driver said.

"Goddamn it, no! Don't go out there! Bring those keys back here!"

Josh had just pressed the talk button to tell Stan he was going to radio for help when something heavy struck hard at the back of his head. He never heard the shots that killed Stan.

EIGHTEEN

Quinn knocked in the agreed upon pattern at the back doors of the ambulance. Kai opened them, letting in brightness, a rush of heat, and—as the wind shifted—smoke from the burning car. He paid little attention to Quinn and went back to stripping the keys and radio off Josh's inert form.

Quinn was momentarily distracted by the blood spattered on his half brother. He found the sight stimulating and odd. Although Kai and Quinn didn't really look alike—they looked even less alike in their currently altered appearances—Quinn felt as if he was seeing himself in a similar act but from outside his body. He forced his attention back to matters at hand and went to work to release the gurney. Looking over at Kai, he said, "Be sure to get his cell phone, too."

"Did you clean off your prints in the cab?" Kai asked.

"Of course. Hurry."

"You have to admit the roadkill was inspired."

"I've already told you I admired your work," Quinn said. It was true. Kai was a genius with electronics and explosives.

They were on a desert road. To the right, just beyond the ditch where Quinn had retrieved his assault rifle, was what appeared to be an abandoned business, surrounded by a high chain-link fence. A large, prefab metal building stood at the end of a short drive. Quinn could already hear the sound of an engine from within it.

They smashed the radios and threw them into the inferno that had once been the following car, quickly removed the SIM cards from the phones and did the same. Next they rolled Nick Parrish from the back of the ambulance and up to the locked gate. Quinn opened it and relocked it behind them.

"Will he be okay?" Kai asked, looking down at Parrish.

"Of course," Quinn said, surprised by the concern on Kai's face. "But we need to hurry. This road isn't traveled much, but the smoke will attract attention from miles away. And who knows how soon someone will try to check in with the guards."

By then they had reached the building. Once they were inside, there was no use trying to talk over the noise of the small plane's engines. Donovan had already lowered the ramp. As they had rehearsed so many times, they loaded Parrish in the back and secured the gurney, closed up the plane, and strapped themselves in.

Donovan had done no more than glance back to ensure they were seated. He taxied out to the single, rough airstrip, and within minutes they were airborne. Quinn looked at the wreckage they had left below as Donovan turned the plane. What he saw provided an unwelcome shock.

"Land the plane!" he shouted.

"Not going to happen," Donovan said.

Quinn turned his anger in another direction. "Damn it, Kai, you didn't kill him!"

Kai, who had been removing Parrish's manacles and handcuffs, moved to a window and looked down. Quinn continued to watch as Josh Enwill stumbled to the side of the road and collapsed.

Kai shrugged. "If he lives, it's not as if he can tell them anything they don't already know."

Quinn bit back a reply and forced himself to calm down. This was not a time for squabbles.

Kai tried to appeal to Donovan for support, but Donovan remained aloof. Quinn smiled to himself. That was all right. Matters would be more easily managed if Kai continued to feel rebuffed by Donovan. In their strange alliance, it was always better if Kai looked to Quinn rather than to their older brother. Better for Quinn, anyway.

Quinn didn't fool himself that what he shared with either brother was closeness. The truth was, all three were incapable of genuine intimacy with anyone—not as friends, brothers, or lovers. He knew it was best to think of them as individuals who were engaged in an enterprise that, if it succeeded, would have rewards for each but did not require real bonding of any kind—or even much trust.

The fact that they could function together at all said a lot for the genius of the man strapped to the gurney back there. The men who shared his impulses were rare, and, among those, he had a trait that was rarer still. Nick Parrish embraced long-range planning. Witness his first escape from authorities. If it hadn't been for Irene Kelly, he'd still be free—and uninjured.

The authorities had all been surprised that Nick Parrish had a helper. A partner, they'd said. What a laugh to consider that one to be something so elevated as a "partner"—"servant" would have been a better word. But the police had seen no further. And they'd congratulated themselves on capturing and imprisoning the so-called Moth. Well, they could keep that one.

Despite the evidence right under their noses that Nick Parrish planned extensively and years in advance, they'd been blind. Apparently they believed they'd put an end to all his plans. How foolish. Nick Parrish always had other plans.

And he had children to help him carry them out.

He had chosen their mothers carefully, and through the years had decided which of his children would later be most helpful to him. Quinn didn't know how many brothers and sisters he had, or how many had been contacted. The one time he had ventured to ask, he'd received a look so cold he had never dared ask again. Not many people could intimidate Quinn with a look. His father could. Quinn had spent hours practicing that chilling look in the mirror, and, although that practice had been useful, he knew he had not achieved his father's abilities.

Nick Parrish had rarely made his presence known to them in their early lives, but he had been watchful. Not all of his children had been deemed worthy to be part of his plans. Some—such as Cade Morrissey—would prove useful if not worthy.

Quinn sat back and closed his eyes, a smile playing on his lips. Killing Cade had been unexpectedly exquisite. Really, the best experience he'd ever had with a male. Cade had been so naïve, so excited about having a brother. And, unlike the two brothers Quinn was with now, Cade actually resembled him.

Quinn had used that, had reflected his emotions to get closer to Cade. He led Cade to believe that he was also given up for adoption, and that he was looking for his own mother. Cade saw him as someone who had been successful and led a normal life, despite having a serial killer for a father. A brother who would act as a go-between to arrange a meeting with his mother.

Killing Cade was almost like killing a little part of himself, and more exciting than anything that had gone before. Once it was done, Quinn felt immeasurably stronger, as if he had absorbed something of Nick Parrish into himself.

Then there was the experience of Marilyn Foster.

Cade had worried over meeting his mother. If he had lived, he might have learned that she had worried over him, too— came right out of the house when Quinn told her that Cade was extremely ill, possibly dying, and wouldn't go to the hospital. Would she please come to convince him, or at least to meet him, as Cade had always hoped? No, Quinn didn't have a car, he didn't have much money, and had used the last of it to ride the bus out here and had walked to her house. In reality, he had parked his van not far away, and Kai had taken him the next day to retrieve it.

But that night she had hurried out of the house, so distracted she'd left her purse and phone behind, and driven with him to the abandoned cannery. She had been appalled that Cade was staying in such a place.

She was under Quinn's complete control within minutes of stepping out of the car.

She had put up a fight, even after he'd bound and gagged her, but he was far stronger, and told her that if she wanted to see her son, she'd have to behave. She became docile then, even though he knew she didn't really believe him. But he'd been true to his word—never having promised that her son would be *alive* when she saw him.

It interested him that she was so grief-stricken. Wept for a boy she never knew.

She'd been enraged for a time, which Quinn had found stimulating. Later, when he'd moved her to the plastic-covered room in the warehouse, he allowed Kai to enjoy her and then kill her. Quinn had left without telling Kai that he'd be at the cannery next door, finishing his artwork on Cade. Kai, at that point unaware of Cade's existence, had thought Quinn was generous. Quinn had hidden Cade's body before going back over to the warehouse.

Kai, who had already been up late turning on the hose at Irene Kelly's house, had fallen asleep when he finished with Marilyn. The hose business was a trick of Quinn's—he had many such tricks, designed to unsettle a victim. Kai was happy to do it and had nearly been caught, or so he said.

Quinn changed the plates on Marilyn Foster's Chevy Malibu, put the originals in the trunk, woke Kai and had Kai follow him as he drove her car to a large storage locker in one of the buildings Quinn owned. There they removed the body of one of Kai's earlier kills, taking her from the freezer in which Quinn had kept her for him—in exchange for letting Quinn practice his designs on her skin. Kai admired the decoration as they put the body in the trunk of the Malibu.

They drove toward the beach and delivered the car to its parking place. These were some of the riskiest moments, because if Marilyn had been reported missing, there was always the chance an ambitious cop might run a plate check and see that these were not originally on a Chevy Malibu. Or even though he wore a hoodie, a wig, and dark sunglasses, he might be seen parking the car by someone who somehow managed to recognize him. Or a cruising patrol car might go down the street while he was changing the plates back. Any of those possibilities could lead to complications.

These dangers had only made it all the more thrilling.

When Kai took Quinn to pick up his van, Quinn mastered a strong temptation to choose a route that went past Marilyn Foster's home.

Kai helped him load the freezer into the van and take it to the cannery, thinking Quinn was going to abandon it there. After Kai left, Quinn hooked up a generator and placed Cade's body within the freezer. He admitted to himself now that there had been tenderness in the way he had done it.

People were easier to love when they were dead.

He set the generator running and went back over to the warehouse. Kai had already moved Marilyn Foster's body to the metal table. Quinn prepared his canvas by removing all her bindings, then thoroughly washing her, including all her orifices and wounds, and cleaning her fingernails and toenails. He dried her, then sealed the buckets of wash water and carried them down to the van.

By the time he came back to the room, she was ready. He used an airbrush and stencils and metal-based paints, permanent markers and calligraphy brushes to cover the bare skin of Marilyn Foster even as her body continued to go through the changes of rigor mortis. When he was inspired, he could work for hours. He stopped only to refuel the generator at the cannery next door.

He wasn't able to spend as much time on her as he would have liked, but she would serve her purpose.

He cleaned up, removing the plastic tarps, and took her to another section of the warehouse, setting her out in a manner that would cause the light from the multitude of high, filthy windows along one wall to bathe her skin and bring out the brilliance of her new colors.

He drove off and called Donovan, who called the police from a stolen cell phone to report the body's location. Donovan destroyed the phone; Quinn destroyed all the other evidence. Quinn was thoroughly exhausted by the time he reached his own bed.

He awoke ten hours later and groggily watched the television news while checking the Internet compulsively. He watched Irene Kelly's press conference with interest—he enjoyed seeing that she was so frightened, even before she knew that Marilyn Foster was dead.

Two moth-covered bodies had certainly set things in a whirl! He could not help but feel pleased. He looked carefully through the online news reports for any reference to the discovery of a third body, but there was none. He had thought the noise of the generator might attract some attention, but apparently either other industrial sounds in the area or all the racket made by the police in the warehouse kept that from happening. He wanted the generator back if he could retrieve it, but not at the price of his freedom.

He went back to bed and thought of Cade before falling asleep.

Quinn kept the generator running for a week, then decided it was foolish to risk being seen going in and out of the building. The police had traced ownership of both buildings to his company, but there was nothing unusual in Moore Properties owning real estate. He was credited with helping to revitalize the area. He had employees who worked on that sort of thing, exactly so that the company's image remained positive.

"He's starting to come around," Kai announced happily from his seat near the gurney.

Quinn smiled, nodded, stretched, and sighed.

Other than the moment when he had noticed the blood on Kai, nothing in today's activities had been arousing. Exciting, yes, but not the sort of thing he ultimately found satisfying. That was all right, though. His involvement in the abduction and killing first of Cade and then of Marilyn, so close to each other in time, had left him sated. Experience said he wouldn't remain so, but the restless edge was off for a while.

Quinn supposed that, as a matter of self-preservation, at some point he would have to kill Kai and Donovan and—saving the best for last—his father. But that could wait. Besides, his father had plans, and like his brothers, Quinn was curious about them. That curiosity would keep them all doing just as Nick Parrish bid them to do.

For now.

The plane landed smoothly and taxied toward a hangar. The flight had been short, as intended. It was a flight that Donovan had completed many times between these two destinations in recent weeks, in part to rehearse, in part to allay the suspicions of anyone who might have noticed the flight today. It was a remote area but not utterly uninhabited.

The plane came to a halt, and they disembarked, but Donovan did little more than help them unload before taking off again. He would eventually meet them in Las Piernas.

The drugs that had been given to Parrish at the prison were finally wearing off. With Kai's help, Parrish came woozily to a sitting position.

"Thank you, Son," he said, and Kai beamed. Parrish looked over at Quinn and gave him a charming smile. "You've both been of great help to me." He stretched. "How good to be free! But we haven't any time to waste. Quinn, you have what we need?"

"Yes, sir." Quinn opened a locker at the back of the building and brought out the wig and clothing stored there.

They changed quickly and packed up all signs of their presence. The gurney was moved to a locked storeroom behind a workbench, covered with a drop cloth, and then loaded up with boxes and other items. Donovan would dispose of it later.

They climbed into the Ford Escape (Quinn wondered even now if irony had determined Donovan's choice of vehicle) parked just outside the hangar. Quinn drove, Kai sitting next to him. Their father sat in the back, looking calm and pleased with himself, and not at all like someone who might at any moment be apprehended as a prison escapee.

When I grow up, Quinn thought with a smile, *I want to be like you, Dad.*

NINETEEN

Before his recovery, every time news about Nicholas Parrish reached me, friends would see its effect and say, "Don't worry. Nick Parrish is paralyzed." Hearing that set off an internal conflict. My rational self said, "Yes, of course, I'm safe from him." Emotionally—that was another matter.

Fear, which knows better than to use mere words, barely loosened its grip. My heart would race, my hands would feel clammy. A brief horror film, rough cut, memories patched together with adrenaline, would play in my mind, take my attention from whatever I was doing.

Therapy had helped me to deal with a lot of that, but try as I might to embrace a calmer view of matters, on some level, I remained entrenched in the belief that he could beat the odds.

He did.

Then I was comforted by well-wishers with "Nicholas Parrish is in prison."

Now it appeared he had beaten those odds, too.

When I heard about Parrish's escape, I called Frank, who had also just heard of it. "I'm on my way over there," he said.

"Where?"

"To the radio station. Don't drive home without me, okay?"

I opened my mouth to say it wasn't necessary, I would be fine, and then decided that I wasn't going to kid myself. "Thanks," I said. "See you soon."

I called Ben. He hadn't heard the news yet, and I didn't take joy in breaking it to him. He swore enough for both of us, then grew quiet. "Funny thing," he said.

"What?"

"I think I've always believed he would do something like this."

"Me, too. I tell myself he's human, not invulnerable, but—"

"He is human. He can be captured." After a long silence, he added, "We'll just have to keep telling ourselves that."

"Is that working for you?"

He laughed nervously. "Not really."

There was a beep on the line, and a moment later he said, "Las Piernas PD is calling. I'd better take it."

We ended the call. Ethan asked for more security for the building, which the station management was reluctant to provide until a couple of detectives from the police department arrived at about the same time my husband did. The detectives were sent to talk about precautions for the staff, especially one of their new hires, who might be a target. The police department was already making plans, assuming that Parrish was going to come after Ben and me.

I'm sure Ben felt about as shitty as I did over all of this, which was no comfort to me.

In the first few hours, most news reports were full of conjecture. We knew that two guards had been killed when the car they were in was destroyed by some sort of mine. The ambulance carrying Parrish had also been attacked, one guard killed, one in serious condition with a severe head injury, and the driver and attendant missing, as was Parrish.

Everyone at the prison, from the doctor to the guard who loaded him in, swore up and down that Parrish was sedated and could not have managed the escape on his own. The other facts supported that view, but it was difficult to see how he had communicated with his accomplices.

The details beyond that information were unclear, owing largely to the remote location where the empty ambulance had been found. Whether the other two men were hostages or participants in the escape was not known. Where they had gone and how they had traveled was a mystery as well.

There was an airstrip, which had caused some excitement at first, given Parrish's abilities as a pilot and aviation mechanic, but it was locked and the FAA said their records showed no unusual activity there. The pilot associated with the only plane using it was in the air at the time the fire was reported and was on a routine run. He had been questioned, but he had not seen anyone lying in wait when he began his flight. The investigators used the time of his flight to help estimate the time of the escape.

When security video taken at the prison was shown, the owner of the ambulance company said that the driver and attendant were not the men sent out on the assignment. Those who examined the recordings were unable to get a clear look at the faces of the men who did show up—and obviously knew where the cameras were—but the owner said with certainty that they didn't match the physical builds of his two employees.

One set of investigators began looking at the GPS tracking records for the ambulance before it reached the prison. At one point, it had veered from its planned route, down a small side road. There had been no radio call from the driver and attendant, both of whom at that point would have been riding in the cab.

Everything about that stop suggested some level of complicity by at least one of the ambulance company employees. The outrage expressed over this was somewhat muted after the bodies of both men were discovered not far away.

There was a lot of chest thumping in some segments of the California political jungle, as those who most enjoy spectacle took the stage and did their usual posturing—just for show, not to do any of the heavy lifting that might have been of real help. The public outcry, rooted in understandable fear, was fierce—but all the same, an outcry from a burdened public that didn't want its taxes increased to improve prison conditions. As usual, most of the drama had little to do with sincerely addressing problems.

In the meantime, Ben and I found ourselves surrounded. The police were not the only ones to figure out that we were Parrish's most likely targets, and the ensuing attention made it hard for either of us to get anything done.

Frank did all he could to reduce the pressure and stress, and we took turns reciting to each other the reasons why we shouldn't let Nick Parrish and his friends dominate our lives, the reasons why Ben and I might be the last people he came after, and how unhealthy speculation could be. I could talk a lot of talk about not letting Parrish ruin my life. And every day, it took every ounce of will I had in me just to walk out the front door.

I knew about Nick Parrish, and not from Sacramento or the Internet or television or any other glass-walled, safe observation point. Nick Parrish had slammed my face into the mud—I had felt his grip on my neck, been utterly in his power. I could have told anyone who cared to listen that Nick Parrish was not going to fit into any ready-made, predictable slot. He was not going to do the expected thing. He had studied other serial killers, seen them as object lessons in failure.

So while the local citizenry worried that he would attack in Las Piernas at any moment, I knew he would make us wait. I remembered other hunts for Nick Parrish that had failed, remembered how capable he was of going to ground.

I knew he blamed me for his previous capture and years of physical suffering.

He would wait.

The public would become distracted, the police would receive other demands on their attention.

Nick Parrish would strike then.

And damn it all to hell, now he had friends to help him do it.

TWENTY

Nicholas Parrish stood at a window and watched leaves drift from the branches of an oak tree to a walkway that led from the lodge to a storage shed. Only a few, at this time of year. Soon the days would grow cooler, the leaves would turn, and color the ground as they died. Death was a gift to the ground, something it needed to bring forth new life. Why did so few people understand the necessity of it?

He decided to go for a walk. He could hardly get enough of being outside, breathing in scents that were not those of a hospital or a prison.

As he moved into the open air, he wanted to shout, to laugh, to scream to the world that he had won again—he had!

He had planned so carefully. Even in the days when he had allowed his first capture, he knew that he would escape— the Moth had helped him. Irene Kelly, as expected, let all the earth know that Nicholas Parrish was unlike any who had gone before. He knew even then there was a possibility that he would be recaptured, but he had already made arrangements for this, his second escape. And while his injuries had been unexpected, and delayed his freedom, he had not let them defeat them, had he?

All the pieces had been in place, and they had waited for him, just as he knew they would.

He had counted on two special devotees, who remained hidden among those who now called themselves the Moths.

Most of the Moths were thrill seekers, rebellious youngsters, and loners who took pride in identifying themselves as outré, unaware of the ways in which they could be easily manipulated.

These two were different. They had been his to control from the time of his adolescence. None of his sons knew who they really were, and he would keep it that way. The two were not gifted in the ways Kai, Quinn, and Donovan were. They were not nearly as bright, and they lacked imagination. But they were utterly loyal and subservient. He wrote to them from prison, seemingly harmless letters. They knew how to decode his letters, and they passed along instructions in a second code to Quinn.

He felt pride in Quinn's abilities. He had kept track of all his children, watching to see which of them would prove most promising. At first he was disappointed to see how few of them exhibited the characteristics he was looking for, but as he considered his own genius, he accepted that they would be rare.

Quinn was not yet out of his teens when he first approached Parrish. Parrish was already aware of him, of course, and when they met, he startled Quinn by telling him that he had found Harold Moore's body. He added that he had made sure it was not going to be found again. He pointed out all the ways in which it was a bad idea to not completely destroy a body if one was about to benefit financially from the victim's death. He had shown Quinn how to do things properly when, together, they had ensured that a certain gossip at the airport restaurant would never again mention a connection between Parrish and Quinn's mother.

It was easy work from there to both charm and dominate

Quinn, to be the father he imagined he was looking for and yet to keep their lives separate and their relationship a secret.

Among the many lessons Parrish had taught him, Quinn learned that if his father needed his help, messages would arrive by mail, labeled in such and such a way, and how to decode them. He was told of a phone number he might call if he had questions or concerns. These would be passed back to Parrish.

And so, when the time came, Parrish's plans had, of course, worked perfectly.

This property belonged to Quinn. He had purchased it to have a remote location when needed. At one time it had been a religious organization's retreat, an irony that amused Nick Parrish no end. The grounds were extensive and included a lodge and twenty small cabins. Yes, Quinn's financial success had proved useful.

Despite a few nagging concerns, he did not underestimate any of his children. He could now admit to himself that he had been anxious when he decided to fake trouble with his spine, knew that the drugs he would most likely be given at the prison would make him unable to fend off any attack his sons might make. He had not expected to be so completely sedated, and waking up—at all—had been a relief. Kai's devotion had reassured him that he had not lost his touch when it came to control of others.

For a time, they would all need to lie low. It would not take long for some new demand to be made on the police, for some new crisis to distract them from their search for him. All the resources law enforcement could bring to bear were being used in the hunt just now, but his sons had followed instructions, and changed vehicles more than once. The trail was already growing cold.

He had found a great deal of amusement in watching television footage of the police swarming over the site where the explosion had gone off. And listening to the commentators (he could not think of them as reporters) had been even more amusing. There was a stiff-haired blonde who could hardly shut up about him. She liked to show photos of some of his earlier victims. That excited him so much he could ignore the idiot psychobabblers she brought on the show. He muted the television when they were on.

Quinn and Donovan were back in Las Piernas now. Thinking of Las Piernas made him think of Irene Kelly.

He thought of Ben Sheridan, too, but while he was angry with Sheridan, the man didn't excite him in the way Kelly did. He could torture her through whatever he did to Sheridan, of course. That bitch would be driven crazy by the mere thought of harm being done to him. Which was, of course, what she deserved.

Irene Kelly was the reason he had been imprisoned. She had nearly killed him to do it. He thought of the long, hard road back from paralysis, and just how he would exact revenge on her for that.

Lying helpless for months, struggling so hard for every tiny victory over his nerves and muscles. Then the surgery, which only led to being transferred from the hospital. The experience of being held against his will—first by his own body, then within the prison hospital, and even during his brief stay in prison—had reminded him of childhood experiences, brought up a wellspring of hatred so strong in him, it had fueled his determination.

He knew exactly who to thank for his years of suffering:
Irene Kelly.

TWENTY-ONE

Persistent rumors were circulating in Las Piernas.

One was that Nicholas Parrish had been seen in town. Plenty of those reports came in during the first few days after his escape, but they tapered off after that. Every now and then, though, there was a spike in the number of calls to the task force that was trying to find him. Aloud, I blamed his fan club for the upswing in sightings—the Moths' blog got more traffic whenever they claimed contact with him. Inwardly, I felt as frightened as any of the more hysterical 911 callers.

Another rumor was that the *Express* was coming back under new ownership. That was a little like being told your good friend Lazarus was up and walking around again. It didn't seem to fit with what one knew about the condition in which he was last seen.

One night, not long after Parrish's escape, I was home alone—if you don't count two plainclothes detectives keeping the house under surveillance from an unmarked car parked nearby. I was wondering what I'd do if someone actually managed to revive the *Express* when I heard Frank's car pull in the driveway. The dogs were at the door and waiting to greet him, but even before he got past them to pull me into an embrace, I knew he had news.

Frank and I have had to hammer out our own set of rules about our workplaces over the years. Essentially, home is home, and conversations there do not go back to our places of employment. So when he told me he wanted to tell me something but needed our conversation to remain private, I didn't hesitate to agree.

Still holding on to me, he said, "We know who the frozen woman is."

I felt myself tense. "The one who was in the trunk of Marilyn Foster's car?"

"Yes. Her name is Lisa King. She was from Nevada."

Lisa King. I said it to myself several times. The real progress in most homicide cases usually begins at the identification of the victim. Most. I thought of Cade Morrissey and Marilyn Foster, named for all these weeks. I thought of Lisa King and wondered if she, too, was somehow related to Nick Parrish. "How old was she?"

"Somewhere between nineteen and twenty-three." He said it in a distracted way, while studying my face. "Are you okay?"

I nodded, although I was a little shaky. "Yes, but let's sit down."

We moved to the couch.

"So," I said, once we were seated, "knowing her name should help you find her killer, right?"

"Maybe. We'll try, but I don't know if we'll get anywhere, even with the ID."

"Tell me about her anyway. Why do you only have an age range if you learned who she is? And how did you find out?"

"She was nineteen when her family last had contact with her. She might have been older when she was murdered, though, because they haven't heard from her in four years. So if she was murdered soon after she went missing, then frozen for all this time, she was nineteen. But if she was murdered more recently, she could have been as old as twenty-three. We're working on narrowing that down, and having a name will help us do that. As for how we learned about her, we caught a break from NamUs."

You live with a cop, you learn acronyms. But this one I knew from writing about missing persons. NamUs offered the best hope for putting names to unidentified dead that had come along in years. It's a national database designed so that any individuals can enter information about their missing family members and search for matches, and also submit DNA samples without cost.

"So who was trying to find her?"

"Her sister. Peyton King. She's three years older than Lisa."

I felt my brows go up. "Not the parents?"

"Father's dead, but the stepfather and mother had not reported her missing."

"What? Her own mother didn't wonder where her daughter was?"

"No, apparently there was a falling-out. Reed went to Nevada to make the notification and see what the locals could tell us—and he said everybody in the family seemed genuinely shocked by the news, and guilt-ridden. He remains suspicious about the stepfather, but not for the murder."

"Suspicious—why?"

He shrugged. "No proof of anything, just a possibility of some kind of abuse. But it might just as easily be what the step-dad said it was—Lisa felt that her mother's marriage to him was a betrayal of her father's memory and never let go of her anger about that. Whatever the case, as a teenager, Lisa King had a history of running away from home."

"Did her sister—Peyton? Did she have any theories?"

"Not that she was willing to discuss with us. She said that Lisa was 'just a free spirit.'" He shrugged. "Again, some people are."

"Some," I agreed, "but if you get them to stop singing 'Free Bird' for a few minutes, you find out there's often more to it."

"Exactly," he said, then fell silent.

"Sorry," I said. "She's—I didn't mean to be flip—she can't tell us her story."

"We'll make sure it gets told."

Seeing the determined look on his face, I felt utterly confident that he would. "So tell me the rest of what you know of that story so far."

He told me that Lisa King had settled down long enough to get a high school diploma but, soon after graduation, started roving again. During the first year she was gone, she called Peyton every few weeks. Lisa also sent pictures taken of herself here and there. In most she was grinning, smoking a cigarette, holding a drink, and shown partying with people she had chanced to meet along the way. She never named those in the photos.

Every now and then she'd give Peyton a cell phone number, and Peyton would call her, too, but most of the time Lisa didn't carry one with her. The calls came less often in the second year, and in the spring of that year, on Peyton's birthday, they had an argument.

"April twenty-sixth," Frank said. "The last time she heard from her. Lisa was in California, but one of the reasons they argued was that she wouldn't be more specific than that. She was acting coy. Peyton lost patience with it, hung up on her."

"So now she's on guilt overload?"

"Yes, even before we showed up. The news we had didn't help, of course, but we tried to let her see that if she hadn't entered the information on NamUs, she never would have had even this much resolution."

"So what's next?"

"We're working with the local authorities to get a look at the phone records, so that we can at least try to figure out where Lisa called from."

Within twenty-four hours, most of what Frank had told me was public knowledge. The police were actively seeking the public's help at that point. Lisa King's last call was placed in Las Piernas, from a phone booth outside a liquor store. The owner of the liquor store didn't remember her, wasn't even sure he still had records showing who had worked in his store that night, and security camera recordings from that date were long gone. Peyton had supplied some of the photos that were now being shown on the evening news—and that Ethan had up on the station's Web site—so I got a chance to replace the single image of Lisa King I had been carrying around in my head. Now I knew what Lisa looked like thawed, clothed, and unpainted.

At least, not painted with moths. She was about five feet four, slender but curvy. She had large, light green eyes and favored heavy use of eyeliner. Her look wasn't goth, though— it was almost Garbo. In nearly every photo, she wore a dark gray cloche hat. It looked good on her—she had a pretty face, a straight little nose, and full lips. She wore a silver cross on a delicate chain around her neck. A silver filigree cuff bracelet was the only other jewelry visible in any of the photos. In most of them, she wore short-sleeve, long, draping tops and dark jeans, and carried a large, cloth shoulder bag that I suspected doubled as a suitcase.

Phone calls started coming in. The hat had made her memorable, and the photos jogged memories. She was a fixture on the local party scene. She had a knack for finding someone who would give her a place to stay for a few days. None of the people she had stayed with—not all of whom volunteered that information themselves—had seen her after the date of the phone call.

Police used the information from the more reliable reports to conclude that it was likely she either met her killer not long after the call or perhaps already knew him by then. They began canvassing the neighborhood near the liquor store.

Two additional "boyfriends" were located, but both of them were college students who had been home for the summer. Neither had been in Las Piernas in the weeks before Lisa disappeared, and she had been seen alive after they had returned to school.

At that point, the investigation seemed to hit a dead end. Police followed up on any information that came their way, but none of it led them any closer to her killer.

Efforts to find Parrish and those who'd helped him escape were also ongoing but didn't meet with any greater success.

I started seeing my therapist again, visits that at first kept me from going completely around the bend and eventually helped me calm down enough to sleep through most nights. She reminded me that Parrish was not Godzilla, and even when I replied that no, indeed, Godzilla was a much nicer monster, she helped me to stop supersizing Parrish and his power in my imagination.

She also reminded me to consider my own power, and the changes I had made since my last encounter with Parrish, including regular lessons and practice with Rachel in self-defense.

Life, as it goes on, always provides variety, and that alone kept me from living in a permanent funk. The days, after all, weren't unrelentingly grim. Guy and Lydia's wedding gave me a chance to celebrate their happiness, and if the presence of two of Parrish's most likely targets meant a visible police presence as well, the occasion lost none of its joy as a result.

I was enjoying my new job as well, finding that the challenges in changing from print to radio reporting were more than a distraction from my fears, and stimulating. If it was a little strange to be mentored in this by Ethan, whom I had mentored at the *Express,* it wasn't the cause of any resentment. I appreciated his willingness to teach me the ropes.

Harder not to resent the fact that I once again had a team of babysitters—a set of bodyguards that rotated between Frank, our neighbor Jack, Rachel, and if none of them were available, one of Frank's off-duty friends from the department. Working out a way to be an effective journalist under these conditions was a more difficult challenge.

My feelings about the protection were, to say the least, mixed. I could easily admit I felt safer knowing that someone was watching my back. But Ethan and Lydia were quite obviously assigning me to stories on the political scene that would kept me in public places or on the phone. I couldn't work the way I usually did, and I wasn't willing to expose the sources I had in city hall to police scrutiny—even from off-duty, friendly officers who probably couldn't have cared less about politics.

And eventually, there was the problem of a lack of solitude. I first began to feel my longing for it on the beach. I liked my runs on the beach with my dogs. Alone. Having Frank along or a friend was fine, but not every day, not every time. For the first two or three weeks after Parrish escaped, I was scared even when someone was with me. After that, I began to chafe at the bit.

It wasn't just on runs, of course. I began to feel as if I were a bug in a jar. I started to notice avoidance behavior on my part— I canceled dinners with friends, begged off when invited on outings. I slept more, found reasons to linger anywhere I might be able to be alone. At home, instead of talking to my minders, who were, in fact, close friends, I pretended to get lost in working on the computer or moved to other rooms and shut the door.

In public, I didn't have that option, and I realized how pathetic this longing for privacy had become when I noticed that I now looked forward to trips to the restroom and dawdled there.

I found some sympathy from Ben, although his work was so different from mine—he seldom traveled alone or made appointments to meet with complete (and often hostile) strangers. Still, he didn't like being constantly accompanied any more than I did. That said, we were both aware of the bull's-eyes on our backs, so there was a limit to our complaints.

As the first month went by, I could see the task of watching over me wearing on those who had taken it on, even if they wouldn't admit it to me. By the end of the second month, little gaps were appearing in the schedule. By the autumn, I was just being warned to be careful.

I was, for all the good that did me.

One afternoon in late September, I was talking to Ethan in my small, shared office, waiting for Ben to show up for lunch with us, when the receptionist buzzed my desk and told me I had a pair of visitors in the lobby.

"Who?" Ethan said over the speaker, before I could ask.

I shot him a frown as the receptionist answered—in much warmer tones—that it was a man named Josh Enwill, who was here with his wife, Andrea.

Ethan raised his brows in inquiry. I was pondering two questions almost simultaneously:

Is Ethan stupid enough to be fooling around with the receptionist?

and

Where have I heard the name Josh Enwill before?

The answer to the second question came to me at the same time it occurred to Ethan: the injured prison guard.

"Escort them to the conference room, please," he said, in a businesslike way that still left me undecided about the first question.

TWENTY-TWO

The conference room was closer to the lobby than my office was, but it took a while for the Enwills to make the short trip. He was walking with a cane, making determined progress, his right side seeming to drag the left half of his body along with it. The counterpoint to this slouched figure was Andrea Enwill, a tall blonde who walked behind him carrying a canvas backpack, her chin up, spine straight. She silently willed him down the hall with a nearly tangible force.

Ethan and I shook hands with them, then Ethan pulled out a chair for Josh but didn't offer other assistance. He looked at Ethan for a moment, then said, with painstaking care but only slightly slurring his words, "Are you the one who got hurt, up in the mountains?"

"No," Ethan and Andrea said at the same time.

"I think you mean Ben Sheridan," I said.

"Oh, yes, of course," he said, ducking his head.

"We'll go over there next," Andrea assured him.

"As it happens," I said, "he's on his way here. He's meeting us for lunch."

Josh looked up at that. "Really?"

"Yes."

"If you don't mind," Andrea said, "could we wait for him? If it won't ruin your plans?"

"No problem," I said.

Ethan offered beverages to each of us, then stepped out to fetch them. I could see the Enwills were ill-at-ease, so I asked them if it was their first visit to Las Piernas. Yes, their first time here. They had driven down from Bakersfield, where they had moved after Josh left the Department of Corrections. There was a world of hurt lurking behind those last few words, so I quickly mentioned that I used to live in Bakersfield and worked for the *Californian,* and that most of Frank's family lived there. So we made Bakersfield small talk and they relaxed a bit. Ethan came back with the drinks—and Ben in tow.

After the next round of introductions, Andrea reached into the backpack and pulled out a notebook and a manila folder. She kept the folder, but she opened the notebook to a page with writing on it and handed it to Josh.

He positioned it with his right hand, and studied it for a moment. He looked up and said, "Excuse me. Since—since I was hurt, I have . . ."

He looked helplessly at Andrea.

"Short-term memory loss," she said.

He stared at her for a moment, then laughed. "As demonstrated!"

She smiled at him. The tension in the room went down another few notches.

"Right." He looked at the notebook again, then said, "I came to Las Piernas for three reasons. Andrea has a sister here who has been wanting us to visit. I wanted to talk to the police here. And I wanted to see Ms. Kelly and Dr. Sheridan."

"Irene and Ben," I said, and Ben nodded.

He wrote our names in the margins of the notebook, then said, "Okay. Irene and Ben, I want to apologize."

"Apologize?" I said. "For what?"

"I let him get away."

"No, you didn't," I said. "It wasn't your fault."

"Irene is right," Ben said, "neither of us blames you for his escape."

"I should have known," he said stubbornly. "Never should have turned my back on them."

"Josh," Ben said, "Irene and I were in the mountains with him when he was shackled and heavily guarded—more people guarding him than you had available. He escaped then, and he didn't have a team to help him do it. We're the last people who will ever believe you were responsible for his escape. We're glad you survived."

Enwill winced and lowered his gaze.

I felt a rush of a familiar, half-forgotten emotion—a feeling that once upon a time had nearly drowned me where I stood. I swallowed hard, failed to fight tears, and said, "It's the hardest part, Josh. Forgiving yourself for surviving."

He looked up at me.

"It took me a long time," I said, "and it damned near drove me out of my head until I realized it was what I had to do. You get so busy healing—"

"At first just dealing with injuries—" Ben said and pulled up his pant leg to show his prosthesis. "Just getting through the next day. So you set aside everything else."

"But the whole time," I said, "it's as if someone's winding up this jack-in-the-box inside you. The tension mounts, and then from wherever inside you all this stuff is buried, that jack-in-the-box flies open, and brings out a memory."

"Sometimes it plays a movie in your head," Ben said. "The if-only-I-had movie."

"Yeah," Josh said. "I know that one."

"Are you seeing a therapist?" I asked. "A good one can really help."

"Not yet," he said and glanced at Andrea.

"He did have a few visits from a social worker at the hospital, but most of that was about dealing with the consequences of a head injury. Can you recommend someone?"

"Yes," Ben and I said in unison, and I wrote down the information.

"If you can't stay long enough in Las Piernas to work with her, maybe she'll recommend someone to you in your area."

"Thanks. I think we could both use it," Andrea said.

"In the meantime, Josh," Ben said, "please understand this— we don't hold you at all responsible for Parrish's escape."

"You hear that, Josh?" Andrea said. She moved nearer and took the notebook, wrote what Ben had said in it. "I'm going to put that on a dozen Post-it notes and plaster them all over the house."

"Thanks," Josh said to us, and for a moment seemed unable to speak.

Andrea studied him, then said, "We had a kind of rough morning with the police. Bunch of assholes—"

Ethan and Ben glanced at me but read my look. They kept their mouths shut about Frank.

"Nah," Josh said, "most of them were okay. Just that last guy we met with, and who could blame him?"

"Who was he?" Ben asked.

Josh looked through his notes. "Detective Vincent Adams." He looked up. "But don't blame him or anyone else there. I wasn't all that helpful."

"Why did you visit the police?" I asked.

He leaned back and rubbed a hand over his close-cropped hair. "I can't really remember the escape at all. I remember them loading Parrish into the ambulance, and Stan . . ." His voice trailed off, then he took a deep breath and went on. "And Stan getting into the cab, and me sitting down in the back. But after that? It's like a tape has been erased. The doctors tell me it's not unusual with a head injury, but that doesn't keep me from thinking that I should remember it."

He fell silent.

Andrea said, "That's been bothering Josh a lot, understandably. Some of the investigators thought if they could question him enough times, hint at things, it would come back to him. The doctors finally told them the memories probably never would return and to stop pestering Josh. A couple of the investigators thought Josh might be in on it, because he lived. So they pawed through his background—and mine—but that didn't pan out, either."

"If anything," he said, "this has ruined us."

"No," she said. "We'll be fine. It was hard at first, because they were holding off on paying his bills, and he couldn't work, and I had to quit my job to take care of him. But we got a good lawyer, an amazing guy who has helped us out, so we sued. We had to sell our house in the meantime, but now that they've settled, we'll be fine. Moving, and the changes and the stress—it's all been hard on us, especially Josh. But as you can probably tell, my husband isn't the kind who gives up."

"And neither are you," I said.

"I've had the easy part," she said, a statement I didn't wholly believe, "but no, I don't give up, either. Which is part of why we have another reason to talk to you today. You're a reporter, so maybe you can help us with the problem with the police."

"I should mention to you that I'm married to a homicide detective in Vince's department."

She shrugged. "I married someone in law enforcement, too. No problem." She turned to her husband. "You okay with me going ahead with my plan to tell her about the photo you saw?"

"Yes," Josh said.

"Like he said, Josh couldn't remember the journey from the prison, but he did remember loading Parrish in the ambulance.

He vaguely remembered the guy who was there in the back of the ambulance with him, the one who probably attacked him while the other one attacked Stan."

"A nerd," Josh said. "Red hair, big glasses."

"They checked, but the ambulance company had never hired anyone who looked like that. So Josh and I have been trying to think of other ways to find him. I know a bit about computers—"

"She's a nerd, too," Josh said with a lopsided smile.

"Yes," she agreed, smiling back at him. "Lucky thing, huh?"

"Yes."

"So, I've been keeping track of the stories about Parrish, listening to your station, and reading the stories about the Moths. You know the stories you had online when you were trying to find people who had known Lisa King?"

"Yes."

"There was one taken at a park, a concert." She opened the folder and pulled out a print made from one of the photos one of our listeners had posted when we asked them to send in any pictures they had of Lisa King. When those went up, the Las Piernas Police Department had been visiting our site more than usual.

Andrea passed the photo to me, and Ethan and Ben peered at it over my shoulders. One of the faces in the photo had been circled. It was not that of Lisa or any of the people close to her, whose faces were turned with rapt attention on the performers, a band not seen in the photo. The face circled was that of a young man in the background, who at the moment the photo was taken was watching not the band but Lisa and the people around her.

He did not have red hair. He was not wearing glasses. He didn't look especially nerdy, whatever that actually is.

"That's him," Josh said, and as if he had read my thoughts,

added, "I realized that the thing that made me say he was nerdy was how he acted, not really what he looked like."

All three of us looked up at him, the same question on our faces.

"I'm certain," he said.

"Josh—" Ben began but was interrupted.

"Show him the other one, Andrea."

She pulled a second print from the folder. She had used software to alter the image, so that the person in the photo now resembled the description Josh had given earlier—red hair, glasses.

"You could do that to a photo of anyone," Ben countered.

"She didn't mess with the structure of his face. She only added the glasses and hair color."

"Well," I said, "since we posted that photo on the Web site, we've learned more about it. The concert took place around the date Lisa King's family last heard from her. It was at Weissman Park, and the band was Needlesmith. The band contacted us when one of their members saw the photo, and they've offered to help in any way they can. They have a fan mailing list. Maybe they can put the word out for other photos from the day."

Ben frowned and said, "Irene—be reasonable. Surely you can understand why Vince was skeptical."

"Yes, but I don't have the limitations set on me that Vince does."

"What do you mean?" Andrea asked.

"The police have to be concerned with convincing judges who sign warrants, district attorneys who worry about conviction rates, and ultimately, juries who will question the way they obtained evidence. That said, Vince might have tried to get you to lower your expectations, but don't assume he's refusing to think about what you told him—did he keep copies of your printouts?"

"Yes."

"Which means you should keep your nose out of it," Ben said to me, "and not interfere with his work."

I ignored that. "Josh, you're hoping we can find out who he is, right? You're not looking for vigilante justice?"

"No, and even if I was, I'm in no shape to deliver it. We just want to keep him from ruining anybody else's life. And besides, I think he killed that girl." He consulted his notes. "Lisa King."

"Andrea, do you have spare copies of these printouts? May we keep a set here?"

"Sure," she said, "keep those."

"Would you mind e-mailing the JPGs to me?" Ethan asked, handing over his business card.

"I'll give you a copy right now," she said. She said she had hoped he would ask for them and had prepared a CD. She handed it to Ethan. We asked for phone contact information, and she gave us her cell phone number and her sister's number.

Ben wrote their numbers down, too, and put a lid on his protests—two facts that told me he was seeing possibilities. Good.

"One other thing," Ethan said. "Josh and Andrea, you've already had a long day, but if you don't mind, I'd like you to let Irene record an interview with you. I think it will help us."

We made it a two-part story. In the first segment, our listeners heard what had happened to the surviving guard. It upped our traffic enough so that the second segment—carefully vetted by our legal team—had a wide audience. We talked about elusive and sometimes unreliable memories, gave the unaltered concert photo a prominent place on our Web site, and asked our audience—especially those who might have been at the Needlesmith concert in Weissman Park four years ago—to help us find information that might lead nowhere or might be vital to a murder investigation: could they identify any of the people who were pictured with Lisa King?

I wasn't too surprised that one of the first of the many calls we received was from Vince Adams, who tried to give me grief. I held the phone away from my ear so that Ethan could hear him yelling. Ethan's grin reflected my own. As soon as Vince took a breath, I told him get the knot out of his tighty whities and call me back when he could be polite. I then hung up on him—which wasn't polite on my part, and, in truth, it was unfair to Vince. But damn it felt good.

TWENTY-THREE

When I walked down Douglas Street, it was in the middle of a sunny afternoon, and I was not alone. Rachel, Ben, and Ethan were with me, as were two of the dogs, Altair and Bingle. The only one officially on bodyguard duty was Rachel, and she was armed, although her martial arts skills made the need for a weapon unlikely.

Thanks to Rachel, my own skills were improving—not that I had advanced much beyond a basic level. Otherwise, I was armed with only the tools of my own trade. I had a notebook. (A paper notebook, not a computer. Old habits die hard.) A pen. And my recorder, ostensibly to record a story about search dogs.

If that had been what we were really up to, it would have been a perfect day for their work—cool, moist air, with a light breeze. Altair and Bingle were wearing their working vests, which attracted a kind of attention that four people walking a couple of dogs might not have otherwise. This was essentially what we were hoping for, and when two kids in the company of their mother and two elderly couples made their way over to admire the handsome canines, Ethan's look was downright smug. The idea to use the dogs as busybody bait was his.

I probably should have objected more vehemently to his

plan—for a number of reasons. Alas, Ethan knew more than a few of my weaknesses, and he appealed to my curiosity and—I'm ashamed to admit it—a desire to royally avenge myself on Vince.

Vince had not only gone public with his objections to my story via scathing interviews with other media but further showed his displeasure by stonewalling us at every turn on that or any other story that involved one of his investigations.

Although it was great publicity for the station and upped our listenership, I was angered on behalf of the Enwills—Vince made more than one public statement in which he said that "reporters at KCLP are being misled by someone police investigators do not believe is reliable." Even that probably wouldn't have been enough to make me go against my better judgment, but then Vince upped the ante by doing all he could to make Frank's life miserable at work.

I heard about this not from Frank but from Rachel. Frank's partner, Pete, never discreet about departmental gossip, ratted Vince out to his wife, who in turn let me know about it. Rachel and I were both furious. Frank told us to ignore it, that Vince was just trying to piss me off. Trouble was, his efforts worked. Really well.

Ethan decided that if Vince wanted to see what life was like without cooperation, he'd be happy to oblige.

So when the calls started coming in, Ethan declared we'd investigate on our own and strictly forbade passing any information on to the police. "This time, we won't contact them until we are certain," he said.

"Certain?" I said. "You planning on setting up a DNA lab in the back office?"

"Okay, until I feel confident."

There wasn't much to feel confident about at first. Dozens of names were mentioned in the calls that came in. Many were clearly hoax calls. Eventually—a word that covers a lot of footwork and Internet searches—we narrowed the possibilities. One of the most promising of those possibilities was a young man named Kai Loudon, who lived with his mother, somewhere on Douglas Street.

Loudon was mentioned by several callers, all former high school classmates. Most didn't know him well. None of them thought he had dated Lisa King, saying that Kai didn't date anyone after his junior year. The junior year was mentioned as a clear memory, because at the beginning of his senior year, he had left school and finished his diploma through online courses. Everyone knew that, because after the start of his senior year, Kai Loudon spent all his time taking care of his injured mom.

The story was a class legend, but I heard a firsthand account from a young man who had accompanied Kai home that day, and had been with him when he discovered his mom lying at the bottom of the basement stairs. At first they both thought she was dead, but even as Kai was dialing 911, his friend saw that she was breathing and had a pulse.

"But she was almost completely paralyzed," he said. "She had both spine and head injuries. Kai had to do everything for her. Feed her, bathe her, comb her hair, give her medications—everything. Luckily, he had just turned eighteen that summer, so he was legally an adult and was able to deal with all of the legal aspect of things. He gave up his whole life to take care of her. I hope you aren't implying he had anything to do with the death of that girl."

The others told similar stories. When I asked them if they had seen Kai lately, they confessed guiltily that they had rarely been in contact with him after the accident. Once in a while they would see him in a grocery store or at the mall. The withdrawal had been his choice, which they saw as Kai spurning pity.

I began to doubt Josh's identification. Weaknesses in eyewitness memories of events had been studied extensively, especially since the "false memory" studies of the mid-1970s. Given his head injury, any confusion he experienced about events of that day was not surprising. Was it possible that we had unwittingly set him up for a false memory? If he was searching for an answer, a face to fill in the blank in his memory of his attacker, perhaps the faces in the photos of Lisa King on the KCLP Web site had suggested one to him that wasn't real.

Despite what Vince claimed in his interviews, though, we had never said that anyone in the Weissman Park photo killed Lisa King, or come close to making that accusation. I had been careful to make the story on Josh about his struggle after his injuries, and the request for information about the photo was not couched as an accusation—we all, Josh included, knew that he could be wrong. We asked for the public's help to find people who might have known Lisa King, and fully acknowledged that identifying the people in the photo might lead nowhere in terms of the murder investigation.

If it was leading nowhere, so be it. But what ultimately bothered me was that it led a little too perfectly to nowhere.

Even for a guy who was caring for an invalid, Kai Loudon was more than reclusive. He seemed to have disappeared. If he had answered the phone when I called and said, "Leave me and my poor mother alone, I was in a photo with a girl who happened to be at that same concert, so what?" that might have been that. But he wasn't answering his phone, and none of his "friends" had seen him for years. I was curious.

Normally, I would have just knocked on his door or camped out near his house, waiting for him to emerge to go shopping or mail a letter or take a walk. But given the now seemingly slight possibility that he was connected to Nick Parrish, there was not a chance in hell that I was going to be allowed to come within a hundred yards of him without an escort.

Which led to Ethan's Plan B.

The dogs were relaxed but in ready-to-work mode, friendly

to approaching strangers but focused on Ben and Ethan, waiting for commands. The two young neighborhood boys asked for and received permission to pet the dogs. They were peppering Ben and Ethan with questions (What are the dogs' names? Are they boys or girls? How old are they? Why are they wearing clothes?), all of which I recorded. After all, I might end up with nothing but the story we said we were there for.

Fortunately, when it came to that *other* story, my three human companions let me ask the questions of the small crowd gathering on Douglas Street.

I told them Ethan and I were from the radio station, and the older couples mentioned that they remembered me from the newspaper. We spent a little time mourning the passing of the *Express* and giving them information on the news programs on KCLP, of which they had been unaware. I told them that I was doing a piece about how search dogs worked but that I hadn't chosen their street at random.

"In connection with another story I'm working on, we're all a little concerned about Kai Loudon," I began. "He lives on this street, right?"

The house—two doors down from where we were—was eagerly pointed out by the kids. The story of the accident on the stairs was soon told by the adults. "Violet was so mean to that kid, I'm amazed Kai takes such good care of her," one of the women said. "I think I would have suffocated her years ago."

Her husband chided her, but the other couple agreed with her.

"No," the man insisted, "she's not so bad. Loudon was the problem."

"Kai's father?" I asked.

"No, stepfather." The man blushed. "I don't think the father has ever been in the picture, if you know what I mean. Loudon was a—" He glanced at the boys, who were eagerly taking this all in. "Loudon was worthless. I think he would have been happy if Violet had pawned the kid off on relatives. Instead, Loudon ended up leaving them. Kai was eleven or twelve, I think." He glanced at the boys, then said, "Kai seemed to have fewer 'accidents' after Loudon left, if you know what I mean."

I would definitely have to talk to this guy when there weren't any kids around to make him censor himself. "Has anyone seen Kai lately?" I asked.

The adults exchanged glances, then admitted they hadn't seen him for quite some time. "But that's not unusual," one of the men said. "He keeps odd hours, doesn't come out of the house much. The Loudons never have been neighborly."

"He doesn't come to the door right away if you knock," the mother of the boys said. "But I'm sure if you keep trying, you'll find him there. He can't go far with her to care for."

"No, Mom," the older of the boys said. I judged him to be about ten. "He's not there anymore."

"Michael!" she said, reddening.

He folded his arms and jutted his chin out, and I could see he was nearly ready to bend double with the effort of not smarting off to her.

"Michael, what makes you say that?" I asked, crouching down to eye level.

"He moved out. I saw him."

"Liar," his younger brother accused.

This led to a brief chase and might have resulted in mayhem, but their mother grabbed hold of Michael before he could punish his accuser, who was ordered to return home immediately. He wisely, if reluctantly, obeyed.

She turned to Michael, still in hand. "And as for you—"

"I'm telling the truth!" he protested.

"I believe you," I said, for which I received a grateful look. His mother sighed and let go of him.

"When did he move out?" I asked.

"Last year," he said. "In the middle of the night!"

"Now, Michael, that's not true," his mother said. "I know I saw him in June or sometime around then." She frowned in concentration. "Goodness, it has been a while—not long before vacation?"

"That's what I mean!" he said in exasperation. "Last year. When I was in fourth grade. This year I'm in fifth."

"When do you get your vacation break?" I asked. Las Piernas was on a year-round schedule.

His mother pulled out a PDA and looked at the calendar on it. "They had six weeks off starting June thirtieth."

Ben, Ethan, and I exchanged a glance. That would have been a week after Lisa King's body was found.

"Has anyone else seen Kai since then?" I asked. The others thought this over, then shook their heads.

"Well, Michael, so you were up in the middle of the night—"

"Barney was sick," he explained, his face suddenly awash in sadness. He looked longingly at Altair and Bingle.

"Barney? Your brother?"

That brought a small smile. "No, my dog. He died."

"I'm sorry," I said. "That's really hard."

He shrugged and kept petting Bingle.

"So you were taking care of Barney," I said gently.

"Yeah. I had to let him out in the backyard. He needed to barf. Then he wanted to stay outside for a while, so I kept him company. Then he heard something—you know, his ears went up. He went to the gate to watch something. So I followed him and saw that he was watching Kai move."

He said that a truck and a van were in the driveway. Kai and another man finished packing up the truck, then the other man helped Kai load Violet ("*her!*" spoken with the air of delight felt by a boy who has seen something rare and freakish) into the van Kai usually drove. The older neighbors confirmed that once in a while they had seen Kai use a kind of gurney to load Violet into the van for doctor's appointments.

"Big, white, windowless cargo van," one of the men said. "Econoline, I think."

"What did the moving truck look like?" I asked Michael.

He frowned and said, "Like a U-Haul, but it wasn't. It was all white."

Michael's failure to mention this to his parents was easily explained—Barney had ended up going to the vet the next morning, so his companion's illness had been foremost in the boy's mind at that point.

It was also clear that the other neighbors hadn't missed Kai and Violet Loudon. They hadn't cared much for them, or about them. Welcome to suburbia.

I studied the exterior of the house from where we were standing. "Its windows are a little dirty, but the yard is cared for," I said.

"Gardener comes by to work on the front yard on Fridays," one of the women offered.

"Just the front yard?"

"Yes. I don't believe there is a lawn in the back."

"Anyone else use that same gardener?"

Another exchange of looks, shaking of heads. None of them recalled seeing any markings on the gardener's pickup truck indicating who he was or how he could be reached. So unless we came back and waited around on Friday, we weren't going to get any information out of him.

We thanked the neighbors and asked them not to follow us as we walked down the block with the dogs and crossed over to the Loudons' yard. Ben and Ethan were just starting to give working commands to the dogs when the breeze shifted, and both dogs alerted.

Their body language suddenly changed. Their ears pitched forward, they went up on their toes, looking back at their handlers as if to ask, "Don't you smell that?" Their excitement was controlled but evident.

Ben and Ethan let them off leash. They ran toward the backyard gate, sniffing there and along the fence, then running back to their handlers. Bingle and Altair also took interest in a small basement window. It was blacked out, as if painted on the other side, so there was no seeing what was drawing their attention.

I began to feel uneasy, wondering if I really wanted to know what was so fascinating to a pair of human remains detection dogs. I told myself not to be so fainthearted, and also not to ignore the obvious approach. Rachel stayed by my side as I went to the front door and knocked, an idea she wasn't too crazy about, especially because simultaneously the dogs became close to frantic with their desire to get into the backyard. But no one answered.

Ben called Bingle back and said, "Time to call the police. We don't have a warrant, we don't want to ruin a case."

I looked over his shoulder and said, "That won't be necessary," just as a black-and-white pulled up to the curb. One of the neighbors must have called them.

Two hours later, there was a bigger crowd on the sidewalk opposite the Loudon house, the closest police would let anyone come. Frank and Pete had shown up, tipped off by the patrolman, who was a friend of Frank's. Their presence and Reed's usual calm demeanor probably kept Vince from going over the edge. Reed and Vince had a warrant.

Attitudes changed not long after they accessed the property. When the gate to the yard was forced open, the reason for the dogs' excitement wasn't immediately plain. A large, slightly raised wooden deck covered almost all of the yard. But the dogs both gave hard alerts as they stood over sections of the deck, and it was soon discovered that many of the boards in these sections were loose. Once those boards were lifted, it was clear that the earth beneath the deck had been disturbed. There were four areas that had been recently dug up—body-sized holes. The soil, when stirred up a bit, had a sharp, unnerving scent that even humans could recognize. No corpses could be seen in the holes, but there were bits of hair, bone, and teeth in each. There was no mistaking that these had been graves and that someone had removed remains from them.

Ben and a team of his forensic anthropology graduate students were going to be busy doing recovery and identification work.

The house itself bore all the signs of a hasty departure. The basement was pristine and was almost bypassed, except that Bingle gave signals that made Ben say, "Not so fast." Turned out there was an exception to all the cleanliness. Bingle's interest led police to the discovery of a false wall, behind which was a hidden room. The thick walls and floor of the room bore stains that Kai Loudon had apparently found difficult to remove.

Or, as Ben suggested, Loudon might have felt a kind of attachment to them, considered them to be erotic artwork.

I tried not to let that thought disturb me.

I also tried to feel proud of our day's work, rather than terrified that this monster had been in my own backyard.

I failed on both counts.

TWENTY-FOUR

Donovan parked on a road that had no direct access to the camp and was not visible from it, then began the hike uphill to the property where his father and half brother were staying. Far from being a hardship, he enjoyed the opportunity to be outdoors and test skills he could not easily use in Las Piernas. Moving silently among the trees in the moonlight, he felt exhilarated, a sensation seldom part of his life these days.

He was armed, though he did not believe that the weapons would be necessary. Still, with these individuals, any possibility was a deadly possibility, so he came prepared. He was an expected visitor, although he was sure there were aspects of his visit that would be a surprise. He didn't know how well they would handle that.

He spotted all the cameras. He had to admit that Quinn's arrangement of them provided good coverage, but would anyone be watching the monitors? He doubted it. He waited patiently and was rewarded with the sound of a car coming up the drive. Quinn. Perfect.

He entered through a side door and was sitting in a

comfortable chair with his back to the large stone fireplace when Parrish and Kai came in with Quinn. He gave them no indication that, inwardly, he was struggling not to laugh out loud at the shocked looks on their faces. A memory he would store away, treasure for another time. Best not to reveal reactions of any kind to these three.

Parrish, not surprisingly, was the first to recover. He smiled broadly and said, "Oh, excellent, Donovan! Quinn, before Donovan leaves, please ask him if he can . . . improve . . . on the security arrangements you have in place."

"Certainly," Quinn said, not quite able to keep the irritation out of his voice.

"You're looking well," Donovan said to Parrish. Parrish, now in his fifties, was not the man Donovan had seen in footage taken of him before his injuries—one of his shoulders seemed to bother him, and his movements were a little stiff. All the same, Donovan knew it would be extremely foolish to think of him as a weak old man.

"Thank you. I continue to improve."

They seated themselves, Parrish lounging back in a large overstuffed armchair, Quinn imitating his posture—all too consciously, Donovan thought—on one end of a matching sofa. Kai sat upright, on the edge of the other end of the sofa. Kai didn't bother trying to look relaxed.

"Now," Parrish said, "why don't you bring me up to date, Donovan?"

Quinn, obviously expecting to be the one called upon to do this, opened his mouth as if to object, then subsided.

Donovan chose his words carefully. "The police obtained warrants to search Kai's home, including his backyard."

"That much we know of from the news broadcasts," Parrish said. "But, as usual, there are so many missing details. How did this focus on Kai come about?"

"Through the surviving prison guard—"

"The one Kai was supposed to kill?" Quinn asked.

"Through the surviving guard," Donovan began again, "the reporters were able to identify Kai and found his home."

"The guard learned Kai's name?" Parrish asked incredulously. Kai tensed.

Donovan saw Quinn tense in response but answered calmly, as if neither of them were in the room. "He didn't know Kai's name, no. I don't think he would have even been able to tell you the fake names Kai and Quinn gave him, if the investigators hadn't asked about them by those names."

"So how . . . ?" Quinn asked.

"The frozen young woman you left in the trunk of the car."

"He couldn't possibly know about her!" Kai protested. "There's no connection between the two of them."

"You are the connection!" Quinn said. "Don't you get that?"

"He didn't know about her," Donovan said, "but he knew that the police in Las Piernas—the town most closely associated with Nicholas Parrish—learned her name, and that the public radio station there has been determined to find her killer. Reporters for the station posted photographs of her on its Web site, and asked those who might have met her and taken her picture to send additional photos in to them. Amazing response, really. You could practically follow her history in the city if you really looked at the details in the photos."

"So what has this to do with the guard?" Parrish asked impatiently.

"The guard recognized Kai as one of the people near her in one of those images."

"This seems weak," Parrish said. "How did he convince the police that Kai and the ambulance attendant were one and the same? The last we heard, his head injury prevented his being useful in the investigation of the escape."

"He didn't convince them. He's quite impaired from the blow Kai gave him, after all. They were sure he was confused, or wanted so much to be of help he created a false memory. But Irene Kelly believed him."

He noticed the reactions that name got from all three of them. Interesting.

"I'm not exactly sure," Donovan went on, "whether it was the station's pressure or her connections to the police department through her husband, but in any case, I believe she's directly connected to the issuing of the search warrant. She was walking around asking questions in Kai's neighborhood just before the police showed up." He paused, then added, "I have it on good authority that, within the next twenty-four hours, there will be news reports about a secret basement room."

Kai came to his feet.

Parrish held up a hand. "Sit down," he said quietly.

Kai obeyed him. Donovan noted that if Kai in any way resented being ordered around by his father, he didn't show it.

"What a mess," Quinn said.

Parrish stared hard at him, and he, too, fell silent.

Parrish returned his gaze to Donovan and smiled. Donovan would have preferred the stare he'd just given Quinn. "You've been reluctant to help us, Donovan, and yet your work is always superior. Your foresight, your perfectionism, these are traits I've passed down to you, whether you acknowledge it or not."

"I have no doubt you're my father."

"Biologically, if not in other ways?"

Donovan stayed silent.

Parrish's smile widened. "Yes! You see, Quinn? He does not rise to bait. You two could learn from him."

"If only he were willing to teach us," Quinn said with false sweetness.

"You could learn just by observing him. I am pleased."

"You're better suited to teach them," Donovan said. "I don't have your experience."

"Of course you don't," Parrish said. "No one does." He turned to Kai. "You'll have to stay on the property for a time. Perhaps even indoors during the day."

"Yes, sir," Kai said.

"What of you and Quinn?" Parrish asked Donovan. "Any renewed police interest?"

"Not since the first questioning."

Quinn shrugged. "I was, of course, shocked that any of my properties had been put to such foul use and have taken appropriate security measures since."

"Both of you must be extremely careful now, but I need not say more on that subject. I can't tell you how pleased I am to be with individuals who truly understand me." He turned to Quinn. "I believe you have a special treat for Donovan before we begin the next phase of our plans?"

Quinn gave a little bow and slid one pale hand into his jacket.

Donovan watched him but didn't show any particular excitement over what could have been a reach for a weapon. He was certain he could outdraw, evade fire, and aim better than Quinn.

Quinn smiled as he handed over a disk in a slender plastic jewel case. "You can watch it here, if you'd like, on Kai's computer."

"I'll wait," Donovan said, tucking it inside his own jacket.

"I'm surprised you care," Kai said, watching this exchange.

Donovan stared at him. "I don't." He turned to Parrish. "If that's all?"

"The security system?"

"No use having cameras if you aren't going to monitor them. Otherwise—Well, I'm sure you've already implemented other defenses."

"Yes," Parrish said, but Donovan saw a bit of doubt in his eyes. Parrish quickly went on. "Well, then, no need to delay your return. You'll have new instructions soon."

Donovan gave an acknowledging nod and stood.

The others stayed seated and silent as he left.

Donovan supposed that idiot Kai was going to watch the monitors now that he was on his way out. He had considered and rejected the idea of going upstairs to visit Violet, something that always seemed to make Quinn and Parrish uneasy, even though Kai almost always accompanied him.

"She can't communicate," Parrish had once said. "She can't move. What do you find so fascinating about her?"

"The same thing you do," Donovan had replied, always willing to lie to his father. "Her helplessness."

Parrish had laughed, and Donovan had known then that he had inadvertently told at least half the truth—that was part of why Parrish kept her around.

Donovan thought of her now, as he made his way back to his car. She would be lying in the dark in a windowless room upstairs, receiving very few visits from anyone other than Kai.

He wondered if Parrish had brought her to the mountains as a living reminder of the fate that had nearly been his own.

TWENTY-FIVE

Nicholas Parrish strolled down a pathway leading to an empty cabin. He walked slowly, apparently relaxed, but anger flowed through every inch of his veins. He was fully aware that Kai and Quinn were not fooled by his show of nonchalance, a fact that led to his further irritation with both them and himself.

Something had changed. Not all that many years ago, he was completely master of himself and anyone he chose to dominate.

But then came the injury.

He thought of it now as *the* injury, even though it was hardly the first time he had been wounded. Before the end of his first few years of childhood, he had become a specialist in enduring pain. Every now and then, memories of those years broke through carefully constructed mental barriers and into his consciousness. They always made him feel a kind of burning rage, for which he had found only one remedy.

Those experiences, he knew, would have destroyed a lesser man.

Injury was not, therefore, something he feared. He had grown taller and stronger and eventually turned on his torturer and repaid her in kind. Many years had passed before he again sustained any serious wound.

Most he had obtained in the course of his hunting. There were those moments—those beautiful, thrilling moments—when he first took hold of a victim. Quite often, those were also the moments in which he suffered minor injuries. He thought longingly now of several of his victims, considered them one by one, reliving that first contact with each: grasping and pulling her against him, her panic as she struggled ineffectively against his superior strength. They were dangerous, those moments before she was completely subdued, because those were the ones in which, despite all his careful planning, there was a slight chance she might escape. So he endured bites, bruises, scratches, kicks—whatever might occur during those struggles—knowing he could withstand much more pain than any victim was likely to try to deal to him.

And then Irene Kelly changed the game.

Even before the injury to his spine, she had been responsible for a serious wound to his shoulder. Had he been an ordinary man, that would have been his undoing. The wound had become infected and caused him a great deal of trouble. That had angered him—surprised him, even—but he had not doubted his ability to achieve revenge.

And then, a few months later, disaster. For the first time in his life, he had failed to kill his intended victims. It should have been easy, doing away with her and her crippled friend. The failure had nearly led to his death.

He felt the bitterness of that failure as he recalled it, replayed it again and again in his mind. Irene Kelly. She had been the one who caused him to be so severely injured—a second time! And worse than the first.

Where was his old self-confidence, his invincibility?

No. He must not let himself fall prey to self-doubt. That would be what anyone else would do.

He was . . . resurrected. Stronger than ever.

He had studied other killers. He had studied criminal profiling. He knew all the assumptions the police, the FBI, and others were making. Men of his type—they believed they had seen his "type" before—were supposed to work alone, or with one dominated accomplice. He smiled to himself at the thought of their current bafflement.

The smile didn't last long. His thoughts had circled back to Kai and Quinn.

He anticipated inevitable problems with each of his sons— lions never remained cubs, and only a fool tried to make pets of them. Kai had not matured enough to control his impetuous nature. Quinn was so power-hungry, he'd find world domination to be nothing more than a good start. And Donovan . . .

Parrish smiled to himself. Donovan might be more like his old man than the other two could possibly imagine. The question was, could Donovan himself be brought to imagine it? In time, in time . . .

Parrish turned and walked back toward the lodge. His temper was back under control now. He could focus his mind on making the best possible next move and face Kai and Quinn in a better state of mind. He would show them, once again, that he was master here—master of his sons and master of himself.

Irene Kelly had meddled again—the invasion of Kai's home at this juncture was a nuisance, but it would not help police as much as she undoubtedly hoped it would. She would suffer for her interference.

He thought of Donovan's report. He was pleased Donovan was keeping such a close eye on her. It was time, he decided, for the next phase of setting the trap.

TWENTY-SIX

At just about three o'clock on a gray October afternoon, I sat alone at a small table in the back corner of the Busy Bee Café, not far from the radio station, finishing a late lunch. I usually ate with a group from the station, but today I had worked through the noon hour to complete a story and hadn't left the building until two.

However busy the bee was, the café was quiet at that hour. Like many small eateries in the district, it catered to the business crowd, open for breakfast and lunch only. So not long before closing, I was the last diner—or thought I was. I was finishing up a turkey sandwich when a florid-faced man came waddling through the door.

He made his way directly to my table, staring so intently as he loomed over me, I felt some alarm. Although his hair was reddish brown, it looked dyed, an act of vanity that was at odds with his otherwise careless appearance. His face was lined and puffy under the eyes. I judged him to be about sixty. He was wearing a sweat-stained, oversized T-shirt and looked as if he was smuggling half a beach ball under the front of it. His arms were brawny and his shoulders wide, making me think he was someone who had once been athletic but had long since devoted himself to inertia as a hobby.

In the next instant, I scolded myself for judging him in this way. Perhaps some illness or injury prevented him from being active. I knew nothing about the man.

"I know you!" he said, startling me. He plopped down in the only other chair at the table, effectively pinning me into the corner. I felt my back stiffen and looked around for an ally.

The place was empty. I heard the kitchen staff clattering pots and pans in the back, probably washing up. The waitress was nowhere to be seen. I took a calming breath, reached for my cell phone, and reminded myself that Ethan, Mark, and Lydia knew where I was. The waitress and other café staff were within shouting distance. Besides, it was nearly closing time, so they would probably be back out here soon—and tell him he'd have to look elsewhere for a meal.

He extended a large but stubby-fingered hand and said, "Roderick!"

When I didn't take it, he pointed at me and said, "Irene Kelly! I've got a story for you."

This happens to me now and then—not the pointing but the pestering. My photo used to run next to my byline in the *Express*, and the paper apparently hadn't been dead long enough to allow me the lack of public recognition I preferred. "Great. Please feel free to call the station and suggest it. Now, if you don't mind, I've got to leave. I'm on a deadline."

"Already tried. They don't get it at the radio station, but I think you will. You can talk them into it. I'll walk you over there."

"No, Roderick, you won't. Now—"

"I just need someone to listen to me! What the fuck is wrong with you people?"

My apprehensiveness went up another notch. If I called for help from the back, he could be over the table before anyone came out to see what was wrong. And they might not do anything right away. I could try using my new self-defense skills, if I could get out from behind the table. But if he was as volatile and hostile as I thought he might be, I should call in the professionals.

"I'm sorry you've been frustrated," I tried in a placatory tone while at the same time pressing 9 and 1 on the phone. Before I could get the next 1 entered, he reached across the table with surprising speed and knocked the phone from my hand.

I drew a breath for a scream, but before I could let it out, a commanding voice said, "Stand up and step away from her table. Do it now."

I caught a glimpse of a tall, golden-haired man before he was blocked from my view by Roderick, who stood and turned angrily toward the stranger. Roderick took a step forward, his right fist raised to deliver a punch.

"You don't want to try it," the man said.

Roderick froze in place, then suddenly looked as if someone had taken the air out of him. His shoulders sagged, and he stared down at his feet. "I didn't do anything wrong!"

"Get out," the man said, "and don't ever bother this woman again. Do you understand me?"

Roderick started to push past him with ill grace, but the man put a flat hand on his chest. "Do you understand me?" he said again, more quietly but somehow with greater menace.

"Yes!" Roderick said.

"Fine. We're going to wait here for you to get down the street and around the corner. Do not look back. Do not try to follow either of us. Understood?"

Roderick nodded. The man stepped aside, and Roderick left.

The man, who looked to be in his early thirties, turned to me and said, "Are you all right?"

I was shaking. "Yes, thank you. That was—that was good of you."

He smiled slightly and bent to pick up my phone, glanced at it, then pulled out his own and asked me if I wanted him to call the police.

I pictured what that might bring on, especially from well-meaning friends.

"No, thanks," I said. I was disappointed in myself—I used to be able to handle the Rodericks of this world without falling apart.

My rescuer brought my phone to me just as the waitress came out to say, "Sorry, we're closed."

I quickly explained what had happened. Her eyes widened and she quickly locked the door, as if expecting Roderick to return. I felt shakier still.

The man spoke up. "Why don't you bring a cup of"—he turned to me—"coffee? Tea?"

"Hot tea, thanks," I said, turning to her. "If it won't be too much trouble?"

"Not at all!" she said. "And for you, sir?"

"Hot tea sounds good," he said, sitting at the next table, giving me, I noticed, some space—and positioning himself to watch the door.

"Thank you again," I said.

"You're welcome," he said. "Is your phone working?"

I tried turning it on. "Hell. He broke it."

"Do you want me to find him, get him to pay for it?"

I shook my head. "No, the less I see of Roderick, the better. I want no excuses for him to remain in contact with me."

He studied me briefly and said, "Are you feeling faint?"

"Just a little wobbly. I'll be okay in a minute."

"Add sugar to that tea," he recommended and went back to watching the door.

The waitress brought the tea, I added the sugar to mine, and with each sip, I felt myself grow calmer.

The man drank his, sitting there quietly, keeping guard.

"I'm Irene," I said. "Irene Kelly."

He smiled ruefully. "At the risk of freaking you out, I know. You used to work for the *Express*, and now you work for KCLP. I've thought about contacting you several times."

"Oh?" I said, surprised but not feeling threatened. His manner was entirely different from Roderick's.

"Yes. When you worked for the paper, you wrote a series about people who were missing—including one about missing children, right?"

"Yes. The series started a long time ago, with my mentor," I said, thinking wistfully of O'Connor. Then the import of his question hit me. "Is someone in your family missing?"

"Yes," he said. "Maybe someday I'll call the station and tell you about it. I won't bother you at lunch, though."

"I'd be happy to help if I can," I said.

"Thanks. But you don't owe me any favors for helping you today." He saw that I had finished my tea. "Is there someone you want to call to meet you here and walk you back to the station? You can borrow my phone if you'd like."

I considered this for a moment, then pictured the combination of bad timing and the awkwardness of the request I'd be making. "They'll be madly working to be ready for tonight's broadcast. I'll be okay."

"How about if I walk you back there? Just to be on the safe side."

I hesitated, then said, "I'd appreciate that."

As we left, I started asking myself if I was nuts. I didn't know this guy any better than I knew Roderick. He was lean and fit, and dressed neatly. Had I let that lull me? I didn't even know his—

"I'm Donovan," he said, not trying to shake hands or even walk close to me. He was watching the street, not me. I relaxed.

"Nice to meet you," I said.

He asked me how I liked working in radio and mentioned an interview of mine he had enjoyed, one with a local physics professor about the Large Hadron Collider.

"Fortunately," I said, "the professor realized I didn't know what I was talking about and dumbed it down for me."

"No, he just made it accessible for nonscientists who were listening to the program. Quite a change from stories on city hall, though."

I admitted that our small staff size meant I covered stories on subjects I never would have covered for the paper. "I'm back to being a general assignment reporter. I don't mind, really— I enjoy the variety." We were at the station doors by then. "Thanks again," I said, "and please do call me if you think I can help you."

"Maybe I will." He glanced back toward the street, then said, "I'll wait here until you're inside. I can see that Roderick has been following us."

"What!"

"He's over by the bank. Trying not to be too obvious, but . . ." He shrugged.

I casually looked toward the Bank of Las Piernas building. Sure as hell, Roderick was pretending to be waiting in the ATM line.

"Do you want to call the police? I have a feeling he's hoping for a rematch with me, but I'm not worried about that. I am concerned about your safety, though."

"If he tries to fight you, maybe I should call the police."

"Don't do it on my account," he said. He glanced back at me and said, "Why do I get the feeling you don't want to call them on your own behalf?"

"I've only recently won a little breathing space," I admitted. "The whole Nick Parrish thing. I'm sure you've heard. If I start setting off alarms, I'm going to be hemmed in again."

"Hmm. I can understand that, I suppose."

"Do you really think he's dangerous?"

He watched Roderick for a while and said, "I'm inclined to say not really, but he strikes me as unpredictable. He definitely needs an anger management class, and I don't like that he invaded your personal space."

I sighed.

"Tell you what. I'll have a little talk with him. If I can't get him to leave when I do, then call the police, okay? And no matter what, promise me you'll get someone to walk you to your car tonight after work."

"I promise," I said and bid him good-bye as I went inside.

I didn't have a very clear view of the bank from the lobby of our building, but I did have the reassuring presence of a security guard standing at his post near the reception desk. Within a few minutes Roderick came tramping down the sidewalk, hands in pockets, casting resentful glances over his shoulder.

Donovan followed a few feet behind him. He didn't so much as glance my way—he was totally focused on Roderick, who flipped him the bird as he got into a battered pickup truck. Donovan ignored him, getting into his own vehicle, a brown Ford Escape. He waited until Roderick started his truck and pulled into traffic before he started the SUV. Only then did he glance toward me. He gave me a quick thumbs-up and drove away.

Back at my desk, I found myself inclined not to make a big deal out of Roderick. I would be careful, but I probably wouldn't mention what had happened to my usual set of keepers. I'd say I dropped the phone, or Frank would be issuing an all-points bulletin for Roderick, who now that I was safely in my office, appeared to me to have been no more than a typical self-involved nut with a story.

So when I ran into Donovan again a few days later, just as I was leaving work, Lydia saw me greet him warmly and heard him jokingly ask if I had figured out why the universe was expanding and not contracting.

She thought I might have met him while working on the physics story Ethan had put me on to and felt sympathy for him when he asked if I had time to talk to him about the missing person case he had mentioned to me. He invited her to join us. Nothing made her feel uneasy about him. When I assured her that he would see me safely to my car, she saw nothing wrong with me walking off alone with him to a nearby restaurant to have a quiet talk about the case.

TWENTY-SEVEN

Kai sat in the darkness in a corner of his mother's room. She was awake. He knew this because she was not breathing the way she breathed when she was asleep. And she was restless, making the small amount of movement she could. He hoped she wouldn't try talking to him. She knew better than to make those awful, meaningless sounds when he was near. He had her so well trained, he could do what he needed to do without really thinking about her. He had bigger problems on his mind.

The lights in the room were out, but a soft glow came from the display of what looked like a clock radio. He had plugged earphones into a jack on the instrument's side and was now listening to a conversation being held downstairs. Donovan may have scorned Quinn's surveillance system, but Kai thought Donovan might have been more impressed if he had known about Kai's own little system. Of course, he wasn't going to tell Donovan about it. Or any of the others. But he was especially glad that his two-faced, backstabbing, know-it-all half brother Quinn had no idea about it. His dad should have entrusted a real electronics expert—Kai—to set up security. Quinn didn't know everything there was to know.

For example, Quinn didn't know that Kai had placed listening devices in every room of this place.

He had been uneasy when Quinn showed up again so soon after his last visit, and just before their next big event. Quinn was supposed to be in Las Piernas, making sure Donovan was obeying orders. Kai thought that was ridiculous. Who was Quinn to ensure Donovan was obedient? Quinn was the one who was disobedient, or he wouldn't be here right now.

In contrast, when their father had whispered to Kai, asking for some time alone with Quinn, Kai had immediately left the room, saying, "I have to take care of Mom. Just call me if you need me."

Before he'd reached the top of the stairs, he could hear Quinn making a remark he doubtless intended Kai to hear.

"I don't know why you don't just kill that crippled-up bitch."

"No," Parrish had said coldly, "you don't."

Kai had smiled to himself and continued on to her room. He knew Quinn's repulsion would keep him away from Violet Loudon's room, and Kai's setup would be safe from at least one pair of prying eyes.

Listening on the earphones now, he could hear Quinn talking to their father.

Urging Parrish to abandon Kai.

". . . I'm telling you, he's going to be the ruin of everything! Look, I've got the money you need to go anywhere in the world. Let's leave Kai and that hideous woman here and take off. I can keep you safe."

"Don't you think Kai might say something to the authorities if he was left here to fend for himself?"

With hardly a moment's pause, Quinn said, "You're right. So we kill them both."

There was a silence, then Parrish said, "Quinn, what do you suppose is happening in Las Piernas right now?"

"You mean, our plan?"

"No. The mood of the town."

"On edge. Terrified, many of them." There was a pause before Quinn added, "I see what you mean."

"I was certain you would. You wouldn't really want to question my judgment, I'm sure."

"Of course not."

"The legend of Nicholas Parrish and sons can only be enhanced by that fear. While I could have wished for Kai to have more time to exercise his talents in Las Piernas, and for our plans to have proceeded at the pace we had hoped for, I am nevertheless proud of my sons. There is nothing to lead the police from Las Piernas to this place. Nothing at all."

"You're right."

"You didn't think this out, Quinn. That's unlike you. But I suppose you were only concerned for my safety."

"Yes," Quinn said. "You understand perfectly."

"Now, I'm going to ask Kai to join us again, and I hope you will be able to control yourself when he returns."

Kai didn't wait to hear Quinn's response. He disconnected the headset and turned off the receiver. He quickly checked on his mother, smiled at her panicked expression, and reached beneath her bed. He retrieved the automatic he had hidden there, assured himself that it was fully loaded and ready to be used, and replaced it as he heard his father call to him. It was one of several weapons he had cached around the house, and he was more certain than ever that he would be making use of at least one of them.

"Coming!" he called back and hurried from the room.

He reached the bottom of the stairs just as Nicholas Parrish's cell phone rang. As far as Kai knew, only three people had that number, and two of them were staring at each other in dislike.

Parrish listened, hung up without speaking to the caller, then turned to his sons. "Your older brother is efficient," he said. "We're about to have company."

TWENTY-EIGHT

I remember this much:

It was about four o'clock. We sat in the bar of the Fireside, a nearby restaurant, quiet in the downtime between lunch and dinner. The place was empty, but that suited us—missing persons stories aren't exactly best told while competing with happy hour in the background. Donovan seemed a little nervous, so I wasn't surprised when he offered to buy me a drink—figuring he needed one more than I did, I accepted. He went to the bar, answered a cell phone call while he was waiting for the drinks, then came back to the table with a tray holding a pitcher of margaritas, two glasses already filled from it, and a little dish that contained a few slices of lime.

"A pitcher?" I said, as he handed one of the glasses to me.

"A friend called. She's going to try to join us a little later—if that's okay?"

"No problem, but I do need to get home—"

"If she's not here by the time you need to leave, I'll still walk you to your car. I'll just text her and let her know what happened."

He picked up his own drink and began to tell me of Denise, his first wife, whom he had married at eighteen. Although he had done well in high school, he didn't have the money for college and, after a couple of years of trying to get by on low-paying jobs, decided to go into the service. He joined the army and was soon sent overseas. Denise filed for divorce less than a month after he left the States.

"Sorry."

"No need to be," he assured me. "We had already started to have trouble getting along—about what you'd expect from a couple of immature idiots—and I think, somewhere in the back of mind, I knew I'd be getting a Dear John letter. I'm not really sure how we managed to stay married as long as we did, except that I wasn't home much during training." He paused. "It wasn't a nasty divorce. For reasons I didn't really understand at the time, she didn't ask for alimony or stake a claim on my pension—which apparently made her attorney crazy—and we were renting, so there wasn't a lot of property to be divided. She took a few personal things, put my stuff in storage for me, and went back to living with her mother."

He fell silent. I sipped at my drink, wondering if he expected me to help him find his ex. If so, I was probably going to have to disappoint him. I was concerned about missing persons cases, and if I could determine that she really was involuntarily gone, I'd do what I could. But so many adult missing persons are hiding of their own volition. Some are avoiding responsibilities, some trying to escape arrest. Plenty of others are trying to survive, to stay safe from someone—especially if their situation is one in which law enforcement can't effectively provide protection. It was entirely possible that Denise was afraid of him. Although I felt relaxed sitting in that quiet restaurant with Donovan, I didn't know what he was like at home—for all I knew, she had good reasons to hide from him.

"Not long after the divorce was final," he said, "I got a letter from her mother, telling me that Denise had died in a car accident."

"Oh—sorry," I said again, thrown completely off stride.

"I probably shouldn't say this, but to be honest, it didn't affect me much. Although I thought it was a shame she had died so young, I was more surprised than sad."

He fell silent again, so I drank and waited.

After a time, he said, "The biggest surprise was yet to come." He reached inside his jacket, brought out a photo, and pushed it across the small table. I picked it up.

A beautiful, golden-haired child smiled back from the photo. A little girl, four or five years old, I'd guess.

I looked up at Donovan.

"My daughter. I'm told her name is Miranda," he said. "She's ten now."

"I don't understand . . ."

"At first, I didn't, either. A year ago, someone sent me an anonymous letter with that photo in it. Said the girl was my daughter, that Denise was pregnant when she divorced me, that she had convinced another man the child was his. I started to do some investigating but didn't need to make much of an effort, because the 'other man' called me himself—his name is Charles Chasten. The letter had been sent by his wife. As it turns out, Mr. Chasten had started an affair with my wife about two days after I left the States."

"Jesus. Denise didn't wait long, did she?"

He shrugged. "I was disappointed that she chose a married man with children—he had two boys and wouldn't leave his wife. I don't think much of him. I have to admit, though, he was generous when it came to giving money for the care of the child to Denise—and, after she died, to Denise's mom. Secretly, of course—until one day his wife, who had long thought he was too stingy, saw a browser window he'd left open after doing some online banking."

"And discovered he had a second bank account she never knew about?"

"Exactly. A joint account with Denise's mom. He'd put money in it for Miranda's needs."

"And how did the wife take this news?"

"Madder than hell. Understandably. Chasten found out that she had sent me the photo and the letter. But I'm getting ahead of myself." He lifted the pitcher, gestured to my half-full glass, but I shook my head. He poured another margarita for himself then said, "After she discovered the account, and after some . . . very heated discussion, let's say . . . Chasten's wife insisted on a DNA paternity test. He was confident of the outcome, but he got a kit and took a cheek swab from Miranda on a visit. Later she told her grandmother, who gave him some additional heat, but he'd already sent the test swabs off by then."

He paused and took a drink.

"Since you've told me she's your daughter," I said, "I can see what's coming."

"Right. He learned he wasn't the father—his turn to be out-raged. Although he told me that he had mixed feelings—he says he's attached to Miranda, but he felt like he'd been duped. He was in for yet another surprise—when he called to talk about the test results, the number was disconnected. He went over to the house, but Miranda and her grandmother had disappeared. Along with everything in the bank account."

"Disappeared? It's actually not that easy to disappear, especially not with a child in tow."

"That's what I thought, at first. Even though I was coming in on all of this a little late—they had been gone two weeks when Mrs. Chasten sent that letter—I thought I could use my skills and contacts to find them." He saw my brows rise and added, "I—I can't give you details, but some of my experience in the military would, I thought, be useful."

I let it pass. I was suddenly feeling a little light-headed and wondered if I should get something to eat. He glanced at his cell phone and read a screen. He looked at me said, "Oh, sorry—my friend's not going to join us after all." He hesitated, then said, "Are you okay?"

"I'm fine," I said, "just shouldn't drink on an empty stomach, I guess."

"Should I order something? An appetizer at least?"

"That might be a good idea." We settled on bruschetta. He went up to the bar again, spoke to the bartender, and came back with a bowl of pretzels. "He's going to bring us an order, but maybe this will help in the meantime."

I thanked him, but my stomach started to feel unsettled, so I let them sit on the table.

"Tell me what happened next," I said, feeling that the most insensitive thing I could do would be to end the conversation at this point but finding it took real effort to concentrate on anything other than my gut.

He studied me and said, "We could save this for another time."

I shook my head, a bad idea, but he went on.

"I sent a swab of my own DNA in, and sure enough, it matched Miranda's."

"Were you happy about that?"

"Yes—but I'd be lying if I didn't tell you that I was also scared."

"Understandable," I said.

"I looked for her, but I kept hitting brick walls. I even tried to get the police interested, but they felt convinced that Miranda's grandmother had disappeared with her voluntarily."

"You don't?"

"No." He hesitated. "Forgive me, but you seem to be feeling unwell. Would you like me to give you a ride home?"

At that point, I was feeling very unwell indeed, and also as if I might pass out. "Thanks," I murmured, hearing myself slur it.

From there my memories of that afternoon become less reliable. There are whole periods of time that I can't remember at all. Some of what I do remember, I wish I could forget.

I recall the sound of a chair scraping on the bar's wooden floor. I recall reassuring bits of words from Donovan, my face forming a giddy smile as he helped me stand. I remember being guided into an SUV, and a drive that seemed to last for days but could have taken a few minutes or several hours.

At some point we stopped. He guided me out of the vehicle and into a room. I have no clear memory of the room or what happened there, or much of anything before we were traveling again. I remember cold air and the smell of pine trees, and being helped out of the car again, and immediately throwing up.

I remember Donovan saying something about telling me the truth, and that he'd help me, that I must understand he had no choice, but I'm not sure that really happened. I felt confused, especially about one odd thing he said repeatedly: "Try not to let them take your parka."

I was barely aware of what was happening at that point, in a state not unlike being roused from a deep sleep—much more interested in falling back to sleep than in anything going on around me. Whole patches of time disappeared—I am sure that I saw Nicholas Parrish, and that he spoke to me, but my only response was to throw up again, which angered and disgusted him. At some point, I was indoors with no idea how I got there or any ability to comprehend where I was. I grew dizzy, and I think Donovan picked me up and carried me.

Parrish argued with Donovan and was saying something to me, and then, just as I felt myself sliding back into unconsciousness, there was gunfire.

CHAPTER 29

Donovan Cotter heard the shots and saw panic cross Nicholas Parrish's face. Donovan's arms were full—Irene had passed out again—and while he was tempted to drop her and pull out one of his weapons, instead he set her on her side behind the large couch and took cover there himself.

"Fuck you!" a voice shouted from upstairs.

More rounds blasted before Parrish, who had stood frozen in the middle of the room, belatedly followed Donovan's example.

"Get up there and stop them!" Parrish said.

Donovan stared at him.

Parrish scowled back. "Do you want her to live or—"

"You know she is little more than a curiosity to me," Donovan said calmly. "I am far more interested in staying alive myself." He thought for a moment, then said, "I'll be right back . . ."

Parrish grabbed him. "You're not going anywhere!"

"I have a—let's call it a first aid kit—in the back of my vehicle. From the sound of things, if anyone survives, we'll need it."

"You fail to return, and I'll—"

"Yes, I know. I'll be back in a minute."

When Donovan returned with his field kit, Parrish eyed it warily, but they were both distracted by screams from upstairs.

They heard more shots, followed by several loud thumps.

Then silence.

Donovan waited.

From upstairs, groaning. Parrish looked increasingly anxious but said nothing more.

They heard another groan.

"Help," Quinn called weakly. "Help!"

"Drop your weapons," Donovan called.

He heard two heavy thumps.

"Kick the guns away from you."

They heard the sound of one gun sliding. "I can't," Quinn said.

"Hurry," Kai moaned.

Donovan strapped his field kit to his back, stood, and made his way cautiously up the stairs, gun drawn. Parrish crept behind him.

He found Kai and Quinn sprawled at opposite ends of the hallway. He glanced between the bleeding men. Kai had a wounded arm. Quinn had a head wound, and his right thigh had been hit. Donovan told Parrish to help Kai. He picked up their loose weapons, holstered his own, quickly gave Parrish a pair of gloves and packet of gauze, and told him to apply pressure to Kai's wound. He then moved toward Quinn.

The hallway was in shambles. Wood, plaster, and a small table lamp had sustained more hits than either combatant. *What lousy aim,* Donovan thought. He made his way over the debris and knelt beside Quinn, who was lying half out of a bathroom.

"That goddamned crazy son of a bitch shot me!" Quinn said, his right hand pressing down on his right leg, the other hand held to his head.

"Looks like you did the same to him," Donovan said. He took a pair of gloves out of the field kit and put them on. After a quick look at Quinn's leg, he decided the bullet hadn't hit an artery and put a thick gauze pad over the wound. He moved Quinn's left hand away to look at the head wound. "Use both hands to keep the pressure on your leg," he told him.

"I feel faint."

"You'll be all right. Press hard." Donovan could see that the head wound was superficial, although he was sure it was painful. He took out another sterile pad and pressed it to the wound, then had Quinn put his hand back on it. He returned his attention to the leg wound, quickly cutting away most of the bloody pant leg.

"Do you know what you're doing?" Quinn asked.

"You'd better hope so," Donovan answered distractedly. The leg looked like hell, and there was a lot of blood, but Donovan had seen many gunshot wounds and knew Quinn was relatively lucky. He'd need to get to a hospital, but it was survivable.

Quinn screeched in protest as Donovan applied more pressure.

"If you'd rather bleed to death, fine. And if someone heard gunfire and next hears your screams, you've bought yourself more trouble."

Quinn gritted his teeth but stopped crying out.

Donovan took a packet of Celox from the field kit and used it to stop the bleeding. He added a field dressing and turned toward Parrish. He was surprised to see him frozen in place.

"Parrish!"

Parrish looked at him blankly.

"How's Kai?"

"I—I don't know."

"Come here!"

Parrish hesitated, then crept forward.

Donovan had done extensive research on his father and his brothers, and on Irene Kelly, Frank Harriman, and Ben Sheridan as well. He knew that Parrish rarely shot his victims but was no stranger to firearms, and certainly the long list of Parrish's psychopathic behaviors included plenty to make one believe he wasn't afraid of blood, wounds, or body parts.

But perhaps, in Parrish's world, he had to be the one who inflicted those wounds if he was to tolerate them.

Donovan regretted that circumstances wouldn't allow him to toy with Parrish's reaction to his sons' mayhem. Instead he sharply ordered him to discard the gloves he had on and put on a new pair, so as not to transfer contamination from Kai to Quinn. Parrish obeyed. "Put your hands where mine are. Apply pressure—steady pressure."

Donovan quickly headed back to Kai, taking the field kit and changing out his own gloves.

Kai's eyes were shut tight, and he was moaning softly. He had been shot in the right arm. *Probably trying to hit your eye,* Donovan thought. *Neither one of you can aim.*

He shook his head. He should have gone for a gunfight with these two weeks ago, shot them dead in the middle of the park. He despised people who carried guns and didn't know how to use them.

"How harmful could it be, getting shot in the arm?" Parrish asked.

"Very. Fatal, in fact. If it had hit an artery, he'd probably be dead. But as it is, it's not too bad." A little too deep to be called a graze, he thought, and undoubtedly painful. Better to make Parrish and Kai worry about it. He could do that and still tell Parrish the truth, in case Parrish knew more about such wounds than he was letting on. "It may keep him from using the arm for a while. He could easily end up with a bad infection. If that happens, he could lose his arm or even die of blood poisoning."

Parrish watched Donovan for a few moments, then said, "You didn't tell me you have medical training."

"Only what I learned in the service. I'm no doctor. You need to get them to a hospital. Soon."

"No. Too big a risk. You take care of them."

"Don't be a fool."

"You'd fucking better make sure I get to a doctor," Quinn said between clenched teeth. "You don't want me to die—I've got a little insurance policy."

Well, Donovan thought, *give a few points to Quinn.* Under other circumstances, Donovan would have found the stunned expression on Parrish's face almost laughable. But the coldness that quickly replaced it ended any desire to laugh.

"What do you mean?" Parrish asked.

"I mean, Daddy Dearest, that I'm not so fucking stupid that I'd come up here to spend time around you and your loving sons without putting something in place to protect myself. If I don't make contact with an associate at arranged times, all sorts of information gets released to the police."

Parrish struck him hard across his bloodied face.

Quinn hit him back, knocking him to the floor—a move that shocked Donovan nearly as much as it did Parrish.

"Stop it," Donovan said. "That won't get us anywhere. Quinn, sit still or you may bleed to death yet."

Kai opened his eyes and frowned but stayed out of the argument. Donovan continued working and managed to get the bleeding stopped. He looked back at Parrish, who was holding a swollen cheek and looking malevolent.

"I may just go ahead and kill you," Parrish said to Quinn.

"You aren't one to make rash moves," Quinn said. "And that would be rash. You need my resources."

"Has it occurred to you," Parrish said, "that perhaps I haven't put my future entirely into your hands? Kai's already a wanted man, and so am I. Therefore, the only thing of importance you could tell the police is where we are. We don't have to stay here, so don't press your luck."

Quinn smiled. "What are you going to do? Finally kill Violet?"

"No . . . ," Kai said.

"No," Parrish said. "I don't think I'll be discussing my plans with you, Quinn."

"After all we've been through together?"

"There's no need for the two of you to fight," Donovan said. "Quinn and Kai need to get to an ER as soon as possible. I'll load the two of them into my SUV and take them to a hospital. I can manage it without being seen."

"They'll both be arrested!"

"Kai probably will be," Donovan agreed. "But if we could arrange your escape, we can do the same for him. There's no reason for them to arrest Quinn."

"Who's going to take care of Violet?"

Donovan nodded toward the stairs. "Irene. She took care of her father when he was dying of cancer, I'm sure she can manage Violet's care."

"No!" Kai protested. "I'm not going. I'm staying here."

Donovan stared at him for a moment, then looked at Quinn.

"While I appreciate what you've done so far," Quinn said, "I want to get professional care."

"Take him," Parrish said. "He thinks he's got insurance?

Well, it's mutual destruction. I've got more than enough on him to ensure he'd end up on death row."

"Exactly." Quinn smiled faintly. "You don't try to stab me in the back, I don't try to stab you in yours."

"They'll catch you, Donovan," Parrish fretted. "They'll know by now."

"They may know, but they won't catch me."

Parrish helped Kai get settled in bed, something he could do without lifting. It was left to Donovan to carry Quinn downstairs. He placed him on a large leather couch and covered him with a blanket. Quinn looked tired and weakened, but there was no sign of shock setting in.

When Parrish joined them, a few minutes later, Donovan spoke softly to him. "Stay with Kai, keep him warm, watch for signs of shock, and especially for signs of infection." He named every sign of dangerous levels of infection he could think of. "Right now, I'm going to take care of getting Irene settled next—"

"I'll stay with you while you do that."

"Look, someone's got to keep an eye on Kai—"

"You don't give the orders around here, Donovan."

Donovan considered testing that and decided this was not the time. "Fine. While I'm with Irene, it's important that you don't say anything."

"Why?"

"The substance I gave her has a number of properties. Among other things, it's a hypnotic and amnestic drug. She'll obey me, but your presence will just confuse her. As it is now, when she wakes up tomorrow, she probably won't remember anything after the moments when she started drinking with me this afternoon."

"What drug was it?"

Donovan looked away, hiding his contempt. "You'd probably call them roofies."

He carried Irene upstairs to another bedroom, one that connected to Violet's through a door on the opposite side of a shared bathroom.

Irene awakened and looked up at him in puzzlement. He set her on her feet.

"There's a bathroom between these two rooms. Take your clothes off and take a quick shower. Shampoo your hair. When you are finished showering, dry off with this towel. I'll set some clothes out for you to change into." She complaisantly walked into the bathroom, although she wasn't steady on her feet, so he helped her take her vomit-stained blouse and pants off, and stayed in the bathroom with her while she took the shower. She seemed a little more alert after that. She dried herself off and changed into the soft, warm clothing he had brought for her, all without argument. At his command, she brushed her teeth. He told her to get into the bed and sleep. She obeyed, falling asleep almost immediately.

He opened a duffel with other clothing suitable for the mountains and hung several of these items, with the exception of the parka (which he kept in the SUV), in a small wardrobe that stood in one corner of the room. He placed the duffel in the bottom of the wardrobe.

Throughout this process, he had been aware of Parrish watching them. He had also been aware that there was something off about the attention, something unexpected. Parrish was interested in her, but not in the way a predator should be interested in his prey.

Donovan placed her soiled clothing in a cloth bag and took it with him.

Parrish and Donovan left the room, locking the doors leading to the hallway, and Donovan saw Parrish look back with a frown as he pocketed the key.

Now or never, Donovan thought. He took slow breaths and made his mind quiet, then turned to Parrish.

"She's changed, hasn't she? Not your ideal any longer. Aged beyond that." He made sure the bag of soiled clothes was between them, the smell of the vomit unavoidable.

Parrish looked at him and answered, "I'll think of something to do with her. *I owe her.*" But his eyes had betrayed him. Donovan had seen him glance to the side before he answered, caught the sign of evasion. Saw his nose wrinkle at the scent emanating from the bag.

Donovan considered how to make use of Parrish's lack of attraction to Irene, which he was sure was not just a matter of having seen her get sick, although that helped. The beginning of a plan came to him.

"Let me have her first," he said.

Parrish laughed. Donovan stayed silent.

"You're serious, aren't you?" Parrish said in disbelief, stepping a bit farther away from him.

"I've been on the hunt for her. I caught her. So yes, I am."

"What about the child?" Parrish asked.

Donovan shrugged. "As I said before, a curiosity. Nothing more. Let's be honest, no one in this . . . family . . . is capable of much more. I doubt you feel much more than curiosity about me."

"Hmm. You do intrigue me. More than your brothers do, as long as we're being honest." He studied Donovan's face, then said, "You'd trade?"

"Her for the child? Why not? I'm no more interested in children than you are."

"Then why have you done as I asked? I was so sure you were not like Quinn or Kai."

"I'm not. As for doing what you asked—well, let's say I've been curious about you as well."

Parrish was silent. He looked uneasily back at the locked door, then said, "I don't see why you shouldn't have a small reward. I'll think about it."

Donovan left it at that. To press too much would backfire, he was sure of it.

He placed the soiled clothes in a washing machine downstairs and started the wash cycle. He took some clean blankets from a supply in the laundry room, then used them to form a makeshift bed in the back of the SUV. He loaded Quinn into the vehicle and drove off, refining his plans.

Quinn moaned as they hit the first curve of the winding mountain road but didn't say anything until he realized they were merging onto 91 West.

"Where are you taking me?" he asked irritably, trying to sit up.

"Stay down," Donovan advised, glancing in the mirror, "unless you want to have to answer some embarrassing questions later."

"The pain is killing me," Quinn complained, although he lay back down. "I thought you were taking me to a hospital."

"I am. In Las Piernas. Just not directly. I'm sure you can understand the need."

"No, I can't. Goddamn it . . ."

"What explanation will you give for being in the San Bernardino Mountains, especially if Nick Parrish's plans continue to get so spectacularly screwed up?"

There was a silence.

"How are you going to explain being shot?"

"I can't think straight—fucking hell this hurts!"

"Then let me do the thinking. If you pay attention, maybe I can keep you from dying. If you actually do what I tell you to, I might be able to keep you out of prison, too."

After a moment, Quinn said, "If you think I'm going to reveal the name of my contact—"

"I don't," Donovan said. "If I asked you, you'd only lie to me, so why bother?"

"You're calling me—"

"A liar? Yes. And for your own sake, you'd better be as expert at it as I think you are."

THIRTY

Frank Harriman knew something was wrong even before he pulled into the driveway. He had caught a drug-related shooting case just after four in the morning, one that had seemed as if it would be relatively straightforward but had kept him busy until nine o'clock that evening. His mind had been on the case as he drove home, until his house came into view and he saw that Irene's car wasn't in the driveway or parked anywhere nearby. The house was dark. As he opened his car door, he heard the dogs barking in excitement—but they weren't inside, they were in the backyard.

He went inside, calling her name, turning on lights, letting the dogs in, and greeting Cody as well. He checked his phone again to see if she had texted a message about being late or left a voice mail—nothing. He looked for a paper note on the counter, didn't find one, and saw that, even though Cody had his usual dish of kibble out of reach of the dogs, the dogs' big stainless steel bowls were up on the counter—they hadn't been fed. His anxiety kicked up a notch. Even if she hadn't been able to get home, she would have called Jack to ask him to take care of them.

Frank told himself not to jump to conclusions and called her cell phone while he was measuring out dog food. It went immediately to voice mail.

He listened to the messages left on their answering machine. Nothing from Irene.

Ethan Shire was catching a catnap on the couch in his office when his cell phone, which he had set to vibrate only, began buzzing, causing it to walk its metal back along the top of the glass table he had set it on, making more noise than if he had just let the sucker ring.

He nearly just slapped it off but saw the caller ID and answered groggily. "Irene? What's up?"

"Ethan, it's Frank. I guess if you thought Irene was calling she's not there with you."

"No—she went home a long time ago. She's not there?"

"No. She doesn't answer her cell phone."

"Maybe the battery's dead. Or she dropped this new one, too." He laughed, but Frank didn't join in.

"Maybe. When did she leave?"

The worry in Frank's voice finally brought Ethan more fully awake. He scrubbed his face with his hands. "Late afternoon— not exactly sure what time. Hang on, I have a beautiful view of the parking lot; let me take a look."

The window was narrow, and the lighting in the parking lot wasn't the greatest, but Irene had an unwavering habit of parking under one of the lights. He let out a breath of relief. "Her Jeep's here, Frank. I fell asleep, and she must have come back here while I was napping. Let me look around the offices and I'll call you back."

"If you don't mind, I'll stay on with you."

"Sure. No problem."

But as Ethan made his way through the station, it became clear she wasn't there. He questioned the staff who were still there.

"Last time anyone saw her, she was with Lydia," Ethan said to Frank.

"Thanks. I'll try her next."

Ethan hung up, sat for a moment, then got his jacket and keys. Irene Kelly and Frank Harriman were, as far as he was concerned, family. Closer to him than any of the losers in his own family had been, in fact. He wasn't going to sit in an office if Frank needed help finding Irene. On his way out to his car, he called Ben Sheridan.

Despite the maître d'hotel's best efforts, Frank, Ben, and Ethan got past him and interrupted the dinner Lydia and Guy St. Germain were enjoying at the exclusive restaurant in the Cliffside Hotel.

Guy saw them first, and he came to his feet as the men approached. "Frank? Is something wrong?"

"I'm not sure," Frank said. "Irene didn't come home this evening, and I can't reach her by cell phone."

Lydia, accurately reading the pained look on the maître d's face, said, "We just finished. Let's talk outside, okay?"

The maître d' accompanied them to the door and started to apologize to Mr. St. Germain, one of his best customers, but the gentleman replied that he would have been far more upset if his friends had not been allowed to speak to him.

He paused, as the others moved ahead of him, and added, "Did I ever tell you how I learned of this restaurant?"

The maître d' admitted he had not.

"Detective Harriman and his wife, Irene Kelly, recommended it."

As he watched them leave, the maître d' felt a headache coming on.

After hearing Lydia's story, Frank exchanged a glance with Ben Sheridan, the only one of the group outside the Cliffside who was staying calm. Or appearing to. Frank appreciated that, in part because it reminded him that if he didn't also stay calm and keep control of this situation, he'd never get the information he needed. Even as he thought this, Ethan began badgering Lydia.

"You're sure you didn't hear his name?"

"Of course I'm sure! I'd tell you if I knew."

Frank intervened. "I know you would, Lydia. Do you think Irene knew who he was?"

"Absolutely. He was definitely someone she knew and felt comfortable with," Lydia said. "I think she might have known him from that astronomy story she worked on. They made some kind of joke about it. But maybe not, because he wanted to talk to her about a missing person case. Didn't set off any alarm bells for me—he was polite and charming, even invited me to join them. But I needed to get home, because Guy and I were going out here tonight." She bit her lower lip. "I can't say why, but I just find it hard to believe he wanted to hurt her."

"He may not have. He might have told her his story and that's all there is to it. But I need to find out who he is and when he last saw her so that I can try to find out what happened after they met." Frank looked down at his notes. "Tall, blond, good-looking man in his thirties."

"Yes—early thirties. Short hair. Green eyes. Neatly dressed—a dark blue suit and lighter blue tie. White dress shirt. Muscular build, but not like a bodybuilder or wrestler. Just in good shape. Looked as if he spent time outdoors."

"He approached on foot? You didn't see him get into or out of a vehicle?"

"Right. In fact, he didn't really approach us. Irene saw him walking down the sidewalk near the station, waved to him, he waved back, and she went over to talk to him."

"And from there they walked into the Fireside?"

"Yes, that I'm sure of. I did wonder if I should go with her anyway, but I watched them and there was really nothing that made me feel worried. She was totally at ease." She hesitated, then said, "Frank, I'm so sorry. If anything has happened to her because I didn't insist that she drive straight home or—"

"Lydia, I'd love to believe that anyone could 'insist' she do anything. This isn't your fault, and I don't even want to assume that something bad has happened to her. She may be perfectly fine. I just need to find her."

"What can we do to help?" Guy asked.

"For the moment, there's probably not much more you and Lydia can do, but if I can find some security camera footage, I may need to get Lydia to confirm that I'm looking at the right guy."

"Call us—don't worry about the hour. I don't think we'll be getting much sleep tonight."

"Do you want us to wait at your house?" Lydia asked. "In case she calls or comes home?"

"If you don't mind—"

"Of course not!"

"I'll call Jack and ask him to let you in. He'll probably want to wait with you."

"We have security cameras outside the station," Ethan said. "I can look through the footage. I should have thought of that earlier."

"I can help you with that," Ben said.

"There's a branch of the Bank of Las Piernas near there," Guy said. "Its cameras will have a good view of the street. All of our cameras transmit images to our main office."

"Can you get a look at the video?"

"Security reports to me, and that office operates twenty-four hours a day. Shouldn't be a problem."

"Lydia, you can take my car to Frank's house," Ethan said. "I'll get a ride back with Frank and Ben. Is that okay with you, Frank?"

"That's fine with me. Let's get going."

It felt good to have a plan, Frank thought. Good to be taking some action. Something to fight the undertow of worry, pulling him toward his worst fears.

Frank caught some luck, if you could call it that, at the Fireside.

The place was busy, and a band was playing loud enough to make conversation nearly impossible. The band took a break, but Frank's conversation with the bartender was constantly interrupted as he served his customers.

The bartender, at first reticent, soon became convinced that Frank was not an irate husband of a cheater but a man sincerely worried that his wife was in danger. This conviction was brought home to him, perhaps, after Frank called the manager over, showed him his badge, and said that although he wasn't working a case, he could get some people in here who would be working one, and do it before closing time.

"Talk to him," the manager said to the bartender. "Use the office. I'll cover for you here." To Frank, he added, "I'm doing you a favor, so please don't take all night, okay?"

Before Frank could reply, the bartender said, "Should I give him the phone she left?"

"Sure. It's in the lost and found drawer. You have the key, right?"

The bartender assured him he did.

As Frank followed the bartender to the small back room, he fought down the despair he felt at learning Irene had left here without the phone. All the scenarios he had imagined, trying to rationalize why he hadn't heard from her—she had gotten caught up covering a story, she had seen an old friend and lost track of time, she was feeling hemmed in and just decided to go AWOL for a few hours, even the ones in which she was hurt but in a hospital, cared for and just not yet located—all those fantasies collapsed.

In the relative quiet of the office, the bartender took another look at one of the photos Frank carried of her and said, "Yes, that's her. She and a big blond dude came in here at the beginning of my shift. I didn't think they were lovers, if you're worried about that."

"I'm not, but tell me what makes you say so."

"In the first place, he was expecting someone else to join them. I overheard him say he had a friend on the way. But mostly, well, they weren't loverlike. I mean, at first I thought she was this good-looking cougar or something, 'cause she was older than him, but she wasn't flirting with him, and he wasn't flirting with her. That's straight. It was almost like it was just a business discussion, him doing most of the talking. Which is probably why she ended up drinking so much more than he did."

"What?"

The bartender explained that the lady had downed the better part of a pitcher of margaritas and was none too steady on her feet when they left.

That wasn't like Irene at all, especially not if she was working on a story, or thought that was the purpose of meeting with the unknown man. One drink, maybe. A pitcher of margaritas?

No way. She didn't drink them more than once in a great while—she wasn't that fond of tequila.

"She was walking on her own when they left?"

"He was helping her, but yes."

"How did he pay for the drinks?"

"Cash."

"Have you seen him in here before?"

"No."

Frank coaxed as complete a description of the man as he could out of the bartender. "You have security cameras," Frank said, glancing toward a pair of monitors.

"Sure, but you have to talk to the boss about that. And quite honestly, they aren't worth shit. I mean, take a look at what it's showing you now."

He was right, they were definitely grainy, and shifted from location to location every few minutes. "Anything will help," Frank said.

"Okay, when we're done here, I'll ask him. Are we done?"

"In a minute. Did anyone else approach them or talk to them?"

"No—although he got a call while he was picking up the pitcher."

"You remember his side of the conversation?"

"Something about making a delivery. I didn't listen in."

"Male or female caller?"

He rubbed his chin. "It's weird, but I'd say it was a dude. Just his tone of voice when he was talking. But I didn't hear any names, so that's a guess."

"What kind of mood was he in?"

"Mood?"

"Excited? Nervous? Happy?"

"No, not happy." He shrugged. "Not a troublemaker. Couldn't say more than that."

He stood up, went to a paper-cluttered counter, and unlocked one of the wooden drawers beneath it. He took out a small plastic bag with a phone in it, the baggie marked with the date and time it had been left.

"I guess I should ask for some way to prove this is hers," he said.

Frank took out his phone, hit the speed dial for Irene's number. "It'll play a few notes from a jazz standard," he said. The phone in the bag rang.

"Ella?" the bartender asked, handing it over.

"Yes," Frank said.

"'All the Things You Are'?"

Frank nodded.

The bartender studied him for a moment, then said, "I'll ask my manager to come back here and look through the video for you. Can I have him bring a drink back?"

"No, no thanks. Thanks for your time."

"No problemo," he said and left just as the band started to play again.

After his first look at the video, Frank called his partner. He had hesitated to disturb Pete, who had looked forward to a rare evening at home with Rachel. But Frank knew this was no longer something he could pursue without the department's knowledge, and he wasn't going to insult Pete by not letting him in on what was going on.

"Did the thought ever cross your mind this evening," Vince said about an hour later, "that we should have been called in on this right away?"

"Vince . . . ," Reed said wearily. He turned to the manager of the bar. "Frank said you have the video cued up for us?"

The office was hot and stuffy now. The four detectives,

Rachel, and the manager crowded around the monitor. The manager pressed a remote, and the screen showed a tall blond man standing at the bar, paying cash for a pitcher of margaritas and then filling two glasses while at the bar, then apparently asking the bartender for some limes. As the bartender turned away to put a few lime wedges in a small dish, the man's right hand moved over one of the glasses.

"Right there," Frank said.

"Yes, I see it," Rachel said.

"I don't know," Vince said.

"Keep watching," Pete advised.

Frank nodded to the manager, who sped the recording up until it showed the "couple" leaving the bar, the man guiding Irene and supporting her with an arm around her waist as she stumbled her way out.

Vince looked back at Frank with raised brows.

"Don't say it," Rachel warned.

"I wasn't going to remark on the fact that they looked awfully cozy," Vince said. "Just wondering if she was overserved."

Frank's phone rang. The others watched and listened, but all he said was "Thanks, we'll be right over."

"She showed up?" Vince asked.

Frank looked at Reed, ignoring Vince. "Guy St. Germain has isolated some footage taken from the bank across the street that shows them going into and out of the Fireside. He'll show it to us in his office."

The images from the bank were much clearer, although taken from a distance that made it hard to see faces.

"Not close enough to identify him," Guy said, "but it's obvious that by the time they reach the car, she's hardly able to stand."

"She's definitely drugged," Rachel said. "Irene has a hard head. Two margaritas would never make this kind of mess out of her."

Guy stopped the playback as the brown Ford Escape drove up the street toward the bank.

"Good shot of the plate there. I've got the number for you."

"Thanks, Guy," Reed said. "This is a real help."

The plate was stolen, taken off a van that had been parked at a repair shop. The alert went out to the media about the missing Las Piernas reporter, the description of the man who was a "person of interest" in the case. Lydia sat down with the police artist so that a drawing that looked something like the man would be ready in time for the morning news broadcasts.

Frank went home, thanked everyone for their help, and tried to think of a way to ask them—as politely as possible—to leave, so that he could smash something to pieces and do it without an audience. Then Ethan's phone rang.

Frank glanced at his watch. It was after three in the morning.

Ethan listened, gave a series of orders, then hung up and said, "Holy shit—Quinn Moore has been shot. They've got him in the ER at St. Anne's."

THIRTY-ONE

Nicholas Parrish held the knife up to the light, its blade glistening, feeling its weight and balance. It was a work of art—a skinning knife made with a stag handle. He loved the feel of it as it warmed in his hand.

He owned many knives, but this one was a favorite. It was neither the longest nor the most threatening in appearance from his collection, but he always felt powerful when he held it.

He unlocked the bedroom door, opened it an inch, and waited, listening. The soft sound of her slow and steady breathing came to him, and he entered the room.

The room was dark, except for the faint glow from a small night-light just inside the adjoining bathroom. He used his cell phone to illuminate his path until he stood next to the bed.

She stirred, moving from her back to her side. He thought of how it would feel to run the knife just below her skin, flaying her in sections. Imagined her awakening to find him in control as he began the process of using the knife the way any good hunter would.

The back of her neck lay exposed in the blue-gray light cast by the phone, and he brought the tip of the knife closer, nearly touching her, and considered slipping the blade between her vertebrae, paralyzing her as he had been paralyzed.

A cough sounded in the adjoining room, startling him. He straightened, angry at his jumpiness. It was only Violet, who was hardly in any condition to harm him, after all. He would think more about Violet later.

He turned his attention back to Irene and thought again of ways to harm her. He might cut off small sections of her at a time—the end of a small toe, the toe, all the toes, and so on. Or perhaps just disable her one muscle group at a time.

He frowned. As appealing as these ideas were as revenge, he was dismayed to notice that something essential to his enjoyment of them was missing: the usual sexual response brought on by his rage was utterly absent.

That realization produced a fresh wave of wrath, but he mastered it. Despite a brief image that flashed through his mind, he knew he would leave the room. He refused to become one of those pathetic creatures who raped with objects—a sure sign of emasculation. He would never let that be said of him.

Perhaps Donovan was right. She had lost her appeal. That must be it. The more he thought about it, the more he became convinced it was true. And perhaps he had strayed too far from his original purpose for her. Things were not working out as they should. He sheathed the knife, closed the phone, and thought about this in the near darkness.

Another cough came from Violet's room, interrupting his thoughts. He again used the light from the phone to navigate his way into the bathroom, then to the door on the other side. He opened it and stepped through, closing the door quietly behind him.

Donovan said Irene could care for the sick. Well, he seemed to be running a damned hospital in here.

Violet was clearly awake. He could have turned on the lights.

But he continued to use the phone, enjoying the widening of her eyes when she realized who was leaning over her bed. She was blinking rapidly, one of her occasional tics, exacerbated by fear, he thought. He had asked Kai if she could communicate answers to yes or no questions by blinking, but Kai had said no, the blinking was uncontrolled. "The doctor tried to get her to do that after she fell," Kai had said. "Kept trying from the time when she was first conscious again, but it didn't work."

"Are you keeping secrets, Violet?" Parrish asked her now. "I'm damned sure that was no ordinary fall down the stairs. How long did you lie there, I wonder, before he could bring a friend home to 'discover' you?"

The rapid blinking continued. Parrish smiled at her, then leaned over and took her mouth with his. She lay passively, having no real choice to do otherwise. She could have moved her head or bitten him, he supposed, but she let him do as he liked, until he moved a hand to one of her breasts.

She made inarticulate gurgling sounds.

He drew back, angry.

Memories of the seemingly endless hours in which he had lain paralyzed flooded his mind. Memories of making that same gurgling sound. A time when he had first suffered head and spinal injuries, thanks to Irene Kelly.

Infuriated, he moved toward the room in which Irene lay asleep and thought of smothering her to death. Thought of choking her to death with his hands. Let that fucking bitch gurgle!

No. Nothing so quick for her.

Some slight rustling sound, one of the few small shoulder movements Violet could manage, brought his attention back to her.

"Your son has been shot," he told her and saw her close her eyes. He took her jaw in a strong hand and pressed hard, until she opened her eyes again. "Be good and I'll try to see that he lives."

She closed her eyes again, and this time he let go. "I've brought a new nurse for you," he said, but she kept her eyes closed. *Ah well. Time enough to have fun with that.*

He checked on Kai, who was sleeping soundly, looking more boyish than usual. *What a troublesome lad you've turned out to be.* Parrish recognized a flicker of some strange response to watching him sleep. Not fatherly love. Not even parental affection, really. Perhaps Donovan had said it best—curiosity. What of himself was there in Kai? Would Kai grow, as he aged, to be more like his father?

Or would Kai fail to conquer his impulsiveness?

There was a legacy to protect here, and that brought Parrish's thoughts back to Irene Kelly.

He suddenly realized that by going out through Violet's room, he had not locked the door between Irene's room and the hall. He hurriedly checked to see that she was still there. She was, still sleeping soundly. The windowless room was stuffy. He would come back later, when the drugs had worn off enough to bring her to awareness. No use terrifying someone who would not remember being terrified.

THIRTY-TWO

I awoke in a dimly lit room, in a bed that was large and comfortable—and not mine. I felt muzzy, as if I had a hangover. It slowly dawned on me that I was dressed in a sweater and sweatpants that were not mine.

I rolled over and found myself face-to-face with Nick Parrish.

For a brief moment I lay paralyzed, too frightened even to draw breath for a scream. Then he smiled at me. I scrambled out of the bed in horror, coming quickly to my feet, and was hit with a wave of dizziness and nausea. I saw an open door and stumbled through it, slamming it behind me and fumbling the lock until it clicked into place.

By the light of the night-light, I found a wall switch and flipped it up.

And jumped as I saw someone next to me—my own life-sized reflection.

I was in a bathroom.

I held my weight against the door, frantically looking for something to set against it to create more of a barrier than the flimsy lock. Unless I got the time and tools together to disassemble the toilet or the sink, there was nothing in the bathroom with enough weight to make even a slight difference.

There was another door, on the opposite side of the room, and I thought of trying to escape through it. But I hesitated, not knowing if it really would be an escape. Who or what might be on the other side? I carefully checked that the other door was locked and hurried back to lean against the one between me and Parrish.

I heard him moving around the room. I tried to stop panicking, which was nearly impossible. It's all well and good to tell yourself that freaking out won't help, but I was discovering that when you wake up in a strange place with a serial killer lying next to you, it takes a while to get a grip.

Eventually I was able to think about defending myself, beyond leaning against a door. I was still feeling confused about where I was and how I got there, but given my immediate danger, I set that aside and surveyed the room for possible makeshift weapons.

There were some toiletries on the vanity counter that looked as if they had been taken from a hotel. The thought of sharpening the end of the toothbrush into a weapon occurred to me. Alas, the toothbrush looked too flimsy to withstand whittling. But I'd see what I could do with it.

A quick look in the cabinet under the sink didn't reveal any cleaning supplies, which dashed my hope of throwing a chemical into Parrish's face before running past him.

As I was considering breaking the vanity into pieces to be used as a barricade between the toilet and the door, he knocked, startling me.

"I'm going to leave you for a while, Irene." He laughed. "But don't worry, I'll continue where we left off."

I heard him move toward the bedroom door, heard it open and close, heard the sound of a dead-bolt lock clicking into place.

And didn't trust that he had left the room.

I sat down on the toilet and tried to gather my wits. That was difficult, because the last thing I clearly remembered was listening to Donovan tell me about his missing daughter. To go from that to waking up in bed with Parrish . . . I shuddered.

What had happened to me?

What had been done to me?

I didn't feel any pain or discomfort other than a bad head-ache and mild queasiness—but that was far from enough to reassure me. I had a vague recollection of being told to take a shower . . .

Obviously, I had been drugged. But after that?

It wasn't hard to figure out that the person who had drugged me was Donovan, and that he had given me a roofie or some-thing else that had wiped out my memories of most of what had happened to me in the time since. How much time? I had no way of knowing. I could have spent hours under the control of Nick Parrish.

A combination of fear and revulsion made my stomach clench.

I told myself to calm down, that I didn't have enough facts to know what had happened to me, and no matter what had hap-pened, there was nothing I could do about it now. I was alive. I wasn't tied up. I wasn't, for that matter, nude. The sweater and sweatpants were a little big on me, and not mine, but I was clothed.

That brought on a vague recollection of Donovan telling me something about a parka. But I wasn't even sure that had really happened.

I waited until I had had enough of sitting in the bathroom and decided to risk going back into the bedroom. Hand shak-ing, I unlocked the door and opened it the barest crack.

The room seemed to be empty. Parrish had left a light on. Without leaving the bathroom doorway, I bent to look under the bed—no Parrish. I left the bathroom door open and crept into the room.

The dead bolt on the bedroom door was a double-key type—there was no key in the lock on my side. That didn't mean Parrish wasn't still in the room—he could have locked it from this side and kept the key with him. There was a large wardrobe at one end of the room, and I made myself open its doors.

Parrish did not jump out at me. There was no one hiding in the wardrobe. I exhaled in relief.

Clothing hung from hangers—two additional sets of clothing, essentially copies of what I had on. But no parka—though if I'd only imagined Donovan mentioning the word to me, it was an odd thing to have dreamed up on my own. No, I believed in that memory. He'd said something about a parka, and said it several times. Unfortunately, when I tried to put that particular puzzle together, there were way too many missing pieces.

A duffel bag sat next to my shoes on the bottom shelf. They looked as if they had been cleaned, which struck me as odd. At least they were my own shoes. They had laces. I wondered if the laces were strong enough to allow me to hang myself if things got really bad.

I hated the thought as soon as it occurred to me, but what came to mind next were horrific images I had seen not many years before—photographs Parrish had taken of one of his tortured victims. Perhaps now was the time to deny Parrish what must seem to him like a long-promised treat. Do it now, while I had the strength and freedom of movement to carry it out.

I shook myself, like a dog throwing off water. Fear was one thing, despair another.

I opened the duffel bag and saw some socks and underwear inside, including a set of long underwear. I was momentarily creeped out by the idea of wearing underwear someone else had picked out for me, then decided that, on the long list of things

I should be getting upset about, that one didn't rank very high. A pair of winter gloves were at the bottom of the bag. So given that and the possibility of the parka, there were obviously plans that I would be taken outside at some point, and not as a corpse. At least, not to begin with.

As I thought again about the parka, a memory came to me, of Donovan saying not to let "them" take the parka from me.

Them.

More than one.

Of course. I knew Parrish had had help with his prison escape. Was Kai Loudon here? Had Donovan been the ambulance driver?

But the word "them" suggested an otherness. Was Donovan saying he was not part of what was going on here? What *was* going on here?

Thinking of Donovan only made me feel more confused. I felt furious with him for tricking me, drugging me, bringing me here, and . . . participating in whatever might have happened after that. But somehow, perhaps with the help of the drug, he had managed to plant the suggestion that he was not allied with Parrish.

How could that be true? He damned well was a part of it.

I rubbed my aching head and went back to work on my search.

The room was windowless, something that would have made my claustrophobia raise my level of anxiety if it could have gone any higher.

I told myself that the last time someone had kept me captive in a small room, I had been in far worse shape and wasn't given the dignity of access to an actual bathroom.

Even with that stretch for optimism, I couldn't reach it, and for a few moments I struggled not to get flat-out hysterical.

You can fall apart later.

The only way I could keep that promise to myself was to live. So I went back into the bathroom, washed my face, took a few deep, slow breaths, and decided to get on with exploring my little prison.

The door to the bathroom also had a double lock. That meant that I could be locked out of the bathroom but also that I could prevent entry into the bedroom from the bathroom—at least as long as the door held.

I moved toward the door at the far side of the bathroom and turned the lock tab on the knob. That didn't mean I could open it, if it was designed like the lock on the other bathroom door. I took a deep breath and tried the knob. It turned in my hand. Unlocked. I carefully released it without opening the door.

If Nick Parrish was on the other side, I sure as hell didn't want to open it. And he would never be so careless as to leave me in an unlocked room. My next thought was that anyone could make a mistake, so maybe this was my chance to get the hell away.

I shut off the lights in my room and the bathroom, except for the night-light, let my eyes grow accustomed to the darkness again, then placed myself in a position that would allow me to slam the door shut again if need be. I cautiously opened it a few inches.

Except for a soft glow coming from the dimmed display of a clock radio, the room was dark. I waited, listened, then turned the bathroom light on again.

Although it was slightly larger than my room, this one was also windowless. Some part of my mind noted a comfortable looking chair, a dresser, a throw rug—even that the clock radio said it was 4:11 A.M. But most of my attention was drawn across the room, to a frail woman who lay on a hospital bed. Her hair was dark and straight, and I thought she might be in her mid-forties, or maybe a little younger.

Her blue eyes were open, staring upward.

I moved to the side of the bed, until she could see me clearly.

"Violet Loudon?" I whispered.

She blinked, several times. She paused, and blinked again.

During the second round, I finally realized what I was seeing: Morse code.

"I'm sorry," I said, still keeping my voice to a whisper.
"Would you repeat that?"

This time, the answer was clear:

-.--. ... --..-- .. .- --

Yes, I am.

"I'm Irene," I said.

Yes, I know.

There was a pause, then she spoke again to me, clearly and
silently:

Please kill me.

THIRTY-THREE

Although I had contemplated something similar for myself only a few minutes earlier, I said, "I'm sorry, I can't. I'll try to get us out of here."

She blinked again. *You are a fool.*

Well, nice to meet you, too, I thought but kept it to myself. Still, even that momentary flash of anger felt better than the pure panic I had been experiencing until then.

I tapped into my anger toward Parrish, but I didn't stay angry at Violet. She had spent several years almost completely paralyzed and utterly subject to the tender mercies of Kai Loudon, so I figured I could cut her some slack. I began to wonder, when her neighbors had said she had been mean to her son, what exactly that meant.

Do not tell them.

She couldn't have known I was thinking about her neighbors, so I said, "Them? Parrish and your son?"

Yes.

"Don't tell them you want to die?" I asked, still whispering.

They know that. Not about Morse. Secret.

"You've spent years like this and haven't let anyone know that you can communicate?"

Her mouth formed a lopsided smile, briefly. *Anyone? Who did I see? Only women about to die.*

"He brought them into your room?"

Bound. Gagged. Doomed.

I straightened and tried to take that in. After a moment, I said, "I can understand keeping secrets from Kai. But why not let the doctors or nurses know?"

Kai always there. Afraid of him. She paused, then added, *They believe he is a saint.*

"Probably not now that your backyard has been dug up."

She closed her eyes for a moment, then signaled, *He is a monster.*

"I'm sorry. I can't imagine how many horrors you've experienced, being at his mercy since you were injured."

He did it.

"He injured you?"

Yes.

"But I thought—oh. Before he left for school that day—"

We fought. He pushed me.

"And left you to lie there?"

He hoped I would die. Later, he forced me to live.

She closed her eyes, and I thought I might have worn her out, or further depressed her by talking.

But she seemed just to have wanted a rest, for she opened her eyes and said, *Good to talk. Glad you know code.*

"Me, too."

Should have tried with doctors. But afraid Kai is a liar. Told neighbors stories. Like his dad.

"Who is his dad?"

Parrish.

That rocked me back on my heels.

Did not know?

"No. No. I'm sorry. How . . . I mean . . ."

Was I raped?

I wasn't sure that would have been my question, but I nodded.

No. See?

"See? See what?"

I am a bigger fool than you.

I was silent, waiting to see if she would say more, when the door to her room suddenly opened. Nick Parrish stood in the doorway, holding a gun.

"Well, well, well," he said. "Look who's been exploring."

THIRTY-FOUR

Quinn looked up at the tall man standing at the end of his hospital bed and tried to discern which held stronger sway over Frank Harriman, worry or anger. He wondered if most people would have detected either emotion and doubted it. He was fairly sure they would have seen the detective as a calm, self-possessed individual.

But Quinn thought there was much more going on beneath that serene surface than met the eye. The ability to perceive the emotions of others—especially the emotions they tried to hide, the ones lurking beneath bravado—had been essential to Quinn's survival from the time he was a child. Later, that same ability had been a key element in his business success—and in his pursuit of pleasure. There were few people he couldn't read. Donovan was one of them, which made his older brother all the more intriguing.

He could see that Harriman was tired and doubted the man had slept much since the previous night, when he would have discovered his wife was missing. Quinn decided that, for just this moment, Harriman's worry was ascendant.

"I certainly want to be of help if I can," he said accordingly.

"I appreciate that." Harriman glanced around. "I'm glad you were able to get a private room."

"Me, too—although I hope not to make use of it much longer."

"I know you're probably tired of talking about it, but would you mind telling me what happened to you?"

Quinn and Donovan had come up with and rehearsed a story during the drive back to Las Piernas, and Donovan had set up at least some matching evidence for that story.

"It began when I was checking on some of my properties last night. Not that late in the evening, about eight-thirty or so, but it was dark," he told Harriman now.

He went on with a story that he had told so many times now, he could tell it with real conviction. He had driven to the warehouse and former cannery where the bodies had been found last summer—checking to see if the security measures he had ordered were still in place. Discovered an entry with a broken lock. Was just reaching for his cell phone to complain to his security workers when he saw the beam of a flashlight, and heard footsteps behind him. At first he thought it was one of the security guards. He turned. Was shot twice, although he was sure other bullets were fired and missed. The next thing he knew, he was waking up in the hospital.

"I'm afraid he blinded me with the light. I never got a good look at him."

"No recollection of being treated by someone with—let's say, advanced first aid supplies?"

"No. I can't figure that part out at all." He touched the bandages on his head and winced. "I'm told this head injury may be affecting my memory."

"Two head injuries. They must be quite painful."

"Two?"

"No recollection of being punched in the face?"

"Oh, I see what you mean," he said, reaching up to carefully touch his jaw, swollen from his father's fist. "No, I don't remember anything at all about that. I suppose that's lucky, but why would anyone hit me after shooting me?"

Harriman shrugged, then said, "You said you were reaching for your cell phone when the intruder blinded you with the flashlight beam?"

"Yes."

"What happened to the phone?"

"I have no idea. As I said, I don't remember anything after the gunfire. Sorry. Did you ask the hospital if it was among my things?"

"It wasn't."

"Damn. That was an expensive phone. All my contacts in it . . . I have that backed up, of course, but what a pain—"

Harriman interrupted. "Which car were you driving?"

"Which car?" Quinn asked, stalling. No one else had asked this question.

"You own several vehicles, right?"

"Yes, I do, but—last night I was driving my Lexus. Isn't it there? The bastard stole my Lexus?"

"Seems so. Maybe that's why you were attacked. What do you think?"

"I don't know," Quinn said, fearing a trap. He held a hand to his head, considered pleading dizziness. But one look at Harriman's face told him that this would be a mistake. Well, he'd put the ball in the other court then.

"Have the police found any evidence?"

"You know it doesn't work the way it does on television, right?"

"Of course not."

Quinn could swear he saw a grim amusement flash in Harriman's eyes before he answered. "Some shell casings that matched the caliber of the slug recovered from your leg were found on a sidewalk near the warehouse, but then we found casings of other calibers, too. You're probably aware that gunfire isn't exactly rare in that area."

"I want to change that, you know," Quinn said, happy to slip into the role of civic reformer. "It's going to take time, but we have plans to revitalize that block. Artists' lofts, galleries, restaurants, shopping . . . perhaps even a theater."

"While I can only hope you succeed, maybe there's someone else out there who isn't too happy about your plans."

"Do you think that's what happened? One of the gangs . . . ?"

"Hard to say. Doesn't fit treating you for your wounds."

"No . . . I guess not."

"You were moved from wherever you were shot, it seems."

"The other detectives mentioned that, but I don't remember anything about it."

"Funny thing is, some of that area was washed down, which a gang probably wouldn't take time to do. Our crime scene evidence team said they can't even find the spatter."

"Spatter?"

"When a person gets shot and bleeds—and you must have bled *somewhere*—the blood makes patterns as it scatters or falls. We'll find everything from fine spray to droplets to pools of it."

"I wish I could be more helpful."

"Hmm." Harriman made some notes, then said, "Our crime scene team will keep looking for evidence, of course. And we'll be searching for any remaining traces of blood that might match up to you."

"Me? But I'm the victim here!"

"Exactly. We have to make sure that if we go to court, we can tell the judge that any bloodstains we find and examine are yours, especially since there have been other crimes connected to your buildings. Don't want a defense attorney saying it was blood from an earlier victim."

"Oh."

"And especially since the doctors here say that you were treated more than an hour before you were found, we'll have to establish exactly where the attack on you took place. You see what I mean? Without physical evidence of your presence, it could be claimed you weren't there at all. And let me tell you," Harriman said, watching him steadily, "that would be awkward."

Deflect. "Will the crime lab need to take a DNA sample from me?"

"It's a painless process, but come to think of it—I can't speak for the investigators on your case, but I imagine we'll just get DNA off your bloody clothing. That was all taken to the lab while you were in the ER."

"Oh," Quinn said again, then forced himself to sound nonchalant as he added, "that makes it easy, then."

"Yes, it does," Harriman agreed. "Anyway, all that washing things down outside your buildings makes me wonder about the shooter and his plans."

"Of course. By the way, is this your case? I thought . . ."

Harriman didn't smile, yet again Quinn sensed he was amused. Amused? How could that be?

"No," the detective said. "I'm pursuing something else. We're just trying to figure out if a couple of our cases may be related. Speaking of relatives, strange thing . . ."

Quinn waited.

"You remember Cade Morrissey?"

"Of course. His body was found in one of my buildings. As was his mother's. That horrified me. That's exactly why I wanted to ensure there was better security. That's also why I wanted to check on the place. Security can grow lax over time.

I'll admit I was just protecting my property when I stopped by last night. I really didn't think the killer was likely to come back to use the buildings after you discovered the bodies there. Do you think I was wrong?"

Harriman studied him for a moment, then said, "I doubt very much that the killer or killers of Marilyn Foster and Cade Morrissey attacked you, if that's what you're asking."

"How can you be so sure?" Quinn asked, hoping he had infused the right amount of panic into his voice. It helped to know that Harriman was at least half wrong.

"You're alive."

Quinn knew he was on dangerous ground. Better take another tack. "You asked me about Cade Morrissey."

"Yes. Had you ever met him when he was alive?"

"The detectives asked me that when his body was found. No, I didn't know him. At least, not that I recall."

"He was Nicholas Parrish's son."

"Nicholas Parrish? The serial killer? You're not serious!"

"I am as serious as can be. Lab was backed up, so it took a while to get the DNA results or we would have known sooner."

"That's—that's so strange. That the son of a serial killer would end up being murdered, I mean."

"It is. But it gets stranger yet. Got some other results just this morning. This time, given that it was so high-profile, the lab put a rush on it for us. Turns out Kai Loudon is Parrish's son, too."

Quinn did his best to look blank, then said, "The one with the backyard burials. Right?"

"Yes. Former burial sites—no question about that. We haven't found entire bodies yet, but we don't have a lot of doubt about what went on there. My wife was one of the reporters who broke that case, by the way. But you probably knew that."

Careful, Quinn thought. "Irene Kelly. Who doesn't know about her?"

Harriman said nothing for a moment, letting the silence stretch, then said, "Irene connected the dots early on. Some people dismissed her ideas, thought she might be a little rattled about Parrish's escape. But she was absolutely right. There is a connection between Nick Parrish's escape and the victim left in the trunk of a car parked near our home. Because of the artwork on the bodies and other factors, we didn't need anyone to point out connections between that victim and the murders of Marilyn Foster and Cade Morrissey. Do you see where I'm going with this?"

"No, I have to admit I don't."

"Well, here's the thing. No one was expecting to find out Loudon had buried people in his backyard, or that he was Parrish's son."

"You're sure that he *is* related to Parrish?"

"Yes. We have Parrish's DNA on file, of course, and you really can't live in a place as long as Loudon did and not leave your DNA behind. So even though Loudon had no criminal record as an adult, we got a familial match."

"Wow. Imagine that."

"Imagine. Of the two children we know about, one helped him escape, and the other ended up dead in one of your buildings."

Harriman paced a few steps, then turned back to Quinn and said, "Cade Morrissey had drawings of moths on him, and similar drawings were found not only on Cade's mother's body but also on Lisa King, the third victim—she was probably the first of the three to be killed, actually. And it seems likely that one of the last people to see Lisa King alive was Kai Loudon."

"So you've solved three murders and identified one of the people who helped Parrish escape," Quinn said.

"No, I'm not so sure we have."

"Why not?"

"The artwork on three of those victims? It's just not likely that it could have survived if those victims had been buried. We think the person who used your property was someone who was careful and very clean and neat. He went to a lot of trouble to preserve his artwork, yet there aren't bloodstains on the walls inside the building or any other sign that those three victims were killed there.

"So even though there's a genetic connection between Loudon and one of those victims, it seems strange to us that Loudon would have this one M.O. of butchering people in his basement and burying them without so much as a plastic sheet wrapped around them, and then a separate operation going on in one of your buildings, with an entirely different M.O. You see what I mean?"

"I suppose so . . ."

"Plus, we're doing a lot of research into Loudon, and so far we haven't come up with anything like art training in his background. His former teachers say he was terrible at it. More of a computer and electronics guy. And our experts agree that the work done on the bodies in your buildings was not amateurish. Someone who really knew what he was doing drew those moths."

"Is all of this questioning going on because I once considered pursuing an art degree?" Quinn asked. "Perhaps I should contact my attorney."

"You can always do that, of course. But what makes you think you're about to be placed under arrest?"

"Victims in my buildings? Artwork?"

"No, I'd never proceed on anything as flimsy as a coincidence like that. As you've pointed out, you're a victim. In fact, you were nearly killed on the same night my wife disappeared."

"Disappeared?"

"She was kidnapped."

Quinn frowned and summoned all of his ability to put sincerity into his voice. "Detective Harriman, I'm so sorry to hear that. Sorry and shocked. How did it happen?"

"I can't really discuss it. Some details will be on the news today." He glanced at the television behind him, mounted high on the wall. "Want me to see if I can find something about it now?"

"No, no thank you—if you don't mind. This is all very upsetting. As I'm sure it is for you."

"Absolutely. Anyway, it just makes us wonder."

"Wonder what?"

"How many sons Parrish has. And if there might be connections." Harriman smiled, but there was no amusement in it. "I'll let you get your rest. Thanks for talking to me."

"I don't know that I did you much good. But please let me know if I can be of help."

"Oh, I will," Harriman said.

THIRTY-FIVE

I had the rules explained to me at gunpoint.

Parrish didn't state them right away. He started with a long lecture about my helplessness, his control, his anticipation of his revenge on me—which would be slow, painful, and humiliating to me. He told me that it was useless to try to escape. That I was his slave now. That I would die, but first I would be brought to the point of wanting death more than anything on earth.

I stayed silent. Even knowing that he would enjoy himself more if I showed fear, I still couldn't hide it.

Fear wasn't all I felt, though, and I found myself hiding those other reactions more carefully. They were mostly a mixture of anger and hope. It wouldn't do to let him see either.

I remembered Rachel's self-defense lessons and positioned myself so that I was balanced over my feet, ready to move quickly. I kept hoping that, while he was going on and on about himself and his power and my weakness, he'd get a little too close, let his aim drop a little, slacken his grip a bit—maybe I'd get a chance to take the gun away from him.

He suddenly paused, smiled a smile I didn't like much, and stared at me.

I stared back.

He looked away first.

I was doing my damnedest to hide the spike of exhilaration that brought me when he started back in on the rules.

The rules weren't too complicated.

I was to attend to Violet's needs and help out with the care of Kai. I didn't have the slightest idea of what he meant by "care of Kai," but I wasn't going to ask. Kai would be brought to this room when necessary. I would not be allowed out of this set of three rooms for any reason until Parrish decided to let me out. Parrish would make use of me for whatever purpose he chose by whomever he chose, but he was going to give me a few days to think about what that meant.

He smiled again but left without a rematch of the staring contest.

He locked the door.

Now that he was out of sight, I allowed myself to sink into the chair in Violet's room. I was still not fully myself. The drug, the fear, the missing hours, the disruption of my normal sleep-wake cycle—I knew all of that had left me unsettled. But the longer I was awake, the more I began to set aside that earlier sense of hopelessness and defeat.

I was also processing some surprising observations:

Parrish looked like hell. When I stopped thinking about his whole catalog of savagery, and thought just about what had happened in his life over the last few years, I realized it only made sense that his injuries and incarceration would have taken a toll on him.

I couldn't afford to ignore the rest of his history or pretend that I didn't know what he was capable of doing to anyone he saw as an enemy or prey. It could be fatal to underestimate his dangerousness, or to forget how much he enjoyed the suffering of others. Still, not only was he not Godzilla but he wasn't Nicholas Parrish. Or at least not as I remembered him.

Which nevertheless left me locked in a room with some-one who had apparently once found him lovable, although she didn't seem so fond of him now. If she could be trusted. For all I knew, Parrish knew Morse code and had been communicating with her all along.

I moved back toward Violet. She was still awake, looking at me.

"Do you know where we are?"

Big lodge. Camp. San Bernardinos?

That gave me a little hope. The San Bernardino Mountains had remote areas in them, but if this was a camp, there was a road nearby that was probably large enough for buses, and that meant there might also be neighbors or even a small town not too far away.

"Any idea what Parrish means by 'care of Kai'?"

Kai was shot.

A memory of hearing gunfire came to me. "Who shot him?"

Don't know. Quinn, maybe.

"Quinn?"

One of the brothers.

"Quinn Moore? The real estate developer?"

Don't know. Has lots of money.

For a few moments, I found it hard to take in. Quinn Moore was well known in Las Piernas—famous as a young man who had inherited a successful but narrowly focused commercial real estate sales company and expanded it into a local powerhouse, transforming blighted industrial buildings into modern lofts, shops, and restaurants.

But then I set aside his public persona, the one he wanted to sell, and thought of the bodies found on his property. Still, the police said he was not suspected in the murders of Marilyn Foster and her son, Cade Morrissey. He had been investigated—I knew that much. He had been very cooperative and had seemed genuinely shocked by the discovery of bodies in the buildings. If he owned this place and Violet had seen him here, though . . .

Then the full meaning of what she had just said began to sink in.

"*One* of the brothers? How many are there?"

Don't know. Three here.

"Now?"

No. Quinn and Donovan are gone.

Donovan.

And I had fallen for what was undoubtedly a made-up story . . .

But she was signaling me again. "Sorry, I was distracted—can you repeat that?"

They have some hold over him.

"Some hold over whom?"

Donovan. Kai talks to me. Likes to brag.

"What hold?"

Don't know. Donovan has to do what Nick says. Kai knows some secret about him.

I had the sense that she knew more than she was telling me, but I decided not to push just now. She was extending a lot of trust just by letting me know she could communicate. I needed to build on that trust.

"Parrish wants me to provide care for you. Are you okay with that?"

What difference does it make?

"I don't know what can be done. I suppose I could just not do anything, but I don't think that would work out well for either of us."

No. Sorry.

"As Parrish mentioned, I took care of my father, but he

doesn't seem to understand that, although my father was weak and bedridden at the end of his life, he wasn't paralyzed. He had stomach cancer. It was almost thirty years ago, so not only am I out of practice but I have no experience with spinal cord injuries.

"Some aspects of your care may be the same, but you'll have to let me know. I'm not a raw beginner, I'm not squeamish, and I am not unwilling to help you in any way I can, but you'll need to give me instructions. Can you manage that?"

Yes. Thank you.

So she began to tell me, slowly and painstakingly, what she needed. She had a C-4 spinal injury, so she could breathe on her own, but her limbs were completely paralyzed. She had also received a head injury that impaired her ability to speak. She could chew, swallow, and slightly move her shoulders. Doctors had tried to get her to use them for yes and no responses, but she had been uncooperative.

I wasn't sure if I should feel honored or disturbed by her willingness to communicate with me. Five years of that kind of lack of interaction with others would have been enough to drive most people crazy. I asked her why she had decided to talk to me.

You know Morse code.

"I can't be the first person you've come across who does."

Second. Learned it from Donovan.

I was surprised, but I didn't reply to that. It was getting harder and harder for me to know what to believe about Donovan—or Violet, for that matter. She was saying more, so I concentrated on reading her signals.

I don't get out much.

There was a look of amusement in her eyes.

What I didn't know about spine injuries was vast, and I wasn't going to be able to get more than a quick summary of concerns in one night. It was simply too wearying for her to blink enough code to explain it all. I had already guessed that this type of injury would require help with feeding, with staying hydrated, with movement to avoid bedsores, with bladder and bowel management, with washing and dressing. That much I had been through with my dad at the end of his life, although even in those areas, Violet's situation was different in many ways.

She mentioned that her spine could no longer carry messages from the brain about heating and cooling, so she did not sweat below her shoulders. That meant that maintaining a normal body temperature was a concern—her body temperature would fall or rise with the environmental temperature. She needed assistance with coughing. There were exercises that were needed on a daily basis to prevent a host of problems. There were complex concerns about her blood pressure, which might rise dangerously in response to pain stimuli signaled to a brain that could not get the message; the potential for injuries she could not feel; and other issues.

It was time to apply lotion to her skin and move her—pressure sores are a serious problem for anyone who is immobilized. I did my best.

I didn't kid myself that her brief instructions qualified me to take care of her, but making the better-than-nothing cutoff eased some of the guilt I felt over my lack of expertise.

She fell asleep not long after that, and after sitting in her room for a few moments, wondering how the hell I was going to get out of this mess and what would become of her if I somehow managed to escape, I decided to go back to "my" room.

I thought again about the contents of the duffel and went through every item in it, including the pockets, wondering if tucked away in one of them I might discover a message from Donovan, one that would explain everything. *Sorry about drugging you and leaving you with a serial killer, but if you look under the floorboards, you'll find a bazooka.*

Alas, nothing. Not even lint.

I searched the room again, found nothing I had not found before, and realized that, between activity and anxiety and perhaps the residual effects of being drugged, I was tired. I decided Parrish was unlikely to find many thrills in killing me while I slept and lay down. I avoided the half of the bed he had touched.

I prayed that someone would find out where we were. That Kai might have been seen driving a van up here, or might have gone shopping or otherwise appeared in public before our story about him broke.

I knew Frank would already be looking for me. I just had to stay alive until he found me.

THIRTY-SIX

Frank Harriman knocked the clock radio off the nightstand as he reached a fumbling hand to find the cell phone. He answered groggily but came more awake when he realized what his lieutenant, Jake Matsuda, was saying to him.

Jake wasn't a ranter, but by the time he had killed you with kindness and long explanations of how you might be compromising a case, you wished he would have just yelled and gotten it all over and done with in one tenth of the time and one one hundredth of the guilt.

At one point, Frank said, "Reed and Vince knew I was going to talk to him."

"Yes, they told me, when I talked to them after Mr. Moore's attorney called me."

"I didn't harm him or threaten him or anything of that nature."

"No. You're far too professional for that sort of thing, I'm sure."

"I hear the warning in that, Jake, but I promise you, I talked everything over with Reed and Vince, before and after. All I really did with Quinn Moore was look for his reactions to a couple things, like the art."

"Under other circumstances, I think it would have been an excellent line of investigation to pursue. Perhaps without tipping our hand to him, however."

"You'll have to forgive me if I don't see it that way."

"Nothing to forgive. Still, I find I have to ask you to choose one of two options here, Frank, or this will end badly for all of us. Either take some time off or let me load you up with so much other work you won't have time to get involved in Reed and Vince's cases."

"If you think I can just sit this out—"

"Oh no, I don't," Jake said mildly.

"I've got three more weeks of vacation time coming to me this year. I'll take a couple of weeks of that now."

"You don't have to use up vacation time. We can call it administrative leave."

"I find myself not wanting to be in the department's debt."

There was a long pause, then Jake said, "All right. Have a good vacation, Frank."

THIRTY-SEVEN

Donovan woke late in the day, momentarily disoriented to find himself in a dimly lit space, staring up at rafters. He listened carefully before slowly sitting up.

He was in the attic of one of the cabins, having easily defeated Quinn's and Kai's pathetic attempts at creating an improved security system.

A few hours earlier, he'd used a disposable cell phone to make the anonymous 911 call that would ensure Quinn got to a hospital. He'd then destroyed the phone and driven to a street in Las Piernas, parked the Escape, and after one brief detour, walked a mile to the place where he had earlier parked a used Subaru Forester. Like the Escape, it had been purchased with cash given to him by Quinn.

He had then made a journey of several hours to the desert. Although by this time he was feeling tired, he stopped by a storage building he owned, picked up equipment and supplies he had not been willing to put in a vehicle parked on the street, no matter how safe the neighborhood, and stored them in the Forester in compartments he had specially built into it, compartments that would not be easily detected. He left his own Honda Accord behind, locking up the building. He realized it was a weakness on his part to keep the Accord, but it was one of a few symbols of what he was reluctantly recognizing as his optimism. His hope—no, his belief—that somehow he would prevail over the mounting odds against him.

He had of course known that the Escape could not be used past a certain point, although it had served its purpose well and would perhaps provide one additional bit of help in the coming days.

He'd driven closer to the mountain camp in the Forester. Despite his exhaustion, he'd parked it at what he considered a reasonable distance and hid it. Then, donning a pack that held a portion of the equipment he had brought with him, he'd hiked back.

He had reached the property just as the sky began to softly lighten in the east.

He had briefly considered simply returning to the main lodge. It had been a long and arduous night. Parrish would doubtless have welcomed him. It would have been easy to accept a comfortable bed inside—but not if he calculated in the odds of being murdered in his sleep.

So instead he had checked the garage near the currently unoccupied caretaker's cabin, assured himself that neither Kai's van nor Quinn's Lexus—which he himself had moved into the garage on the previous night—had been driven recently, then hiked a short distance to one of the more remote cabins on the property.

He had climbed into this dusty attic after obscuring all signs of his arrival, set a few booby traps for anyone who might come too near, and no sooner crawled into his sleeping bag than he had fallen deeply asleep.

Now he awakened among the recreational odds and ends stored and forgotten here—a badminton set, a volleyball net, a raft that did not look seaworthy.

He did not know if Irene Kelly was still alive. His check of the van had told him that, as of this morning, Parrish had not left, or driven it elsewhere and returned, but that was all he had been able to determine.

He disarmed the traps leading to the attic, lowered himself into the cabin itself, and took a shower. He dressed, disarmed the outdoor traps, and made his way back to the lodge.

He heard voices as he approached the lodge, then realized they were coming from a television. A news program, apparently. He cautiously went in through the kitchen under the cover of its noise. As he peered into the main hall, he saw Parrish asleep on the couch, and after a quick look around to see that Kai was not in the room, he entered.

Parrish was still dressed in the clothes he had worn the day before. Other than an automatic and a stag-handled skinning knife lying on the table next to him, he appeared unarmed. Donovan considered his options, including slitting Parrish's throat, but he regretfully abandoned that in favor of pocketing the revolver and picking up the remote, stepping across the room from the couch, and pressing the mute button—his eyes on Parrish all the while.

As the voices abruptly stopped, Parrish awakened, grabbed the knife, and moved to a sitting position. Faster than Donovan had anticipated but far too slow had Donovan been intent on harming him.

Parrish sat wild-eyed for a moment, and Donovan read exhaustion in his confusion. Of course. He had expected to have Kai—young, able-bodied, and devoted—available to assist him in his plans. Perhaps he had planned that Quinn and Donovan would be here as well, and now all of that had changed.

"You're back," Parrish said, setting down the knife. He

rubbed his hands over his face and stretched. "Tell me that you're the one who has my gun."

Donovan held it up, then put it back in his pocket.

"I've been listening to the news reports," Parrish said with a yawn. "Do you think there's a chance that this story of Quinn's will fly?"

Donovan shrugged. "I wouldn't bet against Quinn's ability to be convincing."

Parrish smiled slightly, then shook his head. "No. It won't work."

"It will be hard for anyone to prove anything against him."

"The story is weak, but that isn't why it won't work. It won't work because Quinn is weak."

Donovan didn't reply.

"You think I'm wrong?"

"No."

Parrish laughed, then fell into a brooding silence.

"We'll have to leave," he said.

"We?"

"Of course. They're already looking for you, you know."

"They have precious little to go on. They don't even know my name."

"Oh, I don't think that's going to be true for long."

Donovan said nothing, but the hairs on the back of his neck stood on end.

"Tell me, did you enjoy playing the hero?" Parrish asked.

"I don't know what you're talking about."

"You did, I have no doubt of it. It's in your nature, isn't it? War hero, right?"

"Now I know *why* I don't know what you're talking about—you don't know yourself."

Parrish's mouth thinned into a harsh line. "I don't like to be spoken to in just that tone, Donovan."

"I was not a war hero," he said, keeping his voice calm and low.

"Have it your way," Parrish said. "But if not in war, then in the mean streets of Las Piernas, certainly. For instance, rescuing damsels in distress in cafés."

Donovan hid his surprise as he studied Parrish's smug look, all the while thinking furiously. "The 'mean streets of Las Piernas' seem to be teeming with your bastards," he said. "Is Roderick another one?"

"No. Merely one of the Moths. But I'm rather disappointed that you didn't already figure out he was there because I provided him for you."

"An unnecessary risk on your part. I would have won her trust by telling her the story of the girl."

"Admit that Roderick helped."

He stayed silent.

Parrish lifted a shoulder. "Donovan, you really must accept your heritage. Your fate. You can't escape it by pretending that you belong to the rest of the world. You belong to me, my son. To me. The rest of the world will never come close to understanding you the way I do." He paused, then said, "I would hate to find it necessary to have Roderick talk about you to the police."

Donovan stood and walked over to Parrish, towering over him. Parrish stared up at him coolly. Donovan's own stare grew colder still. "You've never intended to tell me where to find the girl, have you?"

"Now, now. I was told you have no real interest in her. By you, if I recall correctly."

"Admittedly, I'm no more capable of being a father than you are."

"But my dear Donovan, I am your father."

"No, like me, you provided a gamete and the rest was just nature taking its course. Nothing more."

"You think I don't understand you? No, I've always known about your nature, your impulses."

"You don't understand me. And you don't know me."

"You think I've ignored you until now? No. I always knew what was happening in your life, Donovan."

Donovan moved away in disgust. "Then you definitely don't deserve to be known as my father."

"Angry with me for not protecting you?"

"No. Where'd you learn your psychology? Afternoon talk shows?"

Parrish smiled. "Let's not be at odds, Donovan. We both have more pressing concerns. The truth is, I had hoped to let you go on your way until Kai and Quinn decided to play with guns. Help me relocate and I'll disappear with Kai. I'll tell you exactly where I've been keeping the girl and her grandmother, and you—and I'm sure this will delight you—you can play the hero once again."

"And Kai's mother?"

"I'm afraid my plans for her will have to be altered. Kai will have difficulty functioning without her, but I'll be sure to help him make the transition."

"Just how does she help him to function?"

"Fueling his rage, of course. But that's just one aspect of their rather complex relationship. He knows it humiliates her to have him touch her as intimately as he must to care for her. She provides an object of prolonged revenge. Exquisite, really, for one as young as Kai."

"They did let you watch talk shows in prison."

Parrish didn't rise to the bait. He seemed to be waiting for something, and Donovan had a good idea of what it was, but he wasn't going to gratify him.

Parrish smiled. "You never really were interested in fucking Irene, were you?"

"Not if you were going to provide an audience, no. Other-wise— Perhaps it's the effect of hunting her over those weeks and months, but I do find I have some interest there."

"I believe you're lying to me, but I won't make anything of it just now." Parrish stood. "Let's see how Kai is doing, shall we? And return my weapon to me, please. I'd like to make sure he doesn't come near any firearms anytime soon."

Kai was awake but did not stir from his bed as Parrish and Donovan entered his room. Donovan thought he looked pale. When he tried to sit up straighter in the bed, he moved his injured arm, now in a sling, and cried out sharply.

Donovan exchanged a glance with Parrish, who only smiled and said, "He'll be all right. He just needs a little time to heal. When we're away from here, I'll arrange for him to see a doc-tor."

"Who changed the bandage and made the sling?"

"Irene," Kai said. "She's taking care of Mom, too."

"Kai," Parrish said, "we're going to have to leave this place."

"Good," he said. "I'm bored with it. And Quinn is going to talk."

Parrish smiled. "I believe you're right about that."

"Sorry I didn't kill him."

"You made him suffer," Donovan said. "As revenge, suffer-ing lasts longer than death."

Kai cheered up. "That's true."

"I'm afraid we're going to have to go soon," Parrish said.

"Okay. I won't be able to do much, I don't think, but I'll try. Donovan will have to help you get my mom into the van."

"I don't think it will be wise to use the van."

"There's no other way to take her."

"Exactly. That's what I wanted to talk to you about."

"You aren't going to kill her!"

"No."

Kai looked unhappy, yet Donovan could see that he was still in awe of Parrish.

"What's going to happen?" Kai asked warily.

"We're going to need to let someone else take care of her for a while."

"Irene?"

"No, Irene will be coming with us."

"Donovan?"

"He'll be with us, too."

"Then who?"

"Kai. Do you think I've failed to plan for any possibility? That I don't know how much you want Violet to be . . . available to you?"

"I'll get her back?"

"Yes, of course. I promise you'll be together again."

"So what is the plan?"

"One of the Moths is already on the way up here."

"But they have to know how to take care of her!"

"Of course. Don't worry. Everything will be fine."

Kai was unconvinced, and Donovan knew that if he could see it, Parrish could see it. But Parrish seemed to believe Kai could be brought round his thumb.

"Donovan," Parrish said, "we'll need to leave as soon as it's dark. Bring the Escape—"

"I don't have it. I didn't want to leave it around where it might be spotted by police. I switched vehicles."

"Excellent," Parrish approved. "What do you have instead?"

"A Subaru Forester."

After a pause, Parrish said, "I know Quinn gave you the money for the purchase of the vehicles. Is it his sense of humor that results in these model names, or yours?"

"Quinn will tell you I have no sense of humor."

"Hmm. Neither vehicle has real off-road ability, but if that's needed, I suppose we'll acquire something else."

"If Kai needs to be seen by a doctor, you'll want to be near roads."

"If you want him to be seen by police, you mean."

"Hey!" Kai protested.

"I don't," Donovan said to him. "I just don't think that being killed by an infection will do you any good, either."

"It's not going to come to that," Parrish said. "Is the Forester here?"

"No. I didn't want to attract attention to this place with a lot of traffic. Bad enough that I had to drive up here and away last night."

Parrish approved of this as well. "We'll need it now, though. Bring it around to the front of the lodge."

Donovan nodded and left immediately. He did not ask to see Irene Kelly—knowing that his interest in her well-being would be of no help to her.

When he was a mile away from the lodge, and certain that he was not being observed by anyone, he took out a disposable cell phone.

He was not, by nature, an emotional man, but neither were the possible repercussions of what he was about to do lost on him. He quieted his mind, closing his eyes, breathing deep and slow.

He composed a text message addressed to Frank Harriman's personal cell phone:

Re: Irene

He pressed Send, then quickly composed and sent three more messages:

Third step down on beach stairs, underneath.
Jacaranda Street.
Previous destinations.

He cleared the phone's memory of the messages, broke it into pieces—crushing the SIM card—and hid the fragments in one of the compartments of the Forester.

He picked up the dark green parka he had chosen for Irene Kelly. If it was not too carefully searched—if no one opened seams or checked certain lining hems too closely—he could explain why he had placed certain items in its pockets. Ideally, there would not be any search. Everyone would be busy with other tasks.

He took another moment to slow thoughts that wanted to race, to remind himself to stay focused. But one part of his unruly mind insisted on noting a certain exhilaration. One he had not felt since the end of his last tour of duty.

THIRTY-EIGHT

I fed Violet and finished doing what I could to make her
more comfortable, talking to her, without any response on
her side, about exploring the possibility of getting some
of the adaptive technologies now available. I had seen wheel-
chairs that could be operated by blowing into a strawlike
device or by the movement of a person's tongue. I kept thinking that if I had been in her place, cut off from everyone but
Kai and a set of doctors I didn't like, I would have been yap-
ping away at first contact. Apparently, though, she was out of
the habit of social interaction or wasn't interested in what I
had to say. I gave up after a few minutes of the silent treatment
from her.

I was considering going back to my room when the door to
hers suddenly opened.

Parrish with the gun again, and he had someone with him,
but this time it wasn't Kai Loudon. I felt pure rage course
through me as I beheld Donovan Cotter for the first time since
he had placed me under Parrish's control.

I was on the verge of venting some of that anger when I saw
how much Parrish was enjoying it. Hell if I was going to satisfy
his puppet mastery.

"Hello, Donovan," I said, then hesitated. "That really is your name?"

"Yes. Hello, Irene."

"How very civil," Parrish said, choosing to be amused. "Especially for a man who was just searching her closet. Tie her up."

I felt panic set in.

"She needs to change into warmer clothes," Donovan said. "I was going to bring those items in here."

Parrish smiled. "We'll go to her room instead."

They took me there. I thought they would leave, but Parrish said, "Go ahead and change. We'll watch you do that."

The panic heightened. I decided not to strip past my underwear and just to put the longer underwear on over my panties and bra. It was humiliating even to strip to that extent in front of them, with Parrish making comments on my body and what he'd like to do to me all the while, and mocking Donovan for not taking advantage of my state of undress.

"I told you. I don't want or need an audience," he said.

Parrish told me to go back into Violet's room. Once we were there, he again ordered Donovan to tie me up.

"That will make it more difficult to put her into the vehicle. I don't want to carry her, do you?"

Parrish clearly didn't like being contradicted, but he said, "All right, just her hands, then."

Donovan moved toward me with a roll of duct tape. I decided I wasn't about to go along with that without a fight, gun or no gun. I used a move from Kenpo, avoiding his hold and getting in an initial blow—hitting Donovan's brow rather than the eye I was aiming for—when he quickly reacted. I wasn't close to being a match for his skills. He soon had me pinned to the floor and bound my wrists.

Parrish started laughing, so hard that he doubled over with a hacking cough.

Donovan turned his head away from him, and under the cover of that laughter whispered into my ear, "Don't attack. Wait." He then lifted me to my feet, far more gently than I had expected.

I was strongly tempted to ignore that advice, especially when Parrish tucked the gun into his waistband and sauntered within range of a kick. I watched him warily, all the time wondering if I was crazy to listen to a man who had drugged me, bound my hands, and was clearly a confederate of Parrish's to some degree. Violet was sure he was somehow being compelled to participate in Parrish's plans, but that wouldn't make me any less dead if those plans succeeded.

In the end what kept me from lashing out was Parrish himself. Looking into his eyes, I could see anticipation. He *wanted* me to give him an excuse.

My next thought was that he had never needed an excuse for anything he did before, so why hold back now?

Donovan.

The answer came to me with a certainty that surprised me. I had no doubt that Kai, whose unpleasant acquaintance I had made a few hours earlier, would have been egging Parrish on, providing an audience eager to see him inflict pain and humiliation on me.

As if to confirm my guess, Parrish glanced at Donovan, who had taken a step away from me, so that he was within view—and reach—but not threatening. It was as if Parrish wanted to impress him but was not quite sure how to do that. For his part, Donovan was standing still and calm, yet radiating power—it was as if nothing Parrish might do would disturb or intimidate him.

"Did Donovan happen to mention that he's my son?" Parrish asked.

I didn't answer.

Parrish smiled. "It's so ridiculous that you have two layers of underwear on now, you know. He's seen you completely naked. He undressed you. He watched while you took a shower. As did I."

I wasn't able to hide the fact that this news disturbed me.

"Yes," Donovan said calmly. "You had thrown up on yourself and Nick. You weren't in any condition to be left alone."

Matter-of-fact, not salacious.

Parrish frowned, but the frown quickly eased into another of his leering smiles. "He asked me to let him have you before I kill you."

Donovan didn't respond. I followed his lead.

Parrish chose a new tack. "Say good-bye to Violet. While she's doing that, Donovan, get her things."

Donovan didn't argue. He just walked into the other room.

I wasn't able to stay quiet. "What do you mean, 'Say good-bye to Violet'—what are you planning to do to her?"

"Why, nothing."

"Then why—"

"You ask too many questions. All you need to know is that we're leaving, Violet is staying."

"Without someone to care for her—"

"Enough!" he snapped.

I moved closer to the bed. Any further protestations I might make—that it was murder, that it was cruel—were unlikely to be seen as anything but points in favor of carrying out his plan. He thought nothing of murder. He enjoyed cruelty.

Hands bound, I could not touch her. I leaned over and said, "I'm sorry."

I am not. Go.

And then she baffled me with the next string of letters, not because I didn't know what they meant but because this one word had already nagged at my memory:

.--. .- .-. -.- .-

Parka.

"Why not let Donovan stay here and care for her?" I asked, stalling, hoping she'd further enlighten me.

No.

"No," Parrish said. "Although that may be what he'd really prefer. He's made a point of visiting her when he stops by." He called out, "Right, Donovan?"

Donovan either didn't hear or pretended not to.

"Do you have any idea what will happen to her if you just abandon her here?"

"You, my dear Ms. Kelly, have much more to worry about than what becomes of Violet Loudon. Besides, who said she'd be abandoned?"

I didn't find that at all reassuring.

Donovan returned carrying the duffel and—I was quick to notice—a dark green parka that looked expedition-worthy. Parrish held the gun on me as we went downstairs.

Donovan said, "We didn't think this through. She needs to have the parka on in the vehicle. We all need to wear our parkas and keep the hoods up—the hoods will make it harder for anyone in a passing car to identify us. And we're going to have to change the way she's bound," he said.

Not much later, I was carried outside by Donovan. My hands were bound in front of me, and after another struggle— no matter what advice he had to give me—my ankles were now bound, too.

Parrish had been all for taping my mouth shut, but Donovan had dismissed this idea, saying it could easily be noticed by others and be difficult to explain, and it would make it hard to feed me or give me water. "Irene," he said, "given your claustrophobia, do you see that it is smarter for you to stay silent? Otherwise we'll have to tape your mouth and put you down on the floorboards for a long ride." It was not hard to agree to be quiet.

It was dark outside, and cold, although I felt the chill air only on my face and hands. I was placed in the backseat of a green Subaru Forester. I was wearing the parka, the hood pulled up in a way that hid most of my face from anyone who might happen to look at the passengers in the SUV. Parrish was always very close to us. Donovan did not attempt any further communication with me.

Everyone in the car wore parkas, which was why the air-conditioning was cranked up full blast. It was still almost too warm. I noticed Donovan's parka was also dark green. Kai's and Parrish's were a light tan color, and of a higher quality. My parka felt a little lumpy, although of course I couldn't reach my hands into the pockets to discover what they held. My imagination supplied possibilities from hidden weapons to remote-controlled explosives (making me a human bomb) and, more reasonably, energy bars, lip balm, and perhaps a scarf or the gloves I'd found earlier. Depending on which way I leaned against the door or seat and how panicked I was feeling at any given moment, the guesses changed.

Kai was in the front passenger seat, his injured arm tucked inside his open jacket. At first he seemed to be having a hard time getting comfortable, but he soon fell asleep.

Donovan drove.

Parrish sat in the backseat, holding a gun on me, barking directions to Donovan.

After we drove away from what I thought might be the Running Springs area and were winding our way down to Interstate 15, I wondered if we might be on our way out of state. But Parrish's next instructions were to go north on 395.

We were headed toward his old hunting grounds, the southern Sierra Nevada. He had killed dozens of people and slain animals there as well. One of his favorite moments, he had once bragged to an interviewer, came when he watched a victim dig her own grave. He'd had many such moments to treasure.

Two facts about my situation disturbed me. First, he was letting me hear directions. Second, there was a shovel among the gear in the back.

Added together, it seemed likely that I was on my way to my own execution.

THIRTY-NINE

Frank Harriman was alone when the text messages arrived, for which he was grateful. Pete had been by earlier, promising to keep him informed of anything he could learn about the ongoing investigation into Irene's kidnapping. Rachel insisted that none of her cases were anywhere near as important to her as locating Irene, and Frank gladly accepted her offer to help him out. In her years working as a P.I. in Las Piernas, she had cultivated sources who would never talk to the police. That might be especially helpful when it came to the Moths.

Ben, Ethan, Jack, Lydia, and Guy had also offered their help. Irene's cousin Travis Maguire, who owned a helicopter company with Jack, was equally eager to be of assistance. Frank had thanked each of them and promised to be in touch.

"Start with some sleep," Rachel advised. "When's the last time you got any?"

He admitted that, between casework and Irene's abduction, he hadn't been asleep more than four hours in the last forty-eight. Sleep was something he deeply desired but found unthinkable. He told himself that poor judgment brought on by exhaustion wouldn't help anyone.

So they had left, and Frank had lain down, his thoughts troubled but so tired that he had no memory of anything after the moment the cat had curled up next to him, until five hours later, when the chiming of his phone awakened him.

He stared at the text messages for a long moment. He didn't recognize the sender's number, but he tried it. No answer, no voice mail. An attempt to reply by text returned an error message.

He did not give this cell number out to many people.

He was well aware that this could be a trap, that his number could have been tortured out of Irene. He told himself not to let his mind always go to the worst-case scenario.

He had also spent almost twenty-four hours feeling as if there was little or nothing he could do to prevent Irene from suffering and being killed by Parrish. He knew she was a survivor, had managed to escape Parrish before, but Frank had now reached a point at which he was desperate for anything that would increase the chances of finding her alive.

He dressed and put on his shoulder holster and his gun, grabbed his jacket, a flashlight, and some gloves, then called Jack.

"Come with me to the beach with the dogs, okay?" Frank said.

"Sure."

He stepped outside with Deke and Dunk, and found Jack waiting outside his own house. Jack owned a fortune in real estate in Las Piernas and several lucrative businesses as well, but anyone who didn't know him tended to see only the biker he had been—his jeans, T-shirt, and leather jacket might have just been seen as casual cool, but the shaved head, earring, and tattoos gave his look a different edge. He was one of Frank's closest friends.

Frank told Jack about the text messages as they walked to

the beach stairs at the end of the block. Had he been with Pete, his partner would have been spouting warnings and advice. Jack just nodded and said, "I'll take lookout duty."

The beach was all but empty on this chilly October evening. Jack took the dogs' leashes and stood at the top of the stairs, watching for anyone approaching from the street or the beach.

Frank went down the wooden stairs until he was just past the third one, then turned to face the stairs and knelt. Flashlight on, he looked carefully beneath the third step from the top. A casual observer would have missed the slight bump, a patch of green duct tape—green, to match the color of the stairs. He put on the gloves, then eased the tape off, all the while knowing that the lab was going to be pissed as hell at him anyway.

They'd have to get in line to chew him out.

There was a keyless entry fob attached to the tape.

He stood, and climbed back up to street level.

"Want to walk over to Jacaranda with me?"

"Sure. Besides, these two thought they were going to the beach, so that might work as a poor substitute."

"I need to stop by the house for a second, just to get something out of the car."

Frank retrieved a box that would hold the tape without further disturbing its surfaces and grabbed a couple of small evidence bags in case more awaited him on Jacaranda Street.

Jacaranda was two streets over. Frank looked for people sitting in cars or watching out of windows and saw no one. Beyond the barricades that marked the end of the street and the edge of the cliff, he could hear the surf, but otherwise the street was quiet. Halfway down the block, a vehicle he had seen before only on video was parked on the right side of the street.

Even before he pressed the unlock function on the remote, he knew it would light up the Ford Escape.

The plates didn't match the ones in the video, but that wasn't a surprise, either.

He made sure no one was standing near the vehicle before he actually pressed the button. He had even warned Jack that for all he knew the thing would explode, which only made Jack grin and say, "Who doesn't like to see stuff explode? Special effects companies live off this shit."

He hit the key, and all that happened was a friendly blinking of lights and a chirping call. They were standing too far away even to hear the doors unlock.

He looked around again, trying to see if anyone had come to a window or looked out at the street at the sound of the remote operating. He didn't see any movement.

"Why not let me go open it up?" Jack said. "My affairs are in order."

"No, wait here, and if I meet my Maker, the dogs are yours on the condition that you'll accept Cody as a part of the package."

"No deal."

Frank sighed. "Am I being an idiot? Yes, I am."

"Since you're taking questions, let me ask you—why don't you call people who have a bomb squad handy to test things out?"

"Because the minute I call them, I'm cut out. I'll have to wait until Pete can pry something out of somebody, and since he's my partner, people see that coming." He paused and looked at Jack. "Intellectually, I know I shouldn't. In my gut—"

"I understand. It's Irene."

"Right. So, watch this idiot allow himself to be manipulated by Nick Parrish—it's almost as fun as seeing shit explode."

"I may get to see both," Jack said, which surprised a laugh out of Frank.

He walked up to the Escape, used his flashlight to check

over the exterior and as much as he could see of the interior, then decided to open the passenger side door first.

He couldn't help but wonder if he had missed some sign of explosives, but nothing happened as the door opened. He looked more closely at the area under the dash—no sign of tampering. He moved to the driver's side, trying not to smear any prints that might be on the steering wheel or column. He took a deep breath and started the engine. No problem. He looked at the mileage, then turned on the GPS. Called up previous destinations and began taking notes. One of the locations, he noticed, was near where Parrish had escaped. But the most recent one was in the San Bernardino Mountains, not far from Running Springs.

He turned off the GPS, turned off the motor, and locked the doors. He looked the exterior over once again, then walked back to Jack.

"I'm going to see if Lydia and Guy will take care of the dogs and the cat."

"Hey, what I said before—you know I was just joking about Cody!"

"Of course I do. But I thought you might want to join me on a road trip."

"Where are we headed?"

"Running Springs, for starters."

"Sounds great."

As they made the turn onto their own street, Jack said, "I was thinking we should ask Ben and Ethan to bring Bingle and Altair. Take the Jeep."

Irene's car. Frank set the thought aside. "Good idea."

He made the calls, telling Ben, "If you don't want to have another encounter with Parrish, I won't blame you at all—"

"I'm coming with you," Ben said firmly. "And let's take my SUV. We've already got the dogs' equipment packed in it, it will

be roomier, and I'll bet I've had more sleep than you. I'll probably bring Bingle and Boolean. Altair only does human remains
detection. Bingle does SAR and HRD, and Bool can track her if
we just pre-scent him."

As they walked back home, Frank made lists of everything
they'd need to bring. Backpacking supplies, first aid supplies,
radios for communicating, weapons, lock picks—he wondered
if Rachel would let him borrow hers. Irene's toothbrush, pil-
lowcase, and her socks from the laundry basket—all items that
would help to pre-scent the bloodhound Bool. The lists went
on.

They were almost back to the house when Frank said, "What
if this is all a wild-goose chase?"

Jack shrugged. "If this is the only lead you've got, chase that
damned goose."

FORTY

The miles seemed endless. We wove our way on and off the main highway at Parrish's direction, taking smaller roads for long distances. Once out of the San Bernardino Mountains, we drove in the darkness over stretches of desolate country, surrounded on all sides by the Mojave Desert. The air was cold and the sky dark and star-filled. Under other circumstances, I would have found it a peaceful place, a place of renewal. Over those hours, it was a journey through hell.

Parrish eventually grew tired of taunting me with threats and simply barked out directions that sent us east and west and back again, as if the car were a sailboat that needed to tack to reach north. I had been able to determine that we were gradually headed north. We stopped for gas once, but only Donovan was allowed out of the car, and then only to fill the tank and clean the windshield. I tried the door anyway, which made Parrish laugh. "Childproof locks. Don't try anything else childish, or I'll shoot not only you but anyone who tries to come to your rescue."

Kai seemed able to sleep through anything.

At one point, when we were back on 395 but well away from the lights of even the smallest town, the SUV drifted across the center line and rattled over its bumps, then came back sharply into our own lane. A moment later, Donovan pulled off the highway. I didn't see a sign, but this was one of those rural exits that boasted no gas station or, for all I could see, any human habitation anywhere nearby.

"What the hell are you doing?" Parrish snapped.

"Unlike you, I haven't had a chance to sleep."

"There's a place not far from here where we'll be stopping for supplies. We can all sleep then."

"That's great, but I've only had about four hours of sleep in the last forty-eight, and I've hit a wall. Someone else is going to have to drive."

Kai, who had awakened when the car stopped, stretched and said, "I could do it."

Parrish stared at Donovan through narrowed eyes, then said, "I'll drive. Donovan will be back here, with Irene. Kai, I need you to take charge of my weapon. You must be on your guard."

Kai eagerly accepted this responsibility. The doors were unlocked. Donovan moved to the backseat, Parrish to the front. I considered trying to use that moment to escape into the darkness and rejected it—with my ankles bound, I would get no more than a few feet from the car, and Kai was clearly hoping I'd do something to justify making his assignment a brief one.

Parrish locked the doors and began to drive. Kai shifted his attention to Donovan.

I watched Donovan almost as carefully as Kai did, and noticed Parrish angling the rearview mirror so that he joined Donovan's audience. But almost as soon as Donovan had taken his place in the back, he closed his eyes. His breathing grew slow and rhythmic. I waited to see if he was faking it. If he was, he was convincing.

Parrish moved the mirror. Kai returned to staring at me the

way a six-year-old might stare at a batch of cooling cookies. I broke eye contact with him, and only then did I catch movement nearby. Donovan's left hand was on his knee, near the back of Kai's seat. His index finger was moving. His hand could not be seen by Parrish or Kai.

I stretched as much as I could within my bonds, movement that, as intended, kept Kai's eyes on me. Under the cover of rolling my head from side to side to as if I were getting the kinks out of my neck, I watched Donovan's finger tapping on his knee.

If I hadn't just spent hours honing my skills with Violet, I might have failed to recognize his use of Morse code.

... .-.. . . . .--. .. ..-. -.-- --- ..- -.-. .- -.

Sleep if you can.

Right. It was so relaxing being in a car with two serial killers and a kidnapper, I was going to go off into dreamland and let them take me wherever they wanted to go. I wasn't going to pay attention to where I was being taken or watch for any opportunity to escape before they took me there.

He could not be serious.

I watched Donovan more openly, without any need to feign my wariness of him. He stopped signaling me. His breathing slowed. I was nearly certain that he was truly asleep.

I looked out the window into the blackness of the desert and considered the other side of the question of sleep. I had spent most of the last twenty-four hours feeling terrified. I had done the physical work necessary for the care of Violet and Kai. I had engaged in two short, futile fights with Donovan. I was tired. I could feel the effect on my judgment and emotions.

If I did manage to escape, I would need to be as rested as possible to stay free from Parrish. I wasn't going to be able to change anything about where I was being taken. Knowing the general direction we were headed, I had little doubt that we'd end up in the Sierras, where Nick Parrish had spent plenty of time before he was arrested.

I wasn't sure that Donovan was an ally. I felt uneasy about the idea of sleeping while Kai pointed a gun at me.

But I wanted to be able to fight and run and do whatever else was required to survive, and I'd stand a better chance of doing all that if I conserved my energy now and rested. If I was too exhausted to think clearly, escape was even more unlikely.

Nick Parrish glanced at me in the rearview mirror.

I closed my eyes and leaned against the cold glass of the window. The last thing I remember telling myself before I fell asleep was that if Nick Parrish was watching me, it would be safer to stay awake.

FORTY-ONE

In the end, they had taken two vehicles, knowing that it might be necessary to split up for a while, and now, about an hour before dawn, their caravan had reached their destination—or near it, parked about fifty yards from the partially open front gate of what appeared to be a private camp. Signs posted at regular intervals along a tall iron fence warned that this was private property, "Keep Out." A large wooden sign at the gate carried more specific warnings about prosecution. "An unlocked gate and a no trespassing sign," Jack said. "I hardly know what to do with myself."

"Could have saved the time it took me to get the lock picks from Rachel."

"Never know—still might need them."

They got out of the Jeep Cherokee and walked back to where Ben and Ethan and the dogs—Bingle and Bool—waited in Ben's SUV.

Jack had made arrangements with Travis to be waiting with one of their Sikorskys at a nearby location. If Irene was here and needed medical attention, they'd be able to fly her to a hospital faster than they could ever make the trip down mountain roads. Travis had already called to say he had landed the helicopter at the field and was ready to help in any way he could.

This address, in an unincorporated area of the San Bernardino Mountains, was the only recent out-of-town destination Frank had found on the GPS in the Ford Escape.

Frank asked the others to wait in Ben's SUV, with instructions on whom to call at the first sign of trouble. At first all three refused to be left behind, but after a brief but intense argument, it was agreed that Jack would go with Frank while Ben and Ethan stayed back. At Ben's insistence, Frank called Ben's phone from his own and stayed connected to that call, using his wireless headset.

"You understand I'm not going to narrate every step I take?" Frank said.

"Yes, and I'm not going to distract you by constantly talking to you," Ben replied. "But we're not going to be able to see you and Jack out there in the dark, and if you're in trouble, I want to know right away."

Despite his sense of urgency, Frank waited and watched for several minutes before moving closer to the gate and the small house just inside it. The house was clearly a gatekeeper's or caretaker's lodge, painted in the dark hunter green color that must be sold by the tanker truckload to mountain camps.

He gave more than a moment's thought to a set of names engraved on a granite memorial in front of the Las Piernas Police Department, all murdered on the same date, all slain by a trap set by Parrish. Good friends, some of them.

He told himself this had all the earmarks of a similar trap. He didn't know who had sent the text messages. Parrish could have sent them himself. He considered, not for the first time, calling in the San Bernardino Sheriff's Department. It would be the smart thing to do. The right thing. But he knew the result would be calls made to Las Piernas and questions raised there and, in all likelihood, his own detention. He had friends in the San Berdoo office, but even if they responded immediately, it would take time for them to contact their bomb squad and get it up here.

He told himself this was foolishness that might end up getting him killed—and Jack, Ethan, and Ben along with him.

Then he thought of his wife spending even another ten minutes under Parrish's control.

He looked at Jack. His friend's facial features were barely visible in the darkness, but Frank felt as if Jack had read his thoughts. His eyes held a look of determination—and a hint of impatience.

Frank smiled. "You sure you don't want to wait here, Jack?" he said quietly. "If something happens to you, the whole economy of Las Piernas is going to be fucked."

"Then fuck Las Piernas," Jack said. "Let's go."

Frank turned his flashlight on and played it over the house and fence. He noted several cameras and a motion sensor for an alarm system. The cameras, although of a design that allowed them to move, were motionless. The motion sensor appeared to be disabled, but that, he knew, could be deceiving—an entirely different alarm system could be operating.

He took a deep breath and eased the gate farther open. It moved nearly silently. He listened for any sounds of approach, then slipped inside. Jack followed him through.

They waited.

There was a rustling in a nearby bush. Jack turned his own flashlight toward it, and they caught a glimpse of a rabbit fleeing through the undergrowth.

The gatehouse was empty, but a check of its garage revealed a van and a Lexus. Frank knew both plate numbers—everyone in the Las Piernas Police Department had been hoping to find Kai Loudon's van. And he had talked about the Lexus with Quinn Moore very recently.

He touched the hoods of both cars. Both were cold.

"Cabins or main lodge?" Jack whispered.

"Lodge, then cabins, but keep an eye out for an ambush."

They reached the lodge without incident and crossed its wide, covered porch. Jack tried the front door before Frank could stop him—it was unlocked. They stood together just outside the open doorway, playing their flashlights around the large room.

"Hang on a sec," Jack said in a low voice. He moved to the side of the porch and stacked a couple of metal outdoor chairs together, then told Frank to stand back.

"What are you doing?"

"Maybe step off the porch a few feet."

"What are you doing?" Frank asked again, more warily.

"Just a little test."

Frank stepped off the porch and watched as Jack picked up the chairs and threw them over the threshold. They landed with a loud clatter.

"Are you okay?" Ben asked over the headset.

"Fine," Frank said. "That was just the sound of Jack improvising."

Jack looked back at him with a grin.

"So much for sneaking in," Frank said to him.

Jack shrugged. "Two things. We can step in that far without getting blown up, and we can stop whispering."

"Shit yes, we certainly can, because you might as well have

set off a fucking fire alarm." Frank shoved the tangle of chairs aside and stepped into the room.

Jack gave him a look of mock dismay. "You brought me along to provide subtlety?"

"Hilarious. Jesus, Jack. If you don't mind, I'd like the Cirque du Soleil SWAT team to let me take it from here."

"Don't mock—I have my uses."

They searched the lower floor of the lodge, turning on lights as they went quickly from room to room. It was a task Frank would not usually have attempted without backup. Despite the quiet following their grand entrance, Frank could not shake the sensation that they were not alone in the building.

However differently he would have approached entering the building, he trusted Jack and knew him to be a good man to have at his side in a fight. Jack had gained his fighting experience the hard way. In his adventurous—some would say misspent—youth, he had survived any number of down and dirty street fights. So he wasn't going to pass out or run off at the first sign of trouble. They were both armed, and although Jack favored knives—he could throw a knife with deadly accuracy— he was also an excellent shot. He kept in practice, had steady aim, and best of all, could keep a cool head.

The lodge was designed so that it could have operated as a small inn even without the cabins. Several of the rooms were connected by shared bathrooms, which meant that someone could easily move unseen into a room they had already searched and wait for an opportunity to ambush them. Because of that, despite Jack's "test," once they were past the front entrance, they seldom spoke.

The floors were wooden, although there was carpet in the hallways. Once they were off the carpet, it was hard to move quietly. Inevitably, boards in older buildings squeaked.

Frank's flashlight had a strobe setting on it, and as they

entered each room, he used that feature, which would make it harder for any attacker to see them.

One of the first rooms they came across was a small office. Paperwork lying atop a desk was addressed to Quinn Moore.

"So it's his place?" Jack asked.

"Looks like it."

"Could you be in trouble for breaking and entering here?"

"Not as much trouble as I think he's going to be in."

They entered a commercial-sized kitchen, where they discovered a set of concrete stairs leading to what appeared to be a cellar, and as they hurried down them, Frank found himself wondering if he would find Irene held captive there. The heavy door was unlocked. As he cautiously pushed it open, he thought of Kai Loudon's basement and felt a stab of fear about what an unlocked door might mean.

Frank recognized a familiar scent—gun oil. His hand located a wall switch, and the room flooded with light. Even recognizing that scent, he was unprepared for what met his eyes.

"Holy shit," Jack said.

"Everything okay?" Ben asked.

"We've found an arsenal," Frank said.

The room, which had probably once served as storage for food, wine, or kitchen supplies, was now lined with cases holding neat rows of weapons—mostly knives but also handguns, rifles, and assault weapons. A closer look showed additional stores of ammunition and explosives.

"Why leave weapons behind?" Jack asked.

"I don't know," Frank said. "Maybe they wanted flexibility, and these guns and explosives just didn't suit their plans. Maybe these all belong to Quinn Moore and he didn't want to share." He took a closer look at the explosives and shook his head. "They're lucky they didn't blast themselves into the middle of next week."

Ben's voice came over the headset. "Maybe those are supplies for his army of Moths."

"Maybe," Frank said, relaying Ben's guess to Jack.

"Possible," Jack said.

"Let's do a quick barricade of the stairway and then get on
upstairs."

Jack worked with him to block the door into the armory
with some heavy sacks of flour and a table and chairs.

At the top of the stairs leading to the second floor, Frank
saw bloodstains on the hallway carpet. He closed his eyes and
tried to slow his breathing, to stay focused. *Don't assume it's
her blood. Approach it like any other scene. Try to figure out
what happened here.*

He wanted to search the other rooms as soon as possible, so
it was going to be a quick study in any case. He could see bullet holes in the walls and clear signs of bullet damage to a small
wooden table. He did no more than glance at them—he knew
that touching the bullet holes would completely screw things
up for the San Bernardino evidence team—but it appeared that
weapons of differing calibers had been used. And the patterns
of stains and damage seemed to indicate that two individuals
had been hit. The stains were just outside two rooms, a bathroom at the other end of the hall and a bedroom.

Quinn Moore's injuries came to mind. It wouldn't be hard
to compare DNA here to the DNA found on his bloodstained
clothing. Frank made a mental note to mention Celox to the
SBSD lab.

Three of the rooms nearest the gunfight had recently been
slept in—unlike in other rooms they checked, there was bed-
ding on the mattresses in these rooms. One of the pillowcases
had bloodstains on it.

Next they came across the room that housed the security
system's monitors. All the cameras and alarms were off.

"That doesn't make any sense," Jack said.

"It does if you're expecting company. Company you want to give access to or company you want to trap."

They opened room after room with no sign of Irene, their search speeding up until they came to a set of rooms with dead-bolt locks and exchanged a glance as they tried the first one. It opened easily and the room was empty, but it was clear some-one had slept in the bed.

Frank leaned close to the pillow, saw a strand of long black hair on it. Took a deep breath. Drew in her scent.

"Ben," he said into his headset, in a voice that was not quite his own, "bring the dogs in, will you?"

"Sure. Are you all right?"

Before he could reply, Jack signaled for quiet, laying a finger along his lips and nodding his head toward an adjoining room.

Frank looked a question.

Jack drew closer to him and said, in barely more than a whis-per, "Thought I heard footsteps."

"Ben, wait, stay put for now," Frank murmured into the headset.

He listened and heard a faint noise. He motioned to Jack to stay back, drew his gun, and opened the door. It was a bath-room. He checked the shower, which was empty, then stood as still as possible and listened at the connecting door.

He heard it again, an odd sound. But not footsteps.

He turned out the bathroom light and waited in the darkness for a long moment. He had the strobing flashlight ready to go, held out to his left. He had checked the door, noting that the hinges were on the other side, and positioned himself to take advantage of what cover the door itself could offer him, weapon ready. He took a breath, let it out, and then opened the door quickly, strobe light on, moving fast to avoid making a target of himself. But there was plenty of light in the room, coming from an open door to the hallway. Enough light to allow him to see that no one was standing anywhere in the room, although it was not empty.

A hospital bed held a frail woman. Her mouth and neck and chest were covered in blood, but her eyes were wide open. She was staring at him.

"Frank?" Jack said softly from behind him.

Frank hurried over to the bed. "Violet Loudon?" he asked, and she blinked at him.

It took only seconds for him to register that she was blinking in Morse code.

Hurry. He escapes. I am not hurt. Bit his nose.

"You heard footsteps!" Frank said to Jack. "She sure as hell didn't make them or open that door!"

They ran into the hallway, but in the next moment they heard a door slam downstairs.

"Ben," Frank said, "watch out—he may be coming your way."

"Who?"

"I don't know yet. A male with damage to his nose. He just ran out of here."

The man never ran past Ben and Ethan. Jack stayed behind to guard Violet while Frank followed a trail of blood drops leading from a back door toward the trees. The sky was lightening, but he could see no sign of the man. He was just about to call Ben to bring the dogs when he heard a motorcycle starting up. He ran toward the sound but had to move carefully through the trees and over the uneven ground.

He soon reached a narrow dirt maintenance road and heard the bike retreating over it but didn't catch so much as a glimpse of the rider.

FORTY-TWO

B en," Frank said as he moved back toward the lodge, "I'm thinking maybe it's time to give San Bernardino a call. By the time they get someone over here, Jack and I can be at the airfield. I'd prefer to have you come along with us, but I don't want to leave Violet Loudon here alone."

"Agreed. Ethan's offered to stay here. He's been talking to Jack on his phone."

"Good."

"I think you should spend a few minutes with her first, though. Jack's been getting some information from her that you may find useful."

"He knows Morse code?"

"He said he learned it as a Cub Scout but at this point can't remember anything beyond 'SOS.'"

"Jack was a Cub Scout?"

"Yeah, Ethan's already giving him endless shit. Anyway, Jack's pulled up some site about Morse code on his phone. He's been painstakingly writing out the pattern she blinks and then translating it."

"Okay, I'll be up there in a minute, but we need to get the

sheriff onto trying to find the guy on that bike. And the SBSD has the manpower to really search these grounds."

"Will do. Cliff Garnett?"

Ben and Frank had both worked on cases with Garrnett, an old friend and homicide detective with the San Bernardino County Sheriff's Department.

"Cliff would be ideal, at least as a starting contact point—but he's not likely to get the case, since we all know one another."

When Frank reached the upstairs room again, Jack had cleaned off most of the blood on Violet's face, which would probably piss off some lab guy, but there was, after all, lots more on her neck and clothing. Jack was giving her water when Frank walked in.

"Violet says the noseless one has been by here before. She said his name is Roderick Beignet, and he lives in Las Piernas. She described him to me. Heavyset, reddish brown hair, blue eyes. Not young—maybe about sixty."

"That helps a lot. I'll need to make some phone calls to Las Piernas once we're on our way." Frank turned to Violet. "Your doctors led us to believe you could not communicate."

She smiled slightly, but it was Jack who answered for her. "We talked about that. She learned Morse code from Donovan."

"Donovan?"

"One of Parrish's sons. I got this from her in an abbreviated form, but if I made it out right, she said Kai, Quinn, and Donovan are half brothers. Parrish, Kai, and Donovan took Irene from here. Donovan told her that if that ever happened, Parrish would probably take them to the Sierras, not the old location but near there. Parrish is comfortable there."

"Who is this guy Donovan? Other than one of the half brothers?"

They both looked to Violet.

Pilot. Forced to help Nick.

"Forced how?"

Don't know.

"What was Roderick doing here?"

Said Nick sent. He heard you come in. Leaned over me. I bit.

Ethan arrived and introduced himself to Violet.

"You know Morse code?" Frank asked.

"Um . . . no. I mean, just SOS. Dash-dash-dash, dot-dot-dot, dash-dash-dash. Right?"

"That's O-S-O," Jack said, rolling his eyes. "So unless you want a Spanish-speaking bear to come to your rescue, don't ever use that one if your boat is sinking."

Ethan looked at Violet, smiled charmingly, and said, "Will you teach me?"

"Ethan . . . ," Jack said.

But she had already blinked a response.

"Was that yes?"

"Yes," Frank said.

"Christ," Jack said.

"He's a quick study," Frank said.

"Maybe, but we shouldn't leave them here alone," Jack said. "Who knows how many more of his Moths Parrish has hanging around?"

"Just go," Ethan said. "Frank has to get out of here. Cliff told Ben they'd have a patrol car here soon, and God knows how many other cops are going to be here right after that. If Frank is sitting here when they arrive, this is all going to go to sh—" He looked at Violet and said, "Sorry. It's all going to be wrecked."

Violet blinked, and Frank and Jack exchanged a glance.

"What did she say?"

"Something worse than you were going to say," Frank answered. "You have your gun?"

"Yes, and Ben mentioned that I was armed but would not be shooting any deputies today."

"Did Ben mention that Frank and I were here?"

"No, but Cliff is suspicious. Wanted Ben to wait around, but Ben told him he was already gone and wasn't coming back—so you two get the hell out. Find Irene. I've got to learn Morse code."

Frank could see what Ethan wasn't saying, knew that he wanted to be going with them but also recognized that, of the four of them, he was the best choice to stay behind.

"Thanks, Ethan. We'll try to meet up a little later. You want us to leave a dog here with you?"

"No, but Ben wants to drive his car to the Sikorsky because he's doesn't want to shift all the dog stuff to the other car. So leave your keys, if you don't mind."

Frank called Pete as they made their way to the airfield. Pete let him know he wasn't happy with him for not telling him about the text message, not calling in the bomb squad when he found the Ford Escape on Jacaranda Street, not reporting finding the vehicle immediately, borrowing lock picks from his wife (Rachel had insisted that Frank not tell her any details so that she wouldn't have to lie to Pete), leaving his partner of many years behind in Las Piernas, and half a dozen other aspects of the situation—all before Frank told him about anything that had happened once they reached Quinn Moore's mountain lodge.

"Pete," Frank said when his partner finally drew a breath. "Listen up. You can help me, or you can bitch about my doing my level best not to get the captain as pissed off at you as he will be with me."

"You think I give a flying fuck about that?"

"Not for a minute. But I'm not going to ask you to sink your career along with mine."

Pete fell silent. It was an unhappy silence, but Frank took advantage of it and told him about the mysterious Donovan, assuming the man had told Violet his real name. He told him about Quinn's and Donovan's family ties to Kai and Parrish. "There's someone else—he may be headed to Las Piernas right now. His name is Roderick Beignet." He gave Pete the description and told him about the attack on Violet. "Vince and Reed need to know all of this, of course."

"Talk about people who are going to be pissed off at you . . ."

"Like you, they're friends," Frank said. "I hope they'll forgive me for it. Thanks, Pete." He said good-bye before his partner could start a second tirade.

They were within sight of the helicopter when Frank got a text message from Ethan.

All OK. SBSD just arrived.

Then he texted a line of Morse code that spelled out "Tell Jack I said hi."

"Sometimes that kid scares the shit out of me," Jack said.

FORTY-THREE

Ten. Nine. Eight . . ."

Parrish was standing outside the bathroom door, counting down the time I had left in the two minutes of privacy allotted to me—one hundred and twenty seconds of a small degree of freedom.

I had awoken as the SUV stopped before a freestanding cinder-block building with a corrugated tin roof. Parrish pressed a remote, and a metal door rolled up. We drove into the building, he pressed the remote again and shut off the engine.

The men got out of the car but left the doors open. Donovan walked straight back to the bathroom, not doing anything to help me but not asking anyone's permission to move around as he pleased. Marking his territory first?

The others followed suit. Next, Parrish ordered Donovan to bring me to the bathroom. He picked me up as if I weighed nothing, which is far from the case. Although running has kept me lean, I'm five seven in my bare feet. He set me on my feet and pulled out a knife.

"What are you doing?" Parrish asked angrily.

"I'm not going to carry her. There's more tape. I've only got one back."

Not that *heavy,* I thought.

"She's not that heavy," Parrish said, instantly proving he could still unsettle me with no more than a few words.

"You're in no shape to carry her, and neither is Kai," Donovan said. He bent and sliced through the tape that bound my ankles. He straightened. "I'm probably going to end up carrying everything anyway, so I'm not going to risk injury now."

Parrish watched him move the knife toward my hands. "You are not going to free her hands!"

Donovan looked at me. There was something so powerful, so compelling in his gaze—for the first time, I felt frightened by him. I found myself struggling to name that something even as I felt it hit me like a blow.

It was not as if he cast a spell. I would have laughed at an attempt to cast a spell.

He did not hypnotize me. Hypnotism seemed a very weak thing next to this.

It was akin to command but not that, even though it demanded obedience and promised consequences for disobedience. It was sharp and cold and said, in no uncertain terms, that any ideas I cherished about myself mattered not a whit to him, that in this particular moment, all that was true was what he was about to say to me, and whether I liked it or not was utterly immaterial. Giving him my undivided attention seemed all that allowed me to breathe.

My mouth went dry.

I felt sure he knew that, knew my heart rate had quickened, knew I had broken out in a cold sweat. Felt sure that no condition or emotion of mine was unknown to him.

When he spoke, he did not raise his voice. He said, calmly and matter-of-factly, "If you use your hands to attack any of us or try to escape, I'll cut them off. Then I'll bandage your wrists so that you will live long enough to experience things that will make you think losing your hands wasn't so bad—compared to what followed." He paused. "So, Irene, are you going to leave here with your hands attached to your wrists?"

I could not breathe, let alone speak. I nodded.

I felt faint as I watched the blade move toward my hands, arcing precisely and quickly to slice the tape between my wrists. I did not move.

He sheathed the knife and took me gently by the arm. He began to guide me toward the back of the building. I went as easily as if he had me on a leash. We passed Parrish, who seemed stunned, as did Kai. I couldn't blame them.

When we were out of earshot of either of them, Donovan said softly, "Are you okay?"

Startled, I looked back up at him. The icy look was gone. The man who had intervened at the café, the man who had tapped out a little reassuring message to me was back. But who the hell was he?

"You did well," he added. "Keep acting afraid of me."

That wasn't going to be a problem.

Parrish seemed to snap out of whatever daze he was in and told me I had exactly two minutes to use the bathroom before he would come in and force me out of it. Not surprisingly, to someone who was thinking *At least I still have my hands,* that threat wasn't as powerful as he might have hoped it would be.

Even with the time limit, I had a chance to wash my face and hands and spend glorious seconds without Parrish or his spawn sharing the same four walls. Maybe not enough time to completely center myself but enough to get rid of the worst of my shakiness.

I made a quick search of my pockets, in case I didn't get a chance to look through them again. Energy bars, the winter gloves that had been in the duffel. *Cheer up! You're not a human bomb!*

There was no mirror on the bathroom wall, for which I felt grateful. If you had asked me just weeks before if I would have thought of a small bathroom in an industrial building in the Mojave as my idea of a slice of heaven . . .

Well, it's not the past, it's now. Take what you have. I knew I also had to stop thinking about all the horrific things Parrish might do in the future, had to stop wishing that what had happened hadn't. It happened. I slowed my breathing, calmly opened the bathroom door, and walked out when Parrish was still on "five." That was clearly a letdown for him, which made it easier for me to keep my head up.

There was no kitchen per se, but near the back wall was a long folding table surrounded by metal folding chairs and a metal counter that held a small refrigerator. Ian told me to sit at the table and opened the refrigerator, which was stocked with water bottles and ham and cheese sandwiches. I ate and drank what was given to me without protest. No one addressed any remarks to me or discussed any plans, which aided my efforts to calm down.

The meal was mostly silent. Kai had stretched his legs out on the one empty chair at the table, until Donovan raised an eyebrow at him. He then put both feet on the floor.

Parrish kept looking at Donovan in a considering way, as if gauging whether he was an asset or a threat.

Kai also appeared interested in Donovan, although the interest seemed different, almost wistful. Was he longing for a big brother?

What, I wondered, had Kai's childhood been like? For all I knew, he had met some of his half siblings before now. I doubted it, though. He struck me as a loner, but I might have been mistaking his aloofness toward me for a general policy. I thought of my conversations with his neighbors and decided that the bonhomie edition of Kai Loudon did not exist. He had been persuasive with his mother's health care providers but did not seem to have any close friends or go out of his way to seek the society of others. Violet's paralysis made the perfect shield.

Was there ongoing contact with Parrish's other children, if any? If any. How many half siblings were there? Were there daughters as well as sons?

I thought of Marilyn Foster and Cade Morrissey, and wondered how many women might have put their children by Parrish up for adoption, felt ashamed of the connection to him. Or believed it was in the children's best interest to be hidden from their father or left unaware of their connection to him.

At the time of Parrish's first arrest for murder, there had been shocked and disbelieving protests by people who had worked with him or lived near him, saying he was a quiet and charming man. Perhaps he had used some of that charm on women like Violet.

I wondered why he hadn't been sued for child support. Perhaps he had been. It seemed more likely that he would have conned these women, given them phony information about himself, kept most of his encounters short and superficial. I thought of the things Marilyn's friends had said about that evening in the park—perhaps he chose vulnerable women, domineered them during brief relationships, then made them so afraid of him it was unlikely they would protest or do anything to draw his attention back to them once he was gone.

My previous experience with Parrish had eventually led me to take up a grim study, an effort to understand more about serial killers. I did so in part, I suppose, to try to understand why he had chosen me to play a role in his plans but mostly to know my enemy. So the idea of family links between pathologically violent men was not difficult for me accept.

Over the past twenty years, neuroscientists, geneticists, and others had been discovering more about the biology of violent behavior. Imaging systems were being used to study the brains of violent individuals and had determined that, in at least some cases, there were physical differences in the way their brains worked. Magnetic resonance imaging studies of the brains of violent individuals taken while they were viewing images of violence indicated areas of their brains were active that were not active in nonviolent individuals viewing the same images. Discoveries had been made of genetic links to high-risk behaviors. In recent years, scientists had been studying the role of variants of the MAOA or "warrior gene" in antisocial and violent behavior, especially when severe childhood abuse was also a factor. Oddly, a variant of that gene might even be a predictor for credit card debt. I'd put that tidbit to use in a consumer economics story last year.

Other factors played their own roles in violent behavior, of course, and these studies did not imply that every child of someone who killed was destined to be a killer. There was a great deal of work yet to be done before the biology of violence could be thoroughly understood.

Kai's neighbor had hinted that Kai's stepfather abused him. I looked again at Donovan, wondering what his family history had been. I wasn't sure what to believe of what he had told me at the Fireside.

So here I was at the family dinner table, such as it was. It occurred to me that Donovan's display of dominance had not only allowed me to move around without my hands and ankles taped but had probably allowed me to use the restroom with the door closed. It might also be why I was eating at the table, treated not as an object but as an individual during that meal. Donovan was distracting the others from me though not overtly.

"What do you want to do about sleeping shifts?" he asked Parrish.

Parrish puffed up a little with this deference. He checked his watch. "It's ten o'clock now. I want to be on the road again at two. Kai will stand guard."

No one raised an objection. Donovan again took on the role of leading me, holding my upper arm and guiding me to an area where there were five cots. He took me to the one closest to the wall and told me to lie down, that Kai would not hesitate to shoot me if I moved from the cot. He then lay down on the cot next to mine, facing away from me.

Parrish laughed as he took the next one over and said, "Yes, Irene, you'll soon be very busy, so rest up."

Whether Donovan's positioning was protective or possessive, I could not tell. I did not fall asleep as quickly as I had in the SUV. My last waking moments were spent wondering why there were five cots and five chairs at the table. I remembered that Violet had said Quinn Moore was one of the half siblings. I had no idea why he was missing, but I felt a flicker of hope. Maybe he was ratting out his "family." Then again, maybe they had killed him. If nothing else, the extra chair and cot must mean they were shorthanded now. I was outnumbered only three to one instead of an obviously planned-for four to one.

I would have felt better with a different lineup on the opposing team.

I woke with something cold and hard pressing painfully against my forehead and opened my eyes to see Kai Loudon staring down at me. He pushed a little harder, until I thought he might intend to kill me just by driving his gun barrel into my skull.

He smiled. "Wake up, you fucking bitch."

FORTY-FOUR

Rachel had taught me a set of moves that I probably could have executed before he executed me. Even lying flat on my back, I could have disarmed him, especially since he apparently didn't think I was much of a threat. He was right-handed—his wounded arm would make him even more vulnerable. I could make him feel intense pain and possibly disable him enough to keep him from coming after me if I made a run for it.

Which still left two other assholes to deal with. And the run-for-it idea had a major drawback—even if I somehow managed to get out of the building, there was nothing close by that would offer cover or a haven. Recapture seemed inevitable, and the follow-up might include removal of my hands, which would make everything else Rachel had taught me a little more difficult to do.

I decided to save my energy for a later fight, and in the meantime encourage his idea that I was incapable of self-defense. So far, all he had ordered me to do was wake up, and I had definitely obeyed.

————

I wondered, in those seconds of looking into Kai's eyes and seeing his desire to pull the trigger, if it might not be worth it to go ahead and resist while I could still breathe.

"Let's go, Kai," a voice said. To my surprise, it was Parrish's.

Kai's smile grew, and he eased up on the pressure, then stood.

"How's the arm?" Donovan asked, and Kai finally looked away from me.

"Better. Still hurts, though."

"I'm sure it does."

"Kai," Parrish said with impatience, "help me with the car. Donovan, tape her hands and feet again."

"Do you need to use the restroom?" Donovan asked me.

"Yes," I said.

He escorted me, as before, although I didn't need to lean on him this time, my circulation having recovered. When we were close to the bathroom, I whispered, "Why are you helping them?"

"Don't take too long," he said and stepped away from me.

When I came out, Parrish was standing next to Donovan, who was listening to someone on the phone. "That's enough for now," Parrish said, taking the phone away. Parrish was silent as he walked to the far end of the building, then spoke in a low, angry voice into the phone. I couldn't make out what he was saying. If Donovan had any reaction to the call, I couldn't see it.

Not much later, I was in the backseat with Parrish again at my side, my hands and feet bound, although this time, warm gloves had been placed on my hands. The oddity of this bit of care made me wonder if they were designed to keep my hands warm or to keep me from leaving fingerprints somewhere.

Donovan drove. Kai, in the front passenger seat again, had fallen asleep even before we began our ascent into the mountains.

Parrish, I had noticed, looked tired, as if he hadn't slept well. Donovan must have noticed this, too.

"I think I slept better in the car than on that damned cot," Donovan said.

Parrish laughed. "They were pieces of shit, weren't they? I'll have a talk with the person who bought them."

"Didn't do a bad job of supplying the place otherwise, though," Donovan said.

"No," Parrish admitted. "But the main purpose was to have a safe place to rest."

"I wish you had let me set it up. I don't like so many people being able to talk about where you've been or where you might be next."

"Don't worry, Donovan. I have an excellent ability to determine who is and isn't truly loyal to me."

"Right. Like Quinn Moore."

Parrish shot a glance at me, then frowned. "I really would prefer, Son, that you not toss names around quite so freely."

"As if she's going to live to tell anybody."

I moved my head so that all any of them could see was the back of my parka. I fantasized about getting that cell phone away from Parrish at some point, but this seemed so unlikely, I began to ask myself why I bothered dreaming that I was going to escape. I stared out the window, struggling against despair, thinking of people I wished I could see one more time. *You are alive. Stay focused, stay alive.*

"All the same," Parrish insisted, "I require more discretion from you."

"Okay, I hear what you're saying."

"I wonder if you do," Parrish said.

"Of course I do. You really don't think any of your children are stupid, do you?"

"Stupid? No. Disloyal? Well, you've answered that one already."

Donovan continued to puzzle me. What was real, and what was manipulation? What was a show to gain my compliance, what was a show for Parrish and Kai? Violet had said they had a hold over him. At the time, I had still been shaking off the effects of being drugged—by him.

My conversation with Donovan at the Fireside came back to me. What if he had told me the truth even as he drugged me? I tried to focus my mind, recall the details. He had unknowingly fathered a daughter whose existence had been hidden from him by his ex-wife. The ex-wife had told another man that the child was his. The ex-wife had died, and eventually, it had been proved that Donovan was the child's biological father. From there, things were hazy, but I did recall that he had said this was a missing person case, that his daughter had disappeared, along with her grandmother.

So if Parrish and his Moths had somehow taken the child and grandmother . . . would Donovan care enough about them to involve himself in a number of crimes—aiding and abetting Parrish, kidnapping me, making himself an accessory to murder, to name a few—for a child he had never met and an ex-mother-in-law?

I thought about Quinn Moore. There was no question of his involvement now, and the more I considered that, the easier certain aspects of Parrish's escape and ability to remain hidden were to figure out. Primarily, Quinn could bring money and other resources into the picture. And he owned the properties on which the bodies of Kai's victims had been found.

I found myself suddenly sitting upright then. Kai had buried his victims in his own backyard. The frozen victims had not shown the level of decay that would have been evident in remains that had spent even a short period of time in the ground. Were those frozen victims Quinn Moore's?

Parrish noticed my change in posture and began talking about his elaborate plans for torturing me. He was sorry, he said, that they would be without electricity, because there were a number of ways he wanted to use it on me. Kai gleefully pointed out that a car battery would work just fine.

This discussion was interrupted when Donovan asked, "Do you want me to take the usual roads from here? Or do you have a special route in mind?"

Parrish had a special route, of course.

"Quinn knows where we're headed," Donovan said, apparently willing to break Parrish's rule again. "I'm concerned about that."

"Quinn thinks he knows where we're headed," Parrish said. "He does not. Besides, I doubt he'll be so foolish as to cooperate with the police. If he does, neither he nor they will be pleased with the outcome."

As I watched out the window, we drove from areas of dry scrub into forest. We were on narrow, unmaintained, and often muddy dirt roads that twisted and turned in single lanes, and if nothing else, I had to admire Donovan's driving skills—I don't think I would have tackled most of those roads in the dark. The unavoidable jolting bothered Kai and Parrish more than it did me, and I took secret pleasure in that.

The trees were taking misty shape in gray light. Twilight.

I thought of a friend who was an amateur astronomer, who'd told me that, although most people did not think of this time of day as twilight, associating that term only with the end of a day, twilight was also the time before dawn, a period of incomplete darkness.

The sky lightened, and above and around me and within me, the universe continued to expand.

Nick Parrish did not know me.

I was not the person Nick Parrish had known the last time I had been in his power. I was not the person I had been when I first learned of his escape.

Like the rest of the universe, I had changed. So had he.

If Donovan was my ally and not my enemy, we actually had a good chance of defeating my two other captors.

I wasn't sure he was my ally, though. The fact that he was helping them take me into the wilderness with them didn't make it seem likely that I mattered to him, and if I was the price for his child's life—however little he'd had to do with that life—I could not bring myself to blame him for making the trade.

The SUV came to a halt.

"All right, let's get going," Parrish said.

"I'll help you unload, hide the car, then meet you there," Donovan said.

"What the fuck?" Kai said, raising the gun and pointing it at Donovan. "Dad told you to get going."

Behaving as if Kai wasn't sitting next to him, let alone aiming a weapon at him, Donovan turned toward Parrish and said, "I know you planned for Quinn to take care of this, but he's not going to come up here. There's no way in hell he can make it, even if he wants to rejoin you, and you know it. If we leave a car here, we might as well light off a fireworks display announcing where you are."

"No one can trace this vehicle to me."

"If Quinn keeps his mouth shut."

Parrish opened his mouth to protest, then shut it, frowning. He shook his head. "You may be right. But as I'm sure you're also aware, you are needed to carry additional supplies. I don't think I really want to give you the chance to drive off and tell the police where we are."

"You know why I won't do that."

"Really? Do I?"

"Of course you do."

Parrish studied him for a long moment.

Kai said, "I can get rid of the car."

"You, who have no outdoor experience, are going to hike back several miles off trail?" Donovan asked. "Injured?"

"While I wish it weren't so, Kai," Parrish said, "he has a point."

Kai looked angry but said nothing more.

"All you have to do is stay hidden until I can reach you. You've already got more than enough supplies there to be comfortable. You can catch up on your sleep. It won't take me long."

"How long?"

"Depends on how far I have to go to find a place to hide the vehicle, but I don't think it will be more than five hours."

"Five hours!"

"Think. They'll be searching by air. They know you've been active in these mountains before. You want me to leave this car anywhere near you?"

Parrish brooded. The rest of us stayed silent. I would have loved to have added invisibility to my attributes, especially when Parrish's brooding suddenly shifted its focus to me.

"I have some plans for Irene, so I suppose I can make a start on those. If you aren't back in five hours, don't expect to find us at the cave. I don't think I'll just sit there waiting for you to show up with the police."

"If I thought it would do any good to argue with you that the last thing I want right now is to be anywhere near law enforcement, I'd sit here for another twenty minutes to do it. As it is, every minute we're here is another minute when the sun gets farther up in the sky, which will make it easier for this SUV to be spotted on a road that is supposed to be open only to the Forest Service."

The argument seemed to work. Donovan helped me get out of the backseat and cut the tape on my ankles.

The air was cold. I was glad for the parka. I could hear water flowing nearby, a small stream, judging by the sound of it.

The forest carried that rich scent that comes only with autumn, the sharp crispness of pine that had filled the air for the few hours of our drive combined with damp, dark earth, fallen leaves, and decay.

Donovan went to the back of the SUV and unloaded a few things—the shovel and two light packs. Kai took charge of the shovel, a folding type used by campers, which he managed to do only by holstering his gun. He seemed confused and over-whelmed. Parrish took out another gun and held it on me while Donovan helped Kai. He took Kai's parka off and removed his injured arm from its sling, then helped him don the parka again, carefully guiding the injured arm into the parka's sleeve. Dono-van was gentle, but Kai was clearly cold and in pain while this went on. Donovan picked up one of the day packs, adjusting its straps and belt to better fit it over the parka, then arranged Kai's arm in the sling again. He fitted the shovel into the pack as well, trying to center its weight.

Next he helped Parrish to don the other pack, again adjust-ing the straps. Parrish grew irritable as we stood there in the cold and snapped at Donovan to stop fussing over him. Dono-van asked him when he had last carried anything on his back. Parrish stopped objecting and allowed him to ensure that the shoulder harness, sternum strap, and hip belt rested where they should.

Finally, Donovan stood before me. I had thought I was fearful before, but now I realized there were other levels of panic I could achieve. The notion of being left with Parrish and Kai without Donovan suddenly made me aware of all the ways in which he had served as a buffer, in which he had been the alpha dog in this pack whether they saw it or not. He had been subtly controlling them, whatever his reasons for doing so, and now he was in all likelihood abandoning me.

He reached in the hood of my parka and roughly took my face between his hands, which were ungloved and already chilled by the mountain air. He looked straight into my eyes and said in a cold, hard tone, "You'll move faster if I don't tape your mouth shut, because you'll be able to breathe better and drink water as needed. But if you start screaming or do anything else to attract attention, you'll be gagged. Do you understand?"

I stayed silent because, hidden by the hood, his fingers were tapping against my face, and I needed to concentrate on that tapping.

"Understand?" he asked again, more harshly.

I nodded.

He released me. "Good."

He turned back to Parrish. "See you in a few hours."

He got into the SUV and backed it down the narrow road, until he came to a place where he could turn around. We watched its taillights vanish around the first curve in the road.

Parrish turned on a flashlight and began to walk toward an opening in the trees. We were soon making our way along the stream. I was marched behind Parrish, with Kai bringing up the rear. Kai stayed close to me. I could hear his breathing grow rapid. Whether that was because of pain from his wound, altitude sickness, or a city boy's fear at finding himself in the woods at night, I didn't know.

With my hands bound, I began to realize how much I used my arms to help me stay balanced when walking. The uneven route along the stream was especially difficult, and I didn't find it much easier when we were hiking over tree roots. Parrish wasn't moving very fast, but five times I nearly fell, once recovering my balance just before landing in the icy cold stream.

Before long birds were beginning to sing, and squirrels and jays chattered noisily above us. Parrish turned off his flashlight and pocketed it as dawn broke.

"I don't understand why you trusted him!" Kai called from behind me, as if he had been fretting over this since Donovan drove away.

Parrish laughed and called back, "Who said I trusted him?"

I kept my head down, watching my footing. I thought of the message Donovan had tapped out:

Have faith.

Faith. But then, who said I trusted him?

FORTY-FIVE

Donovan drove until he reached a point where he felt sure that if Parrish decided to hike down the road instead of going up his makeshift trail, he wouldn't discover that the SUV hadn't been moved very far. Donovan's next requirement for a stopping place was not as easily met as he had hoped, but it was important that the vehicle could be seen from the sky.

He had studied Irene Kelly. He had read as many of her articles and columns in the *Express* as he could find online, then searched out others in the local public library. He had learned as much as he could about her previous experiences with Nicholas Parrish and, perhaps as important, her thoughts about those experiences. He had learned about her husband's and friends' roles in her rescue.

That was also how he had come across a column published last April, on the birthday of the inventor and artist Samuel Morse, which talked of how his invention of the telegraph—considered by many to be the birth of electronic communication—had changed the world.

She had written about the code itself as a creation that had an impact beyond its use by telegraphers, how—although it was in danger of becoming a lost art—in this day when cell phones and GPS needed signal strength, Morse code could be sent with a mirror, a flashlight, by tapping against almost any surface, and a dozen other ways. The column included a story about her having learned the code as a girl. She used it to communicate secretly with her best friend in school. Years later she was delighted to discover that her husband knew Morse code, too. Although she claimed the slowest ham radio operators were more proficient, Frank and Irene kept in practice by sending messages to each other.

Donovan had thought of the ways this information might be useful and had brushed up on his Morse code.

He had learned everything he could about Irene Kelly, and had also studied Frank Harriman. He knew that their friend and neighbor, Jack Fremont, had sold half his interest in his helicopter service to Irene's cousin Travis Maguire. Both Fremont and Maguire were devoted to Frank and Irene. They had used their helicopters for search and rescue operations in the past, including a mountain search for Irene Kelly.

Which was why Donovan looked for a place that would allow the SUV to be visible from the sky.

Weather changes were frequent and unpredictable in the autumn in the southern Sierra Nevada and obscured visibility or other conditions would keep a helicopter on the ground. There was rain—possibly snow—in the forecast, but it wasn't due for another twelve to twenty-four hours, and so far, it looked as if this would be a clear day. Although snow could be found at the higher elevations of this range even in the summer, Donovan thought that it was unlikely Parrish would hike that far.

Parrish was not at exactly the same location he had once used as his burial ground—that location, at a higher elevation, was undoubtedly covered in snow right now. But he had used another meadow as a makeshift airfield when he brought victims to these mountains, and that meadow was not far from where they were now. Frank Harriman was by no means stupid, and even if he didn't get the text message, or didn't talk to Violet, Donovan hoped he would eventually recall that airfield and make his way there as a starting point.

Donovan knew that all plans rely on likelihood, so no matter how good the odds are *for* something happening, there are always odds *against.* He would do what he could to make it easier for Frank to find Irene if he came here. Ideally, she would be safe by then. He wanted events to go that way, but unexpected things could happen in wilderness areas, and worse things could be expected to happen around Nick Parrish, so in this situation only a fool would let everything depend on his own guesswork—or even his own abilities—to effect a rescue.

Although he could not have brought them in until now, at this point there were many advantages in calling on the resources of the police and other agencies, and the sooner the better.

Donovan told himself to stop hoping about this or that and get back to work. He could do nothing about Frank Harriman or Nick Parrish or anyone else. He had control only of his own actions, and if he and Irene were to remain alive, he must concentrate on his own next move.

He opened the back of the Forester and removed his backpack. It was not quite as full as he'd led Parrish to believe. He opened the covers over the interior sides in the SUV's rear cargo area. He used the screwdriver tool in his pocketknife to loosen the false covers over the bottoms of those spaces. He had considered building these spaces out a bit, but then he would have been betting against the possibility of a flat tire. Given the state of the roads he had been on, that was too high a risk.

From the compartments, he quickly removed two small nylon packs and his field kit. He consolidated most of this gear in his backpack, left behind what he had planned to leave—one item, stolen from Parrish while fitting his pack on his back, he parted from with extreme reluctance—and locked the car. He remained only long enough to make a slight change to the roof of the vehicle.

As he hiked back up to the place where he had left the others, Donovan reached into a concealed inner pocket of his parka, one he had sewn into it weeks ago. He took out a device about the size of his hand, turned it on, and waited. As he watched, a signal showed up on a GPS map display. This check completed, he turned it off and tucked it back into place. He wanted to conserve its battery's life.

He knew where Parrish, Kai, and Irene were going without the help of the small signaling device so carefully sewn into the lining of Irene's parka because he had hiked to that place many times before. Parrish's cave. There were caverns in these mountains—some running miles underground—and abandoned mines, but what Parrish had found barely qualified as a cave.

That was probably for the best, since they weren't outfitted for spelunking.

The cave was shallow, only about ten feet deep and ten feet wide in its widest places, just big enough to keep two or three persons hidden from view. It was reached by way of a climb up a steep rock face, so it was not easily accessible for animals. Although there was no sign of any use of it by anything larger than a rodent, Quinn had set some barriers just out of view of the opening to ensure that the space wasn't taken over by a larger mammal. He had wanted to set traps, but Donovan had convinced him that a dying animal would only draw other animals, if not the notice of rangers, and that the barriers would probably be enough, especially since the space was not all that easy to reach. He wondered, in fact, if Kai would be able to manage getting up to it, even using the ladder that could be lowered once the first climber was in.

He knew Irene was claustrophobic and worried that being in the cave would induce panic, but if so, her fear of enclosed spaces would have to compete with other terrors. Perhaps Parrish had chosen the cave with her phobia in mind.

Still, she had been active in the outdoors, and he suspected that, all told, their surroundings would be more threatening to Kai. Donovan wondered if Parrish had visions of being Kai's wilderness guide and teacher. That should be interesting. Then again, perhaps that was supposed to be Quinn's job.

Unlike Kai, Quinn had spent time outdoors—hiking, back-packing, climbing, rafting, hunting, fishing, and camping. This was true of Parrish as well, until he had been injured and imprisoned.

As part of the endless amount of planning Parrish required, Quinn had been told to prepare certain supplies and leave them in the cave. He had brought Donovan with him. Initially Donovan had thought Quinn had included him in his plans unbeknownst to Parrish, risking an argument because he didn't want to haul all the required gear on his own, especially when it came to getting it up that rock face. As it turned out, Parrish had no objection to Donovan knowing where the cave was, which told Donovan that Parrish did not intend to stay there for long. The small amount of food packed for this trip only verified that the cave was not a permanent hideout. Donovan did not see the permission Parrish had given for him to know this location as a sign of trust—on the contrary, it suggested that he was not slated to survive this trip.

Plans to kill him could have changed, Donovan thought, now that Quinn and Kai had staged their half-baked version of the Gunfight at the O.K. Corral.

Parrish wanted a human pack mule at this point—Donovan had already seen his frustration over the fact that Quinn was missing and Kai was injured. Donovan found it difficult to judge Parrish's physical condition. Each time Donovan had seen him, Parrish had avoided exertion, but Donovan knew better than to judge Parrish by what he chose to reveal about himself.

Whatever Parrish might be hiding about his physical status, there was no doubt he was convinced of his own intellectual superiority. That conviction was, ironically, a weakness— a weakness Donovan intended to exploit as often as possible. Parrish imagined himself to be the ultimate planner. Donovan could plan, too.

So when he was given access to the place where supplies were being laid, he kept in mind that one difference among all the members of his "family" was build. What fit Parrish would not fit Kai, who was more slender. None of Donovan's siblings were as tall or broad in the shoulders as he was, nor was his father. As the person who was sent to buy the parkas, boots, and backpacks, he knew this and had used the information to do what little he could to try to derail Parrish's plans.

Donovan reached the place where the trio had entered the forest from the road. He could have tracked them quite easily—no attempt was being made to hide shoeprints in the muddy ground along the stream. He followed them without disturbing their trail.

Aside from other reasons to be concerned about Irene, he hoped she would not fall. He had seen no way to loosen her hands without raising Parrish's suspicions. She was only in running shoes, and boots would have been safer and warmer. So far, though, Parrish and Kai seemed to be having greater trouble. Kai was favoring one side, probably because of his arm. Parrish seemed to have fashioned a walking stick for himself, probably from a fallen branch. Depressions in the ground showed he was leaning heavily on it.

At the place where it looked as if they had crossed the stream, Donovan realized he was catching up to them. He picked up a few rounded stones, each a little smaller than a golf ball, and pocketed them, then put on some waders and began to make his way across. It was not, he thought, where he would have chosen to cross—a little farther up a fallen tree bridged the stream. Perhaps it had fallen during the time Parrish was in prison so that Parrish didn't know of it.

Donovan stepped out of the stream and hurriedly removed the waders. Once Parrish had brought Kai and Irene to the cave, anything might happen to her. He stood, about to be on his way again—then he saw the bloodstains.

FORTY-SIX

Streams fed by snowmelt are usually calmer in the morning, but that didn't mean the stream we followed was sluggish. In several places, it narrowed and flowed in pounding rapids. At one of these points, almost all of the rocks were wet and mossy, making progress so difficult I expected at any moment to be seriously injured in a fall.

I heard Kai swearing and turned just in time to see him slip on a wet stone. He moved from rounded slick rock to rounded slick rock, higher, lower, left, then right, swaying and trying to counterbalance with his uninjured arm before he finally recovered his balance. In a different situation, I might have found it comedic, but either because I thought my pride would soon "goeth before" a similar loss of balance of my own or because I could see the experience had truly left him shaken, I didn't even crack a smile.

Parrish looked back at us, but he had missed the acrobatics. "Hurry up!" he said and moved on.

I nearly advised Kai to take his arm out of the sling to aid in his balance, then asked myself why I wanted to do anything to help him out. I turned back toward Parrish and kept moving. I forced myself to recall the manner in which

Kai had awakened me that morning, to think of the young women he had killed. If he dashed his brains out on a rock, it would be to my advantage, right? I could hardly claim that I had his best interests in mind. If I got my way, he'd be captured and imprisoned for life at best—disabled or dead if the cavalry never showed up. Whoever the cavalry was going to be at this point. I had a nasty feeling I wasn't going to be able to wait to find out.

I decided to take a risk. "We could move faster if my hands were untied," I called to Parrish.

He looked back at me. "Nice try." He kept moving.

I tore at the tape with my teeth every time Kai became too distracted with keeping his balance to watch me.

I hadn't made much progress when we reached a point where Parrish wanted to cross the stream. It wasn't a bad choice, all in all—the stream had widened and slowed, but judging by the movement of leaves and twigs going by, the current was still strong. It was also deeper and rockier than I wanted to try with my hands bound together. The depth was a little more than knee-high, every inch of it undoubtedly icy cold.

If we had been friends doing some hiking together, things might have gone differently. There are strategies for fording streams as a team—such as crossing with arms linked or crabbing parallel to the flow—but Parrish wasn't used to playing well with others.

Nor did he advise his son to get a branch to use as a walking stick, as he himself had done some way back. The stick would aid him in crossing—it would help with keeping balance, with testing depth, and testing how solidly placed any stepping-stones in the streambed were. And it could make it easier to move in the pressure of the stream's current by parting its flow as he stepped behind it.

He did take his socks off and put his boots back on, and Kai, watching him, did the same. No one gave a damn if I was going to get blisters, so my hands stayed tied and my socks on.

Parrish unsnapped the sternum support and hip belt on his pack and said to Kai, "Be sure to keep her covered. This is where she's most likely to try something."

He began crossing.

If Parrish had looked closely, he would have seen that Kai, who had removed his arm from the sling by then and retied his boots, had been so involved in those processes that he hadn't seen his father unstrap his pack.

I hesitated, then said, "Kai—"

"Fuck you," he said. "I'm not going to cut your hands free."

That nearly settled it for me, but I kept my temper and said, "Fine. But you're more likely to drown if you fall into the stream with a belted pack on. Think about it."

He eyed me suspiciously, then said, "It's not deep. Get going."

So I rucked my parka up as best as I could and waded in. The shock of the cold water took my breath away, and I felt the hard push of the current, but it wasn't too strong to stand up in. I was worried that if my feet and legs grew numb I'd make a misstep, but I didn't want to move so fast I'd lose my balance.

Kai stepped in and swore, something he did continuously and violently as we made our way, but he stayed as close as he could to me.

We were over halfway across when he suddenly lost his balance. He rocked forward and back and forward again, and made a grab for me with his right hand. That was the injured arm, or he might have succeeded in pulling both of us in. Instead, he missed, toppled over, and went in face-first.

The stream wasn't all that deep there, but depth is far from the only danger in water that is moving. His two biggest pieces of luck were that he wasn't hit by debris and that the current wasn't strong enough to easily sweep him away—although it definitely made it hard for someone with weight on his back to stand up again. Kai was young and muscular, and under other circumstances, with some effort he probably could have struggled back to his feet, even on the rocky streambed. But the pack, with the shovel inside, made that much harder. The injury to his right arm, the coldness of the water, even the loose sling—all combined to make the task even more difficult.

He rolled and flailed and eventually got his nose and mouth out of the water. His face was covered in blood. He coughed and spluttered and flailed some more without regaining his feet.

Parrish hurried back, but I was nearer. I thought of leaving Kai there, of making a run for it. For that matter, it probably wouldn't have been all that hard to drown him while he struggled half-stunned in that turtle-on-its-back position. He was close to doing that without any assistance. He saw me, though, and reached a hand out. I told myself, as I took hold of that hand, that it was my only real choice. Parrish had a clear shot and would have killed me without hesitation if I had tried to run for it or harmed his child. I knew, even at the time, that wasn't why I chose not to just stand there and let someone drown in front of me.

I grabbed onto him and pulled back, keeping his face out of the water as I tried to reach the releases on the pack's straps—all the while struggling to maintain my own balance.

Parrish reached us and helped Kai regain his feet, then shepherded him to the other bank, leaving me to fend for myself. I joined them there, cold and far more wet than I wanted to be, although at least the water-repellent parka had stayed dry.

Again, I thought of bolting, but Parrish was watching me now, aiming his gun at me. If I got closer, I could probably disarm him, but then what?

I made a show of stretching and looked around. No real cover.

Kai lay on his side, coughing, vomiting up water. Given the bacteria count in many mountain streams, he might not need to have drowned.

And what if you have allowed him to live so that he can go out and torture and kill another dozen women?

I felt my stomach churn.

"Come here," Parrish said.

Reluctantly, I moved closer.

"Hold out your hands."

I did, and he holstered his gun and removed a knife—a strange knife with a thin, long blade—from his pack. He swiftly cut through the tape between my wrists, then held the tip of the knife under my jaw, just shy of the soft skin there.

"You are going to take this pack off him. You are going to care for his wounds, and you are going to help me get him to shelter. If you try to fuck with me or Kai in any way, I will make you incredibly sorry for it."

He didn't wait for or want a reply from me. He moved out of reach, nodded toward Kai, and said, "Get him into a condition that will allow us to move out of here, and quickly."

A tall order, but I did as he asked. I found myself willing to ignore almost all the first aid training I'd ever had. I found a water bottle, didn't check to see if the water in it was sterilized, and told Kai to drink from it. I used water from the stream to rinse off the cuts on his forehead. I dried his face and taped a big pad of gauze on the worst cut, the only one still bleeding. I paid no heed to concerns about sterile conditions, hand washing, hypothermia, head injuries, blisters, or even athlete's foot. Let him suffer.

While I worked on Kai, Parrish looked toward the stream, walked to its edge, stared, then walked back. He paced this distance several times, then suddenly seemed resigned. I wasn't sure what that was about.

Parrish walked back over to us, and together we helped Kai to his feet. Kai leaned on me while Parrish carried Kai's pack in his free hand—the shovel had been lost out of it, and God knew I wasn't going to point that out or go looking for it.

We hadn't gone far before it was apparent that Kai was more bruised and shaken than seriously hurt. Foreheads can produce dramatic bleeding, but he didn't show any signs of concussion, although those might appear later.

His skin was blue, though, and he shivered.

"Do you have a change of clothes in your pack?" I asked.

"He'll be able to change his clothes not far from here," Parrish said. "He'll warm up as we move. Or maybe I should have you strip and give him your clothes."

I ignored him. As we walked, Kai clung to me, in a way that both unsettled me and at first made it difficult to move. He seemed to figure out fairly quickly that he needed to loosen his hold at least a little, and he did so, but he kept his uninjured left arm around my shoulders.

We walked upstream, past a place where we could have stayed dry by crossing on a fallen log, a fact that made Kai shoot Parrish a dirty look. Not long after that, Kai played with my hair. I stepped away from him. He smiled but didn't try to put his arm around me again. I felt queasy.

We reached a point where trees hid the sheer rock face from view. We left the stream and walked along the foot of this cliff. Moving was good—I warmed up a little.

Not much farther in, Parrish called a halt and told me to give Kai a boost up the rock face to a ledge. It was about ten feet above us.

"How is he supposed to reach that ledge with an injured arm?"

He sighed. "Do not try my patience. Give him a boost."

For his part, Kai obeyed without hesitation. He struggled to pull himself up, but other than giving a grunt of pain as he rolled onto the ledge, he didn't complain. He peered over the edge, his face pale, awaiting orders.

"Get the ladder," Parrish said. "Anchor it the way I showed you at the lodge. And while you're back there, get one of the other guns. Try not to lose this one. Tomorrow I'm going to send you in after the one you dropped into the water, and the shovel, too."

So—that explained Parrish's unhappy pacing near the stream.

Kai's eyes widened at Parrish's threat, but he scrambled to his feet. I heard scraping sounds, and a few minutes later, he dropped the ladder down. It was a fire escape ladder, the kind people keep in the bedrooms of two-story homes. Parrish tested it, then began calling more instructions up to Kai.

"I'm going to change," Kai said. "I'm freezing."

Parrish scowled up toward the ledge, but Kai had already retreated from view.

I was on the ground but knew I would soon be asked to climb into God knew what kind of lair Parrish had set up. He and his son had made it clear that they planned to torture me, sexually assault me, and kill me. If not there, at whatever other hideout he had in mind.

My hands and feet were free. Donovan was nowhere nearby. Kai was above me and injured and not in view.

I had one opponent, and he was reaching for me.

I made my move, a technique known in Kenpo as Covering the Flame. Rachel had been convinced—given who might be after me—that I needed to know this one, and she'd made me practice it again and again.

That practice allowed my next series of movements to go by in seconds. As Parrish stepped forward, I evaded his reaching left hand and continued moving, stepping with my left foot to his right side—his semiautomatic was held in his right hand.

Now facing his right side, I used my left hand to immediately take hold of the back of his right wrist in an iron grip. He began pulling the trigger, firing wildly, but I was outside his range, controlling his aim with control of his wrist. I used that grip to move him off balance even as I rapidly raised my own right hand to my shoulder. I pivoted on my left foot as I stepped forward with my right, landing my right foot behind his right leg, never letting go of his wrist. I brought my right arm in hard to bend his hand in, so that I now pinned the wrist of his gun hand with the bones of my right wrist and used my forearm to force his hand toward his shoulder. Soon my elbow was lodged against his shoulder.

With my hold on his wrist and the way my body was positioned, I completely controlled his movement and balance as I pivoted—twisting his wrist and shoulder and using my momentum. He followed where his wrist was being taken, but his leg encountered the back of mine, and he lost his balance. The motion pulled him down to the ground, so that he landed flat on his back with an "oof" at about the place I had been standing a moment before.

He had lost his grip on the gun, but I still had not lost mine on him. I kept hold of his wrist while I used my right foot to stomp hard on his right arm, his chest, his left arm, then jabbed the knuckles of my right hand into his eyes. He turned his head just before I made prime contact, but I still hit him hard enough to hurt him.

I knew I had taken him by surprise, I knew he had been underestimating me all along. But this was no time to gloat. I didn't wait to see if I could take him in round two. I picked up the gun and ran like hell into the trees.

FORTY-SEVEN

Donovan heard shots and screams. He moved quickly toward the cave, then slowed and approached cautiously when he realized the screams belonged to Nick Parrish. Parrish was yelling something about his eyes and screeching, "Shoot her!"

He was on the ground, curled on his side, rubbing his chest and pressing one hand over his eyes.

By then Donovan was near enough to catch a glimpse of Kai before he turned back in to the cave. He noticed that Kai wore a bandage, looked unhappy—and, oddly enough, had most of his clothes off. Donovan thought over his options, waited until Parrish seemed to have himself under better control, then approached.

"Well, that ought to bring the rangers down on us in no time," he said.

"Donovan?" Parrish said, peering out from between his fingers, wincing. "Where the hell have you been?"

"Exactly where I told you I'd be. I hid the car and then hiked back here." He looked up at Kai. "What happened here?"

"He tripped over his own two feet and landed on his ass in the stream," Parrish said.

Kai frowned, then said, "He got his ass kicked by a woman."

They squabbled and denied and embellished, but out of all that mix, Donovan was able to roughly piece together what had happened.

"Why didn't you shoot her?" Parrish demanded.

"The guns up here aren't loaded," Kai said. "I've never been here before, so I don't know where the fuck you put the ammo."

"Let's deal with your wounds—and change your clothes," Donovan said, hoping to stall long enough to give Irene the chance she needed to get away. He was concerned about the fact that she had no water with her, and he hoped she'd stay away from the stream, since Parrish would undoubtedly hunt for her there.

"Are you going to chase her?" Kai said.

"I'll do that if you prefer," Donovan said to Parrish.

But almost as quickly as he answered, Parrish said, "No!"

Kai gave him a puzzled look.

"We need to stay together," Parrish said.

"I'm getting a crick in my neck staring up at Kai," Donovan said. "You want him to come down, even though he's turning blue, or do you want to go up?"

Parrish decided he could climb the ladder. He made slow progress. Soon after they reached the cave, Donovan set up a couple of cots with sleeping bags on them, then brought out two propane camping heaters while Kai dressed. The contents of Kai's backpack were strewn about, creating tripping hazards.

Parrish seemed glad to have a warm, soft place to lie down. Donovan got each of them to let him look at their injuries.

Parrish was bruised, and his left eye was swollen shut. His right wrist appeared to be sprained. Donovan put cold packs on the eye and wrist, and wrapped the wrist. He did his best to make Parrish believe he was concerned about more complicated injuries without overdoing it. He wanted Parrish to be thinking about his vulnerability, his aches and pains, the possibility of worse outcomes.

He had almost no admiration for Parrish, other than in one

regard: his determination in recovering from his spinal injury. Although Parrish had been luckier than most in the nature of the injury itself, Donovan didn't fool himself that coming back from it had been an easy process. But Parrish's determination to survive and recover could not outweigh all the attributes that made him worse than a monster, or make up for what he had done to his victims. Donovan felt no compunction in using a little psychological warfare on a man whose greatest fears had to include the possibility of suffering paralysis again.

So as he looked over the places on Parrish's upper arms and chest that were red and swollen and would undoubtedly show bruises soon, Donovan said, "I'm glad you weren't lying on your stomach when this happened. She could have permanently injured your back." And a little later, "I don't *think* the ribs are broken, but I'm really not certain." And after gently studying his left eye and looking at what was probably going to be a shiner and not much worse, he injected just a little worry in his voice as he said, "I don't know. Hard to tell."

He went no further than that, and did the rest of his work in silence. There was a balance to be found, especially with someone experienced with abuse. He knew, from Quinn's long lectures on the Legend of the Glorious and All-Powerful Nick Parrish, that Parrish had suffered torture and sexual abuse as a child—as had Quinn and Kai although Kai's and Quinn's had been at the hands of their stepfathers, with their mothers turning a blind eye. Parrish's mother had been actively involved, a partner in the abuse.

Donovan reminded himself that all three had long-standing acquaintanceships with pain, providing fuel for their rage.

"Donovan," Parrish said, "I have a question for you."

Donovan waited.

"Do you have my cell phone?"

"You didn't leave it back at the warehouse?" Donovan asked, letting a mixture of suppressed anger and a little anxiousness creep into his voice. "You know those things can be traced by the police, don't you? It's like having a locator button on you."

"No, I didn't leave it in the warehouse. I had it with me this morning. As for the locator—how would anyone know its number has anything to do with me?"

"For starters, Quinn—"

"Knows nothing about this particular phone."

"Well, that's a relief. But what about the man I spoke to—"

"The Moth who guards your child? Utterly loyal to me." He paused. "I do hope you find it. If I'm not in contact with him within a certain time frame, well, I'm sure you understand what might happen."

Donovan shrugged. "Whatever. At this point I'm more interested in staying out of prison."

To emphasize his supposed lack of concern, he moved toward Kai. "How's the head?"

"Hurts."

Donovan looked at the wound, put some antibiotic on it, and bandaged it again. He changed the bandage on Kai's arm as well. "So far, no sign of a bad infection. You're lucky. But we'll have to keep an eye on it—streams up here can have some nasty bacteria in them."

Kai shook his head. "I hate it here. I want to go home."

"That's not going to happen," Parrish said. "But we'll find a better place to live."

"You like it up here," Kai said, making it an accusation.

"I know you want to live in a city. We'll do that."

"What about my mom?"

"I told you, I sent someone to take care of her. He'll take her to live with Donovan's little girl. There will be people there to take care of her until we can all be together."

"One big happy family?" Donovan asked.

"The idea doesn't appeal?"

"Not something I've ever tried. As you know, I prefer solitude."

"What about when you were a kid?" Kai asked.

"It was usually just me and my mom," Donovan said, trying to figure out what Kai was really asking. Did he still think of himself as a child who needed Violet? Or was he curious about Donovan's own childhood, comparing notes?

"How is she these days?" Parrish asked.

"Why ask a question you already know the answer to? It can't be because you think I don't know the answer."

"That's right. She's dead. Questionable circumstances, as I recall."

Donovan said nothing.

"Was she mean to you?" Kai asked, frowning.

"She did say something terrible to me once. She told me I reminded her of my father."

Parrish gave a crack of laughter, then groaned. "Oh, that hurt." He slowly rose to his feet. "Let's get going. First order of business is to find that bitch and kill her."

Donovan turned off the heaters and said, "Why bother with her? Why not just get out of here, then go after her again later?"

"Yeah!" Kai said.

"No," Parrish said. "I've waited too long already. She's not going to leave here alive."

Every backpack—each fitted for the person who would carry it—had a name stenciled on it, and Donovan picked up his and put it on. It was the backpack that he had especially prepared when he and Quinn were gathering supplies. Now he was the only one who donned a pack.

Parrish, who had been pocketing extra ammunition for his rifle, raised his brows. "A tent and bedroll?"

"If we don't find her by nightfall, are you going to want to drive off, taking a chance that she'll find help? She knows the stream comes to the road, she knows any road up here will eventually take her to other people, rangers if no one else. She may not have food, but there's plenty of water."

"If we haven't found her by dusk, we will come back here."

"Seriously? You think she's going to stay close to this cave? Because otherwise, you're talking about tracking her and then doubling back and losing ground."

Parrish stared at him so coldly and for so long, Donovan knew he had pushed him too far.

"Suit yourself," Parrish said finally and smiled. It was not a comforting smile. "Kai and I will be warm and comfortable. Did you know that there's a good chance of rain, Kai?"

Kai nodded. "You had me check the weather before we left the lodge."

"You see, Donovan? I'm not as unprepared as you may think I am."

"Are we going to be out in the rain?" Kai asked.

"Not if I can help it," Parrish said. "Let's get going."

Donovan said nothing more. He made an effort, after that, not to openly question Parrish's judgment.

"So, Donovan," Parrish said when they had climbed down from the cave, "you have tracking experience. Where did she go?"

He had expected this, and answered honestly, pointing out trampled foliage that would have been obvious to anyone. He was not especially comfortable having Parrish and Kai at his back, but as he suspected would happen, after about half an hour of following him, Parrish insisted on taking the lead.

"Kai, you'll be behind Donovan. Keep your weapon out. Don't take your eyes off him."

Donovan watched Kai for the slightest sign of rebellion. He had been encouraged by Kai's earlier anger with Parrish, but now he saw a look come into his eyes that put an end to any hope that his half brother might be turned away from worshiping Parrish.

"And Donovan," Parrish said, "give your gun to Kai."

If this was going to escalate to a pat-down, Donovan thought, now would be the moment to go for broke. He didn't hide his wariness but handed over the automatic. Parrish watched him, then said, "I think I'll also ask you to leave the backpack here. I don't want to take the time to search it now, but I also don't want to find out you've provided yourself with an extra weapon."

Donovan opened his mouth as if to protest, then closed it. He shrugged and took off the pack, leaning it against a tree.

Parrish smiled. "All right, let's get going. She can't be too much farther ahead of us."

FORTY-EIGHT

Frank had the maps with him.

Topo maps, creased and worn, maps he had thought of throwing away a dozen times or more. But once they had guided him to where he had found Irene, Ben, and Bingle, and brought them home.

Travis and Jack and Frank's own dogs had been with him then, too. Along with Stinger Dalton, a pilot who had later taught Travis to fly. Stinger was in Hawaii this week and would undoubtedly be pissed off that he had missed being part of this second hunt.

They had laid the maps out at Stinger's place and marked them up based on what they knew from various reports about where Parrish might have taken a group of searchers. Stinger had helped Frank to reason out where Parrish was most likely to be. The maps still bore those markings.

Even though he had not since been back to the area they flew over now, Frank thought he could have found it in his sleep. It had been, after all, a place of waking nightmares.

Frank looked down on the pristine expanse of white below him and saw it as he had seen it that day in May, a bloodied field covered with the remains of his colleagues and, as he had at first feared, perhaps his wife's as well. He shook himself. She had not died there. She was not, he told himself fiercely, dead now.

He glanced over and saw that Ben was looking pale. As hard as this was for Frank, it had to be a thousand times worse for Ben. "You okay?" he asked over his headset.

Ben shook his head no but kept staring down at the meadow.

The last time they had been here, Ben's closest friend had been murdered. Ben had left on a stretcher, airlifted in this helicopter.

The vista below was beautiful and serene.

Everything changes, Frank thought, and forced his mind back to the present.

Travis brought the helicopter as low as he could without allowing its downwash to disturb the snow. Even studying the meadow with field glasses, Frank could see no signs of human tracks.

They had already looked in another meadow, one Parrish had also been known to use. They had even explored the ridge between the two meadows. Travis had set the big Sikorsky down there, not far from where it had rested once before. They had trudged through the snow, looking for any sign that Parrish had come back here, even hiked up to a shallow cave, one of the places Irene had told Frank about after she was rescued. But the cave was clearly long-abandoned. Other than stretching their legs and giving the dogs a chance to get some exercise, nothing had been gained.

Travis's voice came over the headset. "Pappy just contacted me," he said, referring to the dispatcher at their home base. "Looks like that storm is slightly ahead of schedule."

"Do we need to go back?"

"Not yet, but we probably only have another hour or so

before we should either go back or put her down and wait it out. She can fly in rain and is designed to survive a lightning strike, but that can still lead to dangerous amounts of damage. I don't want to risk it."

"I don't want anyone to have to rescue us," Frank said. "Do what you need to do." They had all been patient with him, Frank thought. Good about keeping him distracted during the long flight up here. And it was beginning to look as if he had guessed wrong about where Parrish was going. He had thought of this area as Parrish's comfort zone, but nothing said Parrish would stay true to that now, especially once it had been discovered. In Parrish's view, the recovery of remains from this meadow was undoubtedly a desecration of his work.

"Wasn't there a place he used as an airstrip?" Travis said.

"Yes," Ben said. "We started out from there . . . the last time. We hiked up here from there."

"Would it still be there?" Jack asked.

"Yes," Frank said. "It belongs to the Forest Service. They use it to land fire crews—he just took advantage of it." He looked it up on the map, then gave Travis the coordinates.

"Okay. Let's head back that way and check it out. We can look from there, and if I need to land until the storm's over, it might do the trick."

They reached the airstrip. It was in a long, narrow valley, at a lower elevation than the meadows, and was free from snow. They let the dogs out again while Frank studied the maps.

Parrish had often flown his victims here in a small plane. That had been part of his M.O. Most killers who used the mountains for dumping grounds stayed close to roads—bodies are heavy, and it's difficult to carry them far or bury them deep. Hiking any distance involves risking control over the victim, as well as hazarding being seen by others. Parrish took that gamble, sadistically forcing his victims to hike with him and to dig their own graves.

But this time, Parrish had come here in a car, not a plane. He knew the roads—including rough dirt roads and roads open only for use by the U.S. Forest Service. He had escaped from these mountains on just such roads.

And he wasn't alone. He had at least two helpers with him. But were his sons used to being in the outdoors?

If he was here, Parrish hadn't arrived by plane, and he couldn't have reached this airstrip by car. What places, near his old killing grounds, could he reach by car?

Frank searched the maps for roads that were accessible by a car initially traveling from the south. A great many, but far fewer coming into this part of the wilderness. Fewer still anywhere near this airstrip. He included fire roads and roads that would be officially closed to the public by now. He spotted one, not all that far away.

He saw Travis standing on a slight rise, staring toward the north.

Frank called to him. When he came over, Frank said, "Take a look at this map. How long would it take us to reach this road?"

Travis studied the map, then pointed toward the area of sky he had been watching. "See those clouds? I'm concerned about that storm. I know you don't want to hear this, and I don't even want to be saying it, but it might be better to just sit tight and let it blow over. Let me see what I can find out about it, because it's definitely going to affect what we can safely do."

He went into the helicopter. Frank followed him, and the others, seeing them, returned, loading up the dogs and strapping them into their special safety harnesses.

The Sikorsky S-58T was a giant, over fifteen feet high and about forty-five feet long. It had been fitted with turbine engines and auxiliary fuel tanks. It could hold eighteen passengers, but the interior had been altered so that now—in addition to a crew of two in the cockpit, which was a separate area high above the cargo area—the cargo area had seats for ten passengers and carried two stretchers.

Donning their headsets again, Frank and Ben waited while Jack went through the start-up procedures and Travis listened to reports from local air traffic and studied weather radar.

There was a *whump* as Jack hit the ignition, and then the whine of the turbines began to build. The blades of the rotors *swoop-swoop-swooped*, ever faster—within twenty seconds, both the main and tail rotors were spinning at a steady speed.

Everything around them was a roar.

Travis's voice came over his headset. "Lightning often arrives before rain, so keeping that in mind . . . if we leave now, we can probably at least fly over it and get back here before the storm hits. We could at least see if the vehicle is there."

"Could you set me down if need be?" Frank asked.

"Depends on conditions at the time. If it's safe to do that, sure. Depending on the road, I may even be able to land there."

"Let's go, then."

FORTY-NINE

I tucked the gun into one of the pockets of my parka and ran in a zigzagging motion, concentrating on not tripping or falling. I ran until I realized no one was chasing me or firing bullets at me.

I crouched behind a large pine, feeling the rough bark on my hands, and tried to catch my breath.

I knew I was far from home safe, but I could not prevent a sense of exhilaration from sweeping over me. I had defended myself. I had fought Nick Parrish, and taken his gun away from him. I had escaped their control. Now all I had to do was stay free.

And alive.

Time to better assess my situation.

I reached into the parka and took the gun out. It was a .22 semiautomatic. I checked and saw that there were only two bullets left. Better than no bullets. I put the magazine back in.

I was not all that comfortable with firearms. Frank was a marksman, but I hadn't taken the time to do more than learn the basics. Still, I knew those basics, and if Frank managed only to drag me out to a range to practice twice a year, at least I knew I had two bullets and a gun that Parrish did not have.

In addition to the clothes on my back and the gun, I had half a dozen energy bars, a collapsible water bottle, and a survival blanket. A small mirror—which could be used as a signaling device. I peered into it, confirmed that I looked as if this was casual Friday at the insane asylum, and quickly put it away.

What I had thought was lip balm turned out to be a small container that had once held aspirin and was relabeled "water purification tablets, use 2, wait 15 m." So I had food, a way to carry and purify water, and something to help me stay a little warmer and drier. I began to feel more hopeful about my odds. Plus, it was all very portable and didn't add a lot of weight to the jacket.

The item that nearly made me weep was a pair of dry socks. I immediately sat down and changed into them.

I stood and checked another pocket, the flap of which felt a little lumpy, and made a major discovery—a book of matches tucked inside a small hidden space, a sewn-over hem that was just tacked down. They weren't super-duper camping matches, but who cared? I wouldn't be forced to test my ability to start a fire from two sticks. I felt along the bottom hem and found another of those lightly tacked places. I pulled at it and withdrew a long, thin cord that had a strong wire at its core. It took me a moment to realize what it was—a garrote.

I looked at that for a long moment. Not a defensive weapon, the garrote. A tool of self-preservation, perhaps. I wondered what Donovan—because without a doubt, he was the one who had prepared this walking survival kit for me—had had in mind. It didn't take a lot of imagination. If I had a chance to kill Kai or Parrish in their sleep, this was designed to help me take it. I tucked it back into the parka.

I supposed there weren't too many weapons he could risk hiding on me. For one thing, he had to make sure I didn't accidentally hurt myself before I discovered them. For another, there would always be the risk that Parrish or Kai would search

me. So as much as I might wish for a knife—for its useful-
ness as a tool in the outdoors more than as a weapon—I could
understand why this might be the only weapon he thought
could stay concealed.

On the downside, my shoes and the bottoms of my pant legs
were still wet from the stream, which could cause problems,
especially if it got much colder. I didn't have shelter, but I might
be able to manage with the survival blanket.

Oh, and I had just pissed off a couple of serial killers whose
desire to kill me was the nicest thing they had on their Things
to Do with Irene list.

Not to mention that I didn't know exactly where I was. A
consequence of running into the forest in a blind panic. That
thought almost sent me into another one, until I realized that
I could hear the stream. I could follow the stream toward the
road, the road toward help.

I wondered where Donovan was. I thought of him telling me
to have faith. I had such mixed emotions about him. I could not
forget that he'd helped Parrish take me hostage. Yet from that
point, he had taken many risks on my behalf. Actually, I realized, he must have planned to help me even in advance of kidnapping me. I couldn't make sense of it. But right now, thanks
to him, my chances of surviving had greatly increased.

I thought about the warm clothing and realized something
else. Donovan had chosen a parka of a color that blended in
with the forest, would provide some camouflage. His parka was
the same color.

Parrish's and Kai's light-colored parkas, on the other hand,
would be easier for me to see.

I needed to think more like Donovan, I decided. I figured out
that I was overdue for a meal. If I was going to stay clearheaded and
have enough energy to keep moving through the forest, I needed
to eat. So I carefully opened an energy bar, saved the wrapper, and

immediately realized that the damned thing was salty and made me feel thirsty. Okay, next stop would be the stream.

The trouble was, Parrish was a hunter, and water was an obvious place to wait for game. And going to the stream would also mean going back toward the cave, and possibly crossing paths with Parrish and Kai.

I couldn't just hurry to the stream like a rabbit.

I took out the little mirror again, careful not to let it catch the light as I placed it on the ground. I reached down into the damp earth and scooped up a handful of dark soil and rubbed it on my face and hands, checking in the mirror to ensure I was well covered. Parrish had talked of having supplies in the cave, and they might include a pair of field glasses. I didn't want to provide any reflective surfaces to catch his attention. When I was muddied up, I carefully put the mirror away again.

I needed to move differently through this forest than I had thus far. I had to be quieter and reduce any signs of my passage. I forced myself to be as still as possible, and to think through where I was headed next.

I felt a temptation to spy on Parrish and Kai. To stalk them, instead of being their prey. Wait for them to leave the cave and then raid its supplies. But the risks were too great that I would simply be delivering myself into their hands when what I needed was distance.

Frank would be coming for me. I knew that as surely as I knew anything. I needed to make it as easy as possible for him to find me and get me safely back home. Ideally, he'd have an army with him, and Donovan would get out, too.

I began heading toward the sound of the stream. I did not take a direct course. I moved carefully and walked as quietly as I could, thinking about every step, avoiding leaving footprints or an obvious trail of crushed leaves. I wondered what had become of Donovan.

I had no sooner thought this than I heard raised voices. Kai and Parrish. I could not make out the third voice, which wasn't as loud, but I knew it must be Donovan's. What if he was in danger? He might have come back for me, not knowing that I had escaped.

He would figure that out. If I could help him, I would, but in the meantime, I returned to my goal of a few minutes before: to get safely to the stream, then put more distance between me and Nick Parrish and Kai.

Suddenly I heard a faint but familiar sound: a helicopter. A big one, it seemed. My hopes soared. Should I start a signal fire? No. Parrish might see the flames first.

I needed to keep going.

I had taken no more than two steps when I heard their voices again. They were much nearer.

I froze, then very slowly crouched low to the ground. I made myself stay as still as possible.

Too close. They're too close.

After a time, I realized that I couldn't tell whether they'd come closer or veered away, because the wind was blowing harder through the trees. Birds were making one hell of a ruckus. There was less light.

Helicopter or no, Parrish and company or no—a storm was coming.

I tried to hear what they were saying. All I could tell for sure was that Donovan was definitely with them. I had a horrible feeling about that, more fear for him in that moment than for myself. He was, I thought, being taken to his execution. I had to do what I could to help him get away. But what? I strained to hear them and finally caught a glimpse of them moving through the trees.

I took out the gun.

FIFTY

Parrish, Donovan was sorry to learn, wasn't bad at tracking. Fortunately, his injuries slowed him down and probably accounted for his being a little noisy as he moved through the leaf-strewn woods. The injury to his eye, in particular, made depth perception a problem, and he was uncertain as they stepped over fallen trees, roots, and rocky, uneven ground. Kai made even more of a racket, apparently having no notion that stealth was desirable. Soon Donovan intentionally did the same, wanting to give Irene as much notice as possible of their approach.

Her tracks were not difficult to follow at first. He could almost feel her panic by seeing the length of her stride, the broken twigs, vines, and other disturbances showing the path of her initial flight—purely an attempt to put distance between her and the cave, with no effort to conceal her trail. She had run through the forest, but with enough presence of mind to move in an unpredictable manner to avoid giving someone a clear shot at her. Then at a certain point, judging by the way the leaves were crushed and the pattern of her footprints on the soft earth, she stopped to catch her breath. After that, it was more difficult to track her. Still, he thought they were getting closer.

As they stalked her, if their less than stealthy movements could be considered stalking, Donovan began to evaluate his own chances of survival. Time to run a little test. He lagged behind Parrish, pulled a rounded stone from his pocket, and as he moved briefly out of Kai's sight, launched the rock at a tree near Kai's head.

Kai jumped and then crouched low to the ground. Donovan had already moved forward to be nearer Parrish.

"Hey!" Kai called.

Parrish and Donovan looked back.

"She must be back here! She just threw something at me!" Kai looked around anxiously, trying to spot his attacker.

"Threw what at you?" Parrish said.

"I don't know!"

They spent several minutes standing still, listening, waiting. Donovan could hear Kai panting.

Donovan heard other things. The wind was moving more strongly in the trees. Birds were getting louder.

"Are you sure it wasn't just something falling from a tree?" Parrish asked.

"Yes! It was like a rock or something."

"She has a gun. Why would she throw a rock?"

"Maybe she doesn't have any bullets left."

"Let's keep moving," Parrish said.

"It's going to rain," Donovan said.

"Rain!" Kai's face had mutiny written all over it.

Parrish looked at the sky and sighed. "All right, let's head back to the cave."

They had nearly reached the place where Donovan's pack had been left when a faint, distant sound caught his attention. A helicopter. He saw the moment when Parrish registered it, too.

"Stay together," Parrish said. "We may have company."

Kai needed no additional encouragement. He began walking closer to Donovan and Parrish. It did not take much work for Donovan to let him get a little ahead, and then several steps ahead. And when Donovan judged the cover to be good enough and their attention fixed on the noises a deer was making as it ran from them, it was not hard to disappear from Kai's sight. Unlike Kai, he knew how to move silently and quickly in the woods.

Parrish caught a glimpse of him as he moved off, raised his rifle, and fired.

His first shot missed.

The second did not.

FIFTY-ONE

They weren't aware of my presence. Donovan was moving toward me. Parrish was firing at Donovan. I saw Donovan fall, saw Parrish hurry toward him, gun raised and ready to fire again.

That brought him closer to me. I stood, which brought him to a shocked halt, and I used that instant to smoothly raise my weapon and fire. I wanted more than anything to aim for his face. But I had two bullets and only two bullets. I aimed for his body, taking no chances.

Parrish's knees buckled, and he fell.

I turned my aim on Kai, whose mouth had opened in a silent, shocked O. Then he ran. I ran after him, pissed as hell, ready to put an end to this. But he kept going, panicked. He ran past something and knocked it over, trying to block my pursuit.

A backpack. It had Donovan's name on it. Better yet, it had a tent and a bedroll on it.

I let Kai run.

I picked up the pack. It was too large for me, but I put it on anyway and let it jostle against me as I moved back to where Donovan and Parrish lay.

———

320 AF JAN BURKE

When I got there, I saw that both Parrish and I had been less than successful in killing our targets. Parrish was on top of Donovan, trying to strangle him. Donovan was fighting back. I could not see where he was injured, but it was clear that at least one arm was useless. I dropped the backpack, placed the gun beneath it, and pulled out the garrote.

Parrish was utterly intent on killing Donovan. He had not so much as glanced at me. I stretched the wire between my gloved hands, then quickly put my left forearm against his neck, looped the wire and my right hand over his head, and uncrossed my arms. The wire crossed at the back of his neck. I pulled it tighter.

I had his attention then. I had it through the seconds during which he let go of Donovan, while he clawed and bucked and kicked and rolled, taking me with him. I felt him go limp, didn't trust it but slackened slightly.

He didn't move, but Donovan did. He reached into his boot with his uninjured arm and in one swift motion withdrew a knife and plunged it into whatever passed for Nick Parrish's heart.

FIFTY-TWO

Pete called, patched through by Pappy. He was a little more subdued, which made Frank suspicious.

"What's gone wrong?" Frank asked.

"I've got some bad news."

Frank drew in a breath.

"No, sorry, not that. I mean—nothing about Irene. But, well, you already know we are trying to track down Roderick Beignet."

"If you're going to tell me he managed to ride his bike all the way into town without getting caught by the LPPD, I'm not surprised."

"You're mad at me for that last call, bitching at you when you've got so much else on your mind. I get it. And I'm sorry. Seriously. If it's any consolation, Rachel ripped me a new one over that."

"Rachel knows as well as I do that you don't do well under pressure."

"Har-har. I will take that to be an acceptance of my apology."

"So what about Roderick?"

"Still looking. He ditched the bike in the mountains, must

have had a car nearby, because it doesn't sound as if he was in the kind of shape that would let him go long distances on foot. We went to the address the DMV has on file, and no one was home. People in the neighborhood say they rarely see him anymore. But he does have a motorcycle. We'll find him." He paused. "I talked Jake into running DNA on the guy."

"You have a sample?"

"Oh, yeah. We got a warrant and looked around the place."

"Thanks—glad you did. What about Quinn?"

Pete sighed.

Frank waited.

"He's in the wind."

"Fuck me. You have got to be shitting me. You let that son of a bitch out of your sight?"

"I can't be everywhere at once. You're the one playing God, not me."

"You know I meant the PD, not you personally."

"Oh, well, in that case, yes. You wouldn't think we could lose track of a guy in a hospital, but we did. As you know, patients have the right to leave a hospital and refuse care—even against the docs' advice—so they couldn't hold him against his will. He checked himself out before we even decided to send the detail. Apparently he never went home, because whenever we stop by, one of his attorneys answers the door and tells us Mr. Moore isn't in and unless we want to get a warrant or press charges . . . you can guess the rest."

He broke off to have an argument with Rachel, then said, "Rachel sends her love, and says not to pay any attention to me, but I told her you don't anyway, so there you have it."

"Thanks for the update, Pete. I'll let you know if—Well, I'll let you know."

Pete was atypically silent, then he said, in a much different tone of voice, "You are going to find her. I know you will."

He cleared his throat, then said, "That lunatic you married is nowhere near finished making my life miserable, let alone yours."

There was indecipherable shouting in the background, then Pete said, "No need to schedule an ass kicking for that remark, my wife's gonna take care of that for you before you get home. Keep me updated."

The call ended. Travis and Jack sat up in the pilot's and copilot's seats, so he couldn't see their faces, but he could see Ben's. His friend was studying him. After a moment, Ben said, "You think your text messenger is Donovan, right?"

"Right, unless Kai wanted me to check on his mom. That's a possibility."

"Possible Violet's in on it?"

"Possible, not probable. Not probable for Kai to have sent the text, either—he was in the mountains while the car was being parked near my house, so he would have needed to use someone else to leave a message taped to the beach stairs and so on. He couldn't do it without Donovan's cooperation."

"So if it's Donovan, why didn't he give you the info on the vehicle Parrish is using now? Why not just text the plate number and let you put out an APB?"

"I've thought about that. Several possibilities. One is that he didn't have that information at a time he was free to send a text. Another is that he can't—perhaps as far as Parrish is concerned, he's served his purpose. In that case, chances are he's already dead."

"Another possibility is that this is a trap."

"Yes. Another is that Violet was telling the truth, and Parrish has some kind of hold over Donovan."

"It must be one hell of a hold. I mean, beyond Parrish being his father. What would it take to get you to do what he's done so far?"

Frank had no answer for that. He was spared trying to come up with one when Jack said, "There! Up ahead!"

They all saw it then. A green Subaru Forester. On the roof, someone had placed a set of dots and dashes that seemed to have been cut from a roll of white duct tape:

... --- ...

SOS.

FIFTY-THREE

I rolled Parrish's body off me, retrieved the garrote, and came to my feet.

I felt shaky, but I made my way to Donovan, who was lying very still.

I turned him over. He groaned. Under the circumstances, it was a welcome sound. I didn't feel so good about all the blood soaking his left arm. I bent to put pressure on the wound, which was near his collarbone.

His eyes fluttered open. "In my backpack, there's a field kit with Celox in it. Hurry."

I ran to the pack, pulled out the field kit, and following his gritted out instructions, went to work.

I was just finishing up with the bandaging when I heard the helicopter again. It seemed closer, but maybe that was wishful thinking. I looked up in the sky, but all I saw was fast-moving clouds.

"Did you kill Kai?" he asked.

"No. He ran off. I didn't want to leave you here bleeding."

"Thanks." He pulled himself up to a sitting position. "Hand me Nick's gun, would you please? Just in case Kai comes back."

"Is that smart? I mean, your shoulder—"

"He's probably not going to come back, but he might also be lost out there, and there's a chance he'll circle back. I'd rather be ready for him."

So I gave him the rifle and picked up the gun I had been using. "You have any ammo for this one?" I asked.

He shook his head. "No, sorry. There will be lots of it in the cave, but Parrish only brought extra rounds for the rifle. Look in his right breast pocket."

I forced myself to reach into the bloody pocket and found the ammo. I gave it to Donovan. His face was looking pale and drawn.

"Do you have anything for pain in your field kit?"

"Yes, but I need to try to keep my head clear."

A gust of wind reminded me of my next priority. I searched for a nearby spot to pitch the tent. I didn't have to go far, for-tunately—I was within sight of Donovan and Parrish's body. I noticed that Donovan had pulled his knife back out of Parrish's chest.

I went to work on getting the tent set up. The wind was blowing harder, something I seem to be able to make wind do just by putting a tent stake in the ground. But I got it assem-bled—including the rain fly—without letting it blow away and soon had the bedroll laid out inside.

I went back and helped Donovan to his feet, then got him settled inside the tent—an awkward and painful process for him, given the nature of his injury, but a loud crack of thunder made us hurry it along.

The rain began to fall. In torrents.

I set up a rain catcher. Donovan had a canteen we shared while the catcher did its work.

After we had both been sitting there a few minutes, Dono-van said, "They'll be big on you, but I have some extra clothes in my pack."

I looked down at myself. I was wet, dirty, bloody, and stinky with God knows what. I didn't want to think about it.

"Thanks."

He closed his eyes.

At that point, I would have stripped in the middle of Times Square for the chance to be out of those clothes, but he allowed me as much privacy as you can get in a tent without stringing a blanket down the middle of it.

He had a pair of soft workout pants with a string tie, and I changed into those, then stuck my pants outside the tent, hoping the rain would make a start on washing the stench and stains out of them. I took off the parka, which made me cold, and slipped a big flannel shirt over the shirt and long under-wear I had been wearing since we left the lodge. His clothes were so big, I was swimming in them, but they were soft, dry, warm, and clean, which made them more valuable to me at that moment than designer wear.

I kept the wet shoes off, hoping they would dry, and did my best to clean the parka before putting it back on.

"You can open your eyes now," I said. There wasn't much light in the tent by then anyway, and we both thought we should keep the use of the flashlight in his pack to a minimum.

He accepted the offer of an energy bar.

"Thanks for all the help," I said.

He laughed. There wasn't an ounce of mirth in it. "I should ask you to shoot me. And you'd have every right to do it. No jury would convict you."

"No, I'm not going to shoot you. I know you've tried to help me. Besides, there's a little girl waiting for you somewhere, right?"

He looked away. "You remember that?"

"Yes, although I don't remember all of it, at least not clearly."

"Miranda. That's her name. I may have just signed her death

warrant. Parrish told me that if he didn't make a call by a certain time, she would be killed."

"I heard a helicopter. I'm sure they're waiting out this storm
just like we are. But as soon as it's over, they'll find us, we'll get
you to a hospital, and the police can do an all-out search for
your daughter."

"My daughter. With any luck, she'll never know that. If she
survives this, at least she won't have to spend time around her
grandfather or her father. One is dead, and the other's going to
prison."

"Not if I can help it," I said. "I mean, Parrish can stay
dead—"

He did laugh at that.

"And I'll do what I can to help you stay free. I know a great
defense attorney."

He was silent for a long time, then said, "You're kind.
And I—I'm glad you don't think the worst of me, although I
couldn't blame you if you did. Which still makes me the son of
that piece of shit out there."

It occurred to me that, until that moment, I had never heard
him use even so much as "damn" under the most trying of circumstances. Which confirmed me in an opinion I had been
forming for some time now. "You aren't like him."

"You don't know that."

"I do."

"No. You don't."

"Look, Donovan, you're right. I don't know your history.
I don't know your background. I don't know a damned thing
about your past. But I know that whatever may have been in
the past doesn't matter to me. Right here, right now, it brought
you to do things for me at great risk to your own life—and
your daughter's. I wish I could tell you how it felt, when I was
alone, trying to hide from Nicky out there, to suddenly realize

that you were rooting for me to survive. Not just in favor of it but actively helping me. You thought everything out. If you hadn't, I don't think I would have made it this far."

"You underrate yourself."

"Likewise."

We fell silent. I had insisted, over his strong objections, that he sit on his own sleeping bag, rather than give it to me. He lay down now but shifted, apparently unable to get comfortable.

"Donovan."

"Yes."

"Remember the physicist I interviewed about the Large Hadron Collider?"

He seemed startled by the change in subject. "Yes."

"I did that interview because my boss, who was once a lowly underling at the *Express,* got on an astrophysics kick. He came across this sentence, 'The universe is expanding.' He fell in love with that. You know why?"

"Because it's true."

"It is true, but that's not the only reason he has all but come up with a coat of arms to put it on. Do you know much about Ethan?"

"You were his mentor. He took over running the news at the radio station, and after the paper closed, he hired you. He rents a room from your friend Ben Sheridan and is learning to be a dog handler, although his new job has made it hard for him to keep up with that."

I tried and failed not to look taken aback.

"I studied you," he said in a tired, flat voice. "You and everyone around you."

"So—you know that he was a cocky, lying little bastard who hid how shitfaced drunk he was getting every day, then fucked up big-time and brought so much shame on himself and on the paper that he nearly got fired, and probably would have found it easier if he hadn't ever returned to the newsroom, where just about everyone hated him?"

There was a long silence before Donovan said, "No, I didn't come across that information."

"Yes, well, in a nutshell, he changed. He's still cocky, but I kind of hope that never changes. So even though the astrophysicists don't mean it in the same way, he believes we should all embrace the fact that the universe is expanding."

"I don't know what sins Ethan committed, but—it's not that. It's not what I've done. It's who I am. Cold. My own mother knew I had inherited an evil streak."

"What?"

"Parrish raped her. She decided not to get an abortion. But even from the time I was little, I remember her being afraid of me, of who I would become, of my nature. I've always known I'm . . . not like other people."

"Well, thank God for that."

He laughed then, a genuine laugh. He reached for his shoulder.

"Sure you don't want that painkiller?"

"Sure. I need to stay awake. I'm fairly certain Kai would have found his way back here by now if he was going to, but I don't want to take any chances."

"What happened to her?"

"My mother? My stepfather killed her. He's in prison."

"I'm sorry."

He shrugged. "I never felt close to either of them."

After a moment I said, "The world would be a horrible place if all children believed everything their parents said about them."

"It's not just what they said. It's what I know I'm capable of."

"That can be tough. For example, I've learned I can kill a

man with my bare hands. A little earlier today, I wondered if I could bring myself to garrote someone. Guess I answered that. I ran to have the chance to do it."

"To save me. Besides, I killed him."

"Grateful for that, but really, I'm not so sure he wasn't already gone. And besides . . ." I drew a deep breath, let it out slowly. "He's not the first person I've killed, and there are others whose deaths I probably could have prevented."

"You aren't God. And I know about the killings—you were defending yourself."

I fell silent. My ghosts endure. I struggle to forgive myself, but they endure.

I felt weary and lay down, even though I knew I would not sleep.

"I'm sorry if I upset you," he said.

"You didn't. Just something I have to live with."

"Believe me, I understand."

He wanted to stay awake, to stand guard, but blood loss and physical exhaustion trumped even pain, and soon I heard him fall asleep. He was on top of, rather than in the sleeping bag, so I put the survival blanket over him, trying to make sure he stayed warm.

"The universe is expanding, Donovan," I whispered. "However small any of our lives are at any given point, we can draw bigger lines around them."

I lay back on my side of the tent and thought about ways to get the attention of a helicopter that might not also draw the attention of a young serial killer.

FIFTY-FOUR

Travis settled the helicopter on the road, not far from the SUV. Frank had wondered if he'd really be able to do it and reminded himself that Travis did contract work for the Forest Service in these mountains on a regular basis, but after seeing how close they had come to the trees, he still needed a minute before he trusted himself to speak.

"I don't see anyone in the vehicle," Jack said.

"Let's go then," Frank said, and they opened the cargo bay doors. Jack and Travis were going to help Ben get the dogs, but Ben shook his head.

"They won't work well with all this wind. We may need them later, but right now I'd rather not expose them to the possibility of getting debris in their eyes."

As agreed—after debate—the others waited while Frank walked to the Subaru.

Concerned that Parrish had set a trap with the SUV, Frank walked around the vehicle, then got down on his hands and knees and looked beneath it. He stood and peered inside it. Nothing bomblike, but there were some objects in the back. He pulled out the lock picks and went to work. In a matter of seconds, he had the Forester unlocked. He took a deep breath and opened the driver's door. A dome light went on, and nothing more. He exhaled.

He pressed the button that unlocked all the doors, then went to the back. He heard the others coming toward the vehicle.

He found a topo map, a cell phone, a GPS tracker, and a large envelope marked READ FIRST.

He opened the envelope. The sheaf of documents inside were laser-printed but included one handwritten page. He began with the top page:

> If this has been found by anyone other than Detective Frank Harriman of the Las Piernas Police Department, please call 911 and ask that he be contacted immediately. This is a matter of life and death, and concerns the safety of his wife and many others.

Frank's direct number and the general phone number of the Las Piernas Police Department were written on the next line.

> If you are a thief who has broken into the car, by turning in the car and the cell phone you will be eligible to receive a reward greater than the value of either, for you will be aiding in the capture and conviction of Nicholas Parrish.

The next page was the one that began as a printout and ended with a handwritten note:

Dear Detective Harriman,
My ten-year-old daughter, Miranda, and her grand-mother Marguerite Page have been taken hostage by

Nick Parrish, who is my biological father. Parrish is holding them at a location unknown to me in exchange for my cooperation in helping him escape from prison and in bringing your wife to his mountain hideout. If you have not already been to the location I told you about on the Ford Escape's GPS, I have listed it on a separate page of properties owned and used by Quinn Moore, another of Nick Parrish's biological sons, who has closely cooperated with Nick Parrish in a number of ways. (See attached.)

It is important that someone check on the well-being of Violet Loudon, Kai Loudon's mother, at that location. Kai is a third son of Nick Parrish's.

I have, on other pages, described all I know about their crimes.

You must be worried about your wife, so I will tell you that the GPS tracker in this vehicle will lead you to me, and I have a tracker that will be able to lead you to her. I warn you now that I may have Kai Loudon and Nick Parrish with me but will help you in any way I can to take them captive, or kill them if necessary. I have been trying to keep Irene alive, but since I'm the one who brought her to them, I'm sure that seems unbelievable to you.

Also, the topo map is marked where a cave used by Parrish as a hideout is established. I don't think he plans to be there long. Be warned that he has firearms and plenty of ammunition there. Approach with extreme caution.

And then, handwritten, in a strong, clear hand:

The cell phone was stolen from Nick Parrish after he received a call from the person who has my child. I beg of you—whatever I have done, Miranda is innocent. Please

*take steps to have this number tracked down. The person
who called is a male. He has my daughter. Please hurry.*

It was signed by Donovan Cotter.

Jack helped Frank gather the papers and other items in
the back of the car and carry them to the helicopter.

Thunder cracked overhead.

They closed the cargo door just in time to escape being
drenched by a driving rain.

Frank asked Travis to set up a phone call to Pete. While Travis was doing that, Frank turned on the GPS device. It returned
a cannot-acquire-satellite message.

"It's the storm," Jack said.

Next Frank turned on the cell phone and wrote down the
number of the last call received.

Travis contacted Pappy and had them patched through to
Pete.

Frank gave him the information he had, told him where they
were, and asked for reinforcements. "It's raining like hell right
now, and I'm not sure how much daylight we'll have left by the
time it stops," he said. "Obviously, the child has to come first.
Let me know what you find out."

While it rained, they looked over the papers Donovan
Cotter had left behind. Included in them was documentation
that he had gone to the Las Piernas Police Department to file
missing persons reports on Miranda and her grandmother. But
since his ex-spouse had died without acknowledging him as the
father, and since he had never met the child and had nothing
more recent than a five-year-old photo of her, officers had been

skeptical of his intentions. Still, they had made a cursory check and, after talking to neighbors, believed that the grandmother and child had left voluntarily. One neighbor even attested to seeing them move out on their own.

Frank called Pete back and asked him to run that case down, to see who the neighbor was. Pete let him know that the phone number belonged to none other than Roderick Beignet. "Cell phone company is cooperating with us," he said, "so we should be able to locate him soon."

Frank flattened the topo map. Travis and Jack came down into the cargo section and looked it over with Frank and Ben. Frank read Donovan's detailed description of the cave and its contents to the others.

As the others talked over possible approaches to the cave, Ben read through Donovan's notes.

"According to Donovan, Kai is inexperienced in the wilderness," he said. "Parrish is an expert, as we know, but it has been years since he's been outdoors. Quinn—who may not be up here at all—is not the expert Parrish is, but he's not a beginner."

"And Donovan's an expert, with skills none of the others will have," Travis said. "So we have a sense of who we're dealing with in terms of their comfort out here."

"Right," Ben said. "We've got supplies for going in even after dark, and if the rangers call in other SAR groups, they'll be able to do the same. Given the dangerousness of the people out here with Irene and Donovan, they may be reluctant to send volunteers in until Loudon and Parrish are captured."

"Understandable," Frank said. "We don't want to be giving them more hostages or victims."

"That said, the terrain shouldn't be too difficult to work with. It's always possible to stumble over tree roots or trip over rocks, but we won't have to tackle any steep trails, and probably won't need climbing gear. No cliffs to fall from in the dark."

An hour after it broke, the storm subsided. The rangers at the nearest helitack station had been in contact, as had several law enforcement agencies and emergency response units. The helitack unit could aid in the search within the hour. Others had units on the way.

Frank tried the GPS again. He got a signal this time. He watched as it acquired the other unit and displayed a split screen: half showing his current location with a numeral 1 in a circle, half showing the other unit's location as 2 in a circle. The controls included two buttons that were marked, simply enough, 1 and 2. When he pressed 1, the whole screen was dedicated to his location. The other button produced a whole screen of the other unit's location. He left that up and tried a minus button until both circles appeared on the screen. Travis, looking over his shoulder, said, "Cool. Not too far." They all noted the locations on the topo map. Although Travis was unhappy about it, he agreed that he should stay with the helicopter, armed to protect it against Parrish—a former aircraft mechanic who knew how to fly planes and helicopters. This plan would also leave Travis in position to bring the helicopter to a rescue point if necessary.

The others started donning the gear they would carry into the forest. Although they all knew the dogs would be unlikely to perform well just after a storm had washed away scent, Ben got them ready, willing to do anything he could to help find Irene.

Frank kept watching the unit, then said, "One thing concerns me."

Silence fell, and they all turned to look at him.

"The other unit hasn't moved. At all."

FIFTY-FIVE

The rain let up. Donovan slept. I felt too claustrophobic to stay inside the tent. I also didn't like being unable to see who might be approaching. So I rolled up the long legs of the pants I had borrowed from Donovan, tucked the .22 back in my jacket pocket, then quietly opened the tent and stepped out.

The ground was muddy and footing treacherous, but I had my hands free to help keep my balance.

Although the air was cold and damp, it wasn't so cold that it had snowed or hailed or given us sleet. In the aftermath of the storm, the forest was beautiful. The clouds had cleared almost as quickly as they had arrived. The wind was dying down now. I could hear a thousand droplets falling off leaves and branches onto other leaves and branches, onto stones, onto the rain fly. The pants I had put outside the tent were soaked but somewhat cleaner.

There was still light left. I didn't have a watch, but it looked as if it was late afternoon. With the helicopter nearby—Frank nearby—it wasn't hard to imagine that we might survive. I felt my mood lighten, until I caught sight of Parrish's corpse.

He had been the monster in my life for so long, I wondered if even his death would be enough to allow me to be free from him. I kept telling myself I should feel something. Triumph. Revulsion. Something.

I moved closer, forcing myself to look at what I had done. Even with his swollen face and bruises and ligature marks and gaping chest wounds, I could not pity him.

Someone else would. I've worked in the news business long enough to know that, no matter how despicable and depraved an individual may be, there will always be someone out there who is able to feel genuine pity for him. And probably someone who wants to start an online fan club and propose marriage to him, too.

He's all yours, ladies.

I felt a kind of hysterical giggle bubbling up in me, put my hand over my mouth, and tried to settle down. I recognized it for the need to have some relief from stress and fear and anger that it was, and clamped down hard on it. Plenty of time for inappropriate laughter when all this was over.

I took some calming breaths and realized that I should search his pockets. There might be useful items besides the ammo I had found before the storm. I had seen him use a cell phone back at the desert warehouse. Cell phone signals were often nonexistent in the mountains, but there were towers in unexpected places.

I bent over him and forced myself to think only of his parka, not the corpse inside it. I found the key to the Forester in one pocket. I found the strange knife and took that. He had a canteen, but I couldn't bear the thought of drinking out of it. Maybe Donovan would want it. I shuddered.

Okay, maybe the cell was in an inside pocket. I tried not to be squeamish, but I know I was making a face when I took hold of the parka's zipper.

My own hood blocked my view of my surroundings, and I was intent on the unpleasant task before me, so I did not know that Kai Loudon had approached from behind me until, at the very last moment, I saw his shadow.

I was in the worst possible position to defend myself, bent over, hands down, feet on a slippery surface. I half turned and saw that he had a short, thick piece of branch in his hand, and he swung it hard toward my head. I raised my arms in a reflexive protective movement and heard my right forearm break even as he continued to follow through. The arm and the parka provided a small amount of protection or he might have killed me with that one blow.

I fell on top of Parrish and rolled, head aching, stunned from the wallop to my skull, arm on fire. There was no coordination to my movements—the world was spinning. He dropped the club, knelt down on my back, and quickly searched my pockets until he found the gun, the knife, and the garrote, and threw them into the woods. I heard him grunt with pain as he took hold of my parka with both hands and pulled it down over my shoulders, trapping my arms.

I screamed.

He cuffed me hard on the side of the head, yelled, "Shut up!" then stood. He pulled his gun from his own parka and ordered me to stand up. He pushed me forward, almost at a run, into the trees.

I heard Donovan frantically call my name, stumbled, fell, and felt Kai land hard on top of me. Hitting tree roots with my face probably hurt, but the pain of his landing on my arm hurt so much it blinded me to any other source of agony. He cried out as well but brought me to my feet again, holding hard to the parka, which still pinned my arms. He held the gun in his injured hand—however much his arm hurt, he still had a grip— and pressed it into the small of my back. We slipped and slid but made progress.

We came to a small clearing and stumbled again. This time he let go, letting me fall hard to the ground, and yelled something I couldn't begin to understand through the haze of pain in my head and arm. He winced and switched the gun to his good arm.

He told me to strip, and when I didn't obey, he moved closer. I fought with kicks and my good hand. I hurt his left knee and even managed to scratch one of his eyes and bloody his nose, but every time he wanted to subdue me, he just pushed on the broken arm. He was strong and filled with rage. He hit me with the gun, nearly causing me to pass out, then pocketed it and started pulling off my clothes.

Think!

But it was damned hard. He had my parka off—the removal was excruciating—and in seconds had torn off my shirt, pausing now and again to strike me with his fist, as my muzzy-headed efforts at defense did little to slow him. My strikes became fewer and even less accurate. I grabbed at anything I could—his hair, his bootlaces—and did little more than untie his shoes. He hit me on the face again and again, slaps and punches, and pulled at my arm if I put up too much of a fight. He yanked off my pants—Donovan's too-loose-on me pants—and pressed me into the ground as he reached down between us—unzipping his own pants.

Think!

"I killed Nick because he killed your mother," I said.

He froze. His eyes narrowed.

In that one instant of letting up his assault, he heard exactly what I heard—the baying of a bloodhound.

Not Bool, I thought. Bool was trained not to bay. But a dog. Other people. Voices. More than one. At a distance, but if I could hear them—

"Help!" I shouted, earning myself another fist in the face before Kai stood and then grabbed my parka and my pants—Donovan's pants—and pulled up his fly.

He sat on a log, hurrying to retie his boots—a task he

grimaced through as he used his injured arm. The sadistic asshole I should have drowned yesterday, while I had the chance,
was getting away.

I felt a surge of rage so pure it masked the pain. I staggered
to my feet.

He was bent over his bootlaces, but he noticed me. I kept
staggering as I moved closer to him—it wasn't all pretense.

He smiled at me. "Don't worry, I'll find you and give you
everything I wanted to give you today, you cunt."

I really hate the c word.

I leaned forward, as if I was about to fall. Instead, I grabbed
his hair in a death grip with my left hand and yanked like hell
on it, swinging his head down as I brought my right knee up
fast and hard into his face, then extended my right leg and
kicked full force into his balls. When he doubled over screaming, I gave it to him again in the teeth with that same knee, let
go of his hair, and let him fall to the ground. When he curled
up there, I started kicking his kidneys. I circled him, kicking
his head and his face and his arms and his ass. Hard. He curled
tighter, I kicked harder.

In my mind, I was screaming at him, calling him every filthy
name I had ever heard, which was an extensive catalog, but I
must not have been doing anything except breathing hard,
because I heard—eventually—someone trying to get my attention.

"Irene . . . Irene. Irene . . . it's okay. You can stop."

It was that best loved voice. I stopped. I looked up. Saw
Frank putting his gun back in its shoulder holster, slowly walking toward us.

"I knew you would make it," I said. I have no idea if any
of that was intelligible, because my mouth was swollen. Frank
later told me that he understood every word, and maybe he did.

He came closer. I warned him about the arm, which caused

him to look down at Kai in a way that made me say, "Not worth it." He nodded and very gently pulled me into an embrace. I leaned against him. "I'm a mess."

"Doesn't matter," he said. "Doesn't matter at all. I can't tell you . . ." And he couldn't, but he didn't need to.

"Frank, I would not be standing here with you if Donovan hadn't helped me. I don't know what you know about him, and you probably want to kill him, but seriously, I'm alive because of him."

"I know. We'll help him."

He stepped away only long enough to disarm and cuff Kai, and to retrieve my parka for me. The front of the parka had some bloodstains on it, a mixture of them at this point, but the jacket was warm and I wanted it back. I got the pants, too.

Within minutes, the others were there, including Donovan, who didn't look too steady on his feet. Jack took one glance at me, then at Kai, and had such a murderous look in his eye that Frank immediately said, "Irene says he's not worth it. Since I found her on the verge of doing what you want to do, I'd let her be the judge of that."

Ben had Bool with him and was praising him, while the big bloodhound practically pulled him over trying to get to me. "Hello, Boolean," I said softly and felt tears rolling down my cheeks.

"Sorry about the baying," Ben said. "I don't know what got into him."

"Why, Bool and I are old friends. That's what."

"I just hope he didn't endanger you with that."

"No, he helped save me."

"Extra treats for Bool, then," Jack said and, seeing Ben's look as he took in the situation, added, "Frank says Irene's already fed this guy's own balls to him, so Bool won't be able to have those for his treats."

Frank had taken off his backpack and had a blanket and thermos full of hot tea for me. "It's probably not too hot by now, but—anyway, it's got a lot of sugar in it. You know the drill."

It was still warm. It was good to get a little sugar in my system.

"You going to formally arrest this shit-heel, Frank?" Jack asked, nodding toward Kai.

Before Frank could answer, we heard a helicopter overhead.

"Sounds like the rangers are on the way," Jack said. "That's not the Sikorsky, and only their Bell could get here that fast."

"Good. Let the Feds take him in—Las Piernas and all the other jurisdictions can work it out with them from there. We've got a couple of people to get to an ER."

He asked Jack to radio Travis and tell the rangers where to find us. Jack had a device in hand that he used to read off coordinates. Within no time, the rangers' helicopter was overhead. They found a place to land and joined us. I was surprised to see a familiar face among them.

"J.C.!"

"Oh, Irene," he said. "I'm so sorry."

"Parrish is dead," I told him. J.C.—Jay Carter—was among the few survivors of our first journey into these mountains with Parrish.

"So I understand. Thanks." He was looking at me with so much concern, I almost started crying again. "Look," he said, "I know that Travis wants to take you and another victim to the hospital, and he's fired up the Sikorsky. Are you able to walk all the way to the road, or do you want us to give you a lift?"

"Her arm's broken," Frank said.

"How about a lift then?" I said. I eyed Kai uneasily though.

"He'll wait here with a couple of the other rangers until we come back for him. I may even get our rescue guys to take him to a local hospital in a different chopper."

Before long, we were on our way to Las Piernas. Donovan insisted that he'd prefer to be taken to St. Anne's, too. An EMT working with the rescue squad kindly helped to splint the arm for the trip and offered painkillers. We both passed up the offer, tempting as it was.

We had a lot of talking and planning to do.

When I first got to the Sikorsky, Donovan looked so dismayed by my now very swollen face, I said, "Remember, the other guy looks worse."

He laughed at that, and Frank said, "She's right." Donovan laughed harder.

When Frank looked at him a little uneasily, I said, "I know what's it's like. Until you can cry, you have a risk of getting a little hysterical over the oddest things. I got the giggles over Parrish's corpse a little while ago."

"I was going to ask you about that," Frank said. "Stabbed, shot, and garroted?"

"If it hadn't rained on him, I would have thought of setting him on fire."

Donovan laughed over that one, too. He needed bed rest.

"She beat the hell out of him, too," Donovan said.

"Disarmed him and gave him his black eye," I bragged.

"You . . ."

"We have got to do something nice for Rachel," I said.

"I don't know if I can hear any more of this right now," Frank said.

I gave him a one-armed hug. "So tell me about your day."

So Frank told me about visiting Quinn Moore and going on "vacation," the text messages, Roderick Beignet, and all that Donovan had left in the Forester to help him find us.

"So that's what happened to Parrish's cell phone!"

"I took it from him when I was adjusting his backpack," Donovan said.

"I used the first locator to find Donovan," Frank said. "He was looking for you. Then he gave me his, and I went on from there, while Jack and Ben took him back to the helicopter."

I told Frank about meeting Roderick in the Busy Bee Café and apologized for not telling him the truth about the damaged phone.

"I don't care about that," he said. "I know you were feeling hemmed in. I'm just so damned glad you're alive."

That went straight into the Very Big Book of Reasons I Will Remain Married to Frank Harriman for As Long As He'll Have Me, but I was still uneasy. "If I had told you, you would have checked his background, and maybe we would have found out about Donovan's daughter sooner—"

"Or maybe my daughter would have been killed immediately if Parrish worried the police were getting too close," Donovan said.

Pete called not long before we landed. Frank told him Donovan and I were listening to the call. I worried that he might try to accuse Donovan of something, but he didn't. He started off by telling us how glad he was that we'd survived. But he had big news of his own.

"We caught Roderick Beignet. Donovan Cotter, your little girl is fine—not to say she hasn't been scared by all this, but she's happy to be rescued. Not sure if your mother-in-law is going to make it. Roderick's been afraid to refill a prescription for a heart medication she needed, and he didn't bother to try to get it any other way. They've taken her and the girl to St. Anne's."

"We're headed there now," Donovan said.

"Good. Miranda wants to meet the person she calls her 'real dad.'"

He swallowed hard, then said, "I want to meet her, too."

"So what did Roderick have to say for himself?" Frank asked.

"Since I put him under arrest, I can quote him exactly. Ready?"

"Ready."

"'My rights! My rights! What about my rights?' I told him that, other than the ones I had just read to him, I didn't think he had any, but he should check with his attorney."

"He has one?"

"Well, that's the kicker, Frank. He wanted to hire one of his nephew's attorneys."

"Who's his nephew?"

"Quinn Moore."

"Quinn Moore!" It was echoed over at least three headsets.

"Thing is, none of those attorneys were interested in taking his case, mostly because he can't afford them. He's in a bind because we managed to get a judge to agree with us that Quinn's assets ought to be frozen, given the indications we have that he participated in some serious crimes. Enough indication to get a warrant out on him, although we're pretty sure he's out of the country. Just not sure where."

"Yet," Frank said.

"Yet," Pete agreed. "Anyway, turns out old Roderick is Parrish's half brother."

"Half brother?" I said. "I've never heard of him having any siblings other than his sister."

"Same father. The parents divorced, the dad remarried, Roderick is the child of that marriage."

"How many more of them are out there?" I asked.

No one had an answer.

FIFTY-SIX

I spent a lot of time answering a lot of questions from people in law enforcement. Fortunately, our friend and attorney, Dina Willner—who had taken over Zeke Brennan's law
firm after he retired—loves a challenge. I don't know how Dina
managed to find the time and energy to keep all of us out of hot
water, but she did.

I was able to talk the doctors at St. Anne's into letting me go
home two days later. Ethan had visited me as soon as I got back
and told me to return to work only when I really felt able to do so.

"See you next week, then," I said.

"You don't know that yet," he said.

"Neither do you."

This led to a bet, which I won, but he got the best of me
by teasing me endlessly when, on my return, I mentioned that
I noticed the receptionist was gone. He made fun of the way I
had tried to casually ask about it.

"Admit it," he said. "You thought I was fishing off the company pier."

"I wasn't certain," I said. "At least not about you. I apologize for that. But if you're going to tell me she didn't try to
make a play for you—"

"I found a job for her at another station," he said. "I couldn't take much more of her making excuses to stop by my office."

I raised a brow, picked up a pen, and tapped out a message on my desk in Morse code. He laughed and said, "It's not bragging if it's true."

I stayed in touch with Donovan. We were all able to breathe easier when we learned that he was not going to be charged with any crimes. Dina convinced the D.A. not only that Donovan was coerced into all his activities on Parrish's behalf but also that he had a great deal to do with my rescue and the arrests of several Moths. I, of course, would never agree to testify that I was drugged by him, since, after all, I was out drinking with a friend that afternoon. Who could say what had happened?

Then there was the matter of the police failing him when he initially reported his daughter and his former mother-in-law missing, a failure that nearly caused the death of Marguerite Page and put the child at the mercy of a man like Roderick Beignet. That, Dina said, was being looked at by the people in her firm who handled civil cases.

Perhaps the most convincing argument was the way the public embraced Donovan himself. Aside from his story, there was his unblemished record of service to his country. He had a handsome face and a beautiful child, and they both became instant media darlings. The—elected—D.A. is not a stupid man. Besides, the D.A.'s kindness toward Donovan guaranteed the cooperation of important witnesses in bigger cases.

Kai Loudon awaits trial. He has done a lot of talking about Quinn Moore from his jail cell.

Roderick Beignet, in a cell not far from Kai's, does the same.

Roderick has the gift, Pete says, of never telling a story the same way twice. "And still manages to avoid including facts in any version."

Quinn Moore has not been seen since he checked himself out of the hospital.

I spend a certain amount of time in my life trying to convince myself he is unlikely to come after me.

So many kindnesses came my way.

Some that might seem trivial were important to me.

Travis, Ethan, and Jack went back to the mountains and made sure that no gear got left behind. Although law enforcement took everything in the cave, impounded the Subaru, and removed some of what was in our "camp" as evidence, there were a few items still there—and my guys made sure those items got taken out of the wilderness, and spared me having to revisit a beautiful place that was too freshly attached to nightmares.

I would be a liar if I tried to pretend that being able to fight back meant I walked away victorious and that was that. The mind plays tricks. Against fifteen minutes or so of action, I had hours of terror as Kai and Parrish's captive. Even winning a brutal fight does not, it turns out, give a person a mental erase button. In fact, sometimes the replay goes haywire, and where you won in real life, imagination shows you a convincing picture of a different denouement. You pull the trigger and the gun doesn't fire. The garrote breaks in two. A corpse rises and grabs you by the throat. You are held down by someone younger and stronger, who is reaching between you, and nothing you do stops him.

You wake or snap out of it, but not without moments of being unsure of the true outcome.

During those first weeks, Ben and J.C. called often, as did a couple of other survivors of the first trip, talking me through the days when even therapy sessions weren't enough to keep me from feeling the vulnerability and terror that follow being held hostage. Other friends helped, too.

No one was as good to me, or as essential to my getting through those days, as Frank. He was, I realized, always going to be the luckiest thing that ever came of any of my luck.

Because of them, I persevered.

I was surprised when I went to visit Donovan, one day about a month after our adventures, to see that this one-time loner—who had already taken his former mother-in-law and his daughter under his roof—now had a tenant. Violet Loudon had moved in, along with an aide she had hired after selling her house.

Donovan and I sat on the patio, watching Miranda play with a calico cat—another addition. "This is quite a change for you," I said.

"I find I do better with groups of women than I do living with just one." He blushed. "That doesn't sound right."

I laughed. "I understood what you meant."

"Miranda needs her grandmother. Violet needs all of us. I need all of them." He paused, then said, "The universe is expanding, right?"

"Right."

"You call on me, Irene Kelly, any time. I've got your back, however far out you stand on the edge of your universe."

The universe expanded all about me. I could adapt, change, acquire new skills, accept the kindness of friends, accept a new kind of friend. What had seemed to me an impossibility—that I could prevail over such attackers—turned out to be within my grasp. And if that victory had a price, I knew defeat would have had a greater one.

A once utterly unimaginable possibility—that I would not be a newspaper reporter at this time of my life—was a reality. I still grieve the loss of the *Express*. In one way or another, perhaps I always will.

It turns out, though, that what we grieve can show us what we have truly loved and why we loved it, and what we should reach for again in the coming day, should we choose to reach at all.

I choose to reach.

ACKNOWLEDGMENTS

I was once told by a college professor that no classroom lecturer could be held responsible for the mangled information that ended up in his students' notes. Similarly, the individuals who helped with this book should not be blamed for my errors.

I am indebted to my friends who work or have worked for newspapers. To all of you, wherever you find yourselves now, my deepest gratitude for your help. Thank you for your work as professionals in a field that deserves to be better valued.

Edward J. Dohring, M.D., whose name my readers may recognize from previous books, is a board-certified orthopedic spine surgeon, a fellowship-trained spine surgeon, medical director of the Spine Institute of Arizona, and a researcher and teacher on the care of spinal disorders. His help with the passages about Parrish's injury and recovery was invaluable, as was his review of information about Violet's care.

Kitty Felde, a National Public Radio special correspondent and an award-winning playwright, was of immeasurable assistance when I asked her to talk to me about Irene's career change. She was able to offer insights from her own experiences and brought her wonderful imagination to the task of anticipating the challenges Irene would face.

What Rachel taught Irene about self-defense comes from true leaders in the martial arts. Grandmaster Al Tracy (who has been teaching karate for over fifty years) and his wife, Kenpo karate black belt (7th dan) Pat Tracy, who run Tracy's International Studios of Self Defense, generously shared their expertise, read and reread fight scenes, and offered excellent advice.

Among my journalist friends, I must take time to individually thank Debbie Arrington, who from the moment I decided I wanted to write about a newspaper reporter, never has failed to spare me the time it took to answer my questions.

Thanks also to my nephew, Detective John Pearsley, Jr., of the El Cajon Police, who answered my frantic late-night emails on police procedure. Forensic anthropologist Marilyn London answered my questions about age determination and frozen remains. Melodie Grace and my brother, John G. Fischer, helped with questions about legal procedures.

I am also indebted to my sister Sandra Fischer, who read each chapter as it was written and caught many of my errors.

This book received shepherding from Marysue Rucci and Amanda Murray, and most especially from Sarah Knight at Simon & Schuster. I'm also indebted to Philip Spitzer, my agent, for his feedback. Thank you all!

Tim, who has met the challenge of living with me with both humor and bravery, has all my love.

ABOUT THE AUTHOR

Jan Burke is the national bestselling author of thirteen novels and a collection of short stories. Among the awards her work has garnered are Mystery Writers of America's Edgar® for Best Novel, Malice Domestic's Agatha Award, Mystery Readers International's Macavity Award, and the RT Book Club's Best Contemporary Mystery. She is the founder of the Crime Lab Project and is a member of the board of the California Forensic Science Institute. She lives in Southern California with her husband and two dogs. Learn more about her at www.janburke .com.